# THE SHADOW OF ARCADIA

**THE AUGMENT SAGA: BOOK TWO**

# ALAN K. DELL

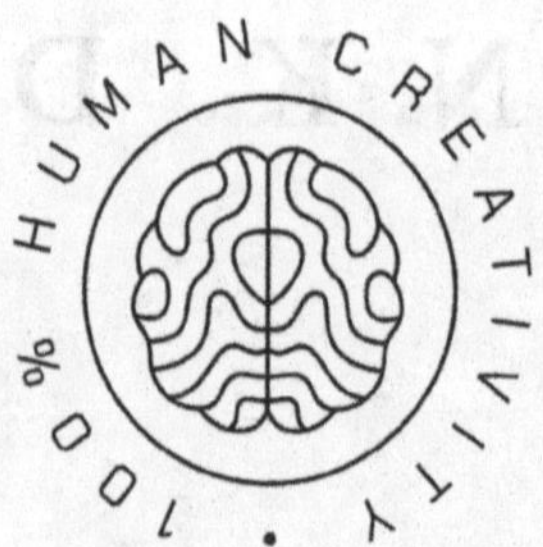
100% HUMAN CREATIVITY

# ACKNOWLEDGEMENTS

ONCE AGAIN, I WOULD LIKE to acknowledge and thank all those who have supported me in my writing journey thus far and who have made the writing of this fourth book and second full-length novel in the Augment Saga a reality. Without these amazing people, none of this would have been possible. *The Shadow of Arcadia* has been a tough book to write, almost entirely rewritten (and replotted several times) from its original form as part of the first draft of *From the Grave of the Gods*. It has been a hard road, and as much as I've enjoyed the process, it has also been in equal parts disheartening and frustrating, and it has taken a lot out of me.

First of all, I would be remiss if I didn't thank my family for giving me the love, support, and writing time that have kept me going over this long, long rewrite. To my wife, Emma, whom I utterly cherish: You have been my rock, and I thank you for all the different ways you've helped me as I rabbited on about this book to you and endured even as I got grumpy about it. To my children, Oliver and Eulalia, who have expressed their pride in my work, even though they're way too young to actually read it.

Next, I must thank my incredible beta readers who agreed to take the time to read through the unfinished manuscript and provide valuable feedback: The stalwart Adam Sadler and fellow indie authors Gary J. Mack and Rari Rajesh.

Oftentimes authors get to a point with our books where we can't see the wood for the trees; we've read and re-read the damn things so many times that everything loses its impact and we fail to notice where things need extra work or just plain aren't working. Beta readers provide fresh eyes, fresh minds, new perspectives. Without these individuals the book would be inevitably weaker. So, thank you for all your comments, thoughts, suggestions, criticisms, and support.

Since this novel originally made the final act of the first draft of *From the Grave of the Gods*, I must once again thank Mr Drew Wagar. It was actually Drew who first suggested that I split the draft into three books, and he was absolutely right. His feedback on this section of the book was invaluable.

To my editor and proofreader Isabelle Wagner, The Shaggy Shepherd, who has made this manuscript all the better with her excellent editing skills and keen eye for detail. Thank you for your speedy turnaround and wonderful comments. They really made going through the returned document a lot of fun. If you're an indie author reading this and are in need of an editor, I can highly recommend her services!

To the wonderful community of writers across the landscape of social media of which I have increasingly found myself a part, who have cheered me on and provided a sense of belonging: Thank you.

Thanks also to author Conrad Altman for designing and providing the wonderful anti-AI icon on this book's copyright page. A true star of the indie writing community.

And finally, to you, my dear readers, both those who are new to the series, and those who have been on this journey with me since the beginning, thank you for buying, reading, reviewing, and championing this series. I hope you enjoy this latest entry and stick around for the rest!

*'Truly, whoever can make you believe absurdities can make you commit atrocities.'*

—Voltaire, *Questions sur les Miracles,* 1765

# PROLOGUE

I BARELY FELT IT AS I SLAMMED against the rear wall of the holding cell. My body and mind had been overwhelmed to numbness by the pain of neural sweeping. I hit the cold metal floor with a thud and lay sprawled on my front, unmoving, for what seemed like hours. This was how they treated me every time and compared to the procedure itself, this rough treatment was almost welcome, comforting, familiar.

It took time for my addled mind to settle from being scraped; even longer for my vision to return.

Peeling my cheek off the floor, I breathed deep and coughed, spattering blood. The red liquid mixed with saliva dripped from my lips in long strands. It would stop soon; it always did. Naked, cold, and tasting iron, I forced myself to a seated position with my legs crossed and scooted back with a grunt. The wall's rough texture provided no salve for my bruised back. It was the same as every wall in these godforsaken ships; white and covered with etched religious texts. Not comfortable to lean against, but it was all I had.

They had what they wanted now. The first few times my Achelon captors had taken me to their machine had been for calibration and they hadn't been gentle about it. Each time, I was returned to my cell half-dead, brain scrambled, and sightless. Why did it have to hurt so badly? Perhaps it was simply how the machine worked. The Achelon communicate through a sort of telepathy and god knows that's painful enough.

This last time, however, my captors had met with success as they delved deep within my mind, dredging up distant memories. Painful, vivid, traumatic memories. It had all felt so real; a sustained surge of pain like electrocution and I relived them all over again. Over and over they'd swept and scraped, as though they'd ripped my skull apart and jammed a whisk into the grey matter, even though the procedure was non-invasive.

They wanted to know my secret—how I had become like them. Except it wasn't a secret. If they'd asked, I'd have gladly told them. As far as I was concerned, it wouldn't have helped them, anyway. But I was inferior. One did not ask an ant how it ended up in the kitchen, crawling all over the dishes.

It didn't matter anymore; they knew it all now. My usefulness had come to an end.

I blinked away the film covering my eyes and the amorphous white light before me resolved into the lit end of a long, and otherwise dark, corridor. My cell was locked shut; it was a simple barred gate, almost at odds with the Achelon's usual aesthetic. The room itself was small and plain but for the ever-present etchings.

There was a small gap in the bars on the floor, presumably for sliding a bowl or tray through to provide sustenance for prisoners. But I had been given nothing. Being like them, they knew I could survive without, and so nothing was offered. I was an abomination to them—an affront to their sense of divine superiority—and depriving me of food and water was just another way to show their disdain.

How long had I been on this ship? Days? Weeks? Months? There was no way for me to tell. In my unnaturally long life, my internal sense of the passage of time had degraded significantly. Time blindness for immortals was so much worse than the regular kind.

All I knew was that it would be over soon. A singular guard would return to my cell—the same one who had escorted me for neural sweeping—this time to take me for execution. No, execution wasn't the right word; it carried too much honour.

Disposal.

This was my last chance to escape.

The etched white walls that pervaded these gargantuan spacecraft were well-known to me. They were a façade, a frontage made of some thin composite covering a more rigid metal core. Ordinarily, they were not prone to separation, but it was possible under a significant force applied in the correct manner. Once broken, the shards were akin to a white obsidian.

I slid my hand back to the etched façade behind and hooked a fingernail into one of the squiggly engraved letters. Its shape had no analogue in any human writing system and it was unique in the Achelon script. That's why I had chosen it. I didn't even need to look to know where it was.

As I pulled, a shard of the white glasslike composite

revealed itself from its perfect concealment. It had broken off a few days ago—days? Perhaps; I couldn't tell—under a precise application of force from yours truly.

*Heh, not really.*

In reality, my guard had thrown me so hard across the floor my elbow had impacted the wall and chipped a shard off. It fit perfectly back into the hole with no visible seam. This way, I hid it from my captors.

The light at the end of the hallway dimmed. The imposing shape of the guard appeared in its mechanised power armour. Its boots clanged on the floor as it approached.

It had been the shape and sound of my nightmares for far longer than a single human lifetime. A deep blue angular suit with a concealed wrist-blade. Its two main arms were huge and it had a second set of diminutive vestigial arms closer together on its chest. The head was uncovered and its kite-shaped cranium glowed with bioluminescent signalling, betraying its emotional state. I never learned the colour codes. Maldaccian historians theorised that in the distant past on whatever planet these Ancient Wanderers had once called home, it had been the primary form of communication among primitive clans; colour codes to warn others of impending danger, in leadership trials, or whatever. The creatures themselves had always been mute; the oppressive telepathy had come much later, a product of experimentation.

The Achelon were tall and intimidating in their suits—terrifying even. But in reality they were mostly a little shorter than humans. They had a similar range of skin colours, but more translucent, and were covered in a fine peach fuzz. Out of their suits they were adept at crawling and scurrying. Their big, dark eyes caught more of the electromagnetic spectrum than any Earth life and their lipless mouths contained teeth that were black and sharp. Surely apex predators in their native environment, whatever that might once have been.

The towering guard stood at the cell door.

'Rise, abomination,' it said, its mental voice forcing its way into my mind. It no longer affected me like it used to. 'Your time draws near. You shall kneel before the Inquisitor.'

I obliged. The guard opened the cell and stepped in. I was naked, cold, feeble, harmless. I clutched the shard just behind my hip, flush with the skin. Flaring my nostrils, I breathed deep, taking in the fusty smell that permeated the ship. I kept my head low, closed my eyes, and focused, slowing my racing heart.

Yes, they knew everything about me. Everything they cared to know. They'd probed my mind and found all they'd wanted. I wasn't one of them.

But I was far more like them than they realised.

My eyes shot open and I leaped, closing the distance with my augmented strength. Before the guard could react, I plunged the molecule-sharp dagger into its skull. Blue liquid poured from the wound as the Achelon officer raised its main arms to swat me away. But I held on. I stabbed, sliced, cut, and pierced again and again with malicious glee, covering myself in its lifeblood as it bucked and swayed. After seconds, the great beast's arms fell limp. Its whole body twitched, then it stumbled and fell with a crash.

I removed the blade from its mangled head, the white composite now stained with both red and blue. With a smirk I held it up in the dim light, my own blood running down my forearm from where I had gripped the razor edge. The unique Achelon letter carved into the flat face of my improvised weapon glinted as it was filled with new colour. What did the glyph mean? Something apt and humorous, no doubt. I'd have to ask when I got home.

I crouched low, making my way out of the cell and down to the lit end of the long corridor. The escape route was ingrained within my mind. I knew the layout of these En-Kadr class warships better than anyone living. Hardly surprising, since humanity had been in possession of one for centuries—albeit a derelict. But the *Righteous Rain* varied little from the one Da'kora had shot down all those years ago. I was confident I could get out without being spotted. A part of me despaired at that prospect. For so long I had fought to suppress the burgeoning monster within and now my desire was torn between getting back to my crew and butchering every living thing on this ship.

It wasn't a question of 'if' but a question of timing.

If I tried anything now in my current state—armed as I was with a tiny piece of composite glass—I wouldn't get far. No, my ship's weapons would make a cleaner, if less satisfying, job of it. It was a war for survival, after all.

*Restraint, then.*

I crept along, hand to the wall, as I turned corners and flew down the long, brightly-lit, carpeted passageways. The occasional patrol came past and I ducked into side-rooms to avoid being spotted. The Achelon engineers and scientists presented less of a problem, I could probably have killed them easily, lacking armour as they were. The security force and higher-ranked officers were far more dangerous.

It wouldn't be long before they discovered the body of the guard and the cell empty. I wondered what the ship would look like on high alert. It was unlikely I'd have to wait long to find out. Despite my in-depth knowledge of the place, this was the first time I'd been inside a fully operational En-Kadr. It was fascinating to see its corridors so pristine and bright, with doors that worked properly and crew going about their business. And all it took was my stupid capture. If I weren't so conspicuous, it would have been a good opportunity to study their operations and tactics from within.

The docking bay was towards the front of the *Righteous Rain*, on the lowest deck. Two decks down from where I was imprisoned and nearly half a kilometre away. If memory served, it sat between the forward ram-scoops behind the flattened nose cone, which housed the main sensor array and communications suite. The bay would be empty. Delegations boarding an En-Kadr class warship were not entirely unheard of but rare. There was no sign among the crew that this was the case; no electric sense of urgency or heightened vigilance that accompanied such an occurrence. At least, that was the case on Alliance ships. One might expect landers, drop-ships, fighters, or other such military sci-fi nonsense to fill the bay instead, but what was the need for landing craft when the ship itself could sterilise a planet from orbit? What was the benefit of fighters when combat took place beyond visual range, sometimes hundreds or thousands of kilometres distant? No, the docking bay would be empty.

I waited until the latest group passed the doorway I hid behind then crept out into the corridor.

An ungodly screech erupted across the ship, piercing and shrill. All the lights went out, to be replaced by a dim violet, the kind that existed on the very edge of human perception.

*Shit.*

My chest tightened and I crouched even lower. Laughter came unbidden from deep within, forcing its way out of my locked jaw and clenched teeth. Whatever I had been expecting, I hadn't considered that their high alert would make use of emergency lighting in the near-ultraviolet.

As my eyes adjusted to the almost pitch darkness, a group of armoured warriors appeared at the end of the corridor. They approached at impossible speed and I darted towards them, dagger aloft.

*Here it is, my death at last.*

But as I ran, I spotted a maintenance hatch in the wall to the left and changed my mind. The security force's giant blades erupted from their wrists with the sound of scraping metal as they closed in on me. Using my momentum and my augmented strength, I wrenched the hatch open and disappeared through. I knew they couldn't follow me through the ship's industrial sections with their bulky armour. Those areas were more suited to the species' naturally lithe frames and proficiency at scurrying.

I could hardly see, but I knew there were pipes and conduits everywhere, lining unadorned narrow corridors that twisted and turned. Here was bare metal, which clanged and echoed as I ran through the darkness. It wasn't all emergency lighting through here, however. The odd spot-lamp still spilled its welcome light over important consoles and machinery.

I wasn't any safer in here than out there. There would be engineers and mechanics, who would no doubt have been informed of my presence. The whole ship would know by now.

Readjusting my grip on the improvised weapon, my palm bleeding afresh, I crouched behind a wall of thick stacked piping, which jutted out into the gangway from deeper within the ship.

There they were. Not fifty metres from my position, a party of unarmoured engineers—three in all—carried their silvery pistols and checked alcoves. Their heads oscillated brilliant colour—fear? Excitement? I wished I knew. They hadn't seen me yet, but they would soon.

I licked my lips and poised myself to strike, stretching the fingers of one hand across the cold metal floor.

Twenty metres.

Ten metres.

One ducked to look behind a conduit on the left. The other two inspected a machine to the right.

*Close enough.*

Like I had done with the guard, I bolted. My bare feet hammered the floor as I closed the gap. All too late, they spotted me.

The first engineer's chest burst open with blue blood as I sliced with my jagged piece of wall material. Its gun clattered to the floor. The momentum carried my body around in an arc as the second turned. I grabbed its arm as it tried to bring its pistol to bear and thrust upward, cleaving its face in two.

The third engineer fired its particle beam and a great searing pain flared up my arm—the one which still held onto its dead comrade—all the way to the shoulder. I screamed and shoved the body towards it, knocking it off balance. As it fell to the floor, I lunged and buried the blade in its throat.

The composite material had served its purpose and so I left it in the dead engineer as I raised myself up. Closing my eyes, I inhaled slowly as I stood over the bodies. My heart slowed and the tingling in my extremities subsided. Gingerly, I prodded my burned arm. It was bad, but it would heal. To anyone else, the dose of radiation alone would have been lethal, but I had endured worse.

I bent down and picked up one of the pistols, triangular, smooth, and shiny. It had been a long time since I'd last held one. Memories came flooding back, closer to the surface than I'd realised—probably a lingering side-effect of the neural sweep. Vivid details I'd thought forgotten. Memories of the man who had set all this in motion.

The corridor was clear for now, but there would be more patrols. It wouldn't do to stay in one place for too long. I still needed to get to the docking bay.

I continued along the gangway apace, ducking and weaving around the machinery, conscious that I could come across more of the crew at any moment. The question was whether they would try to kill me or take me back to that accursed cell. I was bound for disposal anyway, but would they follow some kind of protocol or put me down wherever they happened to find me? If I were a betting man, I'd put money on the latter.

One thing was clear: if I didn't get out now, I never would.

I.

# CHAPTER ONE
## ARCADIA LANDING

### *12ᵗʰ April 2066*

CAPTAIN AUSTIN QUEEN STEPPED OUT of the airlock into the bright, bustling arrivals lounge of Arcadia Landing. The late afternoon sunlight streamed through the left-side panoramic window. Pillars and people, desks and chairs, plants and information boards all cast long shadows across the spacious, if sterile, interior. All about him was activity: young people in their prime rushing around, living enviable lives of adventure on the frontier of human accomplishment.

A smile crept across his wrinkled face and his heart swelled at the sight. These were the hard-won fruits of his—and so many of his former colleagues'—decades of labour.

At the age of eighty-three, Austin both looked and felt very much out of place here in the Martian city. He was short and bald with a scruffy white beard and tanned peach skin, and though he had retained the muscular physique of his youth, he now carried a cane wherever he went.

*An old man with a cane, on Mars of all places!*

He rubbed his hip with the ball of his hand. The preceding five years had played havoc with his arthritis and his hip hadn't healed right after that tumble six months ago.

Gripping the stick's ornately-carved pewter handle, he thought about how ridiculous he looked. If he could have gone without the damn thing for the rest of his life, he would have. At least he didn't need to actually lean on it here; the lower gravity did a good job of supporting his weary joints. Rather, carrying it had become habit.

This was the first time he'd been invited off-world since the International Space Administration had taken over, the first time he'd been into space since the *Magnum Opus'* maiden voyage to Mars over forty years ago.

He shuffled his way to the panoramic window overlooking the dusty red rock-scattered landscape. What met him was a surreal, painterly scene. If he didn't know it to be real, he would have been tempted to touch the reinforced glass to make certain it wasn't oil on canvas.

Half-buried in the Martian dirt, just beyond the outermost reaches of the human city of blocks and domes and tubes, lay the chilling reason for the settlement's existence: the vast wreckage of an alien warship, the *Bitter Authoritarian*.

The kilometre-long derelict loomed large, casting its imposing shadow across the city. A fitting picture of the Achelon's posthumous influence over humanity.

Austin shuddered and turned away. He'd never thought he would see it again and he almost wished he hadn't.

The landing site for Austin's mission was ten kilometres to the south of the ship's impact trench. Arcadia Landing had been built around the original *Magnum Opus* crew's surface habitat but had since expanded to fill the distance in the intervening decades.

What had once been a simple scientific outpost to study the wreckage had become something more: a tourist destination, a colony, or a soon-to-be independent state, depending on who you asked.

After shaking the image of the alien wreckage from his mind, he drank in every detail of the spaceport's interior with wide-eyed wonder and meandered through check-in.

Absentmindedly, he showed his documentation to a beleaguered clerk. The city wasn't used to having so many visitors at once, but despite the uptick in footfall for the occasion, the arrivals process remained fast and efficient.

Austin found himself boarding a mag-lev train before he knew it, which swiftly and silently spirited him away from the small northern spaceport.

Sitting alone and staring out the window, he watched as the city sped past. Wide, clear agricultural domes glinted in the cool glow of the setting sun. Most of the other buildings surrounding them were no more than a couple of storeys tall, all of a modular design, light grey and box-like, connected by tunnels or vestibules into a vast web.

Dust storms had done their part in weathering the settlement, the Martian sand collecting in crevices and reaching up from the base of the utilitarian structures, so nothing looked new.

Few buildings had windows larger than a porthole. Still fewer had airlocks leading to the inhospitable outside world. The panoramic views of the spaceport were a luxury, it seemed.

None of this fazed Austin, however. The fact that humans had a working settlement on Mars within just forty years was remarkable enough. Of course, his own faster-than-light engine had played a key role in the expansion.

As the train approached the heart of the city, the size of the buildings increased. So too did the weathering, the older parts of the city having greater quantities of settled dust.

Austin usually fell asleep on long train journeys these days—especially one so smooth—but the views of this rusted alien world captivated him.

Pressing his face against the glass, he fancied he might recognise some of the natural landmarks from when the area had been a barren wasteland. But the reality was that rocks were rocks.

As the density of buildings increased, he could scarcely believe the scale of the city. It was a shame he'd been unable to see it on approach. The passenger cabin of the *UNSV Magellan*—one of the ISA's four Aurora-class spaceplanes—had no windows. It was simply a cargo bay with added seating.

After a while, the train slowed, coming to a smooth halt at the North-Central station, which connected to the wide geodesic dome in which the treaty signing was to take place. It made a stark contrast to the utilitarian aesthetic of the city's outskirts.

Out of the station and barely a step into the spacious dome, Austin came to a dead halt. He had to lean heavily on his cane, then, as his breath caught in his chest. It was clear no expense had been spared in the dome's development into a lush garden zone filled with trees, shrubs, flowerbeds, and pathways. The landscaping was immaculate. Austin knew a huge chunk of the funding for the city had come from private companies interested in space tourism. As such, it represented a little slice of home amid the rusted wastes. Visible outside, spreading out in a vast ring around the dome, were the city's residential and entertainment districts.

The dome also played host to Arcadia Landing's administrative centre, constructed around the first modules of the early 2030s. Along the eastern edge, many of those modules had been converted into UN governmental buildings, with the scientific facilities relocated to elsewhere in the sprawling city.

In the middle of the dome was a wide-open space, a circular area containing a monument to the first expedition.

Austin wandered along the path to the memorial, taking in the greenery and delicate floral aromas. Despite the sights and smells, there was an unnatural quality to it all. It was quiet, still, sterile. No leaf stirred with no cooling breeze; no birds chirped, no insects buzzed, and the people were surprisingly few, revealing this spot as an unsatisfying simulacrum of home.

*Or am I just being cynical?*

After a short way, he arrived at the memorial: the original habitat his team had made out of their descent vehicle on that fateful day. In front stood five reddish statues flecked with grey, hewn from local rock. Space-suited likenesses of Austin's younger self and his team posed like heroes of old; the only place in the solar system where they were honoured rather than forgotten.

Commander James Fowler, Cosmonaut Yula Merkulova, Specialist Grant Oliveras, and Major Zhu O-Huang.

He sighed and reached up to touch Yula's statue, the smooth, polished stone adding to the softness of her features. 'I wish you could have seen this place,' he said in his Arkansas drawl. 'You would've loved it.'

'Reliving the glory days, Captain?' came a chipper voice from behind in a Pacific Northwestern accent.

Austin grunted without turning. 'Glory days? That's not what I'd call 'em, Nate.'

Captain Nathan Rifkin came up beside him. He was much taller and younger than Austin. Nate had always been a man who took pride in his appearance. A finely trimmed jet black beard adorned his warm sepia face, accentuating his angular jawline. His dark hair was styled in a dense, textured high-top with a low fade.

'Who was she?' he asked, his hands on his hips.

'Her name was Yula, our imaging specialist,' said Austin. 'She was killed aboard the ship by one of the Achelon survivors. A damn tragedy, but she wasn't our only casualty.' He pointed to another of the statues, a bald man with much the same build as Austin looking up to the sky with a hopeful expression. 'This was Sergeant Grant Oliveras, former Spanish Army; he was our geologist, would you believe?'

Nate cocked an eyebrow and looked down at Austin.

'Back then, we thought we were dealing with a comet. He died a couple of years after we got back to Earth. Quit the agency as soon as we got back and went to go work in his father's bakery in Montpellier—probably hoping for a simpler life. But the trauma proved too much for him and he took his own life.' Austin then continued to point out each statue in turn. 'That's Colonel Zhu back when she was a major. She was our pilot at the time, so she stayed aboard the *Magnum* during the mission. Administers the Le Guin Research Base now. And of course you already know Jimmy.'

'Wait, that's James? Apart from the beard, he hardly looks any different. Isn't he nearly as old as you?' said Nate with a snort. 'Like one of those celebrities that never seems to age.'

Austin shrugged. 'Good genetics. I tell you, Nate, none of us who came down here that first time escaped without deep wounds. Some fared better than others. I counted myself among them, but being back here again is…'

'Painful?'

'In a way. More like the shadow of an ache that's been there in the background for so long you can't tell if it's real or you're imagining it.'

Nate squeezed Austin's shoulder. 'I'm sorry, sir. I didn't know. Neither you nor James have ever talked about it.'

Austin waved him away. 'Few remember these days. And it's hard to talk about when you know all we've gained has been paid for in blood. Do *you* remember what I told you when I chose you to command the *Magellan*?'

'"Don't be like the other guy"?' Nate said with a shrug. 'I don't know, Captain, it was five years ago.'

Austin couldn't help but laugh. A joke from Nate was a rare thing, but he was practical and not one for philosophising. Similar to how Austin used to be in his younger days. The last forty years had changed that. The ISA had placed a lot of responsibility on the ageing captain, especially since the first successful FTL flight of the *Aurora*. The Austinium drive that was his namesake had performed wonderfully and opened up a whole new era for spaceflight. The *UNSV Magellan* and its sister-ships, the *Newton* and the *Galileo,* had been built a mere seven years later in the *Aurora*'s template. Captain Queen had been placed in charge of choosing, training, and directing the crews for these new superluminal vessels. It had been a lot, but the personal touch had been nice. It made them feel like a family.

'Never mind,' said Austin, finally tearing his gaze from the memorial—now reflecting the bluish glow of sunset—and turning to the younger captain. 'Where's the rest of your crew, anyway?'

Nate smiled. 'Damien, Petra, and Bill went to get settled into their accommodations. I've given them the night off, so I imagine they'll hit up the entertainment district this evening.'

'And the new kid—what was her name? Marissa?'

'Corporal de Beek,' said Nate with a nod. 'She said she was going to take a tour of the city. First time she's been here, just like you. Speaking of which, the treaty signing isn't until tomorrow morning. Do you know where you're staying?'

Austin scratched at his beard with his cane. 'Yeah, they got me set up in a hotel nearby with the UN ambassadors and ISA big wigs. Got a map on my phone. But before I check-in, I wanna send a message to Jimmy, let him know I arrived safe.'

'I could do that on the *Magellan,*' offered Nate.

With a smile, Austin shook his head. 'Thanks, but I want to do it myself. Plus, it'll be a long-range video out to Ganymede, so it'll need a bit more power behind it.'

The two of them continued talking as Nate led Austin

around to the eastern edge of the dome where the main communications centre was situated. Austin could have found it himself, owing to the large array of parabolic antennae plainly visible through the triangular segments, but he appreciated the company.

Once inside, he bade farewell to Captain Rifkin and enquired at the front desk about sending his message. Soon after, the clerk led him through to a large room full of cubicles. Some were larger than others; some were occupied with their doors closed, while the vacant ones remained open. The clerk showed Austin to one of the smaller booths containing just a chair, computer screen, microphone, and camera. The software and set-up were familiar, similar enough to the ones he used in the ISA headquarters in Budapest. He was used to communicating with the *Aurora* at long-range, though this time he would be transmitting to Catamitus Dock rather than the ship itself.

The dock on the surface of Ganymede was brand new and still under construction, planned as a ground base and orbital shipyard for future exploration ventures deeper into the solar system and beyond. It was, after all, cheaper to launch spacecraft from lower gravity worlds. Captain Fowler had been assigned to ferry parts out to the work crews using the *Aurora*, an assignment that kept him from attending the historic treaty signing himself.

Austin selected the new dock from the list on the screen and pressed the button to begin recording.

'Hey Jimmy,' he said, shifting in the seat to centre himself in the camera view. 'Just wanted to let you know I've arrived safe and sound here at Arcadia Landing, courtesy of Nate and the *Magellan*. I don't recall if you've been here before, but… Honestly, dude, it's incredible. Shame about the ride over though. Nate had me sat next to a bunch of highfalutin, richer-than-god politicians coming over for the ceremony. Insufferable assholes. The journey from Earth only took a few minutes—not counting the take-off and landing—but… Jeez. I was glad to get outta there!

'I don't know why I'm here if I'm being honest with you. Feels like they're gonna drag me out on a stage like some old relic, speak a few platitudes over me, then send me on back to museum storage. Anyway, man, I hope things are going well with the construction efforts. Give my love to Angie when you get back to Earth. Queen out.'

With the press of a button, the camera turned off and Austin sent the transmission. He waited while the progress bar filled the screen.

*An hour or thereabouts from Mars to Jupiter this time of year, with Earth as a relay. Christ, I wish that damned alien database had given us FTL communications too.*

On his way out, he thanked the clerk and made his way back through the dome towards his hotel.

* * *

It was late evening when Nate went down to the entertainment district, much of which was still under construction. At the end of a winding corridor from the central dome, the facility opened out into a large two-storey communal concourse. The Martian night sky was visible through the flat windowed ceiling, which was held up by thick pillars arranged regularly along both sides of the plaza. On the ground floor, between vacant lots, were the few clubs, bars, and restaurants that had opened in the last couple of years, their neon signs bathing the dimly lit arcade in vibrant colour. The upper floor housed the rooms for two separate hotels catering to the mega-rich. People milled about: staff, tourists, and dignitaries alike flitting from bar to club or sitting on the benches around planters and small green spaces.

In the last two decades, tourism had become an important factor in supplementing funding for off-world bases, allowing their important scientific work to continue uninterrupted. The staff—who usually made up the vast majority of residents in a city like Arcadia Landing—rolled their eyes and grumbled about the hoity-toity clientele but were still glad of the new opportunities for relaxation that came with them.

Nate made his way towards the Hephaestus Chain, the barely-contained electro beats growing louder as he approached. He pushed through the throng outside and spoke to the bouncer, showing his officer's ID. The bouncer let him through and he descended a small ramp into the nightclub, tapping his phone on the reader to open the gate.

It was dark inside. The hot, sticky air thumped with music as clubbers danced, bright lights flashing in time with the rhythm. Others sat on sofas around tables on the periphery, drinking and yelling, leaning close to one another to try to make themselves heard above the booming bassline.

The flickering light revealed the faces of Commander Damien Vance and Sergeant Petra Milakova, who were seated around one of the tables, laughing, drinks in hand, watching the dance floor.

Commander Vance had skin of dark umber and wore his light grey *Magellan* flight suit unbuttoned at the top. He reclined with an arm resting behind his shaved head and, unlike Nate, his sharp-featured face was clean-shaven as well.

The top portion of Sergeant Milakova's suit was down with the arms tied around her waist and she wore a plain white tee. Her skin was a pale but warm peach and she had vivid green eyes. Between drinks, she grooved in her seat, laughing, whooping, and cheering at the dancefloor.

Specialist Bill Watkins would be close by, gyrating like a lunatic probably. The crew of the *Magellan* was a tight-knit bunch with the exception of Marissa, but there was still time for her to get used to her crewmates' antics.

*Where is Marissa anyway? She ought to have finished her tour by now.*

Nate looked again at his crew's table, then to the bar on the opposite side of the dance floor.

*Ah well, while I'm here…*

With a drink of his own, he joined the table with Damien and Petra in time for Bill to come back from the floor, drenched in sweat. He wasn't a good dancer, but what he lacked in skill he made up for with enthusiasm. The crew had teased him often, at which he would point to his pasty-white skin and say, 'Do you see this colour?'

At least here with the lower gravity and awkward, floaty movements, nobody else would be winning any awards either, so he blended right in.

'Captain!' said Bill, taking off his square-framed glasses and lifting his shirt to wipe his face as the music died away between songs. 'What are you doing here? Never thought I'd see you in a club.'

The music started up again and a cheer erupted from the crowd of revellers. Nate leaned in and yelled, 'I came to check up on you guys. Early start tomorrow.'

'That's a shame,' said Bill. He ran his hand through his short, tawny hair, still looking soaked. 'You look like you could use a bit of fun.'

Commander Vance looked at his smartwatch. 'We were nearly done here anyway, sir.'

Nate patted Damien's back sharply and gave him a nod. It was easier than shouting.

A wide grin spread across Petra's face and she tapped Bill's hand. She leaned over the table, spoke something inaudible into his ear, and pointed to the dance floor. Bill turned and grimaced as another dancer—a guy in an engineer's uniform—waved at him. His expression grew more contorted as he spun back around to the table, picked up his drink, and finished it in one gulp.

Then, in triumph, Bill stood, declared to the three of them, 'One more dance!' and motioned for them to accompany him.

'You joining us, Captain?' said Damien in Nate's ear as he rose from his seat.

'No, Commander,' Nate said, holding up his drink. If he'd been here to dance, he'd have dressed more appropriately and stylishly. He'd only come for business and so had stayed in his flight suit. 'I'll just finish this and go.' He nodded his head towards Petra and Bill, who were now dancing together with the engineer and another man. 'Make sure *they* get back to the hotel safe and… unaccompanied. Remember we're on duty in the morning.'

'Yes, sir.'

'Oh, have you seen Corporal de Beek this evening?'

'No, sir. Maybe she got an early night.'

Nate nodded and dismissed the commander, who went off to join the others. He watched them dance while he finished his drink, then left the nightclub and headed across the concourse towards the hotel.

* * *

Austin returned to the garden dome the next morning and found it in a much different state than the previous day. A small stage with chairs and a singular lectern was set near the monument in the centre with a seating area facing it. It seemed almost the entire city had turned out for the occasion. Politicians and diplomats, journalists, city staff, security guards, and civilian residents gathered in droves. There wasn't enough seating for everyone.

Above the stage hung a banner emblazoned with the words 'A United Earth for a Better Future'. The aisle dividing the rows of chairs down the middle was taken up by a set of cameras. Arcadia Landing staff busied themselves finalising the set-up on the stage, attaching an array of microphones to the lectern and bringing out a table on which the treaty document would eventually be placed.

Captain Rifkin and the crew of the *Magellan* milled about the outskirts of the seating area. Nate talked with a few of the diplomats, while Bill, Petra, and Damien patrolled with security. Another woman stood to attention nearby, wearing the same light grey *Magellan* flight suit as the rest of the crew. She had shoulder-length curly blonde hair and bright blue eyes.

Austin made his way over to her as she surveyed the gathering crowd.

'You're Marissa, right?' said the captain, stopping in front of her. He leaned on the top of his cane with both hands and smiled.

'Excuse me, sir, but the seating area is reserved for the diplomats,' she said, sparing him a quick glance before returning to her hawk-like observation.

Austin's smile deepened. 'At ease, Corporal. It's a pleasure to finally meet you. Nate has told me… well, hardly a thing, but I do like to get to know my crews.'

Marissa's eyes snapped back to the old man and widened. 'Captain Queen? I am so sorry, sir, I didn't know it was you!'

Austin waved a hand. 'Understandable. We've never met in person, after all. Now, tell me, how're you finding working with Nate?'

Rubbing the back of her neck, Marissa replied, 'Captain Rifkin is an exemplary commanding officer and the *Magellan* is a fine ship, sir.'

'That's not really what I asked, Corporal, but—'

Austin was cut off by a soft chime and the chattering diplomats redoubled their efforts to move to their seats.

'I'll speak with you more after,' he said with a nod.

Marissa gave him a nervous salute and he shuffled down the seating aisle, chuckling to himself.

Towards the front he noticed the chairs were labelled with names. He quickly found his own along the front row and heaved a great sigh as he sat down. Glancing around, he saw there was nowhere good to put his cane, so he leaned forwards and tucked it under the chair.

He had barely gotten himself comfortable again when Elisabeth Schreiber, the administrator of the ISA and German ambassador to the United Nations, sat down next to him. She wore a smart black blazer over her matching flight suit. On her lapel was a pin featuring the UN logo.

'How are you finding Arcadia Landing, Captain?' she said, brushing her dishwater-blonde shoulder-length curls out of her face. 'It is wonderful to finally visit; Dr Azzopardi would be so jealous he did not get to come during his tenure.'

'Yeah, I'm not so sure about that,' Austin countered.

'No?'

'I worked with the man for seventeen years, even after he stepped down as the Maltese ambassador, and not once did he ever express a desire to go off-world.'

Schreiber sighed and looked around the stage. 'It is an exciting time for us all, no? The Treaty on the Confederacy of the United Nations promises to open up wonderful new opportunities for us as a space agency.'

'Spare me,' Austin grumbled.

The administrator looked taken aback. 'The world is finally seeing the importance of our work, of *your* work, Austin.'

'Hey, I'm all for closer international co-operation but *a military arm?* I left the military for NASA back in the day because I hated that culture. Why does the UN need to militarise the ISA anyway?'

'After this, the UN will be the United Earth Confederacy. We are on the cusp of making your engine viable for interstellar travel. All the work you and Captain Fowler have done with the *Aurora* over these last two decades has been toward that goal. It is a symbol of the better future the UEC will stand for. But we cannot ignore the facts.'

'What damned facts?'

'That the spacecraft sitting beyond the walls of this city is a ship of war. Armed to the teeth with planet-killing weaponry. That nearly fifty years ago, by the grace of God, we narrowly avoided being obliterated. We cannot hope to leave this solar system unprepared, undisciplined.'

Austin scoffed. 'Sounds like something Guy Furious would say.'

Elisabeth sat back, her hazel eyes wide and fierce. 'He had a point. For all of his, uh, imbecility, there was always that one grain of truth. You, of all people, should know that is why his following has been so strong, even after his death.'

Austin made to argue back but fell silent, then muttered, 'You have a point.'

Elisabeth regained her composure and relaxed into a smile. She placed a hand on Austin's shoulder and gave it a gentle squeeze. 'I had better go find my seat. I will speak with you more after the ceremony. Please try to enjoy it.'

The captain grunted his weary assent and the administrator stood and moved further along the front row until he could no longer see her behind groups of standing diplomats.

*Try to enjoy it? Pah!*

How could he? The Austinium drive was meant to herald a new era of space exploration, not place the world back on the knife-edge it had worked so hard to come down from this last half-century. There were so many ways the militarisation of the space programme could backfire. Visions of his miraculous engine strapped to asteroids, of warships that could appear and disappear on a whim, raining hell-fire down on unsuspecting countries, had plagued his sleep. In space, any engine was a potential weapon, so how much more an engine that warped the fabric of reality? These threats existed regardless of the administrative structure of the ISA, but Austin distrusted the hawkish minds of generals and admirals.

And yet, he understood the prudence of it. Journeying beyond the safety of the solar system, tearing through space with reckless abandon without any means of defence, was foolish. The Achelon *were* out there, or others like them. Austin knew only too well the threat they posed.

But hope remained in the strength of the international bonds forged by this new confederation. Remnants of old prejudices persisted. Still, nations disagreed regarding the philosophies of governance. Still, gross injustices and human suffering continued to afflict Earth. But there was a new spark of hope and the UEC represented the next step in humanity's slow, faltering, gradual trend towards brotherhood.

Austin prayed it would be enough.

The seats around him began to fill and the chatter grew louder as the time drew near. The butterscotch mid-morning sky bathed the park in warm light. Crisp, clear shadows from the polyhedral dome criss-crossed the stage.

The seats behind the lectern filled and a leather-bound document was placed open on the table. Following this, the din of voices died down and a hush came over the room. The air itself buzzed with anticipation; it was the kind of silence that could wake the dead.

After a long moment, Sasha Barrington, the administrator for Arcadia Landing, crossed the stage. Like all the other dignitaries and ambassadors, she wore a smart black flight suit with subtle detailing and the ISA logo on her shoulders. Her golden hair was a slicked-back textured bob and her wide, square jawline and angular features gave her a stern look. Sasha had led the Arcadia Landing project for the last ten years, having taken over during a brief period of uncertainty about the running of the place when commercial tourism was first floated as an option to secure continued funding. It was no over-statement to say her commanding presence had made the city what it was today.

She scanned the crowd and the line of diplomats seated on the stage with her shrewd, dark eyes as she approached the lectern.

'Today has been a long time coming,' she began, lean-ing forwards with her hands gripping either side of the countertop. 'So I will keep this introduction brief. The people of Mars are proud to play host to the signing of this new treaty, bringing humankind one step closer to unity.' She extended one arm out to the side. 'It is there-fore my pleasure to introduce Secretary-General Masahiro Fujikawa, who will preside over the rest of the ceremony.'

The gathered crowd gave polite applause, while Austin rolled his eyes and kept his arms folded.

Masahiro Fujikawa, the secretary-general of the United Nations, rose from his seat behind Sasha and stepped to the front. His flight suit was similar to hers, except his bore the UN logo on the shoulders. His black hair was side-parted and thin-rimmed glasses framed his round face.

Sasha shook his hand, gave way to him, and sat down in the now-unoccupied seat at the back of the stage.

After a quick, perfunctory inspection of the treaty document, Mr Masahiro approached the lectern.

# CHAPTER TWO
## INTERRUPTION

S ECRETARY-GENERAL MASAHIRO OPENED his mouth to speak, holding his hands out in an invitational gesture. A dull rumble shook the dome, rattling the triangular panels in their frames and cutting him off. The ground trembled and the audience murmured.

A second later, a dull crack like thunder, muffled by the thin atmosphere, sounded to the south and the big spotlights flanking the stage went out.

Nate looked about for his team as the seated audience grew more restless. Mars quakes were a thing but never this intense. And thunder on the red planet was completely unheard of. Something was happening and he didn't like it.

The secretary-general regained his composure and made to restart his speech but was cut-off once again as alarms blared across the city.

The nervous chattering of the crowd grew more intense.

'Power's gone out city-wide,' Bill hissed into Nate's ear. 'It took a second, but we're on the emergency generators.'

The city's security personnel were already beckoning to the secretary-general and other diplomats to come down from the stage.

'We need to get these people out,' Nate said with a nod. As Bill moved off to rally the rest of the crew, Nate clambered up onto the stage and approached the microphone. 'This is an evacuation order. Everyone, please remain calm and make your way to the emergency launch vehicles at North-Central station.'

The dignitaries, tourists, residents, and journalists rose from their seats and proceeded apace through the greenery in the direction of the train station, escorted by the security personnel and the crew of the *Magellan*.

Austin remained behind.

'The fuck's going on, Nate?' said Austin, shuffling over to the stage.

Nate hopped down to meet the captain. 'Unsure, sir. Probably an accident of some kind over at the power distribution centre,' he said, pointing to the south. He remained unconvinced by his own explanation. Why would such an accident even occur? And why would it be bad enough to evacuate the entire city? 'Let's get you to a capsule.'

His words were punctuated by the sound of screaming and gunfire. Residents, tourists, and city staff who had not been present at the ceremony sprinted through the dome towards them from the entertainment district tunnel.

'That doesn't sound like an accident,' said Austin.

'Shit.' Nate drew his pistol from its holster and radioed for his team. 'Everyone back to the stage, we're under attack. Unknown assailants approaching from the south.'

Austin yelped as Nate grabbed him by the arm and dragged him along in retreat. They both ducked down as bullets flew through chairs and bodies and hammered against the stage.

Nate shoved Austin, who fell to the soft grass behind the stage before the *Magellan*'s captain followed suit. The gunfire sputtered against the wood, sending splinters over them, then died away.

A short moment later, Commander Vance, Corporal de Beek, Sergeant Milakova, and Bill skidded down next to Nate, their weapons drawn.

'Anyone have a status update? Just what the hell is going on?' cried Nate.

Bill spoke up first, shaking his head. 'Not a fuckin' clue, but whoever they are, it looks like they sealed off all the evac terminals. Security are there now, trying to pry open the doors.'

Nate and Austin chanced a look around the corner of the stage. There were bodies strewn across the grass in front of the memorial area. Civilian colonists and workers continued to run by, all heading for the train station. Of the attackers, there was no sign.

'They're not advancing into the dome,' Austin said, pulling his head back behind cover.

Nate glanced around the edge again and sighed. 'Alright, our first priority is to protect these people, get them to some kind of safety. With the emergency pods down, they'll be sitting ducks if these guys do decide to advance.'

'What about the *Magellan*?' said Petra. 'Are the trains still running? If we can get people on the trains to the northern port, we can take them back to Earth ourselves.'

Commander Vance nodded and grunted in agreement.

Marissa reached into her pocket and pulled out her phone. 'The network's still up,' she said. 'Looks like the auto-lockdown has been compromised, but security has already sent out a distress signal on ISA channels. The trains are working but only out of North-Central; East and West-Central are sealed shut.'

'And we don't want to go to South-Central. That's past the guys with guns,' said Austin.

Nate holstered his weapon and took one last glance out across the dome. 'North-Central it is, then. Let's go.'

The group made their way cautiously through the dome, keeping a close eye on the receding doors of the entertainment district.

Nate kept a firm grip on his holstered sidearm and the others did the same. As they ran, they all shot anxious glances behind them.

Their time exposed dragged on, but soon they were obscured amid the trees and shrubs, and it wasn't long before they emerged at the station's entrance.

Austin stopped and bent over to catch his breath, leaning heavily on his cane.

Damien put a hand on Austin's shoulder and offered to help him into the station, but the captain shook his head and stood up straight, breathing deeply.

Inside, the train station heaved with people crowding and jostling, shouting and grumbling; it was anything but calm.

As Nate and the crew pushed their way through the throng, he caught snippets of an argument over by the doors for the Emergency Launch Vehicles. City engineers and security personnel exchanged terse words with dignitaries displeased at their lack of progress getting the doors open.

*How long until this turns violent? We need to give these people a solution, and fast.*

Nate spoke with the train operators, who nodded and rushed away. Seconds later, the doors to the nearest train opened and Nate hoisted himself up onto a pillar.

'Attention!' His voice boomed and echoed despite the mass of people. It took a few tries, but eventually the crowd filling the station platform fell silent and turned to face him.

'The *Magellan* stands ready to take you off-world at the northern port, so let's make this orderly,' he bellowed. 'I want UN personnel and visitors to board the train first, then residents and staff. Who's in charge of security?'

A woman in a white uniform stepped forwards out of the crowd, flanked by four others. She had short, bronze-coloured hair in loose curls and her pale peach face was covered in freckles below hazel eyes.

'That would be me, Captain,' she said, crossing her arms. 'Jean Kamzel, head of security.'

Nate dropped down from his perch and gestured to Bill and Petra, who began co-ordinating the refugees.

'Any idea what's going on here?' he asked.

A grim look came over Jean's face as she said, 'Treason.'

'You mean our own people did this?' said Austin, sputtering and leaning on his cane. 'Preposterous! Everyone's vetted before they come out here. The ISA performs extensive background checks, psychological evaluations, and—'

'Yeah, well, something slipped through the net, Queen,' Jean shot back, glaring daggers at Austin. 'Mars ain't like it used to be back in your day.'

Nate stepped between them, palms out. 'We don't have time for arguments. Just tell us exactly what happened, Kamzel.'

Jean huffed and refolded her arms. 'Xander Levine happened. Him and a dozen other engineers. Collins caught sight of 'em on one of the security cams just before you arrived.

'They screwed with the lockdown protocols, the evacuation pods, and bombed one of the power distribution centres.'

'A bomb? That explains the noise. How could a dozen guys do all that without anyone noticing?'

Jean shrugged. 'They know the city better than anyone and we ain't exactly prepared for an attack of this scale, you get me? I mean, we're tens of millions of miles away from the nearest dickwad, or at least we're supposed to be.'

Nate looked at her deadpan. 'You have a city full of billionaire tourists and politicians.'

Jean kissed her teeth in frustration. 'You know what I mean. All those woo-woo alien worshippers and conspiracy wackos.'

'Any idea what Xander and his crew want?' asked Austin, bringing the topic back on track.

'How the hell should I know?' Jean said through an incredulous scoff. 'They've made no contact, no demands. Just started butchering us… Their own people. Jesus.'

Austin dragged Nate aside. 'I know him. Xander Levine; I recognise the name.'

Nate put his hands on his hips. 'Tell me about him.'

Stroking his beard, Austin reminisced. 'I've only seen his file. He's a brilliant nuclear engineer, a specialist in fusion reactor technology.'

'He's not exactly our department, so how did his file cross your desk?'

'Schreiber accepted a transfer to Arcadia Landing from him maybe two years ago. I was having a meeting in her office at the time. You know what she's like, up to the eyeballs in work, multitasking.'

Nate bit his bottom lip. 'But what could've made him suddenly snap and start murdering innocent people?'

Austin turned away and shook his head. 'We've dealt with this kind of bullshit before, way back. The first time James took the *Aurora* out, it nearly ended in disaster thanks to a saboteur embedded within the ISA itself. God, how could we have been so careless as to let it happen again? Maybe our standards are slipping. Give 'em an inch and they take a mile.'

Nate pursed his lips and turned back to the security chief. 'How many people have you got?'

Jean tapped her finger to her chin. 'I have a squad of ten, the rest are trapped elsewhere around the city.'

'Well, I need at least four or five to accompany these refugees to the port to make sure things stay civil. The rest are to come with me and get the bastards killing our people.'

Nate beckoned to his team. Bill and Petra jogged over from the train and Damien and Marissa shuffled closer.

'Orders, Captain?' said Petra.

'Once everyone's on the train, I want you, Bill, and Marissa to get on too. Open up the *Magellan* and make her ready to receive passengers, then start getting them on board. Meanwhile, Vance and I will try to retake the entertainment district with Kamzel's security forces.'

Damien spoke up. 'Sir, I think it would be better if I

got on the train instead. That way, I can take the first wave of refugees on the *Magellan* as soon as they're aboard; I am the pilot, after all. We can only take forty at a time.'

'You're also my most experienced combatant,' said Nate, rubbing his chin. 'But I agree; that makes the most sense. Petra, you come with me instead.'

Nate turned to Austin and gripped his shoulders. 'You should get on the train too. Go with Damien. He'll look out for you.'

'The hell I will!' said Austin. 'I'm coming with *you*.'

'But—'

'I may be old, Nate, but I'm not dead yet and I can still hold a gun.'

Nate laughed, a little too loud. 'That's all well and good, but I ain't giving you one.'

Austin scowled at Nate for a long moment, then turned to Marissa and said, 'Give me your gun, Corporal.'

'But, sir, I—'

'That's an order.'

Without a further word, Marissa made to remove her weapon from its holster.

'Don't do it, de Beek,' said Nate and Marissa paused, looking between the two officers. 'You're not being fair on the rookie.'

Austin groaned and threw his hands up. 'Would ya quit it already, Nate? You're gonna need all the help you can get. Let me do this. Don't make me pull rank on you, too.'

Captain Rifkin squeezed the bridge of his nose, then gestured to Marissa to hand over the gun. 'Fine.'

Austin gripped the pistol in one hand and tested its weight, leaning on his cane with the other.

A short time later, Nate, Austin, Petra, Jean, and five of her security officers made their way back across the embattled dome and arrived at the entrance to the entertainment district's connecting tunnel.

With a glance behind, Nate saw the faint trail of the *Magellan* rising rapidly into the Martian sky.

They arranged themselves either side of the doorway, clutching their weapons, with Austin bringing up the rear.

With the press of a button, Nate opened the door and peeked inside.

'It's clear,' he said, waving his hand. 'Move in. Queen, you stay at the back.'

Austin rolled his eyes but agreed, nonetheless.

Nate shook his head. Why was Austin even doing this? Throwing himself into the line of fire was ludicrous at his age. But he couldn't deny he could use the help, especially with most of the city's security officers trapped elsewhere. They would be facing an overwhelming force, even if it was just a bunch of engineers.

The group crept down the darkened corridor, bathed in the dim glow of emergency lighting. Slowing their pace, they moved along quietly until they reached a bend in the narrow, corpse-strewn passageway.

Pressing himself close to the wall, Captain Rifkin peered around the corner. He heard someone pleading. There was a flash of light and the sharp crack of an electrical discharge. Something sizzled and burned and everything went silent. Nate's heart skipped a beat.

*Shit.*

'One contact,' said Nate at a whisper as he pulled his head back from the edge. Austin's face looked grim even in the dim light and Nate knew he'd recognised the sound. 'He just executed someone with some kind of energy weapon. They must have found the armoury.'

'Plasma rifle,' said Austin. 'From the alien ship. They're nasty things.'

'How bad?' Jean hissed as she crouched behind Nate at the corner.

'War-crime bad,' Austin said, repositioning his cane. 'I've used one myself, a long time ago.'

Remaining tucked behind the corner, Nate raised his voice, 'There's nowhere for you to go. Drop your weapon immediately.' He paused a few seconds. 'I am not going to repeat myself. Do it now or die where you stand.'

In reply, a bolt of plasma cracked and burned through the corner of the wall where Nate stood, just missing him as he jerked back in anticipation.

Then he rounded the corner and fired with his pistol, sending three rounds into the other man. The rifle clattered to the floor and the rest of the team joined Nate in the open.

The two captains stooped over the sprawled body of the terrorist. He was young and wore a black uniform emblazoned with a white death's head logo.

The collar of the suit was open and Austin pointed to the bright orange of the Arcadia Engineering Corps.

'They're just kids,' he said. 'What do they even want?'

'Right now, it doesn't matter,' Nate said with a scowl. 'We just need to stop them before more people die.'

'Or at least hold the line until backup arrives,' Jean said as she approached the body of the man who had been executed by the terrorist. He was slumped against the wall in a sitting position, the cauterised stump of his neck below a hole in the wall where his head had been.

By the blood-stained uniform, he had been a scientist from the salvage division.

'Jesus fucking Christ,' she said. 'You weren't wrong, Queen.' Holstering her pistol, she picked up the plasma rifle and examined it closely.

Nate stepped past the others and continued along the corridor a short way. 'Let's keep moving.'

Austin and the others grunted in agreement and followed. At the end of the corridor through another door was the two-storey concourse of the entertainment plaza. Far from the bustle of activity of the night before, it painted a grim picture. The dead lined the arcade. Some bullet-riddled and bloody, others burnt and missing limbs. The bodies remained where they had fallen, mostly clustered at this end, where the narrow tubular corridors of the city had created a bottleneck, preventing their escape. Some had clearly fled towards the nightclub and the bars but had been gunned down before they had reached the doors.

The *Magellan* captain's stomach churned at the sight and heat rose in his chest.

The dusty Martian sky could be seen through the windowed ceiling, tinting the walls and pillars in its sickly orange.

Creeping through the plaza, stepping over and around the littered corpses, darting between pillars and blood-spattered planters, the team moved apace. There was no sign of the attackers and a disquieting silence hung about the place. Nate's ears strained to their limit, listening for the slightest shuffle. There were a lot of places to hide along the concourse. It was always a possibility the other attackers had heard Nate put down one of their own in the corridor behind and taken up position for an ambush. Or they could simply have fled. Knowing why they had even begun the attack in the first place would've given Nate some indication of where they could be, but it remained a mystery.

As they moved through, Nate motioned for the security officers to break off and check the premises and open hotel rooms along the sides, for both the terrorists and survivors.

Austin lagged behind, a look of sorrow on his face. With his cane he turned a corpse onto its back—a male agricultural worker in a dark green jumpsuit. He tucked Marissa's gun into the belt of his flight suit. Bending down with his stick for support, he shook his head then closed the man's eyes.

'Know him, sir?' asked Nate.

Austin looked up. 'No, not personally.'

Nate chewed on the inside of his cheek and surveyed the strewn dead. 'Once we've neutralised the threat, we can make sure they're returned to their families.'

Austin grunted in agreement and rose to his feet, his eyes back on the man on the ground. 'It's funny. We all accepted the risks inherent in coming off-world. There's so many different ways the universe is hostile to life. Every step of the way, the environment itself seems to want us dead, but instead we get... this. What was it Kamzel said earlier? We're supposed to be millions of miles from the nearest whack-job. But we brought them right here anyway.'

Nate approached the old man and gave him a wan smile. 'We can safeguard against all kinds of natural hazards, but there's no accounting for plain, old-fashioned evil.'

One of the security officers, the one Jean called

Collins—the one whom Nate recalled as a slab of a man with a hawkish face and rough voice—radioed from the nightclub. 'Captain, Chief, we've located a group of survivors. Five total. They were holed up in the backroom. We're sending them out to you now.'

Sure enough, five terrified-looking men and women came out of the entrance to the Hephaestus Chain towards Nate and Austin. One Nate recognised as the barman. The others were in civilian clothing; two men, two women. Tourists, most likely. They stopped and exchanged horrified looks at the carnage about them.

'Get to North-Central,' Nate called, pointing back towards the dome. 'There's trains taking people to the northern port for evac.'

After recomposing themselves, they nodded their thanks and sped off in the direction of the exit.

'More over here,' came the voice of another security officer over the radio. Nate hadn't stopped to ask their names, but this one he knew as the only other woman of Jean's group. 'We've got about a dozen locked away in different hotel rooms,' she said. 'They're not opening up; they think we're going to kill them.'

Jean rested the plasma rifle on the ground and stood up with a groan. 'Then slide your ID badges under the door; let them know who you are.'

Nate's gaze lifted to the rustic sky. Something was off. Leaving survivors—especially in such obvious places—was an odd thing for a supposed massacre. Xander Levine and his crew had plenty of opportunity to go around clearing out the premises, taking out stragglers—if that had been his aim. But aside from the one kid in the corridor who'd taken the time to execute a scientist, they'd retreated elsewhere. At least, it was clear the attackers were no longer in the plaza. So what exactly was their aim, here?

'They're still not coming out,' said the security officer over the radio, her voice tinged with irritation. 'We're up on the first floor.'

Glancing upward, Nate spied the couple of security officers huddled outside of a hotel room beyond the balustrade.

He looked to Jean, who made to bite back over her comms, but Nate held up a hand.

'I'll handle it, Kamzel,' he said. 'You wait here. It doesn't look like our little death squad stuck around anyway, so we need to find them. Be ready to move.'

Nate hopped up the nearest set of stairs, which rose in a sweeping curve to the first floor. Passing some waste bins at the top, he made his way along the walkway towards the security officers.

The officer who had made the call was leaning her head against the hotel room door, her eyes clenched shut in frustration. As Nate approached, his boots squeaking on the polished floor, she looked up and silently moved aside, gesturing to the door and rolling her eyes.

'Have at it, sir,' she said, folding her arms and leaning against the railing opposite. 'I'd appreciate it if you could get my ID card back, too.'

'Is it just this room?' asked Nate. 'What of the others?'

'These four,' the officer replied, pointing out two rooms along to the left and one to the right of the door. 'This one's convinced the others not to open up. If we can get through to her, then the others should follow suit.'

Nate nodded and turned back to the hotel room door. He banged on it with his fist. 'This is Captain Nathan Rifkin, mission commander for the *UNSV Magellan*. Is everyone alright in there? The attackers are gone; it is safe to come out.'

A terrified voice retorted, 'How do we know you are who you say you are? As I told your accomplice, you could be waiting for us to come out so you can kill us.'

'My *colleague* is one of the city's security officers,' Nate said. 'I believe you have her identification.'

'She could have stolen it.'

The security officer pushed off from the railing. 'I've explained all this to her alrea—'

Without looking at the officer, Nate held up a finger. 'Look, ma'am, I get that you're scared. Believe me. I won't lie, it's been a bloodbath out here, and you did the right thing by staying inside. But you're also incredibly lucky to be alive. If the attackers had wanted you dead, this flimsy door wouldn't have helped you none.'

'What do you mean?'

Unlike the rest of the premises in the building—and throughout the city, in fact—the private hotel had opted for lightweight hollow-core doors due to the lower transport costs. Nate knew they wouldn't have held up to being bashed in, let alone a plasma cannon. Xander's crew would have simply burned a hole through it and butchered everyone inside. The rooms weren't very large, so they wouldn't even have needed to aim.

He searched briefly for a tactful way to say it, then settled for, 'I'm saying if we were the bad guys, we'd have blasted the door open by now. In fact, I could sneeze and this door would open, but we'd rather get you out and to the northern port safely.'

A long moment of silence passed. Nate wasn't sure if the guest behind the door had heard him. He opened his mouth to reiterate, then heard a banging, which sounded like it was coming from the internal walls. A short moment later, all four of the hotel rooms unlocked with a click and the dozen guests emerged warily. Some grimaced at the bodies on the ground floor, while others came over queasy. One man vomited over the side of the railing.

Out of the room Nate had been in front of came four people, three of whom were women. None said a word to him, but they all eyed him suspiciously. He couldn't tell which was the woman he'd been speaking to, but as soon as they vacated the room, he stooped down and picked up the security officer's ID.

As he handed the card back to the officer with a smirk, Jean radioed. 'Well? You get them out? We need to find Levine and his nut-jobs.'

'We got them, Kamzel,' Nate said as the other security officers directed the guests down the stairs at the other end of the walkway. 'They're heading towards the dome now. I suggest we move through into South-Central station from here.'

'South-Central? Jesus, if they've boarded a train, they could be anywhere in the city by now.'

'Then let's hope they haven't.'

Nate and the security officers soon re-joined Jean, Austin, Petra, and the other officers from the nightclub. To the south, not far away, was the doorway out of the entertainment district, which lead to another short corridor adjoining the train station. Like all of the city's four central compass-point stations, it was connected to the vast residential ring encircling the dome. There would be many residents who had not been present at the treaty-signing trapped within the ring by the closure of the East and West-Central stations, just like the rest of Jean's security force. It was a lot of people the *Magellan* wouldn't be able to evacuate, so neutralising the threat was imperative.

The mag-lev tube system broke off at several points around the ring to take its passengers outward to the city's scientific and infrastructural modules. Further to the south—beyond the station—was power distribution, from which the initial explosion had come. Further still, the main fusion reactor.

The group approached the doorway to the interconnecting corridor and, as before with their entrance to the entertainment district, they fanned out to the sides with Nate and Jean taking point.

Nate hammered the side of his fist into the button and the door whooshed open. Inside was pitch dark, without even the emergency lighting that had bathed the previous corridor in its ominous red glow. The open doorway spilled enough of the sickly Martian light to see to the far end. Unlike the previous corridor, this module was short and straight, but it bulged slightly in the middle.

They moved to the end, repeating the same formation, and were plunged into total darkness as the door behind them closed.

'This is it, people,' said Nate, reaching his hand up to where he knew the button was. 'If they're in the station, expect heavy resistance. Weapons ready.'

He heard the shuffle of movement as grips tightened and arms poised ready to fire.

Quieter this time, he pressed the button and the door opened.

South-Central station was a mirror image of

North-Central. Small slit windows along the tops of the walls illuminated the area with rays of Martian sunlight; still dim, but it was enough. The emergency lighting had failed here, too. Or perhaps it had been deliberately disabled. But for the window slits, the place would have been just as murky as the previous module. Immediately on entering, to one side were the locked escape capsule bays, while onwards the station opened up to its boarding platforms, complete with benches and slim columns along the length. They weren't as wide or as tall as the ones in the entertainment district, but they would do for cover if need be.

As they knelt in the shadows together by the corner of the escape capsule bay, looking out onto the open platform, Nate noticed a train carriage blocking the nearest tunnel. The lights were on and there was movement inside.

'They're in the train car,' Jean hissed.

Keeping his voice to a whisper, Nate replied, 'I know. We need to wait for them to come out. They have the advantage right now.'

'Fuck that. They've been killing our people; we're taking them down,' said Jean. She gestured to her security officers, pointing towards the pillars, and they readied themselves to move out onto the platform.

'Kamzel, stand down!'

'No, Captain. You Earthers can stay put if you like, but we're ending this. Now.'

'Goddammit, Kamzel,' said Austin, shuffling ahead and grabbing Jean's arm. 'You're gonna get us all killed.'

She pulled away and nodded to her team. They crept out from behind the wall and took up defensive positions behind the closest set of pillars.

'I suggest we follow them, sir,' said Petra.

Nate huffed. 'Agreed but keep low and go quietly.'

The three moved out and were more than halfway across when the platform erupted in uproar and gunfire.

Nate grabbed Austin and dragged him behind a pillar as plasma volleys burned the floor, splashing with an eerie light as they impacted.

Casting a glance out, Nate saw muzzle flashes emanating both from within the cab of the train carriage and to the side at the end of the platform.

He couldn't get a clear shot and so he stayed back behind the pillar, clutching his pistol. His heart hammered in his chest as he leaned against the cool Martian concrete. Austin sat at his feet, panting heavily. Petra had made it to another pillar and synchronised her movements with the security officers. Ahead, Jean's security team gave a good account of itself with the deafening rattle of gunfire, which echoed through the station.

After a few seconds, the assault died down. Over the ringing in his ears, Nate heard Petra shout, 'What's the plan now, Kamzel?'

'Soon as we get a clear shot on these assholes, we light 'em up,' Jean replied.

Austin snorted and called out, 'Simple. I like it. Y'know what I'd like better? *An actual fuckin' plan.*' He hauled himself off the floor and said to Nate, 'How many are we dealing with?'

Nate glanced out. From his vantage point he couldn't get a clear view on the enemy, but during the first wave, there had been at least two plasma rifles and another two with conventional anti-personnel weapons. 'No idea, maybe a half dozen.'

The moment he said this, a yelp of pain came from one of the security officers ahead and he stumbled back from his group, holding his arm. The exchange of gunfire began again in earnest from both sides. Concrete chipped and burned around them.

'How's that plan working out for you, Kamzel?' Nate cried, popping out and firing on a dark shadow behind a far pillar. 'We're outmatched,' he said to Austin. 'What did they hit that officer with?'

Austin leaned out low to the ground and put two rounds into one of Xander Levine's crew. 'Must've been one of the alien pistols; some kind of particle beam, so it's invisible.'

*Great, a tiny silent gun shooting burning shit we can't see?*

'We need to go,' Nate cried between gunshots.

'Fine!' Jean replied. 'I'll lay down suppression. Sergeant Milakova, you get my officer to safety.'

Petra grabbed the injured man by the collar and dragged him backwards across the floor in the direction of the station entrance. Jean and her other four continued firing on the train, ducking behind their pillars as haphazard balls of plasma arced towards them.

Jean and her officers then backed out and snaked their way along the pillars towards Nate and Austin. Another plasma volley caught Collins in the chest and he went down, screaming in agony.

'Fuck, Collins!' cried Jean. She started towards him, but Nate launched himself out from his cover and grabbed her, pulling her behind another pillar just as a hot streak burned the floor.

They stared at one another for a short moment, Nate looking down into her eyes as he held her in his arms.

Then Jean pushed herself away and gave him a grateful nod, which he acknowledged.

'We need to get out of here,' she said during a brief lull in the assault.

'No shit, Kamzel,' Austin said. 'I'm nearly out and I don't know how long the power cells in those plasma cannons last.'

'Back to the dome. We can regroup and try again,' said Nate.

'I'll go across to Sergeant Milakova first,' Austin cried. 'Then we can cover you from there, got it?'

Nate watched as—cane in one hand, pistol in the other—Austin moved out from behind his pillar in Petra's direction. The security officers and Jean were already out and laying into the enemy force.

Three-quarters of the way across, Austin's side erupted in a severe burn and he fell to the ground with a cry.

'Captain!' Nate screamed. Without a further thought or care, he darted out from his cover across the platform to the old man who now lay motionless on the floor. With Petra's help, they pulled him the rest of the way across to the station entrance and turned him over. They rested him leaning up against a planter; his breathing was ragged and his gaze distant.

'Captain?' said Nate, leaning over him as his alertness slowly returned. There was a shrillness to his voice he hadn't intended. 'You've been hit. The burn's pretty bad, but if we can get you back to the *Magellan*, we might—'

Austin cut Nate off with a grunt and a bloody cough. Licking his lips, he shook his head and said, 'No, leave me. Get outta here, Nate.'

'What? Leave you? Not a chance, old man.'

Austin reached up and gripped Nate by the collar. 'Goddammit, you've gotta go. I'll only slow you down.'

'Oh, so now you're worried about slowing us down?' Nate said through a wavering scoff.

'I can cover your escape from here.' Austin coughed again and hoisted the pistol still in his white-knuckled hand. His cane lay at his side.

'You'll die if you don't get help,' said Nate.

'Then get me help, ya idjit.'

'They'll kill you if we leave you here.'

'Not if I get them first.'

'Sir—'

'Go!' Austin roared and shoved Nate away, which left him panting.

Nate looked between his officer and Austin as Jean and her remaining officers came skidding down next to him.

'They're advancing,' she said. 'We're out of time. Oh god, Queen, I am so sorry.'

Austin shook his head as bullets ricocheted nearby. 'My stupid fault for coming along.'

Petra put a hand on Nate's shoulder and pulled on him. Nate leaned forwards and squeezed Austin's free hand. 'I *will* come back for you, sir.'

'I know you will, boy. Now *get*!'

Then Nate, Petra, Jean, and her officers peeled away, running for the door, firing behind them as they went.

* * *

The group of attackers came into Austin's view and he raised his pistol.

*Come on, you bastards...*

His hand trembled and his vision blurred. Letting out a long, slow breath, he squeezed the trigger and fired.

One of the attackers crumpled to the floor. The rest turned their attention away from the fleeing officers and raised their weapons at Austin.

He fired again, missed.

The man in the middle raised a hand and lowered the gun of the man next to him.

Austin pulled the trigger again.

Click.

And again. Click. Click. Click.

*Fuck.*

The man in the middle stopped, lifted his tinted visor, and smirked. The others came to a halt level with him.

'What the fuck, Xander? Why're we stopping,' said one as he lifted his visor. 'They killed our guys and this one just killed Avery.'

'Let them go,' said Xander Levine. 'They'll run all the way back to their precious ship. Lock down the door.'

One of the helmeted men moved off to comply.

Xander folded his arms.

'What do we do with this one, then?' asked the impatient man, gesturing to Austin. 'I could put a bullet between his eyes right now!'

'Patience, Michael,' said Xander as he placed a hand on his compatriot's shoulder. 'Your zeal for the cause is commendable but show some respect. This is the great Captain Austin Queen.'

Austin hurled the empty gun at the group, but it fell short of hitting any of them. He reached out with his other hand for the security of his cane.

Xander chuckled and stepped closer to Austin, stooping

down to his level. 'You're not long for this world, Captain. Even if your friends do return, you will not survive. The radiation from the particle beam will kill you anyway, but... you knew that already.'

'What the fuck do you want, Levine?' said Austin, stifling a cough.

'You'll find out soon enough, Captain. You're coming with us to watch the fireworks show,' said Xander. He turned to Michael. 'Take him.'

Austin's eyes drooped. Weariness and pain overtook him as the man named Michael approached. He hoisted Austin from the floor, supporting him under the arm from the left. The third remaining attacker jogged over and held Austin on the other side.

With a last burst of energy, Austin brought up the cane and pulled the handle free of the shaft. He then rammed the revealed dagger into the chest of the man on his right. The man gasped and fell away, clutching the exposed handle.

'Futile and predictably brutal,' said Xander with disinterest. He made a quick hand gesture.

As the man choked on his own blood, another stepped over him and took his place holding the now disarmed captain.

Together, they dragged him along behind Xander as they moved towards the train.

It all seemed a blur to Austin as his energy gave out and he faded in and out of consciousness. Xander had been right. Austin had known the moment he'd gotten hit with the particle beam that he wouldn't make it out alive. He'd studied Achelon technology enough to know how awful their weapons truly were. Telling Nate would've only been a distraction.

The train rocked him gently as it sped out of South-Central station, curving north-eastwards away from the city centre. James and Angela came to mind, his best friends in the universe; his only regret was that he would never see them again. James would take his death the hardest: a man out of time, already disconnected from the rest of the world and the natural order of things. Austin's stomach twisted; he couldn't tell if it was the guilt or the poisoning.

This wasn't the way Austin had wanted to go, but as he stared out at the Martian landscape, a certain satisfaction came over him. Arcadia Landing was as much his legacy as the Austinium drive. Being able to see it for himself, even just once at the very end of his life, was better than wasting away on Earth.

*My life truly began here, and here it ends. Poetic.*

'Where're we going?' Austin said, his voice hoarse and weak, speech slurred.

Xander stood over him, obscuring the blurry view out the window. 'The science labs,' he said. 'Classified research and development; the heart of sin.'

'Why?'

'Architects of their own destruction,' said Xander with a heavy sigh, his voice a low growl and the sides of his mouth twisted. 'So desperate to make progress for progress' sake, your people pressed on in wilful ignorance, plundering and pillaging; desecrating… inviting wrath.' He leaned in close to Austin's face and gripped him by the chin. 'Well, we shall open the eyes of the blind, this day.'

As Xander stepped away, everything went black once more. When Austin opened his eyes again, he was being dragged through more corridors. Soon, he was lowered to his knees in the centre of a small control room, an annex of the city.

Out of the window to his right was a sight that chilled his bones. He doubled over and vomited, only to be grabbed and brought back up to his kneeling position.

The gargantuan planet-killing particle cannon from the *Bitter Authoritarian* sat outside in its turret. Austin had seen the news weeks before that the Arcadia reclamation teams had successfully salvaged the ship's weapon and managed to power it. The warship had two, but one was trapped inside its bay. The other—this one—had been the easier of the two to remove. Now it was ready for testing.

'Targeting system online,' came a computerised voice. The huge artillery outside the window came to life and raised itself skyward, elongating and unfolding with a motorised grinding.

'Boss, I thought we were leaving some alive?' asked the other terrorist whose name Austin hadn't caught. 'You said we was supposed to make it so someone could tell the story.'

Xander laughed. 'Don't get ahead of yourself, brother. After all, what good are fireworks if there's no one around to see them?'

# CHAPTER THREE
## THE MAGELLAN

NATE, PETRA, JEAN, and her remaining officers sprinted across the dome to North-Central station. Anxious refugees milled about the platform, waiting for the train to return for them.

'Make way! Everyone, make way!' Jean cried over the din, raising her plasma cannon aloft. 'We need someone with a torch, now.'

A member of the engineering corps called out from the other end of the room and made her way over to the group, tool bag in hand.

Panting, Nate pointed back towards the dome and said, 'The door to the station locked down behind us as we retreated. Captain Queen is trapped on the other side.'

With a nod, the engineer called over to a couple of her colleagues and they all ran off in the direction of the entertainment district.

Nate wiped his face and paced back and forth. 'Once

they're through the door, we'll need medics,' he said to no-one in particular. His voice was shrill and trembling.

*Stupid. Stupid old man. What'd he have to go and do that for? He should never have come with us.*

Austin wasn't the only thing weighing on his mind. It should have been so simple to retake the city. They were just engineers—though engineers with advanced alien weaponry. How could it have gone so wrong?

He glared at Jean and heat flushed through his body. *Her.*

If she hadn't been so headstrong, they could've come up with an effective strategy.

*No, I can't go blaming her. She just wanted to save her people.*

Nate huffed and turned away just in time to see the train pull into the station. The doors opened. Damien, Bill, and Marissa had returned and began calling people forwards.

Nate caught Damien's eye. He gestured to the others to continue and pushed his way through the throng.

'The first wave with the secretary-general and the other ambassadors successfully alighted at Skyport, sir, and we've already got another party on board the *Magellan* ready to go,' Damien said. 'Lots more waiting in the departure lounge, though. Wait… Where's Captain Queen?'

'Trapped—possibly captured—and we need to rescue him. Once the engineering corps has the door to South-Central open again, I plan to hit the bastards hard. I want you, Marissa, and Bill to gear up and be ready.'

'Captain,' said Jean from behind. 'If you've got people on that ship ready to go, I suggest you take them.'

Nate spun on his heel. 'And abandon Captain Queen?' *Is she crazy? How could she suggest something like that?*

'It's going to take a while for them to cut through the door. You've got the time and the evacuation is still on, if you hadn't noticed.'

'She makes a good point, sir,' said Petra.

Nate weighed the options. His mind raced. Jean was right, cutting through the door would take time. The *Magellan* needed Damien since he was the pilot, but Nate could stay. Perhaps there was another, faster way to get through the door?

With a sigh, Nate said, 'Vance, get back to the *Magellan* and take off with the next wave of refugees. Sergeant Milakova, you go with him.' He turned to Jean. 'Maybe we could use that cannon of yours to blow the door open—'

'Stop,' said Jean, holding her hand up. 'I get that you're worried and I get that time is of the essence, but you're all over the place right now. There's no sense going on the attack when we're several people down. The priority has to be getting people to safety.'

'I cannot—I will not—leave Captain Queen behind.'

'For fuck's sake, Queen is dead!' Jean cried. The clamour in the room stopped as people turned their attention towards Nate and Jean. 'He only gave you hope so you'd get out of there. He knew full well what was in store for him. You really think, after what we saw them do to all those other people, that they'd let him live? Stop being so naïve. Do your damn job and save my people.'

Long moments passed between them. Nate stared dumbfounded at Jean. Anger welled in the pit of his stomach. How could she just give up like that? Austin wouldn't have let himself be killed so easily.

*The man's a legend, a genius, there's no way...*

At the same time, another feeling in his gut grew: what Jean had said made sense. He hadn't allowed himself to see it before. Austin may have been a legend: one of the first people on Mars, the father of faster-than-light travel, a brilliant scientist. A great mentor and friend. But he was also an old man long past the age of retirement and it had been decades since he'd held a gun. Nate had severely overestimated Austin's abilities.

*I should have insisted, the stubborn old mule. Should've thrown him on the train myself.*

'Fine,' he said, his expression softening. He glanced to Damien before locking eyes with Petra. 'Let's go.'

As the three officers boarded the train, Nate cast one last look to the platform at Jean, who simply nodded. Then the doors closed, obscuring the platform from view, and the train glided out of the station.

The train ride dragged on in silence. Nate sat with his head in his hands with Petra and Damien opposite him, Marissa and Bill further down the carriage. Scared people, mostly civilian residents, sat or stood around them, staring out of the windows at the passing city. The atmosphere of relief was palpable and Nate fought bitterly against it.

There were no tears, but his heart ached. He fought against the grief, too, willing himself to feel nothing. As Jean had pointed out, they had a job to do. He could grieve when the evacuation would be complete. But the silence cut like a knife; the liminality left no room to think about anything else.

The train slowed and pulled into the Northern Port station. Nate could distantly hear the voices of Bill and Marissa ushering the civilians from the carriage and walked as if in slow motion, following Petra and Damien.

The departure lounge was crammed to the walls. Boards and planters and chairs—anything that wasn't bolted down—were pushed to the sides to make more room. It was unreasonably loud and body odour hung in the room like a miasma. Stressed people tended to sweat more.

The crowd did its best to part as the officers moved through. As they reached the other end of the room, Petra opened the door to the boarding ramp and the group made their way up the shallow slope to the *Magellan*'s airlock.

The spaceplane's cramped flight deck lit up as the crew entered, all crouched, and took their seats. Damien and Nate sat up front amid the bevy of control panels. The cockpit's instrumentation was simple: a couple of large touchscreens on the dashboard with some physical controls spread around to the sides and a keyboard below. The others strapped in behind: Marissa and Petra to either side with their own monitoring stations and Bill in-between.

The dusty orange and red Martian landscape stretched before them out of the front panoramic window, a view broken by the intrusion of the half-buried front end of the Achelon warship.

Nate fastened his restraints with a reassuring click and heard the others do likewise. With a tap his screen brought up a view of the converted cargo hold. It was filled with scared passengers in full spacesuits, a mix of dignitaries, visitors, and residents, forty in total. The seats were arranged in ten rows of four with an aisle down the middle. The trip to Skyport and back wouldn't take long, but evacuating the over seven hundred and fifty people in the city forty at a time would soon add up. They needed backup, more ships, and some way to get to those still trapped in the residential ring. Arcadia Landing had more landing pads, if only the other stations hadn't been locked down.

*Damn that Levine.*

He tapped the intercom button on the screen. 'This is Captain Rifkin. We are about to get underway. Please ensure your seat restraints are locked and tight. In the interest of saving time, we'll be docking at Skyport, where you will be retrieved by ISA personnel and brought back to Earth.'

Switching off the intercom, he glanced around to Bill. 'Any response yet to the distress call?'

'No, Captain.'

Nate huffed. 'Well, we're just gonna have to hope to god they get here soon. Vance, take us away.'

'Yes, sir,' said Damien as he flicked switches in front of him. He gripped the throttle control and stick.

A short moment later, the magnetic locks disengaged with a thud and the ship shook as the *Magellan*'s vertical thrusters pushed it up from the landing pad. Clouds of Martian dust billowed around the ship as it rose. Then, the view out of the window careened away from the besieged city towards the open sky.

Nate was pushed back in his seat as the powerful rear engines forced the spaceplane through the thin Martian atmosphere towards the edge of space.

With the deft manoeuvre of a practised hand, Damien smoothly switched the ship's turbojets over to their propellant-burning mode. After a brief moment of silence, the rocket engines ignited. The craft lurched forwards at an incredible pace. Nate felt the familiar squeeze as the ship made its final push into Mars orbit.

Once through the planet's thermosphere, the ship's automated systems turned the rocket engines off and pulsed the reaction control thrusters for orbital insertion.

'Uh, sir?' said Petra from behind. 'I kept monitoring Arcadia Landing during our ascent and the city seems to be experiencing some kind of energy surge.'

'What?' said Nate, turning in his seat. 'What kind of energy surge?'

Petra opened her mouth to respond but was cut off by Marissa. 'Captain, we're receiving a transmission from the surface.'

Without looking away from Petra's concerned expression, Nate said, 'Put it on the screens. It could be news from Kamzel.'

He turned back to look at the panel in front of him. Static flickered and hissed as a man's faced appeared. He was young, his skin pale and head shaved. His face bore a deep black goatee and his expression gave him a look of unhinged confidence with his wide eyes and smug grin.

'Who the fuck is this guy?' said Damien.

'Greetings. I don't believe we have been formally introduced,' the man began. 'My name is Grand Mage Xander Levine. We met in battle, albeit briefly, in the station.'

'Xander Levine,' Nate snarled. 'You're the one behind all this.'

Xander's grin widened. 'I am disappointed to see you leaving so soon, Captain Rifkin. I was hoping you would stay and bear witness to the completion of our good and righteous work... like your dear friend.'

The man swung the camera view around. Austin appeared

on the screen, hunched over and kneeling in a pool of vomit. His breathing was heavy and his eyes sunken.

'Captain Queen!' said Nate. His heart leaped and relief spread through him. 'I knew you were alive; we're coming back for you soon. Hang in there, sir.'

The camera panned back to Xander. 'A noble sentiment, but I'm afraid you won't be going anywhere.'

As soon as he finished his sentence, there was a bright flash of light from the surface, visible out of the side window. Its brightness intensified and the wispy Martian clouds parted in concentric rings.

Nate's eyes widened as a moment later the *Magellan* was struck by an intense particle beam. The cockpit shook and the ship drifted off to one side. Nate cried aloud through gritted teeth, his eyes clenched shut. Then a resounding boom rocked the ship further, sending it into a slow spin as the remaining rocket fuel at the rear ignited.

Nate opened his eyes enough to see Damien fighting hard to regain control of the ship's attitude with the RCS thrusters.

The ship stabilised just before the cockpit was plunged into darkness. A second later, the *Magellan* switched over to emergency power.

'Is everyone alright? Sound off, people,' said Nate.

The rest of the crew grunted and groaned that they were mostly unharmed.

'Corporal de Beek, ship status,' Nate said as he looked out of the windows. Small chunks of metallic debris drifted past outside.

'What the fuck did they fire at us?' asked Bill.

Petra groaned and said, 'Probably one of the alien cannons.'

'The planet killers? How are we still alive?'

'Must've been a glancing blow,' said Nate, rubbing his neck.

'Uh, Captain?' said Damien.

Nate spun. His first officer was looking out of the other side window, his head tracking a large, smouldering triangular chunk that looked suspiciously like the *Magellan*'s portside wing.

*Shit.*

'All propulsion systems are offline, sir, but we still have life support, scanners, and comms,' said Marissa.

'The Austinium drive?'

'Dead, sir. If the initial blast didn't destroy it, the secondary explosion definitely would have.'

'Right.' Nate sighed and wiped his face with his hand. He tapped the screen to bring up the view of the cargo bay; blank. The cameras were dead. They'd need to check on the passengers manually. 'Everyone, helmets on in case of decompression. Milakova, go check on the passengers and make sure to engage your mag-boots. We don't know what's left of the ship back there.'

In unison, the crew pressed a button on their collars and their helmets sprung up around their heads.

Petra unbuckled herself from her seat and stepped to the floor of the flight deck with a clunk. She opened the rear airlock to the cargo bay and ducked through. A moment later, she came back to the cockpit.

'Passengers are all shaken up, sir, but aside from a few bumps, scrapes, and one or two broken ribs, they're okay. They're going to need medical attention, but there's nothing we can do for them right now. It's a miracle the explosion didn't breach the cargo bay.'

Then, the screens flickered to life once more and Xander's face reappeared. 'There, that's better, isn't it? You've all got front-row seats. Now, if you would please direct your attention towards the surface…'

The other crew members unstrapped themselves and floated towards the side windows, crowding around the small openings that faced the Martian surface. The pockmarked Arcadia Dorsa region of the planet was spread out below. They turned their attention to the southern ridge of the enormous Milanković Crater near where Arcadia Landing was situated.

Xander continued, 'You are about to witness the dawn of a new age for mankind, one marked not by such hubris as to think we belong out here. For too long have you plundered and pillaged the grave of our gods, taking what was not meant to be yours, inviting wrath. Now, we are that wrath made manifest.

'Take this message back to your masters: Mankind's journey to the stars ends here. Sidera silere!'

The camera view panned once again to Austin's gaunt face moments before the transmission cut off. Nate's blood ran cold as another blinding flash of light erupted from the rim of the crater. This one, however, grew outwards rapidly. Atmospheric shockwaves went out from the epicentre like ripples in a puddle.

After a few moments, the light began to fade and a huge, rustic mushroom cloud could be seen reaching into the upper atmosphere.

Arcadia Landing was gone.

'No…' said Nate; his voice, barely above a whisper, was hoarse, his throat dry. As he slumped back into his seat, his body felt numb; everything felt numb. His ears rang through the deafening silence. The city was gone. Jean was gone. Austin, his mentor and friend, was gone. Hundreds of fearful people, whom he had filled with the hope of rescue, killed in an instant of senseless violence.

'They must've gotten to the fusion reactor...' said Marissa, her voice shaky and her face pallid.

Damien's eyes streamed and his voice rumbled in held-back rage, sharp and biting. 'This was their plan all along. Force us out so there'd be someone to tell the tale. They played us.'

Minutes passed as the cockpit returned to silence. The crew stared out at the mushroom cloud lingering above the surface and drifting across the rim of the crater northwards with the wind.

A faint beeping filled the void. Marissa floated back over to her console and lowered herself into the seat.

'Why would they do this?' whispered Petra.

Bill said nothing but shook his head and put his arm around her.

'We're receiving another transmission,' said Marissa, puzzled. 'Audio only.'

Nate gave her a sidelong look and said, 'Where the hell from, Corporal? Those cowardly bastards vaporised the city—never mind, just play it.'

The speakers about the cockpit crackled to life as a man's voice came through in an East London accent. It was fuzzy at first then cleared. 'This is Captain James Fowler of the *IXS-17 Aurora*. *Magellan*, do you read me? If anyone's alive in there, please respond.'

Nate looked up to the ceiling and sighed. He wasn't ready for this inevitable conversation.

*Fuck, why did it have to be* him?

The distress call had gone out from Arcadia Landing across the solar system. It would have had to have gone through Earth first. How could it be the only ship able to mobilise quickly enough was the *Aurora*?

Slowly, Nate reached his hand forwards and pressed the button on the screen to reply. 'We're alive, James, just barely. Where are you?'

'Nate! Thank god,' said James. 'I came as soon as I received the distress call. I'm around thirteen kilometres out from your current position. I did reply, so they'll probably get that message down in the city in about fifteen minutes.'

Damien and Nate exchanged looks. It was clear he had no idea about what had happened.

'Is Austin with you?' asked James.

Nate froze. A pit formed in his stomach. How could he tell him? What should he say?

He gulped then hit reply. 'Uh, negative. Listen, we need your help here. We've got a hold full of survivors and we're completely adrift.'

*Deflection? That's the best you can come up with? Nathan Hosea Rifkin, you fucking idiot.*

After a short burst of static, James said, 'Happy to help in any way I can, mate. I imagine the *Newton* and *Galileo* will be on their way shortly an' all.' He paused. 'Hang on a minute, why can't I get hold of the city? What the hell happened here, Nate?'

Nate felt himself squirm in his seat and his gut clenched. The flimsy attempt at deflection hadn't worked, not that he'd expected it to.

All throughout his life, Nate had known what to do in any given situation. At least, that's how it had felt, even from childhood. He'd come from a good home in Portland, Oregon. His parents had been foster carers for many years and as the eldest of six, they had relied on Nate to help with their numerous foster children. So out of all his siblings, foster siblings, and cousins, he'd been the sensible one, the one who'd gotten them out of the trouble he'd had a hand in causing.

This propensity for stability came in handy later as his training required and reinforced stoicism; he mustn't lose his cool. Now, for the second time today, he was unravelling within. He'd already begun to process his grief over Austin's assumed death, then had felt the elation of seeing him alive once more. Now, as his mind struggled with the rebound and his body coped with the shock of being thrown around, he had the added guilt of informing Austin's dearest friend of his demise.

Despite the helmet covering his face, his discomfort must have been visible, as Damien reached across the divide and placed a hand on his shoulder.

'Just tell him, sir,' he said with a tone that was grave, yet full of sympathy. 'He deserves to know.'

Nate tapped to reply and took a deep breath. 'The city is gone.'

A few seconds of silence passed. No response.

Nate opened the channel again and continued, recounting the day's events over the radio, from the start of the treaty signing ceremony to their current situation.

Again, no response.

Time ticked by, long moments laced with tension. Nate kept his eyes on the screen, unfocused as if looking through it directly at the man on the other end of the line. He knew the other captain well. Being the most experienced of Austin's almost ragtag bunch, James had done most of the hands-on training, both Nate's and his predecessor's. It made sense. Captain Fowler had been the original test pilot for the *Aurora*, after all.

James and Austin had been nearly inseparable; they'd worked together for years before Nate had joined, years before even Captains Pritchard and Rose-Hartley had taken command of the *Galileo* and *Newton* respectively. It had been their warmth and approachability that had helped knit the small group into a kind of found family.

The radio crackled again, breaking the long quiet. 'Acknowledged, *Magellan*. I'll extend the tow lines and take you to Skyport.'

Nate slumped back. The voice was robotic, cold, distant.

'He's not taking it well,' said Bill grimly.

'Are any of us?' Nate asked.

At his words, two sharp thuds vibrated through the *Magellan* and a white and black spaceplane—shorter but otherwise almost identical to their own—glided into view. Two lengths of thick cable stretched between the spacecraft and glinted in the sunlight.

The *Aurora* moved away until the cables were taught, then bright blue pulses from its RCS thrusters stabilised the craft and brought it to a halt.

'Standby for jump to FTL,' said James.

Nate watched as the backdrop of stars beyond the *Aurora* shimmered and shifted, stretching out vertically as though being pulled apart by invisible hands.

Then, like the ping of an elastic band, the stars returned to normal and the great curve of the Martian horizon, still visible out of the side window, slipped out of sight.

# CHAPTER FOUR
## SKYPORT

KYPORT STATION LOOMED CLOSE as the *Aurora* arrived in Earth orbit with the wreckage of the *Magellan* in tow, the residual ripples of distorted spacetime from the Austinium drive's operation dissipating into nothingness.

A long, slender cylinder with a rotating habitation ring towards one end, the vast space station was truly a sight to behold, gleaming a blinding white in the light of the sun. Blue solar panels stretched out like wings all around the ring, and modules, cargo canisters, radiators, and fuel containers were laid out along the trunk.

Midway were the station's docking ports, arranged into two groups of four. Attached to one of the berths was the husk of the long-decommissioned *Magnum Opus*, now reduced to a museum piece. The only things still working on the massive spacecraft were the fore and aft habitation rings. Even the command module—an early spaceplane—had been replaced with a non-functional replica. Some said it was a better end for the venerable ship than burning it up in Earth's atmosphere, while others argued destruction would have been preferable to its current ignominious state.

Under normal circumstances, the approach to Skyport brought with it a sense of awe. Seeing the station appear out from the blue haze of FTL travel was always enough to catch James's breath, no matter how many times he saw it, but now those feelings were far away. Nothing felt real; everything was numb. The familiar sight of the *Magnum* in its mooring might even have been painful if he could have mustered any emotion at all. For now, his only driving thought was the need to bring the survivors home.

'Skyport, this is Captain James Fowler of the *Aurora* requesting permission to dock. Two berths; drones to deploy,' said James, his voice hollow and flat.

This wasn't the first time a spacecraft had limped back to the station after suffering some kind of mishap, rendering it unable to dock under its own power. Since the advent of private space tourism, at least once per year a privately owned craft suffered a malfunction in its RCS thrusters, miscalculated its delta-v, or came in too hot; enough to necessitate the development of guide drones.

Ever since the *Aurora*'s inaugural flight had ended in the need for repairs, Skyport had played host to mechanics specialising in making ships fit for re-entry. The *Magellan* would be in good hands.

James stared unseeing out of the window through the long moments before the station replied and the conversation that followed went by in a haze as he relayed the situation to the horrified port crew.

Soon James had detached from the *Magellan* and brought his own ship into dock while a dozen small drones erupted like a swarm of bees from the trunk of the station and surrounded the stricken craft.

He pulsed the ship's thrusters, orienting it side-on to the station's docking port. Using the screen and instrumentation, he made micro-adjustments to align the ship's outer airlock with the port's clamps.

Carefully he inched the ship on until it was close enough for the station's automated systems to grab hold.

The docking clamps locked down onto the *Aurora*, making an airtight seal around the airlock, and the screen showed 'docking successful'.

But James remained in his single cockpit seat. He stared out of the window as the *Magellan*—its back-end a mess of shorn and burnt metal—moved under the power of the drones' tiny thrusters.

For long moments he hardly stirred, his knuckles white as he gripped the throttle and stick. In the dead silence his ears rang. A strange sense of unfamiliarity coupled with slight nausea came on him. He became aware of how surreal his surroundings truly were. Control surfaces. Screens. A window looking out on the deep blackness of space, the pinpoint stars dimmed by the ethereal atmospheric glow off to the right. Everything was as it always had been, and yet he felt like he was in a different world, a different timeline that had broken away from his expectations. He flicked his gaze to the dashboard—a much less sophisticated design than the *Magellan* and its sister ships, with physical buttons and switches rather than touchscreens—and noted the communications channel to the station was closed.

Alone in the silence he tried to process what had happened, what Nate had told him. The thoughts that came were jumbled, without order, a jigsaw with mismatching pieces. He thought he might cry or scream aloud. Visions of thrashing and pulling, ripping panels and destroying controls, rose in his mind. But his arms remained still, his hands on the flight controls disobedient. His eyes dry. Nothing felt real. Even if he had lashed out in the cockpit and even with his augmented strength—minimal as it was—he wouldn't have been able to force the controls from their housings. Austin had made sure of that when he'd designed the *Aurora*.

He blinked. The *Magellan* was gone, docked at one of the moorings around the station's trunk, no doubt. In the glass he caught his reflection, his hair and beard unkempt. For the first time, he truly felt his advanced age, but the same forty-year-old face that would be his for the rest of time stared back, nonetheless. Over the years, it had become harder and harder to explain away his lack of ageing to those around him who weren't privy to the truth. And most weren't. Austin's repeated explanation of 'good genetics' had always been piss-poor, but he'd said it with such confidence people just accepted it. What would James say to the busy-bodies now Austin was gone?

James caught himself.

*Why am I even thinking about something so inconsequential?*

With a frustrated sigh, James pushed all thought to the side. He still had a job to do.

After taking one last look out at the stars, he exited the *Aurora* through the airlock and into the station.

Within the hour, other spaceplanes from the ISA's contract partners had arrived at Skyport and the confused, shaken, and injured refugees from the *Magellan* were ferried onto them. They had only the vaguest idea of what had happened from what had been explained to them by Nate and his crew. From their perspective in the windowless cabin, they, like James, had seen nothing. James had drifted through the whole process as though in a daze, operating mostly on autopilot. He answered questions matter-of-factly and helped direct the survivors with injuries through the station to medical. In truth, he was barely keeping it together. As the weight and truth of what had happened began to settle, he found himself increasingly leaning on the job of getting the survivors through the station to hold back the flood of thoughts, questions, and grief threatening to burst forth.

Now James sat cradling a cup of tea in Skyport's mess hall, which was situated in the habitation ring, watching out of the window as Earth drifted idly by. The simulated gravity here was much less than it had been on the *Magnum Opus*. At about one-third of Earth's it was more akin to walking on Mars, but it meant the ring didn't have to spin as fast.

James took a sip. Cold. Food and drink lacked flavour out here; it was something everyone who worked in the environment of space had to contend with and get used to. But it seemed particularly bland in today's unreality.

*Austin's gone… No, he can't be. Not like this.*

Pressure grew behind his eyes and his vision swam with welling tears. He sniffed them back.

*Keep it together, James. Can't break down here. Not now. Focus on something else.*

He glanced at the entrance as Nate and the crew of the *Magellan* entered the mess hall and clustered around another long table at the far end of the room. Their faces were sullen. Nate's especially.

There was a woman with the four of them James didn't recognise. He'd heard Nate had been assigned a new crewmember—a corporal from the Royal Netherlands Army—but he hadn't been introduced. At any rate, the new woman was the only one who didn't seem thoroughly exhausted. She was clearly in the middle of a heated debate with Nate and Commander Vance and it looked like she was having an anxiety attack.

Within minutes of sitting down, she shot up from her chair and stormed out of the room, leaving Nate and Vance dumbstruck. Sergeant Milakova and Specialist Watkins simply buried their heads in their hands.

James hastily took a sip of his tea as Nate looked up and spotted him watching. A short moment later, the other captain was sitting opposite him.

'James, I... I don't even know where to begin,' he said, clasping his hands together on the table.

James sipped again and said with a wavering voice, 'Having problems with your new recruit?'

Nate blinked. 'Marissa? Yeah, she's taking it hard, transferring already. Can't say I blame her, really. None of us signed up for this.'

'How's the rest of your crew holding up?'

'Shit,' said Nate, rubbing his eyes with the heels of his palms. 'Petra and Bill are pretty shaken, and Vance? I mean, he's stoic as ever, but we both saw some pretty horrendous stuff down there.'

'And you?'

With a heavy sigh, Nate turned his head to look out of the window as the glowing curve of Earth came around again.

'I spoke with Elisabeth briefly before she got on one of the shuttles,' Nate said. 'She wants a full debrief back at HQ as soon as we're done here.'

James pursed his lips and nodded, then finished off his stone-cold tea with a grimace. 'You could come with me on the *Aurora*? I'm sure we can make some space.'

Nate shook his head. 'You go on ahead. I'm gonna stick around here a little longer; make sure the mechanics know what they're dealing with.'

'She'll be in good hands.'

James got up to leave and gave Nate a light slap on the shoulder as he walked past.

The din in the mess hall fell to silence and James stopped in his tracks. The television screens on the walls lit up with the news, which played footage of the Mars explosion in a loop. By the angle and high level of zoom, it was footage taken from one of the new reconnaissance orbiters. The words 'Arcadia Landing destroyed' were displayed prominently in a banner on the screen as the newscaster reported soundlessly on the incident. Gasps of horror and worried chattering ended the silence.

James's heart ached as he watched the blinding flash of light consume the city over and over again. He clenched his fists tightly and heat flooded through him.

'Seven hundred fifty-six,' said Nate.

James glanced sidelong at the dejected captain. 'What?'

'Seven hundred fifty-fucking-six!' Nate cried, slamming his palms onto the table. 'I failed them. I failed them all. We got about eighty people out on the *Magellan* before

Levine blew the city.'

James reached out a hand and touched Nate's shoulder. 'Nate, I—'

'No, James,' he said, brushing him off and burying his face in his hands. 'It's unacceptable. Eighty people out of seven hundred fifty. If only I hadn't been so stupid. Oh god, it's all my fault.'

James sat back down opposite as Nate sobbed into the table. He ran his hands through his hair and groaned; he wasn't ready for this. 'Look, you and your crew barely made it out alive. Forty people crammed onto the *Magellan* in two runs? That's eighty people alive who wouldn't be without your team's intervention. They would have been vaporised along with... with...' James choked on Austin's name. 'This is not on you—'

Nate shot up, leaned across the table, and raised his voice, drawing attention from others in the mess hall. 'No? Then who is it on? Come to think of it, where the fuck were *you*?'

Without waiting for an answer, Nate huffed and peeled away, heading for the door.

*He's right. Where* was *I?*

After a few minutes, the people around him went back to their own conversations, so James got up and left the mess hall.

Before long, he was back in the cockpit of the *Aurora*. After securing himself, he leaned his head back and let out a heavy sigh. Nate was clearly suffering; James knew the feeling all too well. He couldn't blame him for lashing out.

As James closed his eyes, the video footage played over in his mind. Austin's absence stung. James had missed the explosion by a few minutes and so the horror of seeing it broadcast in the mess hall had made it all too real.

His thoughts went to his wife, Angela. He hadn't seen her for a few days, the assignment to help the construction efforts at Catamitus Dock having kept him away from Earth. How would she take the news? Austin had been their closest friend for decades; not only did James and Austin work closely together, but the grizzled old captain had also been the best man at his and Angela's wedding.

With a lump in his throat, James sent the launch request to docking control. The moment the light on the dashboard turned green and the docking clamps released, James pulsed the RCS thrusters, pushing the *Aurora* away from the station.

A couple of hours had passed and James now sat, arms folded, at a long table in a meeting room off the Mission Control Centre in the ISA's headquarters in Budapest.

The room was deathly silent, lit by green-tinged fluorescent lamps suspended above the table. The surface in front of James looked and felt like ordinary lacquered oak, but it was in fact a large touchscreen.

Administrator Elisabeth Schreiber sat at the head end, poring over data, tapping and swiping at windows of reports and videos on the table-top.

The chair creaked as James leaned back into it and puffed out his cheeks. He tapped his arms and swivelled from side to side while glancing at the clock on the wall.

The door flew open, clattering the blinds, giving James a start. Nate marched through and quickly took the seat opposite, muttering apologies.

'You're late, Captain Rifkin,' said Elisabeth without

looking up from the desk.

Nate said nothing as he tapped on the desk, calling up a login portal. He looked haggard, even worse than when James had left him on Skyport. James himself was faring no better. He focused all his attention on the debrief. The best course of action would be to remain dispassionate.

'So, gentlemen,' Elisabeth began, resting her hands under her chin after Nate had logged in. 'A tragedy has occurred on our watch. We have lost not only our most valuable off-world asset along with the seven hundred and fifty-six caught in the blast, but also a number of dear friends. I need to know how this happened.' She paused. 'Captain Rifkin, how is your team doing?'

'Processing. I've put them on compassionate leave. It hit Bill and Petra hard. I haven't had much of a chance to talk to Damien since we got back. Don't worry, they'll all have the mandatory counselling sessions when they come back.'

'What about Marissa?' asked James.

'Gone,' Nate said, leaning back in his chair. 'I think it hit her the hardest. Didn't wait around even for a second. She was furious about the way everything went down and I think it scared her off.'

'Where's she transferred to?'

'No transfer,' Elisabeth interjected, her sharp features set hard. 'I accepted her immediate resignation pending a full medical and a debrief with me after this meeting.

'Now, about how this tragedy occurred: Captain Rifkin and I were both on the ground when the attack began, but I know very little of the events following the initial explosion.'

'It was an inside job,' Nate began as he launched into

recounting the attack from his perspective. He got as far as breaching the entertainment district and finding more survivors before Elisabeth cut in.

'Wait, you let Captain Queen go with you to retake the city?' she said, her mouth agape. 'An old man. With a walking stick. In a combat situation?'

James looked down at his hands and couldn't help but laugh despite himself. Elisabeth hadn't known Austin in his younger days, she'd only known him in his frailty. But James knew. There was no way Austin would have let Nate go without him and no force in heaven, hell, Earth, or Mars could have stopped him.

Elisabeth glowered at James. 'Do you find this recklessness amusing, Captain Fowler? May I remind you these actions resulted in the loss of your friend?'

'No,' said James in a low voice. 'No, you may not, Administrator. And neither do I blame Nate for what happened; Austin's decisions were always his own.'

He tried to give an encouraging look to Nate, which came out as more of a scowl than he would have liked, then folded his arms.

Nate sunk into the chair a little and after a short pause said, 'It's true though. It's my fault Queen's gone. I should have made sure he got on that train with the others.'

'This is supposed to be a debrief,' said James, looking pointedly at Elisabeth. 'We're not here to assign blame, and anyway, you wouldn't have gotten Austin on that train. Never in a million years.'

Elisabeth placed her head in her hands and scratched at her curly dirty-blonde hair. 'Okay, fine. I need to know exactly what happened down there. Continue your report, please, Captain Rifkin.'

As Nate recounted Austin's injury and capture, James felt a twinge of pain. He knew as much about the Achelon particle beams as Austin had.

*He was dead already and he knew it. No-one could've prevented it after that.*

James appreciated Nate's impossible position—his desperation—and his gut knotted.

'Sidera silere?' said Elisabeth, bringing James's attention back to the conversation. 'Are you certain that is what Xander Levine said?'

'What's unusual about that?' James asked, grateful for something else to focus on. He unfolded his arms and scooted his chair closer to the table. 'The anti-spacers have been using that as a motto for years.'

Elisabeth gave him a grim look before calling up one of the digital files in front of her. She flicked it to the centre of the table, just past Nate and James. A hologram came up from the file, projected above the table-top.

'This was broadcast earlier today,' Elisabeth said.

She tapped once more in front of her and the video began to play. It was the head and shoulders of a man silhouetted against a bright background. The black mask he wore featured a grotesque visage that glowed green and his voice was distorted.

'Citizens of Earth,' said the figure. 'For too long your leaders have ignored our warnings. Time and again they have edged mankind towards its inevitable damnation, failing to heed the message of our Founder and Prime Martyr, Guy Furious. In so doing, they invite a wrath that will consume us all.

'You will by now have heard about the destruction of Arcadia Landing. It was our masterwork, designed to put a stop to the ISA's sacrilege.

'But who am I? I am simply a son of Adam with the vision to lead those in the fight for our right to galactic anonymity, for the protection of the beloved children of Terra Mater. Earth is to be shielded and its gift of abundant life cherished. We are Sidera Silere.'

The hologram faded back into the desk.

'Who was that?' said James.

Nate shook his head. 'Whoever he is, he sounds exactly as melodramatic as Xander Levine.'

'The authorities are simply calling him "Son of Adam",' said Elisabeth. 'No one knows who he is and his organisation—this Sidera Silere—has claimed responsibility for the attack on Arcadia Landing. Their manifesto has been posted all over the internet on message boards and across social media. It all appeared at the same time.'

'Wait, the way these people are talking now—Xander Levine and Son of Adam—it's like they're part of one of those Achelon-worshipping cults,' said James. 'I thought they were anti-spacers, not religious nuts?'

Elisabeth nodded and flicked a few of the digital files over to James's side of the table. 'It has mostly flown under the radar, but there have been some indications of growing collaborations between the anti-spacers and the cults ever since Guy Furious died.'

Nate leaned across the table and grabbed some of the files from in front of James, sliding them across to his side. 'And the authorities think this guy has unified them?'

'It is a working hypothesis,' said Elisabeth.

'So what do you want us to do?' said James, looking down at his remaining files. They showed a bunch of intelligence reports, police statements, and articles dating back to the mid-2040s. One thing was clear: governments and intelligence services around the world had been aware something was up for a long time. There were rumours in the reports since Guy Furious' death that his disparate factions had come under a new, stronger leadership, but nothing concrete.

*They have no way of tracking this Son of Adam, no idea who or where he is, nothing about him at all. He covers his tracks well.*

'Go after him,' said Elisabeth.

Nate looked up from the files on the desk. 'Excuse me? You do know we're not police, right? We have no authority to "go after" anyone.'

James considered his words for a moment, then said, 'There's no police force in the world equipped to handle something like this, and besides, there's no clear jurisdiction. If not us, then who?'

Silence hung in the room as Nate looked between Elisabeth and James, bemused.

James stared back at him with a cocked eyebrow. There was something to this: an opportunity to do something, to bring Austin's killer to justice. It felt right, but they needed a plan or at least somewhere to start.

Elisabeth steepled her fingers to her lips and closed her eyes.

'With all due respect, Administrator,' said Nate, creasing his brow, 'I'm an astronaut, not a detective. I don't know the first thing about investigating anything.'

'And I'm a physicist,' James said, showing his palms. 'I don't know anything about detective work either, but that doesn't mean we should just let Sidera Silere get away with this. It's a damn sight better than sitting on our hands.'

'I don't think it's that simple.'

'Why not?'

'Gentlemen,' said Elisabeth, tapping on the table, causing James and Nate to look around at her. 'I understand this is uncomfortable—it is a difficult time for all of us—and outside of your usual remit, but Captain Fowler is right.'

Nate stared at her and opened his mouth to say something, but Elisabeth cut him off, seemingly answering his unspoken question. 'The law has been slow to catch up with our advancements. We are essentially dealing with the very first major off-world crime. There were no national jurisdictions governing Arcadia Landing; it was completely under our remit. We have almost total exclusivity over humanity's off-world ventures; even private flights and tourism boards have to go through us. In lieu of anyone more suitable, the fact is the jurisdiction is ours alone.'

Nate rubbed his temples. 'Aight. I guess it's up to us, but I'm not taking the lead; I've made enough stupid decisions already. What's our first move?'

'I have the list of the survivors here,' said James as he called up a photo gallery. Pulling it apart with his two index fingers, he created copies of the windows and sent them sliding across the table to the administrator and Nate. 'Ambassadors, dignitaries,' he continued, 'but a fair amount of personnel too. They were gonna get a thorough debriefing anyway, right? So let's focus our questions a little. We need to try and establish what triggered the attack, why it started when it did. A broader view would help. Maybe the personnel know something.'

'It's a long shot,' said Nate, looking over the staff

pictures. 'Eighty out of seven hundred fifty: what are the odds we happened to rescue the ones who saw something?'

'It's not vanishingly small. As unlikely as it sounds, it's the only place I can even think to start.'

'I agree,' said Elisabeth. She collapsed the windows on the desk with a gesture like scrunching up a piece of paper. 'Talk to the survivors after they've had a chance to settle in, starting with Arcadia staff. I will clarify our legal position.'

The administrator stood and made to walk away. Stopping and turning back to them, she said, 'Do not forget your own counselling sessions either.'

She gave them both a brief nod and marched from the room.

James watched after her. Through the plexiglass of the door, the Mission Control Centre bustled with activity. He unfocused his eyes so it all became a wash of swirling colour. In his mind he could see Austin's desk out there, from which he had conducted most of the *Aurora*'s test flights.

*Middle row, two to the left.*

Together they had refined the Austinium drive's efficiency tenfold and shared in the wonders of the solar system. James had seen the rings of Saturn up close, skimmed the Great Red Spot, looped around the moons of Pluto, and mapped the surface of Arrokoth, all under Austin's direction. Now he was gone. James knew this day would come eventually; it was the curse of immortality, but it was no less painful.

He'd thought about this a lot over the years; each time Austin had taken a fall, the last time when James had accompanied him to get his walking stick, then when he'd had to take him for cancer treatment a few years back.

During the latter, Austin had made his wishes known: He'd wanted to sit in the cockpit of the *Aurora* and die watching the sun set over Neptune. But the cancer had been cured and the subject hadn't come up again. After that, James had assumed they'd have more time. Facing up to Austin's mortality meant also facing Angela's and that thought was more than James could bear.

'James?' said Nate, bringing James out of his introspection. His voice sounded distant, hollow, broken. 'Thanks for standing up for me, though I don't think I deserve it. I'm sorry for what I said on the station.'

James turned to Nate and leaned on the table with both hands, giving the man as much of a smile as he could muster. His voice trembled as he spoke. 'That? Don't worry about it, mate. We'll give the survivors a week to settle into their accommodations and get the medical checks out of the way. Meanwhile, Elisabeth's right. I think it'd be best if we take some time to process as well. God knows I'm pretty fucking far from okay and I'm sure that's true for you, too.'

Nate nodded.

'Come on,' said James. 'Let's get some rest.'

# CHAPTER FIVE
## INVESTIGATION

JAMES THANKED THE DRIVER, stepped down from the bus, and started towards home. His apartment wasn't far from the bus stop—only a few hundred yards along Csömöri Út, a wide suburban road in Budapest's District XIV—but his feet dragged as though someone had filled his shoes with cement. Angela would probably be worried sick, no doubt having seen the news reports. He could see her in his mind's eye, pacing anxiously around the lounge in her slippers. No lists of names had yet been released to the public; it would take time for the ISA to inform the families of the seven hundred and fifty-six.

*She doesn't know...*

Streetlamps came on, bathing the road in their dim blueish light. James's pace slowed even more. He didn't want to be the one to tell her, but he knew he could never accept anyone else giving her the news. He came to a stop and peered back along the road. No cars, no more busses. A streetlamp was out, throwing a section of road and pavement into shadow beneath a cloudy, darkening sky. Where he stood felt as though it was within an isolating cone of light. He didn't want to move.

A cool spring breeze picked up briefly and he shivered and stuffed his hands into his pockets, the illusion of isolation broken.

'Fine,' he muttered, as though to Austin. 'Fine, I'll tell her. No sense dallying, is there? You old coot.'

A short time later, James was at the apartment door. With the key in the lock, he took a deep breath and turned. He'd barely closed the door behind him when a quavering voice came from the lounge.

'James?'

'Yeah, it's me.'

Seconds later, Angela shuffled around the corner. She was indeed wearing her slippers, paired with her matching fluffy dressing gown. She brushed her long white hair behind her ear, looking briefly as though she'd seen a ghost.

The moment passed and she visibly relaxed, closing her eyes with a sigh. 'Oh, thank god,' she said. 'I've been watching the news reports. They're saying Arcadia Landing was destroyed? What happened? Is Austin okay? I know he was supposed to be at the treaty signing.'

James looked away, his eyes watering, and chewed his bottom lip. Everything he'd held in since retrieving the *Magellan* threatened to overwhelm him.

'What is it?' said Angela, the piercing blue of her eyes interrogating him.

He tried, but the words wouldn't come; he couldn't even look at her. All he could manage was to shake his head as his whole body trembled.

'Oh god, no,' Angela said, stepping back. She put her hand the wall to steady herself. 'Austin's… gone?'

He nodded.

Her expression went rigid, her eyes closed, and she stood like a stone weathering a storm. She said nothing.

James tried to hold it in, but he was coming apart at the seams. He fell to his knees. There, it all came out, all his grief and rage, as he gripped the fibres of the carpet. He roared a guttural cry that broke into heaving sobs.

Angela wiped the beginnings of dampness from her eyes and shuffled towards him, arms outstretched, and they embraced. Still kneeling, he leaned into her for comfort and sobbed loudly, his whole body shaking. She had always been his strength. Angela was the only person he could be this vulnerable with, the only one who could understand the true depth of his pain. It wasn't just for Austin but also for the beginning of a process he'd been avoiding—the process of facing up to the isolating reality of his agelessness.

His heart ached, crushed in the vice grip of grief. Questions flooded his mind and a deep anger, directed towards the holographic face that had hovered above the table in the Mission Control Centre, flared in his abdomen. Why would anyone do such a thing?

Angela pulled away, tears now tracing winding streams down her wrinkled face, and she held James's hand, helped him up, and led him trembling into the lounge.

They sat on the sofa together in silence, subdued, James's eyes unfocused as he stared into the black void of the TV. He knew Angela would be itching for him to tell her everything, but she wouldn't push. Twenty years ago, this would've been uncharacteristic, but the intervening years with James's various comings and goings had forced her into patience.

Eventually his gaze lowered and came to rest on a holograph on the unit below. An image of James, Angela, and Austin on the day James had formally been accepted as the *Aurora*'s permanent test pilot. The way it flickered was so 2040s. The intrusive nostalgia for early mid-century holography immediately struck James as strange, but it represented a time with so much promise, the beginning of something new: endless sky, boundless horizons. Seeing Austin's smiling face beneath that big grey beard was like a bullet to the gut and James had taken his fair share of those.

After regaining his composure, he shifted in the seat and explained everything to Angela.

'I was already in orbit when the distress call came through,' James said. 'I'd launched to take some supplies up to the shipyard—it's like this big claw structure in orbit over Catamitus Dock—'

'James.'

'It'll be attached to the settlement by space elevator when it's done—'

'James...'

'Not something that would work on Earth, of course, but Ganymede's gravity is low enough—'

'James!'

He saw Angela's pained expression and fell silent.

She touched his arm and said, 'You're distracting yourself.'

'Sorry,' he said with a small chuckle. He sighed and wiped his eyes. 'Elisabeth's put me in charge of the investigation to catch Son of Adam. I don't think that's such a good idea; I'm no detective.'

'Mmm, if I recall correctly, you like to skip that part and go straight to getting yourself captured.'

James ignored her attempt at levity. 'Why couldn't she have picked Nate instead?'

Angela raised an eyebrow. 'Why wouldn't she pick you? You're the most senior member of Austin's team.'

'That's true...'

Scooting closer and gripping his hands in both of hers, Angela said, 'I also believe you can do it.'

'Really?'

She nodded solemnly and touched his cheek. 'Out of everyone, I know you'll go to the ends of the Earth for Austin and heaven help anyone who stands in your way.'

'That sounds more like you,' said James, leaning in and kissing Angela's forehead.

'Once,' she whispered, turning her gaze to the holograph. 'All that's behind me now, but I like to think I've rubbed off on you. Something of me to take with you into endless time when I'm gone.'

James winced and his heart ached. He hated it when she talked like that. For the last year, she'd become increasingly morbid, more keenly aware the end of her life was approaching. Her health wasn't in the best state. Her knuckles were swollen from arthritis and her hips and knees often troubled her. Just like Austin, she walked with a cane when out and about, but unlike the cantankerous captain, she'd embraced what she had called her 'grumpy old woman' phase with glee and often waved the stick around threateningly. But now, as she settled into the role she had made for herself, the joy had faded and she'd begun to speak of her life as finished, like she was standing on the threshold of eternity with one foot out the door. Though, perhaps the unique situation of being married to an immortal was affecting her mental health in ways neither of them had anticipated. Angela had always played it off as a benefit—that as she aged, James would be like her toy-boy—but for a long time now, James had felt it had become a mask. They hadn't spoken about it properly since before they'd gotten married. They'd argued over it when James had first told her he was biologically immortal and the matter had been laid to rest. Or had it?

James felt the pull of fatigue. A discussion for another day. So, he simply smiled and patted her hands.

'Have you eaten?' Angela asked as though everything she said had been totally normal.

'No, I had a cuppa in Skyport, but I've not felt much like eating. Nothing tastes the same in space anyway.'

Angela rose with difficulty and grabbed her walking stick from the coffee table. 'I'll fix you something.'

'Y'know, you really should use that thing in the house more,' said James, pointing to the stick and thinking of how she had been pacing without it when he'd come through the door. It was ornate, featuring a chromed handle in the shape of a raven. 'For someone who said they loved it, you seem to leave it lying around a lot when we're at home.'

Angela jabbed him in the knee with the end of the cane and then moved off towards the kitchen. 'Don't you start that old shit again.'

A week had passed since the destruction of Arcadia Landing. James and Nate walked northwards together along the eastern waterfront of the river Danube, under the Elisabeth Bridge, passing restaurants and hotels on their right and busy river tour operators seemingly every hundred yards on their left. Budapest's city centre thrummed with activity: tourists idling and admiring the monuments, locals walking with purpose or resting in the sparse green spaces, boats gently cruising up and down the river, and trams trundling past. A warm and clear spring afternoon.

The two captains had taken public transport from the ISA headquarters at the airport into the city centre.

The two of them couldn't have looked more mismatched walking together. Nate wore an immaculate, pressed blue and pink suit and designer sunglasses, which made James feel out of place. His outfit was far simpler: an ISA branded bomber jacket over a plain tee and ripped jeans.

They'd given the refugees from Arcadia Landing long enough to settle and it was time to find out what—if anything—they knew. The ISA had set the survivors up in a hotel near to the waterfront; many of the dignitaries were visitors to Budapest and were afforded top notch hospitality. This was also extended to the handful of long-term residents who had made it out of the Martian city on the *Magellan*, especially since some had no other homes to return to. A few had lived and worked on Mars for a decade or more and found readjusting to the environment of Earth a challenge. Whatever their situation, the survivors had been instructed to remain in the city until full debriefs could take place. And that included interviews with James and Nate.

'Who do you think we should start with?' asked James, twisting his body out of the way of a group of inattentive tourists, his jacket flapping open.

Nate brought up the list on his phone and showed it to James. 'We go in order of importance: dignitaries first to get them out of the way, then we can move onto Arcadia staff and residents. Personally, I think we should start with this guy: Jason Laplace, one of the aides to Secretary-General Masahiro.'

James frowned. 'Why him?'

'Petra said she'd seen him heading off on the same city tour as Marissa the day before. It included all the power generation buildings. Maybe he saw something? Sure as hell can't ask Marissa. She got the all-clear from medical then boned out. Didn't show up for counselling either.'

Leaning over, James swiped through a couple more profiles. 'If we're doing it in order of importance, then shouldn't we start with the secretary-general himself?'

'Hey man, I'm just thinking about who's most likely to get us the intel we need.'

'Alright, fine, we'll do it your way. But we've got to get through everyone anyway. Eighty people... Won't get them all done today, that's for sure.'

Nate nodded and put his phone away into his blazer's inside pocket. 'Six hours or so, by my estimation. We'll do as many as we can this afternoon and come back tomorrow.'

As they passed a small garden plaza with an ornate fountain, there was a loud rhythmic clanging from workmen hammering metal, which reverberated across the street.

James's heart picked up speed and his throat tightened. He stopped in his tracks and stumbled across to a nearby railing. It took Nate a moment to notice and turn towards him, his face etched with concern.

A flash of memory sent James back to that fateful day aboard the *Bitter Authoritarian*. He saw a huge blade glinting in the darkness of the medical bay. The clanging of hammer on metal became the footsteps of the mechanised Achelon warrior as it stalked towards him. A scream sent a chill through his bones. Yula hung dead and bleeding from the blade as the armoured assailant looked at James, its cranium glowing with orange bioluminescence.

He gripped the railing tightly, ran his fingers over the surface of the metal, counting the raised flecks of paint, and took deep breaths. He felt the weight of a hand on his shoulder.

'James, what's going on, man? Are you okay?'

Nate sounded panicked. It was the first time he'd had an attack in front of any of his colleagues, but focussing on the sound of Nate's voice helped the vision to fade.

'Yeah,' he said, panting and patting the railing as he pushed himself off of it. Other concerned people stopped in the street and looked like they were about to come over to him, but James waved them off. 'Yeah, I will be.'

Standing upright again, he took a deep breath. 'I'm sorry you had to see that.'

'What happened?' asked Nate, calm returning to his voice.

'Flashback,' James replied. 'To the Mars mission. It's been a long time since I last had one. All this with Austin and Arcadia Landing has me off-kilter.'

This last week had been hell for James. His grief over the loss of Austin had brought back the nightmares of years past that he'd worked so hard to rid himself of. Evening palpitations and an increased jitteriness had also returned.

'I know you and Captain Queen never really spoke of what happened on that ship, but from what I've heard, it sounded pretty traumatic. If you need a rest...'

'No, no, I'm fine,' said James, straightening his jacket.

'And you don't know the half of it. Let's just get to the hotel. It's not far now.'

Before long, they arrived at the hotel that the ISA had booked out for the survivors at quite some expense. It was a newer building constructed with ornate architecture and sat across the street, overlooking the tramline and the waterfront. The space agency had also reserved one of the hotel's conference rooms for drop-in group therapy and of course the survivors could book one-to-one sessions if they wished.

The two strode through the golden-hued foyer between seating areas full of soft couches and under a row of three extravagant crystal chandeliers.

After speaking with the concierge, who directed them to the right of the check-in desk, they ascended a short staircase and boarded a lift to the upper floors housing the ambassadorial suites.

As they stepped off, Nate pulled out his phone and they began the long process of going door-to-door.

After around two hours, they had exhausted the list of dignitaries and politicians—less time than they had expected. Most of the interviews took place with not just the VIPs but their aides present also, cutting down on the number of individual conversations they needed to have. But, to Nate's chagrin, his potential lead in Jason Laplace turned out to be a dead-end. In fact, none of those they spoke to all afternoon had seen anything or been aware of any plot to destroy the city. They had been just as surprised as everyone else when the shooting had started.

James was wary; could some of them be lying? It was known that some of the ambassadors had initially opposed the confederacy of the United Nations, though they had come around in recent years. But some nations even now had far-right minority parties whose entire purpose was campaigning to stop the treaty signing. It was the politicians that James distrusted the most. The mega-rich energy barons and business tycoons with ministerial positions and ties to the far-right, funnelling tax money to their friends via lucrative contracts for this or that, never to be seen again. It was the same as it always had been. They might have plenty of reason to want the city destroyed and this Sidera Silere group could provide plausible deniability. Yet he could detect no subterfuge, though he suspected that their inability to do so was more to do with their inexperience as first-time detectives. Why had he agreed to this?

Mentally drained from having to listen to pompous officials for hours on end, James and Nate finally stepped out of the lift on one of the lower floors.

'That was a colossal waste of time,' said Nate, leaning against the wall, his head on his forearm. 'Even if any of them knew something, I'm damn sure they wouldn't tell us.'

'Oh, I agree,' said James, resting with his back to the opposite wall. 'Plus, if it was ultimately a political hit, there's no way the ISA will want to get involved. Aside from the secretary-general himself, they've all got motives, reasons to lie, opportunities, resources. But their ideologies just don't jive with Sidera Silere's.'

'You think the politicians wouldn't work with those nuts?'

James bit his lip and shook his head. 'No, I don't think Sidera Silere would work with the politicians. Remember, they're conspiracy theorists of the "new world order" and "lizard people from the centre of the Earth" variety mixed with radicalised alien worshippers. Distrust in governmental institutions is their bread and butter.'

'Mmm, you may be right.'

'So who's next, then? We're onto the Arcadia Landing staff now, right?'

Nate checked his phone. 'Yeah, how do we want to handle these guys? Alphabetical? Departmental?'

James pushed himself away from the wall and paced the corridor. 'Departmental this time, I think—'

'Oh, ho, ho!' cried Nate, cutting James off. 'Except for this guy. We need to do him first.' He turned the phone screen around to show James. 'Augustus Syracuse, barman of the Hephaestus Chain and a long-term resident. He's in room two-one-seven.'

'Hephaestus Chain's the nightclub right?'

Nate nodded and put his phone away. 'Bar staff hear things.'

'I didn't think anyone heard anything in a place like that,' said James with a chuckle. 'Alright, we can go back to the departmental list afterwards. And as luck would have it, he's on this floor. After you, Dick Tracy.'

Nate gave him a quizzical look and began to walk along the corridor. 'Who's that?' he asked, to which James simply responded with a knowing smile.

'Y'know what, never mind,' Nate said, finally stopping outside the door to room two hundred and seventeen. His knock was loud and fast, a product of his growing impatience.

The man who answered the door looked like Hephaestus himself: olive-skinned, broad-shouldered, and imposing, sporting a full, dark beard and long braided hair. He wore an open checked shirt over a black tee, which had one of those scratchy indecipherable death metal logos that had somehow never gone out of style in the last half-century. By contrast, on his lower half he wore sensible jeans and loafers.

'Augustus Syracuse?' asked Nate before pointing to himself and James. 'Captains Nate Rifkin and James Fowler. May we come in?'

The man nodded. 'What can I do for you, Captains?' His voice was deep and gravelly with a Canadian accent.

James and Nate stepped through the doorway. The bartender sat on the edge of his bed and motioned for them both to take a seat in the armchairs by the desk.

The room was small and immaculate, bright white. The bed was made, looking hardly slept in. Apart from a thick, crumpled fantasy novel on the bedside table, there was no evidence of it being lived in at all.

Syracuse clasped his large, gnarled hands together, the faded scars on which spoke of a man not shy of hard labour.

As James and Nate lowered themselves into the chairs, a look of recognition flashed across his face and he pointed at Nate and said, 'Hey! I remember you. You were there, that day in the plaza...' Syracuse trailed off and his expression turned grim.

Nate returned the man's grave look. 'It's been a rough time. How're you holding up?'

Syracuse let out a bitter laugh. 'Not every day you lose your job, your place of work, all your friends, and your home all at once. I've been talking with the other survivors. A couple of the newer transfers, man, they don't get it. They have places to go back to here on Earth. Families. I'm glad for them, of course I am, but...'

'Not you?'

The man shook his head and turned to look out of the window. The warm light bathed his face. 'Feels wrong. This is midday light; sunset is cold. And I feel heavy.' He turned back to Nate. 'I've been a resident of Arcadia Landing for near twenty years. Started as part of the reclamation team. It was great. Before that, on Earth, I was a forge hobbyist. I'd always be digging around scrapyards for bits of metal I could use to make stuff. So rummaging through that old wreck felt familiar.'

'So, how'd you end up tending bar in the Chain?' asked James.

Syracuse smirked. 'I had some disagreements with management, shall we say. I got fed up and put in a transfer request as soon as I heard they were opening a bar. It's good to change things up every once in a while.'

'I understand,' said Nate. 'We have some questions, Mr Syracuse.'

'Please, just call me Gus.'

'Alright, Gus.' Nate sat back in the chair. 'We're trying to establish how the attack began and you work the bar, so you seemed like the best place to start. Did you hear anything?'

Gus was shaking his head before Nate finished the question. 'No, if you're asking if I heard any conspiratorial talk, I can't help you. Sorry.'

'Nothing at all?' asked James, leaning forwards. 'Are you sure? Doesn't have to be directly related. Anything unusual.'

Gus thought for a long moment, his gaze fixed off into the distance. 'Now that you mention it, some of the comms guys seemed stressed out about something the morning of the treaty signing. I only heard it because

I was there cleaning. The Chain was always open; we sometimes did breakfasts.'

'Any idea what agitated them?'

'Arcadia Landing got a lot of transmissions,' said Gus, his eyes glazed as he reminisced. 'All kinds, even some that would make you blush. So many people there under different circumstances going back and forth with their families and friends on Earth, the Moon, or even Ganymede. Rarely did I ever hear of anything that worried the comms guys, except for that morning.'

'What was it?'

Gus shrugged. 'You'll have to ask them. One of them survived. His room's just down the way. A guy called Galen Hughes.'

Nate and James thanked Gus for his time and left the room. James called the front desk and asked for the room number for Galen Hughes. It was only a little way along the corridor as Gus had said.

'What do you think?' said James.

Running his hand along his fade just above his ear, Nate replied, 'I say we carry on with this lead. It's the best we've had so far.'

'It's the only thing we've had so far.'

This time, James knocked on the door and Galen greeted them. He was around the same height as James, pale, and had dishevelled short blonde hair. There were dark bags under his eyes from a lack of sleep and, in contrast to Gus, his room was a complete mess. More than that, things were broken and there were impact marks on the walls. It was clear he hadn't been taking things well; it was good the ISA had the funds to repair a few busted rooms.

Galen wasn't nearly as accommodating as Gus had been, but James and Nate eventually managed to get him to open up somewhat.

'We got a strange transmission from the Le Guin Research Base on the Moon,' said Galen, jittery, pacing up and down his room while James and Nate stood by the door. 'Encoded. Nothing we recognised and it got relayed elsewhere in the city. It was only a couple of hours before the whole place went to shit.'

'And that kind of transmission is unusual?' said Nate.

Galen stopped pacing. 'Not just unusual, downright worrying. If only we'd paid more attention, alerted someone instead of bickering about it over breakfast. Chaichana was certain it was—Oh god, Chaichana. I think I'm going to be sick. You need to leave.'

They were shoved out of the room and the door slammed closed behind them. James leaned against the wall and sighed as a muffled retching sound came from the other side. He hadn't expected to get any leads from the survivors at all, much less for the trail to lead to the Moon.

'Le Guin Base,' said Nate, shaking his head.

James nodded. 'The plot thickens. I've never been to the Moon before.'

'You're expecting us to go there?'

James stroked his beard and pulled out his phone. 'Well, Elisabeth told us to investigate, so we go where the trail leads.'

With a groan, Nate paced back and forth along the corridor. 'Le Guin's one of ours though, like Arcadia and Catamitus Dock. Everyone there is on staff. Why do *we* need to go? Just send the info to Colonel Zhu and let her deal with it.'

'Mmm,' said James as he scrolled through the ISA's launch schedule on his phone. 'Hey, look at this. The *Galileo* is set to go to Le Guin next week for maintenance on the FSBL radio telescope. We could join Captain Pritchard.'

'Why?'

'What?'

'Why? If Schreiber wants us to go as a priority, surely she'll slot us in before that.'

James rolled his eyes. 'And what happens if the person who sent the transmission to Arcadia Landing intercepts a message to Zhu or gets wind of the change in schedule? It'll be pretty conspicuous. Wouldn't take much of a leap to figure out why we're there. Remember, they're likely to be one of us. No, our best bet is to double up with an existing mission to stay under the radar.'

'I get you. We go under the guise of helping with the telescope maintenance, it's less likely to tip off our target,' said Nate, pacing back and forth. 'I still don't like it.'

After shoving the phone back into his pocket, James folded his arms and regarded Nate. Something was off; he had never known him to be so hesitant, so negative. After what had happened, he had thought Nate, of all people, would have been leading the charge to bring Austin's killer to justice. James had known the younger captain for five years—ever since Captain Buck Ashcroft had transferred out—and he'd always been ready to step into difficult situations with a collectedness James envied. He thought back to his prior conversations with him and the language of blame he'd used. It was understandable to feel that way to a certain extent. After all, James blamed himself for not arriving at the scene sooner and wondered what would have happened had he insisted on accompanying Austin to the treaty signing. But he knew deep down he had done everything he could; he may be immortal, but he wasn't prescient. All he could do was move forwards. The attack was still fresh in his mind and raw. In the blessed moments when his revived trauma didn't assail him, he found himself thinking of Austin and crying silent tears. But with Angela's help he was coming to terms with it faster than he could have alone.

Who did Nate have? As far as James knew, the man's family was still very much alive, but he never seemed to make plans to visit them or check in. Perhaps they were estranged? James knew little about them or their relationship to Nate. He always seemed the closest to his own crew. With Sergeant Milakova, Commander Vance, and Specialist Watkins on compassionate leave, could it be Nate had no-one to lean on? Could it be the attack had changed Nate in a much more profound way than James had realised?

'You don't like the plan?' said James. 'What don't you like about it, specifically?'

Nate stopped in his tracks and turned to James. 'Well, y'know...'

He looked like a deer caught in the headlights.

James took a step forwards and placed a hand on the man's shoulder. 'Are you doing okay?'

'Yeah, fine,' Nate replied, his voice clipped.

James sighed. 'I ask because I see you there hesitating, second-guessing, pulling back, and that's not the Nate I know. You've been with us long enough by now to know we're a family. I don't want to push, but what would Austin say right now?'

Nate's eyes were red and damp. He looked up to the ceiling and exhaled heavily. 'He'd say, "I ain't got time for no goddamn tea party, let's have some real talk".'

James nodded and squeezed Nate's shoulder. 'That's right. So let's have it then: real talk.'

'I—I'm not ready yet,' said Nate, looking James in the eye.

'Alright, but I'm here for you when you are. Just tell me this: will it affect the investigation?'

'No.'

'Good. We need to follow this lead to get justice for Austin and for the other seven hundred and fifty-six souls we lost out there. If that means going to the Moon, then that's where we need to go.'

'Understood,' said Nate with a nod.

'Come on, I've had enough for the day. Let's report back to Elisabeth and we can come back to interview the rest tomorrow. Who knows, maybe she's got an update on the jurisdictional issues.'

The two captains made their way back through the streets of Budapest, first on foot, then by tram and metro, to the ISA headquarters in silence.

As they entered the foyer James was reminded of his first time coming here. He had just received the summons from Dryden, the deputy assistant director at the time, and Angela had accompanied him. It had been the first time he'd seen Austin in years and the first time he'd seen the *Aurora*.

*It was a good reunion. The start of something amazing.*

James and Nate went through the winding beige corridors and entered Elisabeth's office off the Mission Control Centre.

They told her what Galen had said about the mysterious transmission and James requested they join Captain Pritchard and the *Galileo*'s mission to the Moon.

'Granted,' said Elisabeth as she opened the launch schedule on her table screen. A few taps and swipes later, the desk was blank once more. James's phone pinged, then Nate's a moment later. 'There, you both have one week to familiarise yourselves with the mission briefing. You will be working alongside the maintenance crews of Le Guin Research Base, replacing parts for the radio telescope. The both of you will need to travel in the *Aurora* since the *Magellan* will clearly not be ready in time. I suggest you liaise with Captain Pritchard directly for the finer details. Only Colonel Zhu will be privy to your true purpose on the base, so you should conduct yourselves with discretion.'

James nodded. 'Of course, and what about our jurisdiction?'

'It is as I suspected. Police will not get involved and the Security Council has approved the ISA to carry out this investigation.'

Nate scoffed and folded his arms. 'No one wants to get their hands dirty.'

'It is a sensitive matter,' said Elisabeth, rubbing her temples. 'No single member state is willing to take ownership. To do so would be tantamount to taking responsibility for Sidera Silere and, by extension, for the attack. At least, that is how they see it.'

'And we're supposed to be moving towards a united Earth,' James said, shaking his head.

'Will that be all, gentlemen?' said Elisabeth, tapping her fingers on the desk. 'You have done well today. After you have completed the rest of the interviews tomorrow, you will have a little under a week to get mission-ready. So I suggest you use that time to familiarise yourselves with the workings of the radio telescope. It is quite unlike any other.'

# CHAPTER SIX
# THE GALILEO

Captain Erin Pritchard pressed the button on her collar and her helmet came up and locked into place as the view of the night sky streamed across the cockpit window. There was a muffled hiss as the RCS thrusters fired to halt the ship's axial rotation. Slowly, the Moon came front and centre, crystal clear and blindingly bright, surrounded by countless stars.

She sighed heavily, lessening the tightness in her chest. The sight of the endless frontier of space had once excited her, but now the unfading stars seemed at best uncaring, at worst cruel.

*I miss her so much.*

It was a deep sadness she couldn't let show. There was something else in there amid the mess of emotions, something dark, a feeling she couldn't identify that had grown in the depths and haunted her dreams. All she knew was she didn't like it.

The rest of her crew went about checking systems, flicking switches and calling out 'nominal' for each in turn. Erin glanced at the large screen in front of her, showing the *UNSV Galileo* parked safely in orbit over the Earth and correctly oriented for their journey. A routine trip for the ISA's second-longest-serving mission commander, after Captain Fowler, of course.

Erin had been to Le Guin Research Base so many times in the last sixteen years she felt she could almost see it on the surface from here, her eyes boring a hole through the lunar crust to its approximate location on the far-side.

'Ready to go, Captain,' said Major Rhys Jones from the helm position. His helmet was already on and his voice was muffled.

'Forgot to turn on your suit comms again, Major?' Erin replied, her voice sounding brighter than she had expected.

Rhys paused then looked down at his suit and pressed a button on the front. His voice came through clear as he laughed and said, 'Oops! I'd forget my head if it weren't screwed on, I swear.'

Erin smiled at the big grin on his thin pink face; Rhys never failed to lighten the mood. She pressed the broadcast button on the dashboard. 'Mission Control, this is the *Galileo*, snug as a bug. Awaiting your go. Over.'

The voice of the flight controller came over the radio. 'Roger that, *Galileo*. Proceed when ready.'

Rhys tutted and shook his head as he powered up the Austinium drive. 'Right-o, all set. Truth be told, sir, we've done this loads. I can't see it as really necessary to call Mission Control every time.'

'Just get a move on, Major. You complain more than

my mother!' Lieutenant Commander Sai Suresh called from the back.

'Oh! Is that how it is? I'll turn this ship around, so I will. I don't appreciate back-seat driving,' Rhys called back. 'Anyways, the drive's primed and ready, Captain.'

With a laugh, Erin raised her arm and said, 'Punch it, Major.'

There was a sudden crack as the view outside swam in the Austinium drive's distortion and the Moon shot towards them and halted, filling the view with its cratered surface.

'Tidy! Low Lunar orbit achieved, Captain,' Rhys said, letting out a deep sigh as he relaxed back in his seat.

'Mission Control, we have arrived safely in low Lunar orbit,' said Erin. 'Approximately fifty minutes until descent phase and final approach to Le Guin. Over.' She removed her helmet and seat restraints, and the rest of the crew quietly followed suit.

Erin ran her fingers through her short, messy black hair as she watched the pockmarked surface slip by below them.

Lieutenant Commander Aisling Simmonds and Specialist Tom Lando started up a relaxed conversation behind while Sai floated forwards to gaze out of the front window between Erin and Rhys.

A soft chime came from one of the crew stations.

Tom pulled himself back into his seat and looked at his screen. 'Sir, I'm picking up the *Aurora*'s signal,' he said with a hint of confusion in his voice.

'Already? Are you sure?' said Erin, turning in her seat.

'Yes, sir. Captain Fowler is already on the surface; his ship's signal is bouncing off Gateway Station.'

'How'd that bastard beat us here?' Erin spat, the shock overtaking her melancholy. She hadn't been in the mood for friendly wagers, but equally she couldn't back down once James had approached her on the runway with that shit-eating grin on his face. Anything less would've revealed too much. James might've had the most flight experience, but Erin and her crew knew the Lunar run better than anyone. But why did she have to put money down on it?

Rhys laughed. 'I told you. Looks like you proper owe him that fiver now!'

* * *

James and Nate looked out at the landing pads through the atrium's large panoramic windows as the *Galileo* lowered itself slowly onto the pad next to the *Aurora*. The ship hovered in place for a moment as its landing gear extended, then it touched down. A dull thud reverberated through the building as the pad's magnetic restraints engaged and a boarding bridge extended outwards to the *Galileo*'s airlock.

The Le Guin Research Base had grown significantly over the last sixteen years, from its humble beginnings as a set of small habitation bubbles serving the nearby Far-Side Breccia Lens Radio Telescope to a full metal construction the size of a small town. Unlike Arcadia Landing, Le Guin Base remained a purely scientific facility; space-tourism was kept to a minimum.

As James watched, lost in thought, Nate groaned and rubbed his back.

'Y'know, we really need to get the *Aurora* some proper seating,' Nate said.

'It's got proper seating.'

'Really? Is that what you call it? It's a cargo rack with a seatbelt in the payload bay. I've sat in more comfortable pews.'

James shrugged. 'Did you get thrown around like a ragdoll, though? No. So stop complaining. The *Aurora*'s a test vehicle, not a pleasure boat.'

Nate went back to staring out of the window and James allowed his gaze to wander. The rim of the three-kilometre-diameter crater in which the radio telescope was situated was visible beyond the few sparse buildings to the north. The radio telescope was an amazing feat of engineering that had been in the works long before the *Bitter Authoritarian* had crashed on Mars. Some considered it the last purely human space project.

Squinting, James could just make out one of the four small anchor points for the radio receiver on the rim, which was suspended across the bowl of the crater. It was little more than a grey box from this distance. Most of the maintenance work was set to take place on the floor of the crater, repairing the reflector mesh, but there were electrical components at the anchor points that needed replacing too.

As he stared, the airlock doors behind them opened with a hiss and five suited astronauts walked through into the atrium carrying large briefcases. James turned and walked towards them with a grin and Nate trailed close behind.

'Ahoy, Cap'n Pritchard,' he called as the team retracted their helmets. 'What took you so long? We've been here ages.'

'Oh god, who made you the welcome wagon?' Erin said with a smirk. 'Service round here's really gone to the dogs.'

The two captains stared at one another for a long

moment, then laughed and hugged.

'And don't think I've forgotten about that fiver though, Cockney lad like me...' James said, tapping his forehead.

'Oh, don't worry, *butt*. I'll buy you a drink later.'

'Holding you to it,' said James.

Erin then peered around him and her eyes lit up. 'Nate! C'mere and give us a *cwtsh* then,' she said, opening her arms wide.

Nate moved forwards and embraced her tightly. The two hugged for what seemed like forever and both had red eyes when they let go.

'How're you holding up, *bach*?' she said.

Nate waved his hand and said, 'I'm good, I'm good.'

Erin put her hands on her hips and raised an eyebrow. She regarded him for a short moment and her expression softened to the typical deep care James knew Erin held for them all.

She touched Nate's arm. 'Are you sure? I hope you don't think any of us blame you for what happened to Austin? I even spoke to April, so I did, and she agrees.'

Nate looked down at the floor and rubbed the back of his neck. 'I appreciate that, Erin. Truly. It's hard and I do still blame myself sometimes, but I'm doing okay.'

James stared at Nate. How truthful was he being with Erin? He still hadn't taken James up on the offer to talk through their shared grief. It certainly hadn't escaped his notice that the taller man's attention to detail in his appearance had begun to waver. A five o'clock shadow blurred the edges of his sharp beard line and the thick texture of his hair had lost some of its uniformity. It wasn't much—almost imperceptible, unless one was watching as closely as James was now—but could it be a sign that all was not well?

*Maybe I'm wrong; maybe he's doing fine on his own. I could be reading too much into it.*

Nate cleared his throat. 'So, uhh, you gonna take the tour before we get started on the telescope repairs?'

'Oh, come on,' said Erin. 'I already know every rivet and bolt in this place three times over!'

James laughed as Nate looked at her quizzically. 'Captain Pritchard and the *Galileo* crew pretty much built this place back in 2050,' he said. 'We have some time, though. I'll go and see Colonel Zhu; you have a look around, mingle a bit, see if you can find anything interesting.'

Erin ran her hand through her hair and said, 'While you two boys are off gallivanting, my team and I'll get started on unloading the *Ol' Gal*.' She turned to her crew. 'Right, let's get a move on, then. Rhys, Tom: I want you two to arrange a removal vehicle for the big stuff. Meanwhile, Sai, Ash, and I will bring what we can through the airlock.'

The group parted ways in the atrium with James and Nate heading off deeper into the facility. They walked together, passing through vestibules and along narrow interconnecting tunnels, making their way along the web of modules towards the base's administration buildings.

Movement through the facility took some getting used to, though having come recently from Ganymede, James adjusted quickly. Nate had a harder time, his normal steps turning into a lope.

Along the way, Nate wondered aloud at the clear differences between Le Guin and Arcadia Landing, to which James listened intently. The lunar facility was smaller and far more utilitarian than its Martian counterpart. James in turn noted its striking similarities to Catamitus Dock.

At every opportunity afforded by a rare window, both men stopped and stared out at the lunar landscape for minutes at a time, taking in the stark beauty of the barren, craterous world. The sun was low in the dark sky, throwing deep shadows across the facility and picking out the smallest craters, mounds, and outcrops across the grey regolith.

'This is how space is supposed to look,' said James.

Nate laughed and leaned against the module wall, peering out of the small porthole. 'Says the old man who got to be the first human to stand on Mars and who got to be first to travel faster than light. You spent the last two decades flying around in the *Aurora* and now you finally recognise you're in space? What gives, man?'

'Cheek, I'm not that old.'

'You're in your eighties!' Nate cried incredulously before examining James more closely. 'Shouldn't you be walking with a cane like Queen did? Come to think of it, you have pretty clear skin for an octogenarian. I know Queen said you have good genetics, but Jesus man, how good are they?'

James sighed. It was inevitable. Barely two weeks from Austin's death and the questions had already begun. They hadn't even had a chance to memorialise him yet.

The thick beard helped hide James's youthful appearance, but it wasn't meant to hold up to scrutiny. Working so closely with Nate, it was bound to happen sooner or later.

James smiled a melancholy smile at Nate. 'A story for another time, mate. And as for the space question, remember I grew up in an era when all we had were pictures from the Apollo missions. No one had gone anywhere else; I know this, because I was the first to go somewhere different. But despite Mars, my mental image of a truly alien world will always be this,' said James as he pointed to the landscape beyond the window.

Before long they came to the administration offices and the two parted ways, with Nate heading off to the base's recreation centre.

James made his way along a wide grey upward-slanting corridor towards a set of double doors at the end. He pressed the buzzer and entered. An expansive control centre greeted him and a small number of personnel sat at computer terminals in rows, monitoring base systems. The front wall was a large, segmented window overlooking the rest of the base in the direction of the Far-Side Breccia Lens Radio Telescope.

As he crept forwards, James gave perfunctory nods to the curious staff members. Looking out of the window, he noticed how high up the control centre was compared to the rest of the facility. He must have climbed at least two storeys without noticing. Directly below, he could see vehicles driving out from under the building. He watched as they snaked their way around the web of modules and arrived at the *Galileo* parked on its landing pad.

*Must be the removal crews Erin ordered.*

'Magnificent, isn't it?' came a voice from behind, warbling and wavering but instantly recognisable.

James spun on his heel with a grin.

Colonel Zhu O-Huang stood before him, smiling, her hands on her hips. It had been many years since James had last seen her, but the years had been kind. Her skin was a warm beige with slight wrinkles around the eyes and her short black hair was streaked with white. She held herself upright, but James knew from prior conversations that, had they been on Earth, she would have needed support like Austin.

'James! It's wonderful to see you again,' she said as she shuffled forwards and hugged him. 'It's been so long. I'm sorry it's not under better circumstances. First Yula and Grant, now Austin.' She sighed.

'Death comes for us all in the end,' James said grimly.

'All except you, it seems,' Zhu said with a hushed tone and raised eyebrow. She stepped away and spoke once again at a normal volume. 'Come with me. We have much to discuss.'

James followed her towards a room at the back of the control centre, off to the right from where he had come in. It was a small office, much the same as Elisabeth's back in Budapest, but Zhu had added a much more personal touch. Everywhere James looked was memorabilia from her previous postings: a hologram of the International Space Station sat rotating above the corner of her desk and on the other corner sat the official group photo of the first *Magnum Opus* crew. Zhu had always been the sentimental type. James looked at Yula's beaming face.

*We were all so young, so full of life and hope.*

Tearing his gaze from the photo, he looked up and saw a model of the *Magnum Opus* itself sitting on the shelf behind Zhu's chair next to what must have been a fist-sized chunk of moon rock. Zhu had led a much more adventurous and successful life than any of them: from decorated Chinese air force pilot to Mars astronaut and pilot of the *Magnum Opus* to administrator of Le Guin Base. It warmed James's heart to know she had done what she'd wanted to do and so much more besides.

'Schreiber has already briefed me on your mission here,' said Zhu, lowering herself into her seat behind the desk and steepling her fingers outward. 'Needless to say, I'll happily give you access to whatever you need in order to bring these murderous bastards to justice. It's deeply troubling to me that the order that led to Austin's death possibly came from here, while under my watch.'

James sat down opposite her and leaned back in the chair. 'We all missed it, Zhu. From Nate's report it was absolute chaos on the ground. The ISA isn't prepared for a threat of this magnitude.'

'Exactly. I'm in the process of putting together a proposal to tighten security around here. I can't wait around until after the UEC treaty gets signed.'

'If it ever does,' said James. 'What kind of measures are you taking?'

Zhu relaxed back with a groan. 'Anti-air defences for a start but also a better-trained security force. Arcadia Landing's clearly wasn't adequate and we've got none to speak of. They only needed it because of all the tourism. We don't have that here... yet. But it's only a matter of time.'

'Anti-air...' James mouthed. 'What?'

Zhu laughed bitterly. 'If there's anything this attack has taught me, it's that there's no lengths these people won't go to. They went all the way over to another planet for a suicide-bombing! We're much closer to Earth, so imagine me waking up in cold sweats for the last week, expecting to have a spaceship ram itself into the fusion reactor at any goddamn moment. Hence, air defences.'

James nodded. It struck him as a bit reactionary, but he also couldn't think of a better response. He got up from the chair and wandered to look at another photo on the left-hand wall. It was from Zhu's posting to the ISS after the first mission to Mars. He didn't recognise any of the faces, but the interior was unmistakable.

'I'll need access to the communications system at the administrative level,' said James, moving on to the next photo: a cheesy selfie of Zhu in the *Magnum Opus* command module making a peace sign with Mars in the background. He chuckled and pointed as he looked at Zhu. 'Very twenty-thirties.'

'That was from my final resupply mission to Arcadia. Mock all you like, it went viral on the 'gram,' she replied with a shrug. 'And granted. I'll send the permissions to your phone. You should re-join the *Galileo* crew,' Zhu continued with a glance at her desk computer. 'Looks like they're ready to get started.'

'That's a shame. I thought I'd have a bit more time to make a start with comms.'

Zhu smiled as she stood slowly and shuffled around the desk to James. 'I understand your eagerness to get on with it. You feel like if you sit still for too long, you'll start thinking about him again, right? I miss him too. But maybe this will help you take your mind off of things. In the meantime, I'll do some digging too, especially considering this worrying trend. We can reconvene later and perhaps have a proper catch-up as well.'

James folded his arms and cocked an eyebrow. 'Worrying trend?'

'You haven't heard?'

James shook his head.

'There's been a spate of murders on Earth over the last few years. I've been keeping an eye on it ever since it came to my attention. All the victims are people who formerly worked on the original *Magnum Opus* project back in the day. It's been sporadic but enough to be a pattern. Now with Austin gone, you and I are the only ones left who were part of that original team.'

'What?' said James, standing up straight. How had he not heard about this before? Lots of people worked on the original *Magnum Opus* project from around the world, but Zhu must have meant the core team, none of whom now worked for the ISA. Who would want to kill a bunch of elderly engineers and scientists who'd worked on a now-decommissioned spacecraft from half a century ago?

'You think this is linked to Arcadia Landing and Sidera Silere?'

'I don't know,' Zhu said, stepping back and sitting on the edge of her desk. 'There's no connection in terms of method and why would Sidera Silere even be interested in them at all? It could be one person operating over several years, several people working in concert, or a remarkable coincidence. Though with Austin's death, coincidence strikes me as unlikely. Perhaps I'm being paranoid, but… be careful, James.'

James snorted. 'You know me, always careful.'

'That's what I'm afraid of. Anyway, I will call you if I find anything.'

After saying goodbye to Colonel Zhu, James sent a message to Nate and went back to the atrium. There he found Erin, Sai, and Aisling seated on the edge of some planters and talking. He hadn't been there more than a few minutes before Nate arrived and the group then headed to one of the base airlocks. The *Galileo* crew waited while James and Nate donned their spacesuits.

'Colonel Zhu's given us access to communications. Did you find anything?' said James as he adjusted the suit gloves.

Nate locked down his helmet with a satisfying click. 'I found some comms crew members and asked them what it had been like here on the day of the attack. I didn't go into detail, but none of them gave me the impression they'd seen anything unusual.'

'Yeah it was a long shot we'd get anything useful when we can't risk showing our hand,' said James. 'We'll check what the logs say after this job's done.'

Once James and Nate were ready, they stepped into the airlock with the other three. Erin explained Rhys and Tom were already making their way over to the telescope in the removal vehicles. She then depressurised the airlock and stepped out.

James allowed everyone else to go on ahead as he took a moment to appreciate his first steps on the lunar surface. The grey soil was soft but clumpy, like walking in powdery snow. With each step, he kicked up clouds of dust to the front of him and he quickly reverted to loping. He stopped and bent down to touch the regolith with his gloved hand, a thin layer of dust immediately sticking to it. It felt somewhere between a fine sand and talcum powder and reminded him of trips to the seaside. James grinned and stood before bounding after the rest of the group.

# CHAPTER SEVEN
## The Telescope

James soon caught up and the walk across from the base to the crater's rim took around twenty minutes. The base's chief engineer set them to work, splitting James, Nate, and the *Galileo* crew amongst the teams from the base to work on different parts of the telescope.

Nate jumped on one of the transports bound for the eastern anchor point. Erin, Sai, Aisling, Tom, and Rhys descended in a buggy into the bowl of the crater towards the reflector mesh and James remained at the southern anchor point with some more of the base's repair crew.

Over the course of a few hours, James and his team finished replacing dust-covered electrical components in the southern point and rotated around to the western one, then to the north.

The view down into the crater was spectacular with the reflector mesh gleaming in the sunlight across the bottom of the bowl. The anchor points themselves were actually the remains of four of the robotic rovers that had deployed the wire mesh. With their powerful tracks they had crawled out of the crater, stretching the mesh out across the floor and pulling taught the suspended antenna. They had then settled themselves on the crater's rim, where they had drilled into the lunar regolith to become the anchor points. There had been more than four of the autonomous rovers initially, but once the anchor points had been set, the others had descended into the bowl again to complete work on the mesh and secure it down.

Eventually, James found himself working alongside a single engineer by the name of Phillip Hargreaves who, by his own admission, had not stopped for a break since arriving.

After helping Phil pull the access hatch on the side of the anchor point open and helping him to pull the old parts out, James handed him a large capacitor. It was weighty even in the lunar gravity.

As Phil turned to take the unit from him, James noticed through the man's helmet he was breathing heavily, much more so than he should have been.

James glanced down at the oxygen indicator on Phil's arm as he moved away.

'Hey, Hargreaves,' said James, tapping the man on the shoulder. 'You alright, mate? Looks like you're running low on air, fella.'

'Ah, I'll be fine, Captain,' said Phil, panting. 'I'll just get this installed. Then I'll go and get another canister.'

Because it was such a long job, the teams had been provided with ample spare oxygen canisters from the base, which sat in the back of their transports nearby.

The rest of James's team had gone off for a break, but Phil had insisted on getting this anchor point finished before taking one. Seeing as James's enhanced stamina prevented him from becoming tired, he'd opted to stay with Phil until the job was done.

'Cutting it awfully close,' said James. 'I know I can't order you about, but I'd feel a lot better if you stopped and grabbed some O2. You just hold on; I'll go get you one now.'

As he said this, Phil reached into the anchor point opening to heave the capacitor inside.

'Ah, fuck!' he shouted, pulling his right arm out of the hatch.

There was a large tear in his sleeve venting oxygen. Phil scrambled to clap his arm over the hole as he turned to face James and began to choke.

'Hargreaves!' James shouted, darting forwards to catch the man as he dropped to his knees. He reached over and grabbed some black tape out of Phil's toolbox nearby and closed up the tear in the suit, but it wasn't enough. Phil continued to choke and his eyes rolled back in his head. A glance down told James the engineer's oxygen was almost entirely depleted.

'Shit. Hold on, mate, you're gonna make it.' James quickly disconnected the pipes from Phil's suit and swapped them with his own before reopening the supply. He watched with relief as air flooded into the other man's suit and he gradually began to breathe again. Then James hit the emergency button on both of their suits.

Cradling the unconscious man, James's predicament sunk in. He didn't need the oxygen; his augmentation, which allowed him to work without tiring and made him biologically immortal, also allowed him to survive in a vacuum environment for a protracted period. How long for, he didn't know, but the scant few Achelon survivors he and his team had encountered on Mars all those years ago had lain dormant without a breathable atmosphere for five years before humans had shown up.

The bigger problem was how it would look to everyone else. He and Phil were at the northern edge of the crater, three kilometres away from Le Guin Base. It would take time for medics to get to them.

*Maybe I could get us over to the transport and get a new canister?*

Craning his neck, he looked to the vehicle. It was a good fifty yards away. Perhaps he could make it if he carried Phil?

James shifted, trying to pick up the man. The air pipe between them pulled, so he stopped.

*Damn.*

He couldn't risk moving Phil in case the air supply broke; the pipe wasn't long enough to take that kind of jostling.

No matter what way James looked at it, by the time anybody arrived, it would be obvious he had survived for far longer than humanly possible without oxygen. Everyone would know about his abilities.

James sighed and looked up to the daytime stars. No matter what would happen to him, it was the right thing to do. He couldn't let the man die in order to save face.

*I'll have to take it as it comes. Might even be able to finally get rid of this beard.*

He thought of Angela and all the people who knew them. Most thought she was his mother or maybe his aunt anyway, the apparent age-difference between them was so great. The few who knew they were married simply thought Angela was into much younger men. The beard had always been a flimsy disguise and James didn't really like it.

It was twenty minutes before a medical team from the base turned up and found the two men tethered together by James's oxygen supply.

As they rushed over, James assured them he was fine with a gesture, having run out of air with which to speak, and pointed to Phil. Nevertheless, after they had hooked up the engineer with a new supply, they reconnected James's and loaded both men onto a vehicle.

The journey back to Le Guin Base was filled with silence. A thick, stifling quiet. The paramedics shot nervous glances at James, but no questions came. Drawing up his knees, he cradled the last vestiges of his humanity close to his chest. Every glance othered. Their eyes said, 'You should be dead.'

When they arrived, James helped the paramedics get Phil inside before he was forced to remove his suit and submit for examination.

An hour passed and James sat at the end of his bed in a hospital gown, having been given a clean bill of health by the doctors. There was a clamour outside the medical bay, so much so, the doctors had locked the doors to prevent a swarm.

Phil's close friends, clearly desperate to see how he was, had been allowed entry but many more gathered outside the door.

A couple of the engineer's friends came over to James and thanked him for saving his life. When James asked about the crowd, they shrugged and said news of the accident had spread like wildfire throughout the base, along with rumours that James had done the impossible. Now the medical bay was empty again save for the doctors checking on the engineer.

One of the doctors noticed James looking and meandered over.

'No need to worry, Captain,' said the doctor with a smile. 'Mr Hargreaves will make a full recovery; you saved his life out there.'

'That's good. I should've noticed sooner he was running low—'

The doctor held up a hand and shook his head. 'You did what you could.' He feigned looking at James medical notes then continued in a hushed tone, 'Which, incidentally, is more than any of us would have been able to do.'

'Good genetics,' James said, standing. He reached across the bed and grabbed the stuff bag his clothes had been put in.

He took a single step when the doctor moved around the bed and intercepted him.

'Not so fast, Captain. You were out there without air for a full twenty minutes. How is that possible? By all rights you should be dead.'

James scoffed and leaned on the bed. 'Thanks, doc. If this is how you make friends, I'd love to see how you make enemies.'

'I didn't mean it like that!' said the doctor.

James rolled his eyes and pulled the clothes out of the bag. If he was going to be interrogated, he might as well be fully clothed.

'I just mean it's a medical impossibility,' the doctor

said, his tone pleading. 'Who are you? What are you?'

'I'm just me, doc. It's…' James glanced around the room and continued at a whisper, 'I don't like to talk about it, alright? The incident was over forty years ago.'

The doctor blinked rapidly. 'Over forty years? Wait, you don't mean to tell me you're *that* James Fowler, the first man on Mars? The one who fell into a coma, right? But that would make you eighty-one years old.'

James chuckled as he zipped up his flight suit. 'Look good for my age, don't I?'

He bundled up the hospital gown on the bed and pushed past the doctor, leaving him dumbstruck.

*I've got to get out of here.*

The door unlocked and slid open as James approached and he was met with a human wall. He stopped and the raucous crowd fell silent.

'Excuse me,' James said, keeping his eyes to the floor. The crowd remained unmoved, their stares oppressive.

James stepped forwards and the front row moved back in unison. He pressed on with his eyes to the floor and the quiet crowd parted for him.

A single clap split the silence and James stopped in his tracks. Then another and another.

The one pair of hands was joined by a second, then a third, and gradually more.

He spun around to the applauding crowd. Erin and the crew of the *Galileo* were among them. Whoops and cheers came from further back.

Nate stepped out of the crowd and drifted towards James with a grin, clapping along with the others.

He placed a hand on James's shoulder. 'You ain't getting away that easy, man. Look at this, you're a hero! So much for keeping a low profile, huh?'

*Hero? No way, I'm no hero.*

Nate frowned at James's bewildered expression. He leaned in close and continued, 'Hey, it's all good. But you've got some explaining to do. C'mon, let's hit the bar. I'm buying.'

'So you're immortal?' asked Nate before polishing off his beer. 'All that stuff about "good genetics"—'

'Technically true,' said James. He leaned forwards on the table around which he, Nate, Erin, and the crew of the *Galileo* sat.

The bar was dimly lit; shutters were closed against the long lunar day and warm lamps glowed above each of the room's circular booths. It masked the utilitarian aesthetic of the base well. But if one simply turned up the lights, they would see the room's bare metal structure and its cold, clinical walls.

'What happened to me in that chamber changed me at a genetic level,' James continued. He brought up his fingers and counted his augmentations off one by one. 'Let's see... I literally haven't aged a day since the incident. I'm slightly stronger, I don't tire out at all, I can hold my breath almost indefinitely and survive in a vacuum environment.'

'But can you get drunk?' Erin said as she slammed her bottle down on the table.

Nate leaned back on the upholstered bench and pointed at her. 'That's the question!'

James shook his head. 'Believe me, I've tried.'

'Aw, that's rough, *butt*,' said Rhys.

'Are you even still human?' asked Aisling, throwing

back her long red hair. It reminded James of Angela's in her youth, but Aisling's was more crimson. Her eyes were a deep brown and she had soft, pale skin across which sat a colony of freckles.

He stared at her for a couple of seconds. In James's experience that question was loaded, masking disdain or prejudice, but he detected no malice in her voice. She had an earnest look in her eyes, which caused a disconnect that made his mind feel like it glitched out for a moment.

'Err…' he started.

'Ash! What kind of question is that?' cried Erin, gawking between them. 'Of course he's still human… You are? Aren't you?'

This kicked James's brain back into gear. 'Y—yes, as far as I know, I'm still human. We did extensive research back in the day. It's a shame none of it survived.' He recounted the way Dr Joshua Hales had betrayed him and how he'd supposedly created his own Elysian Serum using the research they had done together.

'So no one ever found it after his death?' asked Sai, stroking his short, black beard. His skin was medium brown and he had soft features with a rounded jaw and cropped black hair. He took a swig of his drink. 'I find that hard to believe.'

James shrugged and drank some more of his beer. 'He had this "mysterious employer", so I guess all his research got taken. It's not turned up in nearly half a century, so it might even be lost.'

At that moment a loud cheer went up from the other patrons around them. A crowd formed by the doorway.

'Hey, it's Hargreaves!' shouted Tom; he had been seated next to Aisling, almost opposite James, and he now stood on the bench, craning to see over the crowd.

James was on one of two stools with his back to the door. He stood and turned in time to see the crowd part for Phil as he walked through. Hands reached out to tousle his hair and slap his shoulders.

Phil greeted some James recognised as his friends from the medical bay. They turned and excitedly pointed towards the booth where James sat. At this, Phil's eyes lit up and he made a beeline for the officers.

James and Phil clasped hands amid more raucous cheering.

'You saved my life,' Phil said, his grin wide and eyes gleaming. 'I don't understand how you did it. People are saying you're immortal. I don't care. You warned me, but like a fool I decided I knew better. Let me buy you a drink.'

James let go and waved him off. 'I'm just glad to see you up and about, mate. Next time, watch that O2 more closely, eh?'

Hargreaves nodded and James allowed him to go off with his excitable colleagues to the other end of the bar.

As James sat back down, he noticed Erin had remained seated. She had a dejected look and tears streamed down her face.

'What's up?' James asked.

At his words the others fell silent and lowered themselves back into their seats.

'Oh, I'm alright,' she said, wiping her tears.

Aisling leaned over and placed a hand on hers. 'Are you sure, Captain? There's a lot to celebrate and you're sitting there looking miserable.'

There it was again, Aisling's earnest directness. Out of

any other person it would have sounded rude.

'Real talk, Erin,' said James.

Captain Pritchard exhaled heavily and looked up to the ceiling. 'Alright, since it seems to be an evening for truth. Real talk. For Austin.'

She breathed in deep and closed her eyes. Slowly she opened them and glanced at everyone in turn, her gaze landing finally on Nate.

'It's about Cheryl,' Erin said, looking down at her hands. She turned the wedding ring around on her finger. Cheryl was Erin's wife and a fellow member of the ISA, though it was hard to keep track of what department she was in since it changed almost every time the topic came up. James and Angela had met Cheryl many times over the years, especially when they'd played host in their apartment. She was a hard-working, determined engineer with a big heart—enough to rival Erin's. James had even worked with her directly a few times at Catamitus Dock. She was no stranger to going off-world.

More tears came to Erin's eyes and she sniffled.

James's stomach knotted. This was no ordinary job change, which came with its own challenges to Cheryl and Erin's relationship but was usually accompanied by minor outrage and grumbling, never by tears and silence. He anticipated her next words with dread.

Eventually, Erin spoke again, her voice quavering. 'Six months ago, she transferred to Arcadia Landing to be on the salvage and reclamation crew there. That's where she was when, when—'

Erin fell to silence and the quiet among the group deepened. James's heart ached for her all the more and he felt ashamed at his lack of intuition for his friend.

He'd acted like they'd shared a common bereavement in Austin, but all the while, Erin had been holding in her grief for Cheryl. The names of those lost in the explosion had been published only a few days after the survivors had gotten settled and the difficult work of informing the families had begun. James hadn't been able to bring himself to look at the list. He knew Austin would be on there already, but he hadn't anticipated anyone else he'd known personally.

He couldn't imagine what he would do if he had lost Angela in such a way. Questions swam through his mind: Why hadn't she said anything? Why was she still working? Did Elisabeth know about this? He pushed them aside; now was not the time.

'When I heard about what happened, my first thoughts were of Austin and Cheryl,' Erin continued, her voice wavering, rising in pitch. 'I hoped against hope they got out. But she wasn't on the initial drop from Skyport, nor the one after that, nor the one after that.

'That's when I learned there were only eighty who got out on the *Magellan* and I knew. The list only confirmed it.' Her voice broke at her last few words and she began to sob.

Aisling and Rhys reached their arms across her shoulders from either side.

James looked over at Nate; he looked sickly, distraught, withdrawn.

'Captain, I'm so sorry, but why didn't you say anything?' said Tom. 'We would've understood; we could've put our missions on hold.'

Erin sniffed and choked back her tears. 'I thought if I carried on with work, I would be okay. Like it didn't happen and I could look forward to seeing her again. I begged Elisabeth when she came to see me to let me carry on and to not tell anyone else. It's stupid, I know.'

'No, it's not,' said Aisling, gripping Erin's hand. 'Everyone grieves differently, reacts differently. But Tom's right, we would have supported you.'

'Yeah, how long have we worked together, *cariad*?' said Rhys, squeezing her shoulder. 'We're practically family, innit.'

'And I wouldn't have given you so much shit,' said Sai with a smile as he took another swig of his drink.

Erin spurted out a laugh and then offered a tentative smile. She looked left and right to her crew and pouted. 'Aw, I love you guys, I really do mean that. I just wish I could do something about the bastards what did this. I feel so helpless.'

'We may be able to help with that,' Nate said in a low voice.

James froze. What was Nate doing?

Erin chuckled and stammered, 'What do you mean, *bach*?'

'Our real mission here at Le Guin,' Nate continued. 'We're not just here to help you with the telescope.'

'Nate, that's enough,' said James, standing. He placed a hand on Nate's shoulder. 'I'm so sorry, Erin. I think Captain Rifkin's had a bit too much to drink.'

'No!' Nate cried, shaking James off. 'It's not fair. First Austin, now we learn about Erin's wife, too? We should be all hands on deck to bring Son of Adam down. We should at least give Erin the opportunity to help us.'

Erin sat forwards, bewildered. 'James, what's he talking about?'

James pinched the bridge of his nose and groaned.

'It's true. Just before the attack on Mars, they received an encrypted transmission. It came from here. We were sent to investigate and it was supposed to be classified.' James looked pointedly at Nate.

'So, helping us with the telescope?'

'A cover so as not to potentially tip off the perpetrator. Only Colonel Zhu knows the real reason for our being here.'

New life seemed to flicker in Erin's eyes. 'I'm in.'

'What?'

'Oh, if you're going after Son of Adam, you'd best believe we're coming too.'

Just then, James's phone pinged. He fished it out of his pocket. It was a message from Zhu that read, 'Meet me in my office after lights-out.'

'What is it?' said Nate as James put the phone back in his pocket.

'Zhu has something,' said James. He looked at Erin. 'How long until lights-out?'

'The base has an artificial day-night cycle keeping it concurrent with Earth time since it's a month to a day here.' She checked her watch. 'Lights-out is two hours from now.'

Two hours passed and the window shutters across Le Guin Research Base came down, signalling the end of the day. Personnel retired to their quarters, leaving the corridors and hallways empty. Tomorrow would see more work on the radio telescope since the job was left unfinished after Hargreaves's rescue.

The bar closed. James and Nate headed to the administration building and up the slope to the control centre.

The *Galileo* crew still had a job to do so decided to turn in and get some rest. Nevertheless, Erin requested the two captains keep her in the loop about what they found.

The control centre door was open when they arrived. Inside was dark, computers left running, no staff present. The sight set James on edge and Nate voiced what James was thinking.

'Where is everybody? There should be a night shift.'

James clenched his jaw. Something was very wrong. He checked around the walls near the entrance and found a light switch.

'Shit,' he said, scrunching his nose as the room illuminated. 'There's the night shift.'

Bodies lay on the ground unmoving by the desks, fallen from chairs or slumped against keyboards. There were fewer staff than James had seen before, all different people. Night shift was a skeleton crew. All dead.

'What the fuck happened here?' said Nate, panic rising in his voice. He cleared his throat and centred himself before taking another look around. 'Gunshot wounds, some killed at their desks, others as they got up to run. How could this have happened without the colonel noticing?'

Lightning shot through James, rooting him to the spot. 'Zhu!' he cried and bolted.

He turned the corner and flew to the door of Colonel Zhu's office. Without waiting for Nate to catch up, he slammed into the door with his shoulder and it opened with a crash.

Zhu's office was dark like the control centre but by design. A single lamp illuminated the desk at which she sat. Her body slumped backwards, eyes towards the ceiling, mouth open, bathed in warm light.

A cold numbness seeped through James's body, crawling up from his fingers and toes. Not Zhu. Surely not her, too? At any moment she would wake and greet him, apologise for looking so stupid. She was elderly, after all; perhaps she fell asleep at her desk?

James approached. Her arms were splayed to the sides; she had two bullet wounds in the chest that ran with blood. He moved closer; there was an entry wound between the eyes, the wall behind her head spattered in crimson.

Trembling, James leaned on the desk and bowed his head. His breathing quickened and he sobbed, droplets falling slowly in the lunar gravity to wet the desk.

He heard Nate's jogging footsteps come to an abrupt halt in the doorway behind him.

'No,' hissed the other man. His voice seemed distant.

James balled his fists as he leaned, scraping his fingernails on the desktop. His trembling intensified, his cheeks flushed, and he ground his teeth.

*I'm the only one left. The only one. Yula, Grant, Austin, Zhu... me.*

Nate's steps were slow and measured, but each one reverberated like a drum in James's ears.

The other captain stopped a few feet from him. His voice was croaky as he stammered a few words in disbelief.

After a few seconds, James's mind cleared enough for him to speak. 'Inform Erin,' he growled. 'This base is on immediate lockdown.'

James spun round and marched past Nate, clipping his shoulder. Tears ran down his cheeks and his fists remained clenched shut.

'Lockdown?' said Nate, rubbing his shoulder.

'No-one is to leave this place, not one ship, not one transport, not one *fucking* moon buggy. Got it?'

The main computer in the control centre was easy to locate. James used the access code Zhu had given him to log into the system. He initiated the base's lockdown protocol, which was clearly marked on the administrative interface. An alarm sounded and an on-screen map showed doors across the facility closing one by one. Doors to staff quarters, doors between modules, airlocks, the hangar bays, and even the docking clamps on the landing pads.

With every mode of exit sealed shut save for the administrative building, James opened a broadcast channel across the facility. He explained the situation quickly and with little tact, then closed the channel abruptly.

He heard footsteps behind and glanced around to see Erin, Aisling, Tom, Sai, and Rhys in the doorway. They slowed, surveying the carnage. The colour drained from Rhys's thin face. Tom's jaw clenched, but he too looked a little green.

Erin marched up to James and demanded an explanation.

'Zhu's dead,' he replied, then gestured to the rest of the room. 'Everybody's dead.'

'The whole night shift?'

James nodded without taking his eyes off the screen.

'So we've got the base locked down and you've managed to treat everyone like petulant children over the radio. What's next?' said Nate.

'I'm going through the security feeds to see if it caught who did all this,' said James. 'Nate, I want you to do what we came here to do: check the communications logs for the transmission that went to Arcadia Landing. Erin, you and your team spread yourselves out over the base and make sure no one gets out. I'll give you all access, just make sure you lock the doors again after you pass through.'

Erin nodded. 'Good idea. It'll make it easier for us to get someone on the perpetrators once you've identified them. Rhys, north; Tom, you take the south; Ash, Sai, east and west. Go!'

After being given codes to unlock the doors manually, the *Galileo* crew went off and James turned his attention back to the security footage. He combed through the recordings of the different cameras in the administrative building and watched in horror as the staff were gunned down at their desks by three hooded assailants.

It wasn't long before he came across the feed for Zhu's office showing a view from above the doorway, facing the desk; it was the only camera in the room.

He watched as the hooded man walked in, flanked by the two others, his back facing the camera. Zhu was already standing in alarm, about to shuffle around her desk. A look of terror came across her as though she had seen a ghost and she stepped back. There was no audio and James was no lip reader, but as she conversed with the mysterious stranger, her body language suggested familiarity. Then her expression hardened and she spat her final words as the man raised his weapon and fired three rounds without hesitation. Zhu fell back into the position James had found her in and the stranger and his entourage left the room.

James stopped the recording and leaned on the desk, his head bowed. Utterly spent, he lowered himself into the chair. In his thoughts he considered the frailty of life. Just like Austin, one moment Zhu had been there, ageing and unsteady on her feet but full of vitality, and the next, she was gone. Simply gone. The moment of her death played over and over in his mind. She'd been so much herself—defiant and dauntless—even to the end. She hadn't flinched when the stranger had pulled the gun on her. She hadn't even blinked as the shots had ripped through her body. Zhu had made damn sure that, no matter what they'd do to her, she would remain undefeated.

At this, James's moment of enervation gave way. His mind raced. Zhu knew her killer; how? Before he could ponder this question much more, Nate's voice broke through the reverie.

'Hey, James, I've found something,' he said. 'Come and see.'

Captain Fowler hauled himself out of the chair with a groan and shuffled over to Nate, who sat at one of the front-row terminals overlooking the monochromatic landscape.

'Is it the transmission to Arcadia Landing?' said James, folding his arms as he stood behind Nate.

Nate shook his head. 'No, not exactly. It looks like the record has been wiped, but not very well. There's no message here, but there is a gap in the normal transmissions the base sends out, like they just snipped it. I've cross-referenced the timestamp of the gap with things like recorded movements of the base's communications antennae and staff lists—'

'And the long and short of it is…'

'It was definitely pointed at Mars and I can narrow down exactly which terminal—and whose—it came from.'

'Great!'

'No.'

'No?'

Nate sighed. 'They weren't here. The guy's name is Sergio Amos and according to his social media'—Nate switched tabs and brought up Sergio's profile—'he's been on vacation in the Azores since last week. Airtight alibi.'

James rubbed his temples and groaned.

'Was there any security footage?' asked Erin.

Nate shook his head again. 'Nothing useful. I found a single view of our phantom using the terminal at the right time, but the base's facial recognition system couldn't pick them out.'

'Maybe we could get some forensics done on the terminal?' said James. 'Fingerprints or DNA or...'

Nate scoffed. 'Are you kidding? You really expect to get anything like that after a week? And it's not like the dude sneezed on it.'

'If it's a dude,' Erin interjected.

The others turned to look at her, perplexed.

She shrugged. 'Could be a woman or an enby. No gender on crime, innit.'

'Hold on...' said James to Nate. He thought back to the footage he watched of the attack on the control centre. 'You said the base has facial recognition?'

Erin moved away, gesturing that she was going to check-in with her crew.

'Yeah, and not just facial, but biometrics and other data,' said Nate, giving Erin a nod and looking back up at James. 'Everyone's movements about the base are monitored. In any given frame of security footage, if there's a person in it, the computer can tell us who it is.'

'And this… "phantom"?'

'That's what's so strange. The base computer has no idea who they are.'

'Shouldn't that be a big red flag?' said James, shifting his weight to his other leg and pulling on his beard.

'Naw, software's not that sophisticated yet. Our "phantom" is such because he—or she or they—is pretty much invisible to the base's computer.'

James pulled on his beard more, twirling the ragged end around his finger as much as it would go. 'Someone who is invisible to the base's automated systems but can blend in well enough to not arouse suspicion from the rest of the staff… Someone for whom the ISA has no data.'

'Not just the ISA,' said Nate. 'The system uses world-wide law enforcement and intelligence data. Birth records, medical history, and so on. It ought to be able to identify—at least to some degree—any human.'

'That's pretty dystopian.'

Nate shrugged.

'So, what about the others?' said James.

'What others?'

'Well, our phantom wasn't working alone, were they? They had two accomplices. If the software can identify any human, who were they?'

'Oh,' said Nate, tapping and clicking around the computer. He brought up two photographs. 'Ah, one's Shane McMurdo, a systems engineer who had only recently transferred over, and the other… Jeremy Slater, who worked right here in the command centre. Day shift.'

James paced around, eyes to the ceiling in thought. 'Perhaps if we could find his terminal, it could provide us with some more clues as to our mysterious stranger?'

'No can do; it's this one I'm using right now and I already checked through it. It's scrubbed clean.'

'Damn, looks like we'll have to have a word with—'

'James, Nate,' Erin cried out, panic-stricken. 'I've lost contact with Tom!'

# CHAPTER EIGHT
## LOCKDOWN

JAMES FLEW BACK TO THE MAIN COMPUTER and brought up the map showing the lockdown. Tom had been surveying the south section of the facility. On the screen, there were doors open that ought to have been closed.

As James watched, another adjoining door opened a little further along the corridor.

'Shit, someone's circumventing the lockdown to the south,' James hissed. 'We lost contact with Tom in module SSE-8. Where could they be heading?'

'If it were me,' said Erin, pointing at the lockdown map, 'I'd be looking for a way out of here.' She tapped on the screen. 'There's a transport docked at the eastern port.'

'Conventional?' asked Nate. 'Are they really that desperate they'd spend two days in space to get back to Earth? We could easily catch up to them.'

Erin shook her head. 'All the old transports were retrofitted with Austinium drives weeks ago.'

James slapped the desk. 'Damn it. So if they get on that transport…'

'Zip! Gone,' Erin replied with a snap of her fingers.

'More to the point,' said Nate. 'How did they get the access codes?'

'I don't think we have time for that right now,' said James as another door opened on the map.

In another window, he brought up the live security feeds and flicked through each camera, hoping to catch a glimpse of their target or at least to ascertain Tom's status. But when he switched to module SSE-8, he found the cameras offline. Flicking to the cameras along the route of the unlocked doors showed more of the same.

*Damn, they're taking out the cameras so they can't be identified.*

He fished his phone out of his pocket and logged into the base's network using the permissions Zhu had given him. It provided him with the same map view as the console.

'Erin, radio your team to converge on SSE-8. We'll meet them there,' said James.

It wasn't long before James, Nate, and Erin arrived at the module where they had lost contact with Tom. It was a short cylindrical corridor containing laboratories, one on each side.

Sai, Aisling, and Rhys were already there, huddled around Tom, who sat on the floor at the far corner, rubbing the side of his head.

'He was hiding in the lab,' James heard Tom say to Aisling as they approached. 'I was just walking past the room, when the next thing I knew, the door opened and I got slammed against the wall. Must've hit my head, too.'

'Did you see anything?' said James as he knelt down next to Tom.

Tom shook his head and winced. His russet hair was matted with blood. 'Didn't even see which way they went, but I guess if you guys came from that way, they must've gone the other. There were definitely more than three of them, though.'

James looked at his phone. Their phantom was now five modules away, based on the string of unlocked vestibule doors. It was taking time for them to get through each doorway; probably hacking the control panels one at a time, which meant they didn't have access codes. At that rate, James and his team could catch them before they reached the eastern dock, but they'd have to be quick.

He gripped Tom's shoulder and nodded before standing. 'Simmonds, Suresh: take Specialist Lando to the med bay,' he said sidelong to Aisling and Sai. 'Erin: we need to go now if we're gonna have a chance of catching the people who did this. Me, you, Nate, and Jones. Let's go.'

As Aisling and Sai helped Tom up off the floor, James led his group through the doorway and into the next module, setting off at a run.

They'd made it to through to the third before anybody spoke.

'I take it we're working on the assumption these people are the same ones who shot up the command centre?' said Nate, breathless.

They sped past more sealed laboratories under the sickly fluorescent strip light—a standard for these smaller, utilitarian modules.

'I think that would be reasonable to assume,' said James.

Erin touched his shoulder. 'D'you reckon they're also

the ones who sent the kill order to Arcadia Landing?'

James slowed his pace and came to a halt. 'Not only that,' he said as he told her about the *Magnum Opus* murders. 'Colonel Zhu seemed to think it's all linked. She thought it was just paranoia and I would've agreed. I mean, she placed an order for anti-aircraft weapons for the base, for crying out loud! But that was until she...'

'Sounds like she was thinking five steps ahead of the rest of us,' said Erin, squeezing James's arm.

A buzz in James's pocket told him another door had been unlocked further on. Walking again, the group crossed the module apace.

'Can't you make it harder for them to keep unlocking stuff?' said Nate. 'Cycle the security or something?'

James pushed open the next set of doors. 'Be my guest. I may be old and wise, but it might surprise you to learn I don't know everything.'

'I know a thing or two about computers,' said Rhys. 'I could give it a go if you like, *mun*?'

James shrugged and handed his phone over as the group continued along their fourth module: a wide, dimly lit space of storage units and materials processing suites; a factory.

After a short way, Rhys cried aloud and threw up his hands, catching James's attention.

The three of them gathered in front of the Major, who looked at each of them in turn. His victorious expression faded to sheepishness and he lowered his arms.

'I got 'em,' Rhys said after clearing his throat. He turned the phone towards the three captains. 'Just in bloody time, too. Any longer and they'd have been through the airlock and scot-free.'

James took his phone back and regarded the map; Rhys was right. In their pursuit through the base, James and his team were now at the entrance to the eastern port. Its small departure lounge was two buildings further along. In fact, the port itself was a protuberance from the main circuit, so if the fugitives wanted to go anywhere else, they'd have to come back through the module James's team was currently in.

He scrolled the view to the departure lounge. At the far end, he could see the airlock leading to the waiting transports had been secured by whatever magic Rhys had wrought.

'So, they're trapped in there?' asked James.

Rhys rubbed the back of his neck. 'Well, "trapped" is a relative term. If they're the same people what killed everyone in the command centre, we won't be much of a barrier if they decide to come back this way.'

'They've got all the guns,' said Nate with a nod. He folded his arms and shifted his weight. 'We've got nothing. My sidearm's still on the *Aurora* and James doesn't carry one at all.'

James shrugged. 'Not much to shoot at on Ganymede, nor here… usually.'

'So, how do we plan on dealing with them, then?' said Erin, placing her hands on her hips.

James paced back and forth. The incident at the telescope flashed through his mind: Hargreaves gasping, choking, flapping wildly to seal the tear in his suit.

He shuddered, then stopped pacing. 'We can incapacitate them,' James said, pulling his phone out. Would it be possible? Zhu's codes had given him access to the security system, but what else could he control? After a short while searching, he found the options he was looking for.

Nate, Rhys, and Erin gathered in front of him with quizzical expressions.

'Look,' he said, turning the phone around so they could see. 'We vent the room. Just enough to cause a panic. They drop their weapons, we restore the air supply, go in, and take them.'

Rhys scratched at his hair and said, 'Great idea, except for one thing: they'll still be able to pick up the guns before we get to 'em.'

Nate and Erin murmured in agreement.

'That's why I'll go in first,' said James, lowering his arm. 'I'll relieve them of their weapons, then bring the oxygen back so you lot can back me up.'

Erin gasped. 'Are you crazy, *butt*?'

'You already know I don't need the air,' James said, looking to Nate for support. 'I'll radio when it's safe for you guys to come in.'

Nate seemed distant, staring into nothingness as he stroked his chin. 'I hate to say it,' he said after a long moment, 'but it's a good plan and our best chance of catching these guys.'

Erin huffed and turned away, shaking her head.

James smiled. 'Major, how long would you give them before they break through your cyber-wotsit?'

'I'd love to say "indefinitely", I would, Captain,' Rhys said, looking at his watch. 'But it was a bodge-job to say the least. If they've got someone even half competent, I'd give them till maybe five-and-twenty past at the most.'

'Jesus, Rhys, that's only a quarter of an hour away. What's wrong with you?' cried Erin.

'We'd better get moving then,' said James as he strode

off through the abandoned port's entranceway, leaving the others to follow on.

The group moved swiftly and silently through check-in. The eastern port was mainly used for receiving shipments of industrial supplies and sending samples so the area for people was much smaller than the spaceport to the north where the *Aurora* and *Galileo* had landed.

Soon they were into the next module: a round-ceilinged registration area featuring automated machines with conveyor belts for smaller cargo lining the left and right walls.

James motioned for the group to separate to each side so they'd be out of view of the window in the vestibule door at the end. He and Nate took the left, while Erin and Rhys took the right.

Kneeling beside the doorway, he nodded to Rhys and Erin then took out his phone again. With the press of a button, he heard the muffled whirr of the vents opening on the other side of the door. He started counting.

*One... Two... Three... Four... Five...*

After thirty seconds had elapsed, James slipped through the first vestibule door. There was just enough room for him to stand between the modules as he locked it behind him. Another button press and the pressure equalised, so he opened the second door into the departure lounge.

No sooner had he stepped through than he heard a muffled shot, barely audible in the last remaining vestiges of air. He recoiled and cried out as the slug caught him in the shoulder. Without a second thought he threw himself behind the nearest row of chairs.

*Fuck, one of them must've had a suit.*

Pressing his palm against the bleeding wound, he shuffled along and peered out around the edge of the row. He had chosen well: a blank departure board broke his line of sight with the airlock at the end. Around the floor were bodies—he couldn't tell how many—and some had guns nearby.

In the scramble he'd lost count of the time, so he quickly pulled up his phone and pressed the button to repressurise the room.

'Whoever you are, lay down your weapon and surrender,' James called through gritted teeth as the air returned. When no response came, he continued, 'Y'know, your crewmates probably have brain damage now, thanks to you.'

*Nothing.*

James swore under his breath and looked back to the open door. There had been a fugitive stationed to one side, now passed out on the floor. He recognised the face as that of Jeremy Slater. Closer to James, a pistol lay on the ground.

*Won't be getting anything out of him, then. Thanks for the gun, at least.*

He let go of his shoulder and reached out. Quickly he grabbed the weapon and drew back, cradling it to his wound.

Erin's voice crackled in his earpiece. 'Are we clear to come in? We heard the vents close.'

Bone conduction earpiece technology had become the standard for off-world operations, as it allowed the transmission of sound should the wearer find themselves in a rapidly depleting atmosphere or in a total vacuum. James had argued the case in their favour due to his augmentation. He'd received little resistance. They were cheap enough to produce that the ISA had no qualms about adopting them.

'Negative,' James hissed back. 'Someone survived. I've been shot. Everything's under control.'

'It doesn't sound like everything's under control!'

James groaned. 'Standby.' Then he turned and crawled out, keeping the board between him and the airlock.

He stood with his back to it and ventured a glance around the board, which was met by a sharp crack as a bullet ricocheted off the frame near his face.

'Stop shooting, idiot!' said James as he lowered himself back to the ground. 'I've just brought the air back. You want to vent it all over again? It's over. You've got nowhere else to go.'

'That's where you're wrong, Captain James Fowler.'

James's blood ran cold at the sound of the male voice, eerily familiar, muddled aspects catching in the back of his mind. A blend of North American overlaid on an original European accent—possibly French or Spanish, it was hard to place—indicative of someone who had lived in the US for many years. It didn't help that it came to James muffled.

'You know who I am?' James asked.

The voice laughed. 'You've made quite a name for yourself already. The Indestructible Man.'

'You're thinking of someone else,' said James as he winced through a twinge of pain in his shoulder.

Silence fell once again. James readied the gun in his blood-stained hand and rose against the board. There was only one way to end this stalemate. The main aisle to his right was strewn with unconscious fugitives.

There were more here than he'd anticipated. He'd only expected three, but there were at least half a dozen. It depended on the severity, but if they truly were brain damaged from the oxygen deprivation, James and his team wouldn't get anything useful out of them. No, he needed this guy, whoever he was. He closed his eyes and exhaled slowly, his heart pounding in his ears.

Then, he stepped out, his acquired pistol levelled.

A man stood at the end, facing James, also pointing his gun. To the left on the wall, the control panel for the airlock hung down by its wires.

The man wore a simple work suit typical of Le Guin staff, but his head was covered by a black mask, which James recognised instantly. A bright green, grinning grotesque, the same one he'd seen on the hologram during the debrief with Elisabeth. The leader of Sidera Silere: Son of Adam.

James's breath caught in his chest at the sight of the mask. Heat rose uncontrolled from deep within and his gun arm trembled.

'You,' he snarled. He could feel the trigger, warmed beneath his finger, every little imperfection. How he wanted in this moment just to squeeze it. That was all it would take: one squeeze to end the man responsible for Austin and Zhu's deaths as well as the deaths of hundreds of others.

'Yes, me,' said Son of Adam. 'And what're you going to do about "me", James? I thought you'd come to arrest me, but I can see right now you'd rather evacuate my brains across the airlock door.'

The urge was strong. He'd felt it once before, years ago, that day in the warehouse as Dr Hales had lain in his sights. Who did this 'Son of Adam' think he was, anyway? He could dress up all he wanted, play around with people's lives, wage his little "holy war", but he was still mortal. James was a god by comparison.

'Let's not kid ourselves,' Son of Adam continued. He lowered his pistol and tucked it into his belt. 'You're not going to pull that trigger and neither am I. It wouldn't be fitting. I have much bigger plans for you anyway.'

'You're testing me?' said James, incredulous. The audacity. Sweat dripped from his nose, his knuckles white around the handle of the gun. Then he noticed it. His rage shattered in a moment of clarity. How had he not seen it before?

*He's not wearing a spacesuit!*

Stupefied, he lost concentration for a fraction of a second. His eyes lost focus and the gun dipped. The next thing he knew, Son of Adam had the airlock door open and was through. Before James could react, the airlock closed and locked tight.

'No!' He ran to the door and hammered on the reinforced window with the butt of the pistol to no avail. Son of Adam simply stared back at him as the door to the docking tunnel opened behind.

A moment later, he was gone, around the corner and up the ramp, James knew, to the waiting transport.

'Damn it!' James hit the door once more with the pistol, turned, and sank to the floor. He tapped his earpiece and said, 'Erin, Nate, Rhys, you're clear to enter. I'm going to lift the lockdown. We need to get the paramedics in here.'

James found the menu on his phone, opened the base's doors, and paged the medics as his team entered from the other end.

'What the… Shouldn't they be awake by now?' said Nate, stepping over unconscious bodies.

Erin rushed over to James and knelt beside him. She checked his wound, both sides, pulling the hole in his shirt to and fro. 'Wait, what?' she said with a stutter. 'I thought you said you got shot. You're not bleeding or anything!'

'I did. Bullet went straight through.' He saw her bewildered expression and explained, 'It's another part of my augmentation; I heal fast.'

'Tidy,' said Rhys.

'Did you get the guy?' said Nate, now standing over James, full of nervous energy.

James shook his head and stood. 'It was Son of Adam himself. He got away.'

'Wait, you're telling me you let him escape?' Nate cried, his face contorted. '*The* Son of Adam, right here, right in your grasp, and you just—What the hell's wrong with you, man? Christ.'

'I don't know, I—I had him at gunpoint and then I lost concentration.'

Nate kissed his teeth and turned away.

'You don't get it,' James continued. 'He wasn't wearing a suit. He should've been on the floor like all the others. I don't understand…'

'It doesn't fucking matter!' Nate spun on his heel and pointed at him. 'You had the chance to get Austin's killer—to get Colonel Zhu's killer. All that alien warrior DNA or whatever and this random dude just slips through your fingers? What good is that?'

'Hey! You two stop that shit right now,' said Erin, standing between them. 'Nate, you know James didn't just let him go, alright.'

'No, I messed up,' said James, balling his fists. 'It won't happen again.'

'Yeah. Better not,' Nate growled.

James glared at Nate. 'How's that?'

'You heard me.'

Erin held James back as he took a step forward. 'Cut it out,' she said, looking between them both. 'Nate, what's gotten into you? We're all on the same side here. Working towards the same goal—'

'Are we?' said Nate, still glaring at James. 'Because it sure don't look like it from where I'm standing. This was our best chance to end this madness. He had him at gunpoint, Erin! He should've pulled the goddamn trigger.' With that, Nate spun round and stormed from the room.

'What's going on with him? Acting like he's the only one who's lost someone,' Erin muttered, staring after Nate. She turned back to James and said, 'I'll go talk to him, see if I can calm him down.'

'Leave him,' said James as the paramedics entered. Rhys directed them and they began seeing to the unconscious fugitives Son of Adam had left behind.

'But he's all over the place,' said Erin.

James sat down on the floor and pushed his palms to his eyes. Sparks lit up the blackness and he groaned. He then blinked as he looked up at Erin. 'I think he's feeling guilty, y'know? Like Arcadia Landing was somehow his fault and he needs to atone. I noticed something was off with him before, but he said he wasn't ready to talk about it yet.'

'We're all still hurting,' Erin said. 'But that's no excuse to act like a total *coc oen*. He needs to buck his ideas up, like.'

James sighed heavily and picked himself up off the ground. 'At least now we have a few theories confirmed.'

'Such as?'

'Son of Adam murdered Zhu immediately after she let me know she'd found something. And I have no doubt that something was the original encoded transmission to Arcadia Landing. Perhaps she decoded it, too, but we'll never know.

'I also think Zhu was right. The *Magnum Opus* murders and Sidera Silere's attack on Arcadia Landing are connected. What's more, Zhu knew Son of Adam's identity.'

Erin scratched the back of her neck and yawned. 'Could be any number of people, though. The Colonel's list of contacts must be a mile long.'

'I agree; on its own, it gets us nowhere. One thing bothers me, though.'

'What's that?'

James crossed his arms and shuffled his feet. 'That I recognised his voice. At least, I get the feeling I've heard it somewhere before. Add that onto the fact he seemed to survive us sucking all the air out of the room like it was nothing, it's definitely got a lot more complicated.'

They walked together in silence back through the facility towards the med bay. What he'd said wasn't entirely true. One more thing bothered him: the urge to pull the trigger. It wasn't like him and he'd spent decades convincing himself Dr Hales had been wrong, that there was no "warrior instinct" threatening to take over his mind. But he knew with an ache in his heart that, if he hadn't been distracted in that moment, he would have done it.

Icy fingers of fear crept through him then. He'd never killed anyone, even during his time in the RAF. But that was mainly because he'd never been deployed. He wondered what dark path lay beyond that threshold; what could it unlock for someone with his abilities? From all he knew of the Achelon, they seemed ruthless and effective killers. Could this be a by-product of the elysian enzyme that had given James his biological immortality?

*What is happening to me?*

# CHAPTER NINE
## FAREWELLS

AUSTIN NEVER SMILED IN any of his portraits. At least, that was the revelation James had as he looked at the two framed photographs sitting side-by-side on the trestle table. The one on the left had a younger Captain Queen in a full mock spacesuit, his jaw clenched. It was from the shoot on the eve of their launch to rendezvous with the *Magnum Opus*. He held a prop helmet in his lap. On the right, a more recent image: Austin as the 'youngsters' knew him, taken barely a month ago.

The table was draped in a white cloth and adorned with artefacts of Austin's life, matching the eras. A model *Magnum Opus* just like the one in Zhu's office on the Moon, a model *Aurora*, but also a folded United States flag, a US Navy cap, and some tealight candles. Everything was arranged as symmetrically as possible. James himself had placed a small photograph of the captain's old dog,

Poochie, on the table. He never did get another.

There was no formal funeral for Austin or any of the seven hundred and fifty-six who'd lost their lives on Mars; no committal with no body to recover. Instead, the small group of those who had known Austin best sat on fold-out chairs in the draughty hangar of the ISA headquarters where James had first laid eyes on the *Aurora* all those years ago. Angela sat next to him, draped in a blanket, and squeezed his hand. Along from her forming a semi-circle were Nate, Erin, and Captain April Rose-Hartley of the *UNSV Newton*.

Like everyone else, April wore formal attire, but clearly in protest. Her shirt was untucked and the top button undone, cravat loose about her neck. Elisabeth's doing; Austin wouldn't have cared how she dressed, but April made it work. In the nearly ten years he'd worked with her, James struggled to remember a single instance of April wearing anything more formal than ripped jeans, leather jacket, and a band tee. She'd even sewn music-related patches onto her flight suit. All 'ancient' bands, she'd said, which had thrown James into a mild existential crisis, as they had all been classic artists from the nineteen-sixties and seventies through to the early two-thousands.

As April leaned back and ran a hand through her hair, styled as usual in a pink and white undercut fauxhawk, James laughed inwardly, imagining Elisabeth trying to convince her to change it and take out her piercings.

On James's right in a wheelchair was Cass Spilka, Austin's old friend from his days at NASA's White Sands facility. It was remarkable her being here at all. She had fairly advanced dementia, but her memories of Austin remained for the time being.

*The man certainly knew how to leave an impression.*

After a couple of minutes, Elisabeth stood in front of them with the table behind her. She said a few words about Austin's life and work. He'd had no remaining family, being an only child and celibate, and his parents had died long ago, before the first Mars expedition.

The old captain had never really had all that much to say about his upbringing, but from the little James had gleaned over the decades, his relationship with his father—a decorated and highly conservative vice-admiral in the US Navy—had been combative, with heavy expectations. From attending Pride marches to eventually quitting the Navy and joining NASA, Austin's father had always had scathing criticism and little in the way of praise. But they had made peace in the end.

Elisabeth's words were beautiful, rehearsed well, but she only knew the broad strokes of Austin's past: his distinguished service record and many professional accomplishments. At the end of her talk, the wind whistled approvingly through the gaps in the hangar roof as though Austin gave his blessing in spirit.

*He'd have loved to have been spoken of so highly.*

Elisabeth invited each of the ISA staff in turn to give short eulogies as she sat down in the horseshoe. James went last, having known Austin the longest.

Clutching his handwritten speech behind his back, crumpling the pages as the tension in his throat rose, he looked to Angela and began. 'I knew Austin for the better part of forty-two years. We of the first *Magnum Opus* expedition trained together as a team a short time before our rendezvous launch. But it was aboard that ship, in the long gulf of space, where we truly bonded. He led our team with wisdom, duty, and integrity. And more than that, he was the first and only person from the space programme to come and visit me after I woke from my coma.

'Captain Queen looked out for us—Angela and I—sometimes at great personal risk to himself. His love and loyalty to his friends was strong and lasting. I will always regret that we lost touch for those twenty years as he worked on the *Aurora* project, but our reunion was touching. It was as though no time had passed.

'Working alongside him and under his command again, flying the spaceplane that will now serve as his legacy, was the greatest of honours. You all knew him as a kindly mentor or a father-figure or a gigantic pain in the arse.' He looked at Elisabeth and gave her a wan smile. 'But for me, Austin was the best friend I ever had.' He choked out the last few words; tears ran down, but he held his head high and Angela gave him a supportive smile.

He turned to face the portraits and memorabilia on the table and bowed his head. The paper in his hands, now brought round to his front, was well and truly ruined.

Under his breath, he said, 'I'll miss you, you old coot, and I vow to keep your memory alive, even into the deepest time.'

After the tables and chairs were cleared away, April approached James, who stood holding the framed photographs.

'So, immortal, eh? Dude, I did not have that down on my bingo card, that's for sure.'

James snorted but didn't look up.

'Y'know,' April continued as she pulled off her cravat, 'I still can't believe you're the same James Fowler who went to Mars with Austin.'

James made a sceptical expression. 'Really? I didn't think my poor excuse for a disguise was that good.' He gestured to his beard.

April threw her arms up and paced back and forth. 'Man, you gotta understand. I thought you were his son or something, like James Fowler the second or some shit. I know a guy, right? Name's Jack. His son's name is Jack, his pops' name is Jack, his grandpappy's name is Jack. My god, even his daughter's name is Jacqueline; goes by—'

'Jack?'

'You got it. So you see my predicament?'

'Yeah, I get it.' James packed the photos away into his bag, gave a last melancholy huff, and looked up at April with a smile. 'Heard you and your team discovered Planet Nine finally.'

April's eyes brightened and she took a victorious stance. 'Hell yes. With a hundred and fifty TNOs to our name, it's about damn time we hit the jackpot. Score one for the Planet Hunters! We named her Hecate.'

'I thought it was "Newton's Reach"?'

'That's the largest moon—a captured dwarf planet, a bit like Triton.'

James felt a tap on his shoulder. It was Erin and she looked concerned. 'Elisabeth wants to see us—you, me, and Nate. Oh, are you looping April in, too?'

'Hey Erin,' said April in a chipper tone, placing her hands on her hips. 'Long time no see. You gonna give me—what was it—a clutch?'

Erin laughed. 'It's *cwtsh*, you ding-dong, and o'course I am!'

James couldn't help but smile as Erin and April

embraced. It had been a very long time indeed since any of them had seen April; the nature of her work as the captain of the Planet Hunters on the *Newton* kept her away at the outer reaches of the solar system for months at a time. It was pure coincidence she had been in range to hear about Austin's memorial service at all. According to April, they had made planetfall on Newton's Reach the day Arcadia Landing had been destroyed and hadn't received the distress signal until hours later—not that the *Newton* would have made it in time anyway. The Austinium drive might have revolutionised travel around the solar system, but it was far from instantaneous.

The Planet Hunters considered themselves a romanticised cross between frontiersmen and pirates but were more akin to ancient sailing cartographers, seeking out uncharted bodies too dim and distant for telescopes to pinpoint.

'So,' said April, releasing Erin and eyeballing James. 'What's this you gotta loop me in on?'

After speaking with Angela about the meeting with Elisabeth, James left her in the hangar happily reminiscing with Cass and her carer.

The three captains walked and talked as they made their way through the facility to Elisabeth's office. James hadn't intended on burdening April with their investigation and was irked Erin had forced him into it. But the feeling soon passed; excluding April was unfair. No matter how unlikely it was she could help them, she deserved the chance to make the decision for herself.

April listened in uncharacteristic silence as James recounted what had happened on the Moon. As they reached the door to Elisabeth's office, she leaned casually against the door frame and stroked her chin as though wrestling with what to do with the information.

'So, are you in?' asked James after a short while.

April bobbed her head back and forth, then said, 'Nah, ain't my vibe.'

'What?'

'Oh, come on, April!' said Erin with an impassioned groan. 'We're avenging Austin and Cheryl and all the people who died, like.'

'Bringing Son of Adam and Sidera Silere to justice,' James corrected her.

'Right. That, too.'

James squeezed the bridge of his nose. 'I don't get it, April. Why not?'

April shrugged and stood from the wall. 'Like I said, not my vibe. And it sounds like you guys got it handled. Good luck catching him, though. Keep me posted, alright?'

She shoved the door open and stepped through.

In the office, Elisabeth sat behind her desk, fingers clasped, and Nate stood in the corner, leaning against the wall with his arms crossed. James hadn't seen Nate leave the hangar; he guessed he must have rushed out as soon as the memorial service had finished. Nate had said barely a single word to James since Son of Adam's escape from Le Guin. James had found him waiting in the cargo bay of the *Aurora* and they had made the trip back to Earth in such silence James had felt the need to switch on the bay camera to make sure Nate had still been conscious after take-off.

The door had barely clicked shut behind James when Elisabeth spoke. 'We tracked the stolen transport after it made LEO. It has taken a while to pull together all the data. Of course, we had Skyport and our own satellites, but getting the orbital hotels to co-operate was a nightmare.'

'Sounds like great news,' said James, but Elisabeth's expression hardened and his heart sank. 'There's a catch, isn't there?'

Nate scoffed. 'Satellites lost track as soon as it entered free-flight.'

'So it's in the wind?'

'Might as well be. It was picked up again on radar as it came in over Saudi Arabia and crossed the Persian Gulf.'

Elisabeth cleared her throat and Nate fell silent. 'That is not—Wait a minute. Captain Rose-Hartley, what are you doing here?'

April examined her fingernails and said, 'James and Erin brought me up to speed. It's all good, Lizzy-baby.'

After a short moment glaring dumbstruck at April, Elisabeth glanced back at Nate and continued, 'As I was saying, that is not the issue. We have triangulated its position to an area in central Kyrgyzstan. We think it landed on a disused runway outside of Kazarman.'

'So what *is* the problem?' asked Erin.

Elisabeth tapped on her desk and brought up a map of the country. 'The Kyrgyz government. James, you will recall what I said about the precarious political position of this investigation, yes?'

Erin and April looked at James and he returned it with a glance to them both. 'It's a powder keg,' he said. 'That's why we got saddled with it.'

'Correct. The ISA is under a lot of political pressure to catch Son of Adam and none of the other member states are willing to lift a finger to help. That includes helping us to locate the terrorists even after they landed on their soil. There is also the fact that Kyrgyzstan is one of the poorer countries in the region with few resources. Their situation has, in fact, deteriorated in recent years.'

'What a crock of shit,' said April, stuffing her hands in her pockets. 'Surely if they help and you catch the guy, it'll look great for them?'

'Yes, I have made that case to their ambassador,' said Elisabeth. 'However, he countered by saying that if they helped and we failed, it would reflect badly on them.'

'And our track record ain't exactly spotless, now, is it?' said Nate, giving James a dirty look.

Elisabeth tapped her palm hard on the desk. 'Captain Rifkin—'

'No, no, Administrator, it's fine,' said James, stepping towards Nate. 'It seems the good captain has something else he'd like to say to me. Something novel, no doubt.'

Nate pushed himself off of the wall and glowered at James with his arms crossed. 'Yeah, as a matter of fact, I do. Administrator, I cannot fathom how this man, whom we hailed as a hero on the Moon mere hours previously, would hesitate for even a second to take down Son of Adam. And yet, here we are. Now, why is that, I wonder?'

'I have already given you my reasons—the same reasons I have given in my report,' said James with an edge to his voice. 'The situation changed. It's no longer a simple matter.'

'With respect, Captain, I remain unconvinced.'

James scoffed and glanced at Erin, who rolled her eyes. 'With *respect*, it's not up to you. The administrator placed me in charge of this investigation after you deferred. The final say on whether my reasons were justified lies with her.'

Nate stepped away with a look of disgust then turned

back to Elisabeth. 'Administrator, clearly Captain Fowler is not capable of conducting this as anything other than a farce. His methods are sloppy, ineffective, and his inconsistency is a liability. We cannot rely on him.'

'Sloppy and ineffective?' said James, now openly scowling at the man. He could feel the heat rising into his cheeks. 'That is uncalled for, Captain. As I recall, I was the one who had to practically drag your sorry arse to the Moon.'

Nate gave him a sidelong glare, his voice trembling. 'They carried out another massacre right under your nose, James. Killed our only lead, managed to evade your lockdown. Then, to top it all off, you let Son of Adam simply walk away through the airlock and steal a spaceship! Just watched as he fucked off into the ether. And now we're left to fix your mistakes.'

'If you have something useful to suggest, I'm all ears,' said James, turning away from Nate.

'Step aside. Let someone else take the reins.' Nate leaned on the desk with both hands and addressed Elisabeth, who watched with a weary look. 'Ma'am, you said this is totally in our jurisdiction. No one else will touch it. We know where he's holed up for now. We'll assemble a strike team, go there, and take him down.'

The colour drained from Elisabeth's face and she bristled. 'A strike team? *Mein Gott*, that is enough, Captain. Even if we could put together such a team— because, may I remind you, we are not yet a military organisation—I would not sanction an invasion onto sovereign soil. Imagine the backlash.'

'So, we just let Son of Adam jump the border and disappear forever?'

'We—*I*—have to go through the proper diplomatic channels and that will take time. I may be the administrator here, but I am still the Deutsche ambassador and I will not risk dragging my country into an international incident over this.'

'I can see the headlines now,' April chimed in, laughing. '"Germany uses ISA for proxy war with Central Asia." What a fuckin' stupid idea, Nate.'

'You got anything better?' said Nate, folding his arms.

April snorted. 'Hell no, man.' She raised two fingers facing outwards and grinned. 'I'll leave y'all to it. Peace out,' she said before slipping out of the office.

The room fell to a pained silence and after a short while, Erin raised her hand. 'I kind of agree with Nate—oh, don't look at me like that, James! I don't mean all that rubbish about you being unfit or whatever. I just mean… Why can't we move in on the bastard now?'

James groaned. 'Elisabeth *just* explained—'

'I'm not talking about sending a strike team. I mean, we could go, plus our crews. Hardly an invasion force, innit? It's only ten of us; mine and Cheryl's hen-do was bigger and no one accused us of invading Pontypridd!'

James, Nate, and Erin stared at Elisabeth, who returned their stares with an inscrutable expression. 'Thank you for the suggestion, Captain Pritchard, but the answer is no. I will go through the proper diplomatic channels'—she caught Nate's exasperation—'the *proper channels*, Captain Rifkin. You will all stand down until I give the go-ahead and you will need to be ready to move at a moment's notice.'

Nate chewed his bottom lip and shook his head. 'He's gonna get away again.'

'And if he does, we will find him,' Elisabeth said, the impatience in her voice palpable.

Nate kissed his teeth.

Elisabeth frowned and looked down at her notes on the desk. There was venom in her voice. 'You are dismissed, Captain Rifkin.'

'Yes, Administrator,' said Nate and he left the room, shooting James a withering look as he went.

'May I speak freely?' asked James cautiously, to which Elisabeth nodded. Keeping his tone soft, he continued, 'We're *astronauts*, Elisabeth. Give us spaceships to fly and science to do and we're golden. Mass murders, investigations, and chasing after fundamentalist nutters are all so far beyond our remit, it's no wonder we're starting to fray. I can't blame Nate for getting riled up. It's way outside our wheelhouse.'

Elisabeth held her head in her hands and exhaled slowly, then shook herself and looked to James and Erin. 'For what it is worth, James, I do not think you did anything wrong. Your report about Son of Adam's apparent ability to survive an airless environment is worrying, however.'

'Yeah, it sounds a bit like your augmentation,' said Erin.

'That is my concern,' said Elisabeth. 'I will have a look back through what is left of the old ESA records.'

A vision flashed before James's eyes of an old man lying on the rough ground of a dark back alley, eyes open yet unseeing, a glistening red stream pouring from a hole in his head. As quickly as it came, it was gone.

James blinked away the last vestiges of the vision, put his hands on his hips, and said, 'I'll see what I can dig up, too. This could be linked to Dr Hales in some way.'

Elisabeth nodded and motioned to the door. James and

Erin left, ensuring to close the door gently behind them.

April awaited them, leaning her back against the corridor wall. 'Hey.'

'Hey, I wasn't expecting you to stick around,' said James.

'Yeah, well, here I am,' April said without looking up, preferring to examine her nails. 'A thought: Colonel Zhu said the Arcadia job and these other murders are linked, right?'

James folded his arms and leaned against the opposite wall. 'Right.'

'So, why not see for yourself? I'm sure ol' Liz can get you access to the police reports,' April said with a gesture back to the door, then with a cackle added, 'Probably some real grisly stuff in there.'

Erin raised an eyebrow and smirked. 'And here I thought you said you didn't want to be involved.'

'Yeah,' said James. 'That could be your job in all this. "Many hands" and all that.'

April puffed, pushed herself off, and began to walk away. 'Whatever, dudes. Take my advice or don't.'

# II.

II

# CHAPTER TEN
## Day Drinking

BILL WAS FIRST TO ARRIVE at the bar. Nate watched from his dark corner, nursing his third pint of the hour, which he'd already drained to half. He shifted in the worn upholstered bench and picked absentmindedly at the beer-soaked gouges in the table. He noticed Bill's hair was dyed blonde with lowlights and he wore double-denim; a lighter blue jacket paired with navy skinny-jeans—a bold choice in the current climate of bright clashing colours, but Bill liked to make a statement. He was freshly groomed, which made Nate realise how little attention he'd paid to his own appearance the last few weeks, particularly his beard. His clothes were uncharacteristically plain—black jeans and a matching puffer jacket over a white v-neck and he wore a black beanie on his head. Sleep had also eluded him. He thought he'd masked it well, but the heavy bags under his eyes that drew his attention every time he saw his reflection screamed otherwise. He hadn't kept up his usual skincare routine either.

It had been a few weeks since he'd last seen any of his crew; the *Magellan* was still undergoing repairs at Skyport and Nate's three remaining crew members took their impromptu shore leave with a lot of enthusiasm. As it was, Bill and Damien had been the easiest to get hold of; they, at least, hadn't left the country. Petra was a different story. She'd been in the midst of visiting family in Russia when Nate had called, but she had dutifully booked in on the next available flight to Budapest anyway. Nate hated to do that to her—she didn't see her family enough as it was—but this was important and something that couldn't be conveyed over the phone.

For a moment, Bill looked confused, as though deciding whether he'd picked the wrong place. He glanced down at his phone, then up again. This time he spotted Nate and made a beeline to the table.

The two exchanged pleasantries; Nate offered to buy him a drink, but Bill declined.

'Isn't it a little early for that, Captain?' said Bill, taking his seat on the bench next to Nate. He took his phone from the pocket of his jeans and dropped it on the table. It was a new model holo and the screen was already cracked in three places, just like his last.

Nate scoffed. 'Never heard of day drinking?'

'Oof, we're well acquainted. Things been that bad since I've been away?'

'You don't know the half of it. How's the shore leave?'

Bill put his hand to his heart. 'Ouch, you wound me, Captain. I'm guessing that means you've not had much of a vacation?'

Nate shook his head. 'Didn't get the chance and it's been a hell of a time. It's good to see you, Bill.' He swirled his drink gently in the glass, watching the refracted amber light dance across the table. Then, he took a swig and set the glass down, aligning the bottom perfectly with the ring of condensation on the table.

'It's good to see you, too, sir,' said Bill. 'But I imagine you didn't call me in because you missed me.'

'Perceptive. I'll tell you more when the others get here.'

It didn't take long. Damien and Petra arrived together and Bill jumped up to greet them.

It was unusual to see Commander Vance in anything other than his flight suit. The fact he now wore a baggy neon-pink basketball tee and sweatpants caught Nate off-guard. In fact, the man looked like he'd just come from the gym—the top of his head glistened.

Sergeant Milakova, on the other hand, wore purple jeans and a patterned teal top—very much her usual. Her chestnut brown hair was tied back in a short, braided ponytail. She gave Bill a tight hug then sat down opposite.

Damien sat adjacent and reached across the table to fist bump Nate.

Once everyone was settled and had declined to join Nate in his day drinking, he explained to them what had happened since their return to Earth from Skyport. They'd already heard the news of Captain Fowler's immortality, which was laced with rumour and half-truths by the time it had reached them.

'I heard he walked out on the surface of the Moon without a suit,' said Bill. 'Bare-ass naked, in fact.'

Petra laughed so hard she nearly fell off her chair. 'He did *not* walk out bare-ass naked, Bill!'

'Shame,' said Bill, leaning forwards with a wistful stare and his chin in his hands.

'He's old enough to be your great-grandfather,' Damien said with a chuckle.

Bill scrunched his nose and sat up straight. 'Nope. Ruined it.'

'Guys,' said Nate, a little harsher than he'd intended. 'I didn't bring you here to talk about Captain Fowler's augmentation.'

'That makes one of us,' Bill said with a smirk.

Silence fell among the group and after a few seconds, Nate continued, bringing them up to speed on the investigation.

'Jesus,' said Damien, clasping his hands together on the table top. 'How can we help, sir?'

Petra folded her arms and leaned back from the table, glaring at Nate. 'He wants us to go to Kyrgyzstan. That's why we're meeting here in this shithole bar instead of on the base.'

'But the administrator—'

'She doesn't know,' said Nate, mirroring Petra's body language. 'What I'm proposing is an off-books mission. Schreiber's got her head too far up Captain Fowler's ass to see this is the right course of action.'

'Are you sure, Captain?' said Petra. 'Because it sounds like you've gone off the rails. I mean, look at you: hunched over in a dark corner, bags under your eyes, at the end of god knows how many beers, asking us to fly halfway across the world with you on a mission that, if it doesn't get us killed, will definitely get us fired!'

'I will take the heat,' said Nate.

Petra scoffed. 'Well, excuse me if that doesn't fill me

with confidence. What's really going on here, sir?'

Nate picked up his glass and held it up to the light, then downed the last drops of beer and wiped his mouth with his sleeve. 'I gotta catch him, Petra. I just gotta. He's taken too much from me.'

'Captain Queen—'

'It's not just Queen.' Nate's voice became unsteady. 'I—I can't sleep. When I lie down, there's a tightness over my chest like an anvil; I can't breathe. And I see them. When my eyes are closed, I see Austin getting shot over and over. I see Cheryl—that's Captain Pritchard's wife; yeah, she was there that day, too. I've only met her once on the base, but her face is burned into my mind. The knowledge that I failed her; I failed them all.

'But it's not just them. It's the essence of myself. I feel thin, like some part of the man I was before got left behind on Mars. Bringing Son of Adam down is the only way I'll even come close to making it up to them and it's the only way I'll feel whole again.'

Damien leaned across the table and put his hand on Nate's shoulder. 'It wasn't your fault the way things went down, but I get you. Seeing the city go up like that from orbit; I can't shake those dreams neither. Maybe it'll help the both of us.'

Bill nodded. 'Whatever you need, Captain. I'm in.'

Nate smiled and gave a slight nod to the both of them, then said to Petra, 'Will you help me?'

She bit the side of her lip and rolled her eyes. 'Fine. I'm not about to let you all get killed. Someone needs to look out for Bill, right? Let me know when you're ready to go.'

Bill huffed and puffed as Petra rose from her seat and

started to walk away. 'Wha—The audacity! The nerve! Petra? Petra! Come back here.'

* * *

James and Erin took April's advice. Elisabeth had sent their request through to the Metropolitan Police in London and the Interpol database without hesitation and case records from the *Magnum Opus* murders arrived on the ISA network within the hour.

Now both captains sat in James's apartment with Angela, all huddled around the coffee table, perusing the documents on its smart surface, mirroring them to their phones as they read. They'd been at it for two and a half hours already.

Angela sat in her usual armchair, reading glasses on, looking through the ballistics report for the most recent murder. She had enlarged her phone's screen using its holo-projector.

By contrast, Erin was on the floor at the other end of the coffee table, her legs stretched out underneath. She wiggled her toes as she compared three different analyses directly on the smart-surface.

James had the sofa, slouched back with one leg cocked, reading the earliest of the police statements from back when the cases had still been assumed to be unconnected.

There were hundreds of documents to go through. One of the first things James noticed was just how far back the records went—over twenty years, a fact that surprised him. The murders seemed to have begun around the same time the disparate groups that would eventually become Sidera Silere had started to employ more extreme tactics. Tactics such as launch pad bombings for uncrewed missions and fitting an explosive device into the drive unit of the *Aurora*.

It wasn't only the *Magnum Opus* murder reports James had requested, but also those pertaining to Dr Hales and the ESA's internal files relating to Project Augment—the very ones Austin had Cass hack into all those years ago.

He recalled Dr Hales's words the night he'd died: 'My employer is very interested in you. Oh yes, very interested indeed, and perfectly content to play the long game, especially since I've completed the serum.'

Dr Hales had lied and exaggerated about so much, it was difficult to know what was the truth, but it was clear the man had expected to have a part in whatever future schemes his mysterious employer had planned. For the briefest moments before the sniper round had ripped through the doctor's skull, James had feared the old bastard might have taken the Elysian Serum himself. Could that still have been possible? Could Son of Adam actually be an immortal Joshua Hales back from the dead? What happened when an immortal died was a question James had never explored. It seemed silly, after all. The essence of James's immortality was biological; his natural ageing had stopped and he was immune to certain diseases like cancer. But a bullet to the brain would surely still kill him… or would it? That was what he'd always understood, anyway. But he'd already recovered handily from severe radiation poisoning and other wounds also healed faster, so why not a headshot? Not that he fancied testing it for himself.

In fact, he realised, for all the experiments—both hinged and unhinged—the doctor had done on him, they had never discovered where the augmentation was controlled from. Was it centralised in the brain like every other bodily function? Could it be independently activated from individual cell nuclei?

Suddenly, the prospect of Dr Hales's return didn't seem so far-fetched after all and he felt sick.

*No, no… No. The old man's long dead. Definitely… Absolutely dead. What am I even thinking?*

Then there was the question of this mysterious 'employer' of whom there had been no sign in nearly forty years. Could they be tied in some way to Sidera Silere?

James set aside the idea of Dr Hales's resurrection as ridiculous once again, but what if the doctor had managed to hand over the serum to his employer? Hales's fear of his own mortality had made him a threat specifically to James and Angela but essentially harmless to the wider world. After all, who doesn't dream of having longer to do the things they love? But if this 'employer' had taken the serum for themselves, ordered the hit on the doctor, and followed it up with decades of unsolved murders, then they were dealing with someone incredibly dangerous.

The trouble was, James feared there was nothing here. The police had assumed everything had been separate and there had been no reason to think otherwise. They'd had no access to the Project Augment files and Dr Hales's assassination had happened sixteen years before the first *Magnum Opus* murder—and the rate of progression for those had been slow. The details of the Hales case didn't fit the pattern for the later serial killings either. There wasn't enough to connect anything together. All James had was Colonel Zhu's hunch, Son of Adam killing her— the motive for which wasn't clear—and his apparent augmentation. They needed something else.

'Well, that's bloody weird,' said Erin, breaking James's ever-spiralling thought-train.

'What's that?' James said, dropping his phone down onto the cushion beside him.

Erin pulled more files towards her on the coffee table. 'Take a look at these ballistics reports. I've checked through all of them and—apart from one or two—they're all using the same weapon.'

'Mmm,' said Angela, peering over her glasses. 'That's probably what made the police realise they were looking at a serial killer in the first place. Not too surprising.'

Erin frowned and swiped away all but one of the reports. 'Then... why is the same weapon also present here in the Hales case?'

James and Angela froze. They looked at one another, mirroring each other's wide-eyed expression.

'What?' they said in unison.

'Yeah,' said Erin, pointing to a picture of the bullet. 'Seven-point-six-two by fifty-one NATO sniper round and the patterns match the gun used in most of the *Magnum Opus* murders. All but three were committed at long-range. There's a note cross-referencing the other cases where the gun was used in some of the later reports.'

That was it, exactly what they needed.

'You mean they were aware it was the same gun being used again?' asked James as he shuffled to the edge of the seat cushion and stroked his beard.

'The MET records illicit firearms in the Interpol database,' said Angela, shifting her glasses up her nose again. 'It's been that way for decades. When the gun shows up again in another crime—ping! A bullet connects to a type of gun, but without actually having the gun to examine, you can't tie it to a person.'

James blinked at her a few times. 'How do you... Oh, writing.'

Angela smiled impishly. 'For the crime short story collection. Didn't think I'd be using my research for investigating an actual crime, though.'

'What they didn't have,' said Erin, wagging her finger in thought, 'was the connection with Project Augment. They didn't know the perpetrator was augmented.'

'We still don't really know that Son of Adam is the *Magnum Opus* murderer though,' said James. 'He definitely killed Zhu and massacred the command centre. But he didn't use a sniper rifle; it was a pistol. And she was aiding me and Nate in our investigation of Arcadia Landing.'

'First of all, it doesn't matter about the sniper rifle; the other *Magnum Opus* murders were committed with a pistol—the same one each time, like it was the murderer's preferred sidearm or something.

'And secondly, back to Zhu, do you really think it's a coincidence she just so happened to be the last person besides yourself connected to the ship? And Austin just so happened to get caught in the Arcadia Landing attack?

'Son of Adam couldn't have known Colonel Zhu was helping you; remember, you went to great lengths to stop anyone knowing why you were really at Le Guin to prevent just this sort of thing!

'Come on, James, that's the final two people on the killer's list, both dying within hours of each other and both killed by Sidera Silere.'

James fell silent; it was hard to argue with Erin's logic. It seemed all too convenient for Son of Adam to have been at Le Guin. Why else kill Zhu if he didn't know she was looking into the bombing? It came back around again to her hunch.

Angela gave a sceptical expression. 'We're gonna need more than that. It's very circumstantial. It won't hold up.'

'We don't need it to hold up in court, you ding-dong,' said Erin. 'We're not police, remember? We're just trying to understand how Son of Adam could have gained James's powers, innit.'

*Powers? What am I, a superhero all of a sudden?*

In all the decades since he'd learned of his augmentation, he'd never considered himself to be powerful. To the contrary, his condition felt like a burden, that in setting him apart, it made him less-than. He'd worked for many years to dismantle that mind-set, but it still plagued him. It was a thought pattern that made the contrast to the unbidden feelings of superiority and godhood he'd experienced at Le Guin all the starker.

'So… We're not going to the police with this?' said Angela.

'Of course we will,' said Erin. 'They can do the legwork to make the solid connection once we catch Son of Adam. But we need to know as much about him as possible.'

James nodded. 'Know thy enemy.'

'Exactly, so he can't blindside us again.'

Angela took her glasses off and put her phone down on the arm of the chair. 'What about Colonel Zhu's murder? We know Son of Adam killed her—there's clear video footage. Have we got anything from that here?'

Erin shook her head. 'It's still ongoing. And just like with Arcadia Landing, the jurisdiction is tricky because it happened off-world, but the police are working with Elisabeth on it.'

'I guess that's how she managed to get these case records for us so quickly,' said James.

'It's just,' Angela mused, 'I'd be very interested to see if the pistol you say Son of Adam used matches the one in the minority of the *Magnum Opus* cases. That would provide us the solid link between them and therefore a direct line back to Hales.'

'The Interpol system will make that connection automatically, right? As soon as they do the ballistics for Zhu,' said James. 'Ping! As you said.'

Angela nodded.

Erin extracted herself from under the coffee table and stood, stretching up with a loud yawn. 'It's so frustrating! Even if all that rings true, it still doesn't tell us who Son of Adam is.'

'We've got some clues, at least,' said James. 'He'd surely have to be ex-military, specifically a trained sniper, to be able to pull off these long-range kills.'

'Both the MET in the Hales case and the Interpol data from the *Magnum Opus* murders support that, too,' said Angela. 'The first thing they did was question all living ex-snipers associated with the space agencies at the time. It wasn't a long list. Trouble is, most of those have died now and the rest are getting on in years.'

'Ah, but if he's an immortal like me, age won't factor into it,' said James.

Angela tapped her bottom lip with her finger and said, 'He definitely wouldn't have been amongst the group they interviewed, then. Remaining youthful as the years went by, he'd stick out like a sore thumb.'

'Thanks.'

'Oh, you know what I mean!' Angela snapped.

Erin sat down on the armchair by the window and put her head in her hands. 'So we're looking for an immortal cult leader who *might* be an ex-sniper with a grudge against the space agencies, but he's not on any military registers and is also totally invisible to facial recognition systems. Fuckin' cosy.'

'We've got our work cut out for us, that's for sure,' James said, rubbing the back of his neck.

The trio sat in silence for a long moment and a general feeling of weariness blanketed the room. The warmth of the lamps bathed them in orange and drew them down into sleepiness.

'It's getting late,' said Angela, finally breaking the silence. 'There's a lot still to go over. I suggest we break for the evening, get some sleep, and revisit it tomorrow night. Erin, you're more than welcome to come a bit earlier for dinner.'

Erin smiled through heavy eyes and nodded but said nothing.

James grunted in agreement. 'We've got to check in with Elisabeth in the morning anyway.'

As Erin stood and began gathering her things, Angela leaned over and turned off the smart table and James made to see Erin out.

'Meanwhile,' said Angela, prompting Erin and James to turn back to her, 'I'll do some digging into these remaining ex-snipers, see if I can bring up a list of past personnel—living or dead—associated with NASA and the ESA.' She paused, then said, 'James, can you ask Elisabeth to get us the ballistics report from the Le Guin massacre as soon as the police have it?'

James shrugged. 'Won't hurt to ask. I doubt the police will tell us of their own accord if they find that link with the serial killings.'

'Goodnight, you two,' said Erin. 'Angela, thank you for having me. Sorry, I've come over all tired. It's been a long day.'

# CHAPTER ELEVEN
## KAZARMAN

NATE, DAMIEN, PETRA, AND BILL stepped off the passenger flight and made their way through the arrivals lounge of Manas International Airport, Kyrgyzstan. After going through customs, they boarded their smaller connecting flight south to the central-western city of Jalal-Abad. From there, they hired a car and it was a further four hours before they finally arrived in Kazarman.

It was a fairly small village on the south bank of the Naryn River, surrounded by picturesque snow-capped mountain ranges with main roads in a poor state. The journey had been rough going. Out of Jalal-Abad the roads had taken them northeast through the mountains and they'd skirted several smaller villages on the way. Two-thirds of the way to Kazarman, Nate had begrudgingly been forced to use his status as an ISA staff member in order to get through the Toguz-Toro mountain pass, which was normally closed in the spring. It was here Nate had been thankful Petra had agreed to come; though the authorities in Jalal-Abad had been conversant in English, here on the Naryn border, Petra's Russian was a lifesaver.

The crew had taken it in turns to drive and it was late evening when they arrived, a fact for which Nate was thankful. At this time of year, tourists to the area were totally unheard of. Even during the peak season, they were few and far between. Their arrival during the daytime would have been noticed and Nate wanted to keep as low a profile as possible.

Petra drove now, navigating only by headlights down the dusty side streets to their guesthouse.

The comfortable warmth of the day had given way to a chill night, the cold air rolling down from the mountains surrounding the triangular valley. From what little light there was while driving through the village, Nate could understand why the area was so run down. The closure of the pass cut them off from the outside world for much of the year and the airport where Nate suspected Sidera Silere were holed up had long been out of use.

They were greeted jovially by the owner of the guesthouse as soon as they stepped out of the car. A bald, squat, older man in a simple white shirt and black trousers, he seemed unperturbed at the lateness. He called his sons, two men in their mid-twenties, to help the crew bring their bags from the car and then usher them to their rooms.

The owner's sons took them through the house and up the stairs. Nate glimpsed through an open doorway a dining room with decorative wallpaper and bench seating. Upstairs was a long hallway with two doors along each wall and one at the end, which one of their hosts pointed out was the bathroom. A long floral rug ran the corridor's length.

The group had booked two identical twin rooms across the hall from each other. Nate and Damien took the one on the right, while Bill and Petra took the left. The rooms were laid out symmetrically, with a single bed either side of the window and a bedside table and wooden chair each in between. Other than the ornate red and gold rug covering the floor, the rooms were plain, the only decoration on the walls being a few cracks in the plaster.

Nate sat on the bed. The mattress was thinner than he would have liked and the springs dug into the back of his legs. He stared out of the window between the beds while Damien got himself ready, turned off the main light, and laid down flat on his back. Within minutes his breathing shallowed.

Nate used to be able to do that, but he'd not slept soundly since the attack; he'd wake several times in the night, his heart racing and thumping uncomfortably in his chest, his pillow soaked.

Now he surveyed the not-so-distant mountains lit by the light of the Moon. He thought of Le Guin Base on the far side and how they would undoubtedly still be dealing with the aftermath of the massacre. The bodies of the command centre crew would be making their way back to Earth soon. Perhaps the ISA would hold another memorial service, particularly for Colonel Zhu, who had served just as long as Austin.

Apart from a few wisps of cloud rolling over the snow-capped peaks, the night was clear. Kazarman had little in the way of light pollution, so the stars hung crisp and bright in the caliginous sky. He could see the faint band of the galactic core rising up above the mountains. The night was still and filled with natural beauty.

He inhaled deeply through his nose, trying to capture a portion of that serenity, craving resipiscence. Some calm came, but his body anticipated something more, a frisson of excitement. He was finally doing something useful, making progress where they had, under James's leadership, failed. While he sat around back in Budapest, probably waiting on his hands for Elisabeth to make her negotiations or doing useless 'research', Nate would take the fight to Son of Adam himself. The ISA's indolence in the matter rankled. This was not a time for research but for decisive action. Tomorrow would bring a reckoning for Sidera Silere, he could feel it in the air. They just needed some weapons.

With a sigh, he pivoted away from the window and lay down, still dressed, his fingers interlinked over his torso. He stared at the ceiling until the cracks and blemishes—highlighted in the moonlight—blurred.

Yes, he would rectify the mistakes he'd made at Arcadia Landing. He thought of Jean Kamzel and her security team; they'd probably still been fighting to cut the doors open to South-Central station when the city had been vaporised. But she'd known. She'd known Austin had had little chance of survival after the wound he'd suffered. But Nate hadn't wanted to hear it. Maybe he couldn't have saved Austin, but if he hadn't been so adamant about going back for him, maybe Jean could have come with them on the *Magellan*. Or maybe if he had prioritised the evacuation rather than the assault in the first place, they could have at least saved two more ships' worth of refugees, maybe more.

It was the same cycle that ran through his mind every

night before bed. Second-guessing himself, replaying scenarios, noticing small errors in judgement. Errors that had cost lives.

His thoughts pivoted once again to what James had said about Son of Adam and he was filled with distrust. They only had James's word to go on about Son of Adam's supposed augmentation. There was no way of knowing what had really happened in that room. What if Son of Adam had managed to sway James, another like himself, and that's why the captain had let him go? Nate reasoned Son of Adam must be extremely charismatic to do what he does. Was it so far-fetched James could have been convinced to join Sidera Silere? There was precedent for it in Xander Levine and his group and even with the woman who'd sabotaged the *Aurora* over twenty years ago. If true, James was much more than a liability.

The bed creaked and groaned as Nate rolled onto his side and he tried his best to clear his mind. Throughout the night he drifted in and out of fitful sleep. The bed didn't help matters; at least at home he could find a comfortable position.

Nate woke with the dawn to the smell of freshly baked bread. Perhaps it was the mountain air, the change of scenery, or the feeling of making progress on his quest, but he felt more refreshed than he had in ages. A glance at his watch told him his sleep had stabilised during the latter part of the night, despite the initial restlessness.

He yawned and stretched then roused Damien and the two dressed silently in casual clothes before knocking on the door to Petra and Bill's room.

Once they were all together again, now looking like

a bunch of tourists, they were met downstairs by their cheerful host, who invited them for breakfast. The enticing aroma that pervaded the hallway made Nate's stomach growl and kept him from refusing.

On the dining table were bowls of porridge, baskets of warm round loaves, and a selection of fruits, meats, and cheeses. Nate, Damien, Petra, and Bill sat cross-legged around the low table on cushions. The host joined them at the head of the table and gestured for them to begin while one of his sons poured tea. The young man then retreated from the room.

They ate in silence. It was a welcome feast after a long previous day of travelling with only car snacks for sustenance. Nate and his crew had arrived so late they had skipped dinner entirely.

After a while, between bites of the delicious bread and cheese, Nate said, 'Petra, we need intel on Sidera Silere's presence here before we can make a move. Do you think our host knows anything about the transport?'

Petra wiped some crumbs from her face then turned to the host and spoke to him in Russian.

The man's face froze. His cheerful demeanour disappeared and he replied, shaking his head vigorously.

'He says he doesn't want to talk about it,' said Petra. 'And that it's best if we don't pry.'

Nate pinched the bridge of his nose and leaned towards the host. 'That's not an option,' he said while Petra translated. 'We need to find that transport. Is it still here?'

The host glanced worriedly between the two of them then spoke to Petra.

'He doesn't want any trouble,' she said.

'Look,' said Nate. 'If Sidera Silere are causing problems here in the village, we can help. We can protect you.'

Damien crossed his arms. 'How much trouble could Son of Adam cause here in just a couple of days, though?'

'You don't understand,' said the host through Petra. 'They have been here for years. Kazarman is a good base for the zealots. We are cut off from the rest of the world for much of the year; we are poor; our airport is out of use. It keeps prying eyes away. You cannot help us. I cannot help you. Do not speak of this. You will only make things worse. They are thugs, thieves, and many are outsiders who have no respect for our ways.'

Nate shook his head. 'We can't let this go. We have to catch Son of Adam. If you know of anyone with weapons we can use...'

'Weapons? This village is an old Soviet barracks,' said the man. 'Many service weapons were left behind. There are some down in the market who keep them as artefacts. Collectors. If you are so determined to get yourselves killed, you can ask there, but be wary. There are too many in Kazarman who have joined Sidera Silere. You are lucky I am not one!'

'Soviet service weapons?' said Bill under his breath. 'Are we really gonna rely on hundred-year-old guns?'

'I don't see that we've got much of a choice,' Nate replied.

'This is as far as I can help you,' said the host through Petra. 'If you choose to go, you heard nothing from me. Now, I suggest you finish your food and leave.' He rose from the table sharply and left the dining room.

After a long moment's silence, Damien popped an orange segment in his mouth and said, 'Captain, I do believe we've worn out our welcome.'

Nate grunted in agreement and stood. 'Come on, we'll pack our bags then head down to the market.'

Petra leaned across the table to Nate and, keeping her voice low, said, 'I'm not sure about this. If the guy doesn't want anything to do with us, then why has his son been skulking out in the corridor this whole time?'

Nate raised an eyebrow and glanced sidelong to the door. Sure enough, there was the shadow of a teapot on the wall opposite.

'You thinking trap?'

'I'm thinking the Sidera Silere problem here is more widespread than he was letting on.'

Nate shrugged. 'Maybe he doesn't know?'

'What does that matter? Either way, we're fucked if we don't deal with this guy.'

Damien picked a knife up from the table. 'I'll do it,' he growled and took a step.

Nate put a hand on his shoulder and stopped him. He shook his head. 'Not here, but keep the knife. If he tails us down to the market…'

'Woah, woah, hold on a second,' said Bill before lowering his voice. 'Have the three of you totally fucking lost it?'

Petra ran her hand through her hair. 'Bill—'

'No, Petra. What is going on here? Less than twelve hours in this town and you're all casually talking about shivving a dude? Captain, I know I said I'd support you on this mission and I even accepted we might need to defend ourselves. But this? We don't know for certain he's even involved.'

'We need to do whatever's necessary, Bill. You know what these people are capable of.'

'Relax, the both of you, I wasn't gonna kill him, just… scare him a bit,' Damien said as he jabbed the air with the knife.

The tension in Bill's shoulders visibly evaporated and he looked sheepish. 'Oh, right.'

Nate nodded in solidarity with Damien. 'Petra's right. All bets are off after Arcadia Landing, þut there's a difference between villagers falling in line out of fear and hardline zealots. I'd rather not kill the locals if we can help it.'

The four left the dining room and returned to their rooms. Nate noted the immediate disappearance of their teapot-wielding eavesdropper from the hallway. Within ten minutes they had packed up their stuff and deposited it in the boot of the hire car.

Nate brought up a map of Kazarman on his phone. It wasn't far to the market, so they set off walking along the dusty, unkept streets, keeping a surreptitious eye out for signs of the guesthouse host's son. Nate knew Petra didn't like the idea of potentially walking into a Sidera Silere trap and neither did he. The non-zero chance their presence had already been reported was greater than he would have liked. But there was nothing else they could do; they could pack up and go home, but for Nate, backing out wasn't an option. He needed to see this through to the end and that meant forging onwards. To make any progress at all, they needed weapons. Sidera Silere would brook them no quarter. It hadn't been viable to bring their own into the country, so it had always been the plan to source them locally. Initially, he'd thought of trying to find a black market contact, but he liked the host's idea better. Even a few pistols would be better than going in with nothing.

Twenty minutes passed and the team found itself at one end of the town centre's small market. There had been no sign of the host's son the entire way and Nate began to suspect they had misjudged his curiosity. It was a relief; he didn't want Damien to hurt the guy. Despite what they had told Bill, Nate knew Commander Vance's history well and it was a real possibility the younger man would have walked away missing a finger if he was lucky.

The street was lined with colourful stalls with locals in traditional dress selling their wares, from pottery and textiles to phone repair services. It was a fascinating blend of the ancient and modern. To Nate's surprise many spoke good English and were, like their guest-house host, initially friendly. Still, Petra took the lead with conversations in Russian. She was deft and tactful, feigning interest in their personal lives, hearing their stories, asking about the history of the village.

After an intense, jovial conversation, an older woman wearing a colourful embroidered headdress decorated with feathers gestured for the team to follow her as she left her stall and tottered off further along the market.

Petra echoed her wave and said, 'Come. Imanaaly said she'll introduce us to her friend's husband. He's one of these "collectors" the guesthouse owner mentioned.'

They followed through the thinning crowds until, two thirds of the way along the market street, the woman turned and disappeared into the building behind one of the stalls.

As Nate, Damien, and Bill approached, Petra leaned with her hand on the table of the stall and a middle-aged man appeared from the doorway. He wore a brown felt shirt with matching trousers split by a white leather belt with a brass buckle and on his head perched an ornately-embroidered kalpak hat.

He examined the group with an intense stare for a long moment then nodded and disappeared once again into the building.

Minutes passed. Bill paced back and forth with his hands in his pockets, Damien shielded his eyes from the glare of the sun and looked up past the buildings towards the mountains, and Petra drummed her fingers on the stall table.

'So, were we supposed to follow him in or…' asked Nate.

Petra shrugged. 'I assume they're getting the weapons ready and will call us in.'

'It's been a while,' said Bill. 'How many weapons do you think the guy has?'

'With any luck, enough,' said Nate.

There was a rumbling along the street. During the whole time they had been there, Nate hadn't heard or seen a single car except for the ones parked for the stall-holders. Now, three approached. They were ex-military vehicles; one an old and battered-looking desert-camo Tiger armoured personnel carrier, which was flanked by two equally aged Jeeps.

Nate's heart sank as they approached in a tan cloud, their wheels kicking up dust from the road. Judging by the reaction of the stallholders, many of whom had already abandoned their stores and retreated inside, there was no way this was a routine occurrence.

It had been too much to hope the *Magellan* crew's presence would go unnoticed here. It was clear from the guesthouse owner's words that Nate had badly mis-judged the situation in the village. He had been working under the assumption Son of Adam was trying to jump the border and disappear further into Central Asia. But now it all became clear. *Of course,* Son of Adam brought the transport here on purpose and not simply out of convenience! His plan had never been to ditch and run but to consolidate. Kazarman was in an advantageous position: difficult to reach most of the time and easy to mark who came and went.

*Damn it.*

If only he'd waited for Elisabeth.

Nate felt a tap on his shoulder and he took his eyes from the approaching vehicles. The man had reappeared in the doorway with another woman who Nate assumed was his wife and the older woman named Imanaaly. The three held the weapons Nate was after but not in an inviting manner.

'Captain, I don't think we're getting those weapons,' said Damien, leaning close.

Nate shook his head and frowned. 'They probably sold us out.'

'I'm sorry, sir,' said Petra as she backed away from the stall. 'I don't understand it; I didn't give anything away.'

'Don't be. It's not your fault. It's not theirs either. They're just trying to protect their way of life. I'm the one who's fucked things up again. I'm sure we were marked when we checked in at the guesthouse.'

'You were marked when you crossed the mountain pass, Captain,' said a deep voice from behind. It was a male voice with a Norwegian accent.

Nate became aware the sound of the vehicles had stopped.

The man's words were accompanied by the patter of many feet on the dusty ground, followed by the slamming of doors.

'I'd tell you raise your hands, but I already know you don't have any weapons,' said the man. 'Turn around.'

The crew followed his instruction and turned slowly, instinctively raising their hands anyway. A group of men and women in desert clothes stood beside the Jeeps and APC, holding assault rifles much more modern than the ones the stallholders had. All were pointed at Nate and his team.

The man with the Norwegian accent stood forward of his associates; he carried no gun—at least none that Nate could see—and wore green fatigues. He was tall, athletic, and had a square jaw and short blond hair with blue eyes. His smug face looked very punchable; if only he wasn't surrounded by armed guards.

Nate glared at the man. 'The mountain pass?'

The man chuckled widely, showing his perfect white teeth. 'Flashing your ISA credentials to get you through the checkpoint is possibly the least intelligent thing you've done on your little excursion thus far and that's saying something. Your coming here was really putting the, shall we say, pigeon amongst the cats!' He paused, looked up to the clear sky, and started pacing back and forth. After a short moment, he recited, 'Captain Nathan Rifkin, commanding officer of the *UNSV Magellan*, and his formidable crew: First officer and former US Navy Commander Damien Vance, Sergeant Petra Milakova, former Spetsnaz, and engineer Specialist William Watkins—or is that "Bill"? I don't wish to be rude.'

'You have us at a disadvantage,' said Bill.

'Are you Son of Adam?' Nate asked through gritted teeth.

The man stopped and locked eyes with Nate, never losing his grin. 'Oh? I can tell you wish with every fibre of your being it were so. But alas, it is not. You may call me... *Fangevokter*.'

'What do you plan to do with us? Execute us in the street or make us dig our graves in the woods first?'

Fangevokter rolled his eyes and then made a gesture to his associates. Immediately three of them slung their weapons over their shoulders and approached, pulling rope and fabric from their pockets.

'Don't worry, Captain. Your lives are not forfeit yet,' said Fangevokter. 'You are to be Son of Adam's guests of honour. They are so looking forward to meeting you.'

As they began binding the crew's hands, Nate caught a last glimpse of their jailer returning to the APC before his eyes were covered and he was shoved towards one of the vehicles.

* * *

Elisabeth listened intently behind her desk as James and Erin recounted their first evening of investigative work.

'So far, we're pretty sure Son of Adam is the *Magnum Opus* murderer, but Angela wants to do some more digging,' said James. 'There are more puzzle pieces to fit together. Any idea how the police are doing on the Le Guin massacre?'

Elisabeth shook her head lightly. 'The bodies are still in cold storage on the base. They are due to be moved onto transports tomorrow. There are no forensic facilities on the Moon, so any analysis will need to be done here on Earth.'

*Damn. Ange's request will have to wait.*

There wasn't much more he or Erin could do with the information they had already been given, but Elisabeth seemed at least preliminarily convinced of their hypothesis anyway. Working to the assumption Son of Adam was indeed augmented in all the same ways as James—possibly including his biological immortality—meant they were far less likely to underestimate him on their next encounter.

'Have we had any more news on Kyrgyzstan?' Erin asked.

'In terms of getting you into the country, no,' said Elisabeth. 'But I fear Captain Rifkin was right about the amount of force we will need to exert in order to reach Son of Adam.'

James cocked his head to one side.

'According to the Kyrgyz police force,' Elisabeth continued in response to James's look, 'Kazarman is a Sidera Silere stronghold and has been for quite some time. They have someone on the inside—one of the local officers—keeping an eye on the situation. Needless to say, this revelation has complicated matters with the Kyrgyz ambassador.'

'I'm concerned this is taking so long, Administrator,' said Erin. 'Are we no longer considering that Son of Adam could get away?'

'I do not think so,' Elisabeth replied. 'The undercover agent saw Son of Adam arrive with his own eyes and asserts that he has thus far remained there. If the village is acting as a home base for the group, it is unlikely they will be in a hurry to leave.'

James nodded to himself. Finally, something positive. If Son of Adam wasn't preparing to move on somewhere else, then it would give the ISA time to come up with a plan.

He made a mental note to find Nate and give him the good news. He'd not seen him all day.

As though reading his mind, Elisabeth said, 'Have either of you seen Captain Rifkin today?'

Both Erin and James shook their heads.

Elisabeth pursed her lips and scratched her temple. 'I wanted to give him the latest progress on the *Magellan*'s repairs. It is nearly ready to bring back from Skyport and I thought I might schedule a transport for him to collect it personally.'

'Oh, I'm sure that would cheer him up!' said Erin.

'My thought precisely. If either of you see him, send him to me.'

James and Erin left the administrator's office. In the short corridor, James stopped and looked down at his watch. It was a bit late in the day for Nate to not be on the base.

Erin came to a halt a few steps ahead of James and then turned around. 'What is it?'

'Nate's normally here first thing in the morning,' James said, folding his arms. 'It's unusual for neither of us to have bumped into him at all yet.'

Erin tapped her lip. 'You're right. He might be avoiding you, though.'

'Maybe,' James said absentmindedly. 'I just hope he hasn't done anything stupid. Tell you what, I'll give him a ring.'

Erin held up a hand and pulled out her phone. 'No, if he's deliberately avoiding us, then there's no way he'll answer a call from you. I'll do it.'

She put the device to her ear and paced back and forth as it rang. In the silence of the corridor James could hear the connecting tone. After a short while, it rang off.

'No answer,' Erin muttered, creasing her eyebrows as

she examined the screen. 'I'll try again. He'd better not be ignoring me too.'

As they stood together in the corridor, with James now intermittently tapping his foot, Erin tried three more times to reach Nate unsuccessfully.

She looked up at him. 'I won't lie to you, James. I'm getting worried.'

'What about his crew?'

Erin put her phone away and shook her head. 'They're still on leave and not due back until next week. Sergeant Milakova isn't even in the country. They wouldn't know where he is any more than we do.'

James bit his lip. 'Damn it. We need to find him.' He checked his watch again. 'I'll look for him around the base. You go check his apartment.'

Erin nodded and started off down the corridor. 'He lives nearby. Meet back here in an hour?'

'Right,' said James.

# CHAPTER TWELVE
## The Airport

THE CRACKLING OF SMALL STONES under the APC's wheels subsided and the vehicle came to a rough halt, jolting Nate in his seat. Owing to the blindfold, he had seen nothing of the inside of the vehicle, but it smelled musty and the suspension had been hard on his back, which had made the journey feel much longer than it had really been. Of conversation, there had been none. The crew had been instructed to remain silent and what little snippets Nate had caught from his captors had been in another language.

Moments after they'd stopped, the door beside Nate opened with a click and the inside of his blindfold brightened considerably. He was grabbed by the arm and pulled from the vehicle. Outside, the air around him was noticeably cooler with a breeze coming from his left and the residual light filtering through the blindfold was dimmer than in the village. The ground was also smoother with little in the way of dust and gravel underfoot and the smell of oil pervaded the place. It was preferable to the stale body odour permeating the vehicle's interior.

He guessed their captors had taken them to the disused Kazarman airport as it was the place where the stolen transport had touched down.

The echo of the vehicle doors closing gave him a sense of the size of the area. It was most likely a hangar and the breeze told him one end was open, possibly onto the runway.

For a short moment, Nate considered it strange they needed the blindfolds at all if they knew Sidera Silere had set up a base in the airport anyway. Yet the blindfold remained on as he was pushed and pulled. They were led out of the breeze, down winding corridors, and up several flights of stairs.

Nate quickly lost track.

The quality of the filtered light changed and flashed and became slightly greenish in tint like fluorescent tubes. The floor changed from the hard, almost squeaky surface of the hangar to a thin carpet. The blindfold remained on until he was shoved into a final room and seated before being secured to the chair. When it was removed, he realised he had no bearing for where he was in the facility, but his crew was beside him at least.

The room was small and featureless; a former office, though everything but the chairs they sat on and a six-foot desk had been removed. There was one large window covered with a white Venetian blind on the longest wall.

Bill's blindfold was the last to come off, then the door was locked and they were left alone.

Bill shook his hair and said, 'So, now we've success-fully infiltrated the airport, what's the plan, Captain?'

Nate grimaced and looked away. He then heard Bill yelp as Petra kicked him in the shin.

'I still have the knife,' said Damien. He tugged impotently against his restraints. 'The one from the dining room.'

'Great, then cut us loose,' said Bill.

'I haven't got it in my hand. I can't reach it like this,' Damien spat. 'And even if I did, the door's locked.'

'We could smash the window—'

Damien laughed. 'How far do you think we'd get after they heard us smashing glass? There's probably a couple of guards outside, too.'

'Hey! Can it,' said Nate. 'The commander's right, we're stuck here for now. Frankenstein—'

'Fangevokter,' said Petra.

'Whatever.'

Petra gave him a withering look.

'Look, the guy—whatever he calls himself—said something about us meeting Son of Adam. This could be our opportunity. We could turn it to our favour.'

'Just like how everything else so far has gone our way?' said Bill.

Nate sighed and hung his head. 'I'm open to suggestions.'

Bill groaned, his voice filled with venom. 'Okay, here's a suggestion: Petra, if I ever agree to go on another off-books mission with the captain, smash me over the head with a bottle.'

Nate rolled his eyes. This was Bill all-over, always volunteering for things and then complaining about them later. He couldn't blame the man in this instance, though; things certainly had gone sideways. But the complaints had never before been about Nate's decision-making and it stung. Nate felt like a shadow of his former self and Bill directing vitriol his way for the first time made the contrast even clearer.

The door unlocked and swung open.

Fangevokter sauntered in with a chair and placed it down facing the prisoners. He then stepped over the back and sat down, his legs spread wide and hands steepled between his knees.

Petra snorted. 'Where'd you learn to sit like that? Let me guess, making room for your "massive" balls?'

Unperturbed, Fangevokter shrugged with his hands and said, 'Back problems. What can you do? And I'm sure you will have noticed by now how uncomfortable these chairs are.'

'I doubt you've got us tied up here just to show us how bad these things are for our posture,' said Nate, testing the restraints. Tight; his hands were secured fast. 'Get to the point already.'

'Here is how it will work, Captain Rifkin. You will be brought to Son of Adam for the brief audience you so desired in coming here and you will tell us what you know of the ISA's movements within Kyrgyzstan. It is quite simple.'

'What movements?'

There was that punchable smug expression again. 'Come now. You do not seriously expect me to believe you came alone, do you?'

Fangevokter clicked this fingers and two armed guards entered, one of whom Nate recognised immediately as the guesthouse owner's son, the one who had been skulking around to eavesdrop on them that morning. He made no effort to look away from them.

*So he* was *with Sidera Silere after all.*

The two guards untied the crew from their chairs in silence and Fangevokter motioned for them to stand.

Nate exchanged a hopeful look with Damien and Petra, who both gave a slight nod in return. Bill wouldn't meet his eyes. It was understandable; this trip had gone from uncertain at best to downright bad. Had Nate's desperate need to atone doomed his crew? The thought was at the forefront of his mind and the temptation to give in to despair was strong, but he couldn't; he mustn't. He'd gotten them into this mess and it was his obligation to get them out of it again. Damien still had the knife and in that knife lay hope.

Nate knew from his service record that the man was capable, reliable, and deadly. That was why the commander had been his first choice to accompany him in trying to retake Arcadia Landing. Petra was terrifying on her own, too, but Damien was something else entirely.

He was terrifying in such a way that made Nate wonder why someone with such high-level combat proficiency would become a space scientist in the first place.

In some ways, Commander Vance reminded Nate of his father, especially in the early days of his posting as the *Magellan*'s mission commander. A hard man with high expectations, it had taken a long time for Damien to warm to him. At least he'd given his approval in the end, unlike Nate's father who still disapproved of his transferring out of the US Air Force to the ISA. 'Wasting his opportunities to become nothing more than a glorified chauffeur,' he'd said. It had driven a wedge between them and as a result, Nate rarely talked to his parents or siblings anymore.

*I wonder what Dad would think now? Fresh disappointment, no doubt.*

Fangevokter left the room and Nate jolted as the guesthouse owner's son shoved him in the shoulder.

Nate and his crew followed along single-file, flanked by additional guards who had been waiting outside the room.

The jailer said nothing more as he led them through the bare administrative corridors of the airport. Here, dust had seeped in and covered everything in a fine layer. The offices they passed looked as though they had been ransacked, but it could also have been natural ageing. There were plenty of broken windows, mould-covered walls, and fallen ceiling tiles. It was a wonder the place still had electricity at all. Officially, the buildings had stood empty for over fifty years—barring a singular abortive attempt to rejuvenate it and bring it back into service—but in actuality, it had played host to squatters prior to Sidera Silere moving in.

They crossed through a short skyway to another building. Broken glass crunched under their feet and a cool breeze whistled through gaps in the walls. The bridge would have been completely enclosed but for the rusted and warped mullions that had allowed the glass to fall.

With every step, Nate's apprehension grew, or was it a strange form of excitement? Either way, he could feel his heart pounding in his chest and the tips of his fingers tingled. He flexed them as best he could; the rope tying them behind his back was tight around his wrists.

They eventually came to a larger meeting hall, another

room stripped bare and ravaged by time. In the centre, flanked by two more armed guards, Son of Adam stood at ease in the proper military style: back straight, feet shoulder-width apart, arms behind with hands tucked into the small of his back. He wore a navy-blue flight suit under a black tactical vest and carried a pistol in the holster on his hip. Nate's eyes, however, were drawn to his most distinguishing feature: the black and fluorescent green mask covering his entire head.

The creepy painted smile felt like constant derision; without needing to utter a single word, it mocked everything Nate had been through, their pitiful plan to bring him to justice, and their hope of escape.

Nate's budding excitement turned quickly to anxiety and he felt beads of sweat forming on his brow. Their chances of turning the tables here became vanishingly small.

The crew of the *Magellan* came to a halt before the Sidera Silere leader and was forced to their knees. The ground was hard and cold. The thin carpet had been worn through to the concrete below in this exact spot.

Nate wondered how many prisoners Sidera Silere had taken here over the years. It didn't take much of a leap to imagine other local chancers trying to stop the group's occupation or perhaps some community pillars had been kidnapped and executed here to send a message. Perhaps the off-world massacres had simply been the latest in a long line of killings this terrorist group had carried out. At this point, Nate could put nothing past them.

Fangevokter continued in his casual saunter to the man's side and, with his back to the crew, said something inaudible to Son of Adam.

The masked leader nodded and dismissed the jailer,

who made his way out through a door at the far end of the room. Then, with a wave of his hand, Son of Adam dismissed the guesthouse owner's son and his companion guards as well.

The masked man turned his attention to his captives.

'Hey, Nate!' he said, stepping forwards and cocking his head to the side. His natural voice was masked through a vocal changer and replaced with a gravelly, unhinged tone.

'Commander Vance.' He saluted. 'Petra… and Bill, too. Ah, it's so lovely to see you all again.'

Nate frowned and looked to his crew; they looked at one another, clearly just as confused as he was.

'You've done well to track me down,' Son of Adam continued, now pacing back and forth along their line with his arms tucked behind his back once again. 'All the way here from the Moon. It really is impressive.'

Out of the corner of his eye, Nate saw Damien wriggle his shoulders and as Son of Adam turned away to walk back along the line, he stole a glance. With no guards behind them to see, the commander had managed to retrieve the concealed kitchen knife.

Nate knew it; Vance would never let him down. If he could just bring the terrorist leader back this way.

With renewed boldness, Nate said, 'You didn't have to go to all this trouble just to congratulate us. You could've just handed yourself in and saved us the effort.'

Son of Adam chuckled and turned on his heel. 'Where would be the fun in that, Captain? Now, I'm sure you're all aware of why you're here.'

'Your pompous errand boy filled us in already. You won't be getting anything from us.'

'Let's not waste time here, Nate. You wouldn't come

here without backup and I've got lots of questions. So what is it? You're the scouting party? How many troops did the ISA send? What kind of weapons are we talking about? When are they planning to attack? You know, that sort of thing.'

'How about you answer our questions first?' said Petra. 'What do you mean that it's lovely to see us again? Who are you?'

Before Son of Adam could answer, Damien roared. With a snap he flung his arms up and leaped to his feet, brandishing the knife. Within a split second he closed the distance to the smaller man.

But Son of Adam's reaction time was faster.

There was a sharp crack and Damien fell to the ground and screamed in pain. The knife fell from his grip and bounced away across the floor. Red stained his trousers above the knee.

Nate, Petra, and Bill cried out in unison.

Son of Adam stood above him, pistol now removed from its holster and pointed down at the commander's head, his breathing heavy.

He reached up, grabbed the bottom of his mask, and pulled it off, allowing it to drop to the ground with a clatter as the voice changer came with it.

The sight under the mask set Nate's world spinning.

Removing the mask had revealed a mess of shoulder-length curly blonde hair and a woman's face. She had bright blue eyes and flustered red cheeks.

The face of Corporal Marissa de Beek.

'Don't do that again,' she said, breathless.

'Marissa? What the fuck?' Nate said. His heart pounded in his ears and his mind raced. How could this be Marissa? Had he missed something somewhere?

He blinked hard a few times, but the sight would not change; she was really there, standing over a whimpering Damien and holding a gun to the back of his head.

After a long moment, Marissa holstered her pistol. Then the two other armed guards, who had not moved at all during the altercation, grabbed Damien and dragged him back to the line between Nate and Petra, leaving a thick streak of blood across the floor.

One of the guards bent down, tied an old rag taken from his pocket around Damien's thigh, and told him to keep pressure on it. The two then retreated back to their former positions and stood sentinel once again.

'I'm—I'm sorry, sir,' Damien said between held breaths and gritted teeth.

'So you should be,' said Marissa.

At this, Nate's mind cleared and he gained a renewed focus as he glared at his former corporal. He clenched and unclenched his hands behind his back and tremors came unbidden.

'How the hell are you Son of Adam? What is going on, Marissa?' said Bill, his voice shrill and trembling.

'We worked together,' Petra added. 'We trained together. We trusted you!'

Marissa laughed and held up her hands in a shrug. 'I guess it goes to show you never really know someone, right? All those months of training, infiltrating the ISA, and getting posted to the *Magellan*, having to listen to that stuck-up bitch Schreiber? Such a drag.'

She paused, looking at each of them in turn. 'Oh, you thought I *liked* you? You thought I liked being treated like the newbie and going off on our fun little space adventures? Wow. Fuck me, you guys are gullible.'

Nate stared down at the floor in silence. Could it really be true? Had they worked with Son of Adam all this time? It would mean they had shown Sidera Silere everything, they'd even transported her directly to…

'Arcadia Landing,' said Nate as he looked up from the floor and glared at Marissa. 'That was you.'

Marissa beamed from ear to ear and clapped her hands. 'Yes! Well done, Nate. You're so smart. I hope you all enjoyed my handiwork. It was my magnum opus—if you'll pardon the pun. That Xander, God rest his soul, he was such a great guy to work with, very forthright.'

'And you made us all culpable,' Bill spat.

Marissa put her hands on her hips in an exaggerated way. 'Oh, Bill.' She sighed. 'Bill, Bill, Bill. You were already culpable long before you took me where I needed to go. You don't get to escape judgment for your sins by simply following orders.'

'You fucking bitch!' cried Petra. She tried to stand but stumbled.

Marissa pulled her gun from its holster, pointed it at Petra, and wagged the end of it like a finger. 'Ah, ah, ah. You guys have such short memories; I can see why it was so easy to pull one over on you.'

She was right. It had been far too easy to fool Nate. He should have known better, should have seen it. Questions were forming in his mind: How much of it had been real? Was her background a fabrication? Did she also fake her qualifications? Was Marissa even her real name? Was there something within the admin he should have spotted as her CO? The old guilt began to gnaw at him afresh. Not only had he failed to save

Captain Queen, but in bringing Marissa along, he'd unknowingly facilitated the attack.

'What about the transmission from Le Guin?' Nate asked. His brain was working on automatic, focussing on the puzzle pieces as though they were a mere curiosity. Anything more and he'd slip into madness.

Marissa lowered the gun. 'Oh, that? That's what set off the first bomb, silly. Xander's signal to begin. Very clever man; did you know it was his idea to shut down all the escape pods? I had to remind him to keep the trains going.'

'And what did you say to James in the spaceport?'

At the mention of Captain Fowler's name, Marissa's expression hardened. 'Don't even get me started on that filthy hybrid. You and the ISA are idiots stumbling in the dark, but James Fowler is an abomination, the embodiment of mankind's sin. Your transgressions pale in comparison to the threat that alien poses to mankind's purity.'

*Guess that means he's not working with her, after all...*

'But, why?' Petra shouted, tears streaming down her cheeks. 'What was the point of any of it? All that death, and for what?'

'Because Guy Furious was right and all the years of pleading and protesting and harmless sabotage did nothing!' Marissa squeezed her eyes shut and rubbed her temple with the side of the pistol then paced erratically. 'You people respected neither his position nor that of the religious leaders who wanted you to stop desecrating a holy relic.

'The Achelon, whether divine or not, are powerful and malevolent. Are they truly gods? Who knows; some of us believe they are, some of us don't. But regardless, they're so far beyond us, they might as well be. And we know they are wrathful.

'So, what's five, six, seven hundred, or even a thousand lives in exchange for the security of our species? We're trying to prevent Armageddon here. Whether that comes from spirits angry that you touched their stuff with unclean hands or fleets of attack ships charging at us from the edge of space because you people broadcast our position to the entire galaxy. It's irrelevant. In the end, we still lose.'

'Marissa—'

'We lose, Petra.' Marissa stopped in her tracks and pointed the gun at each of them in turn. 'And Sidera Silere are the only ones who realise that. The ISA must be stopped at all costs. We are done here for now.'

Marissa holstered her pistol and scooped the mask up from the floor. With it back over her head and the voice changer reactivated, Son of Adam continued, 'You will return to your makeshift cell. I will give you some time to think over the gravity of your situation and then you'll be brought back here. If none of you volunteer the information that I want, then I'll start with the maiming and the torturing and the killing until one of you breaks. My money's on Nate.'

Without a further word, Son of Adam marched away through the door at the far end of the room.

Fangevokter re-entered along with the contingent of armed guards.

'Well, I hope you got everything you wanted from your meeting?' said the jailer.

'Eat. Shit,' said Damien through ragged breaths. He spat on the ground at Fangevokter's feet.

'How rude, Commander Vance. This is not the way to ingratiate yourself to me.'

'If I could walk, you'd be ingratiating my foot up your ass.'

Nate wanted to bite back in solidarity with his first officer, but he couldn't speak. His stomach churned and he could feel a burning at the back of his throat. This was it, their last hope of escape gone. There was now nothing keeping Nate from despair and he embraced it silently. Marissa was Son of Adam; Nate's culpability for the Martian massacre was now greater than he had imagined. It was too much to bear.

The crew was forced to stand. The guesthouse owner's son hoisted Damien up, still bleeding, and supported him as they made their way back through the corridors and across the skyway to the small office-cell.

* * *

Angela's holographic avatar hovered above James's phone screen as he held it horizontally and spoke into the microphone.

'I've made a good start on this list of ex-snipers,' she said. The holo-avatar was just a head and shoulders, but as she spoke occasionally a hand would come up into view. It was a bit of a modern gimmick and James preferred ordinary video calls for practicality, but he couldn't deny it was sci-fi as fuck.

'Have you stopped for lunch yet?' James said. He knew how she could be when she got deep into the weeds and it was quite late in the afternoon.

'It's fine. I had some toast earlier.' She gave a dismissive wave. 'It's a surprisingly long list. I've been scouring the internet for information on them. There's not much I can access, but so far I've not found anything that matches up.'

James nodded. 'Listen, I won't be able to get you the information from the Le Guin massacre for a while. They haven't brought the bodies back to Earth yet for autopsy.'

'Understandable. This has never happened before. There are bound to be hold-ups. At least this time there are remains to bring back. I've got this list to keep me occupied for the next few days.'

James gave her a pained smile; he wasn't convinced how useful Angela's line of enquiry would be to their investigation overall, but there was no reason to stop her. He'd rather be thorough than potentially miss something anyway.

'Have you had any luck finding Nate?' Angela asked.

James shook his head. 'He's not here. I asked around and no-one else has seen him either. I'm waiting for Erin to get back from his apartment.'

'Well, I hope he turns up soon,' Angela said. She squinted at something on her end outside of James's view. 'Oh, hey, that's a name I've not seen in a long time.'

'What?'

'A lot of the people on the list for the original inquiry are dead now, but I wanted to go over them as well anyway, just in case. Trouble is, the list of the deceased isn't formatted for the investigation. It's just a mix.'

'Right...' James leaned against the wall and tucked his free hand under the opposite armpit.

'Well, Grant Oliveras is on here. Wasn't he part of your crew on the *Magnum Opus*? Says here he did a short stint in the Spanish Army, made the rank of sergeant, and took the Desert Sniper course.'

James laughed. 'Grant? An army sniper? I had no idea. Didn't think he had the constitution for the military.'

Angela tapped her bottom lip. 'He took his own life, right? At least, that's the official report. What if he was the first *Magnum Opus* murder victim?'

'Even before Hales?' James was sceptical. It was starting to sound a bit 'tinfoil hat' to him. The police hadn't even considered Dr Hales part of that particular string of serial killings. That had all been in the connection James, Angela, and Erin had made via Project Augment. Specialist Grant Oliveras had died over a year prior to that, before James had even found out he was augmented, before he had worked with Dr Hales, and therefore before the ESA or NASA had known about it either. No, Grant's death had been a tragic consequence of the horrors they had encountered on the *Bitter Authoritarian*.

'I suppose it is a bit far-fetched,' Angela said finally. 'Just thought it was interesting.'

James smiled. 'That it is. You said you're scouring the internet for this stuff?'

Angela looked at him sheepishly. 'Most of it is publicly available.'

'Most?'

'Some.'

'Ange…'

'Don't worry. I'm not diving that deep. This isn't like when I researched that book.'

'And almost got arrested.'

Angela chuckled. 'I'm definitely on a few watch lists.'

James pinched the bridge of his nose. This was *exactly* like when she had researched that book. She'd gone from poet to streamer to author, then briefly to international fugitive before the charges had been dropped. 'Just be careful; don't talk to strangers.'

'Yes, Dad. Besides, what are they going to do to a harmless old woman anyway?'

'Angela, you are anything but harmless.'

# CHAPTER THIRTEEN
## A GAME OF STRATEGY

THEY SAT IN THE DIMINUTIVE OFFICE tied to their chairs for what felt like hours. Nate hadn't said a word since the group had returned. Hearing the others speak was like listening from underwater. Some part of his mind took in what his crew discussed and understood it, but he couldn't engage with them.

'Marissa and Fangevokter seem convinced we know something,' said Petra. 'What are we going to tell them when they drag us back in there?'

'You mean, do we tell them the truth: that we're here all alone with no authorisation, no backup, and no exit strategy?' Damien replied, wincing with every small movement. Shortly after Fangevokter had locked them in the room, a guard had visited and seen to Damien's leg, patching it up as best as he could. The bleeding had stopped for now.

'If we do that, there'll be nothing to stop them killing

us,' said Bill. 'Marissa could have shot the commander dead when he leaped at her, but instead she kneecapped him. She could have shot you as well, Petra, when you tried to get up. For all her nervous energy and rambling, right now she needs us alive.'

Bill was probably right, but Nate couldn't bring himself to verbalise his agreement. At the same time, he wished they had wanted them dead. It would have been preferable to living with the knowledge he had been instrumental in the murders of so many.

How desperately he wanted to cry out his aching heart, but the tears wouldn't come; to howl, but his throat was dry; to pour forth his despair and chill the bones of his enemies outside that door, but all he felt was numbness.

Instead, he stared at the wall with eyes unfocused and his mind played the scene of Marissa revealing herself from under the mask again and again. Every replay drained him a little more.

'But if we lie to them about some impending strike, they'll think we caved and kill us anyway,' said Petra. 'And if we stall… same deal but slower.'

'Maybe if they think we've been useful to them, they'll keep us alive longer,' said Bill. 'It's clear our presence here has caused some disarray. Marissa expected the ISA to pursue her and she knew we'd be able to track the lunar transport. But… it's just us. There's no army, no large-scale assault. Just us. They don't know what to do. They're still expecting the rest of the strike team. Threat or no threat, we're valuable as hostages—they could bargain for us.'

'But what would they get in exchange for us?'

'They return us and the ISA backs off.'

'That doesn't make any sense.'

Damien groaned and snapped, 'It doesn't have to make sense! You heard Marissa; she's completely lost it. They're all through the looking glass in this place. You've seen the way Fangevokter stares, right?'

'I've never met a man who blinks so little,' Bill said with a melodramatic audible shudder, 'and I've seen them on all kinds of drugs, believe me. Serial killer vibes.'

'Truth, lies, misdirection: It doesn't matter. The real problem we need to address is how we're getting out of here. My plan was terrible; I don't recommend it.'

Petra sighed. 'That was the only knife, wasn't it?'

Damien nodded.

'Then we'll have to improvise,' Petra continued. 'Especially since our fearless captain has crumbled like Circassian cheese. We should keep our eyes open and watch for any opportunity.'

'And hope the captain is amenable to joining us,' said Damien.

Bill scoffed. 'If he wants to wallow in self-pity rather than help us escape, he can stay here.'

'That's out of line, Bill.'

'How? He dragged us along on this horseshit mission, gave away our presence before we even got into town, got us captured, and would now rather stare at his own dick than help us get out of here.'

'We've been over this,' Petra said with a groan. 'You agreed to come; we all did. Sure, this hasn't gone according to plan, but we were prepared for this, right? We all knew it might happen. It was a huge risk to come out here alone with no weapons and no support from the ISA, and we took it. The captain's not to blame for that. He asked; we said yes.'

'More fool us,' said Bill.

Petra called over to Nate. 'Sure would be nice if you snapped out of your funk and helped though, sir.'

Nate sighed but said nothing. Why bother? They were locked in here with no way out. Even being optimistic about their chances, they wouldn't be able to try anything until the next time someone came into the room and that would be to take them to their doom.

As if reacting to his thoughts, the handle of the door depressed and the door opened slowly. It broke Nate out of his stare and he looked up.

The guesthouse owner's son entered the room, carrying his assault rifle slung over his shoulder and a black rucksack on his back. He looked frantic and closed the door behind him as quietly as he could then locked it again.

He crouched down and put his finger to his lips then showed his palms. After a short moment, he removed the assault rifle from his shoulder and placed it on the ground, followed by the bag.

'Captain Rifkin. We do not have much time,' he said with a furtive glance back to the door. 'I am here to help.'

Nate stared at him. Was he hallucinating? This man had sold them out to Sidera Silere, had been part of the contingent that had brought them to this godforsaken place, and had escorted them right to Marissa. Surely Nate had misheard. What did he mean by 'help' anyway?

The man tilted his head at Nate's confused expression then looked to the others in the room. 'I owe you all an explanation. My name is Alinour, son of Nour-Islam—the owner of the guesthouse you stayed at. No doubt you recognise me, perhaps even suspected me as Sidera Silere.

'This is by design. I am an undercover agent for

the Kyrgyz police and have been investigating Sidera Silere's presence here in Kazarman for the last year. I can help you escape.'

'Why should we trust you?' said Damien. 'How do we know this isn't some weird game from Fangevokter?'

Alinour shook his head and crept around Damien's back. 'You have no reason to believe me, but I hope I can convince you by my actions.'

There was a slicing sound and the rope binding Damien's hands fell to the floor. The commander rubbed his wrists as Alinour moved on to Petra and Bill.

'I have left a message for ambassador Schreiber inform-ing her of your capture,' the man continued, releasing the two crew members. 'She will undoubtedly send someone to extract you. We just have to get out of the airport and to the car park. The further I can get you away from Kazarman, the better. My father was right; many have fallen in with Sidera Silere here out of self-preservation.'

'They're waging a holy war for the future of humanity,' said Bill, stretching as he stood from the chair. 'And they don't care how many innocents they drag into it.'

Finally, Alinour freed Nate of his restraints. His arms slumped to his side. He wanted to leave them there, but his hands tingled and he couldn't help but shake and rub away the discomfort.

Alinour pointed to the bag he had left on the floor and, evidently realising Nate was uncooperative, addressed Damien. 'Check the bag. I brought weapons. But it is my hope we will not need them; I would rather not jeopardise my operation here. If Anders Larsen—the one you call Fangevokter—finds out I am helping you, that is a year's work wasted and he will abandon this base because of everything I know about it.

'It has been a strange time here the last few days. The arrival of the lunar transport has changed many things. Never before has Son of Adam visited Kazarman personally. At least, not a visit I have been privy to. And now your arrival…'

Nate spoke through a cynical laugh in a low voice, his throat hoarse and gravelly. 'So, it's been more than a year.'

'Captain?'

He fixed Alinour with a glare. 'The rest of the world only found out about Son of Adam and Sidera Silere's existence after the attack on Arcadia Landing two weeks ago. You're telling us the cops knew about all this for more than a fucking year? And did nothing?'

Alinour knelt before Nate and put a hand on his shoulder without breaking eye contact. 'You have to understand, Captain, things move strangely and secretly here. The groups that formed Sidera Silere have been operating for decades around the world, you surely know this. We have been on them from the start, but there was never any sign they would carry out something like Arcadia Landing. As for the situation here in Kazarman…' He shook his head sadly. 'We are forgotten.'

The man moved back, grabbed the bag, and pulled out a gun, then handed it to Nate. He passed the bag to Damien, who began distributing the remainder.

'Come,' Alinour said, retrieving his own weapon. 'Hope is not lost, Captain Rifkin. I can get you out of here. Stay close.'

Nate took a moment to handle the weapon. It was a new Vakoconn Arms VAS-67 submachine gun, compact and lightweight and jet black in colour. It had a bullpup configuration with a stubby rubberised foregrip immediately forward of the trigger. The barrel was angular and incorporated its own suppressor and at the rear the weapon featured a short adjustable chassis-style gunstock. These weren't supposed to be on the market yet, but Nate vaguely recalled the news reporting on a theft of the initial consignment from Vakoconn months ago that was never recovered.

After Damien had finished handing out the weapons, the bag was empty. They would have to make do with a single magazine each. Nate hoped they wouldn't get into any protracted combat.

Still, as he held the submachine gun in his hands, he felt that glimmer of hope like a spreading warmth. Alinour's optimism was contagious. If the man was telling the truth about contacting Elisabeth, maybe everything would be alright after all. Sure, Nate would probably have to face consequences for his unsanctioned operation when they got back, but at least he and his crew would be alive and free. Even though he had failed his primary objective, he was armed with knowledge that would surely help them bring Son of Adam—no, Marissa—to justice.

'Alright, let's get out of here,' said Nate, nodding to Alinour as he stood from the chair. He gave his crew an apologetic expression. 'I'm sorry for shutting down—'

Damien held up his hand. 'Sir, later. Let's just focus on getting free of this place.'

Alinour beamed. He unlocked the door and inched it open. 'Stay behind me, move slowly, quietly, and only when I move.'

One by one, with Bill supporting a hobbling Damien,

following the undercover agent's lead, the crew of the *Magellan* exited the room.

* * *

James met Erin by chance as she came through the foyer entrance. One wide-eyed look from her was all it took to tell him what he needed to know: Nate wasn't at home. A knot tightened in his stomach and he feared what it meant.

The two captains rushed through the ISA head-quarters towards the Mission Control Centre. James had received an urgent summons on his phone from Elisabeth and it seemed Captain Pritchard had, too, just prior to her return. It was nearing the end of the day and James hadn't expected to hear from Elisabeth at all following their morning meeting. He had expected to rendezvous with Erin so they could report to Elisabeth about their worrying suspicions together. But it seemed Elisabeth had beaten them to the punch.

'I've already put my crew on alert,' said Erin. She didn't offer a reason, but it was clear they both feared the same thing and neither of them needed, nor wanted, to vocalise it. Her cheeks flushed and she huffed and puffed as the two ran through the corridors side-by-side.

James simply kept on, pushing open doors and dodging the odd alarmed flight controller or engineer.

Before long, they arrived outside Elisabeth's office. James opened the door for Erin and followed her through.

Elisabeth swiped away a call from the desk as the two entered. She leaned both her elbows on the surface, put her head forwards, and gripped it in both hands.

'Fuck!' She slammed her palms on the desktop hard,

shot up from her seat, and paced, holding her forehead. Her cheeks were flushed. There was a sizeable circular crack in the glass surface where her left hand had impacted.

James and Erin said nothing.

The administrator stopped and composed herself, then said, her voice clipped, 'That was the Kyrgyz ambassador. Their undercover police agent in Kazarman has made a report. Captain Rifkin is there, along with Commander Vance, Sergeant Milakova, and Specialist Watkins. They have been captured by Sidera Silere and are being held in the disused airport.'

James took an unsteady step back and swayed. It was exactly as he had feared, the reason neither he nor Erin could find him or get hold of him.

'The whole crew?' he said in half a daze. Surely not? Surely Commander Vance and Sergeant Milakova wouldn't have gone through with something so monumentally stupid? Why couldn't Nate have taken personal time like a normal person? He'd been under so much stress and struggling with his grief, so it would have been the most reasonable thing for him to do. Everyone would have understood. But this? Flying off to Kyrgyzstan with his whole crew in tow to capture Son of Adam himself? No authority, no support, no backup. It was a miracle they knew he was there at all. Though James had suspected it from the man's absence, Elisabeth's confirmation still floored him.

Erin covered her mouth with her palm and went pale.

Elisabeth groaned and hissed something in German then followed it up with, 'I have a headache. Jesus.' She riffled through the drawer in her desk and pulled out a small box of painkillers, cracked two pills from the blister-pack, and swallowed them with a glug of water.

James stuttered. 'Of all the impulsive…'

'Have we got diplomatic clearance to go there?' asked Erin. 'I have my crew standing by.'

'Fuck diplomatic clearance,' Elisabeth spat, leaning on her desktop. 'They are stonewalling me anyway. No more delays. I want both of you to go to Kazarman and extract our people. Take the *Galileo*. Go in armed. Just get them out of there.'

'We're going with the strike team idea? What about causing an international incident?' asked James.

'It is too late for that now,' said Elisabeth. 'Captain Rifkin has made the decision for us.'

Erin put her hands on her hips. 'Are you sure you want us to take the *Galileo*? It is a spaceship, like.'

'It is also a spaceplane,' Elisabeth replied. 'Emphasis on the "plane". It will be faster than a passenger flight or a private jet. Do not wait. Get ready and go. It sounded like the undercover agent is going to help them get out of the building, but you need to be there.'

Erin pulled out her phone and brought up a map. 'Forty-two-hundred kilometres from here to Kyrgyzstan. We can get there within two and a half hours if we go suborbital.'

James scratched his cheek then crossed his arms. 'It'll be less than half an hour if we go to LEO and back down again.'

'Yeah, but the *Gal*'s a shuttle, not a bloody missile! The up and down'll fuck us right up, especially if we need to fight when we get there. Plus, I don't want to damage the heat shield again after it's literally just been refreshed. I think suborbital is the way to go.'

'Do it,' said Elisabeth.

Erin nodded. 'I'll prep the *Gal.* James, meet us in fifteen minutes.' Then she left the room.

'Captain Fowler?' Elisabeth said as he turned to follow. 'Your first priority is rescue. Everybody gets out alive. Ensure Captain Rifkin does not dodge the consequences of his actions by dying.'

James chuckled. 'If he dies, I'll kill him.'

'But what if Son of Adam is right, y'know?' said Lieutenant Commander Sai Suresh as the *Galileo* cruised along the edge of space at Mach three.

'He's not,' said Erin.

It was cosy inside the *Galileo*'s cockpit. James was much more used to having the extra space in the *Aurora*. He sat at Specialist Tom Lando's station on the starboard side of the craft with the seat locked in the forward position. For this flight there was no need for them to make use of that console, so Tom had given his seat up for the captain and volunteered to travel in the cargo bay. Luckily, even in the *Galileo* there were emergency fold-out seats along the bay's rear wall, either side of the Austinium drive's access hatch.

On the port side sat Lieutenant Commander Aisling Simmonds and directly in front of her Lieutenant Commander Suresh. In front of James in the captain's chair beyond the entranceway was Erin and next to her Major Rhys Jones kept a steady hand on the flight controls.

James had never noticed before, but the cockpit windows were different in the *Aurora*'s sister-craft. Instead of a single panoramic pane up front with triangular side windows, the front view held a series of trapezoidal panes in vertical strips similar in style to the old Handley Page Victor bomber jet.

Sai shuffled in his seat. 'But what if he *is*?'

This time Aisling and Rhys joined Erin in repeating, 'He's not.'

But Sai was persistent. 'Look, I'm not saying he is. I'm just saying, *what if* he is?'

Rhys turned in his seat. 'Would you stop being such a pillock? No-one wants to play devil's advocate with you, *mun*.'

'It's worth debating, Major,' Sai snapped back. 'Some of my father's friends have started falling for it, reading things on the internet, memes on social media. The usual.'

Rhys rolled his eyes.

'Well, regardless of the point he's trying to make,' said James after a long moment. 'The ends do not justify the means, especially when the means involve mass murder.'

Sai's expression brightened at James's response. Rhys threw up his hands and went back to piloting.

'Does he have a point though?' said Sai. 'That all our advancement out into space is endangering our species?'

James shook his head. 'No. Pootling around our own solar system in our silly little spaceships, setting up bases in our own back garden, poses no more threat of attracting hostile aliens than the radio transmissions we've been sending out incidentally for the last two hundred years. The only way we'd be in any danger is if the *Bitter Authoritarian* had sent a targeted distress call. It didn't.'

'How can you be sure?'

'Because he was there, numbnuts,' said Aisling.

James laughed and nodded. 'Yeah, I went inside the thing, remember? The ship's comms were busted. All that stuff about there being danger was just Guy Furious's conspiracy bullshit, reinforced by neo-religious dogma.'

Sai pursed his lips and nodded. 'Thank you, Captain. See, Major, at least someone knows how to engage in a question dispassionately. People need to know whether or not their claims of danger are legitimate.'

Rhys groaned. 'I swear to god, Sai, I will come back there.'

Sai shrugged. 'Well, it's put my mind at ease. I'll hopefully be able to use this to help prevent my father from following along with it. That's the last I'll say about it.'

James leaned back against the headrest. Sai had a good point. Sidera Silere's methods may be horrific in the extreme, but they had built on Guy Furious's foundations effectively. Guy had been in just the right place at just the right time and had capitalised on people's worst fears with an effective network of misinformation. Ordinary people who would never have counted themselves as conspiracy theorists found themselves wondering if there mightn't be more than a grain of truth in the anti-xeno rhetoric.

It was far too easy for people like James, Erin, Nate, April, and all those who worked in the space industry to assume theirs was a universal experience, when really the outside world was struggling to tell truth from fiction.

'Less than twenty minutes out from Kazarman, Captain,' said Rhys. 'Starting descent phase. I'll put us down at the far end of the runway.'

'That's is fine, Rhys. Right then, you lot,' said Erin, turning to face the crew. 'Things are likely to go fast when we touch down. With any luck, Nate and his crew should be waiting for us by the time we land. Quick'n tidy in-and-out.'

Alinour led them slowly through the winding corridors of the airport office building. Nate's back was starting to ache from all the crouching and Damien's face had taken on a sickly tinge from working his injured knee so much.

It was taking much longer for them to make their way out than it had done to get to their makeshift cell on the way in. Alinour kept stopping them while a patrol of Sidera Silere faithful went past.

More than once they took refuge in an empty room while they waited out a group of armed guards who stood around chatting. It gave Damien some much-needed respite, at least, and gave them all a chance to eat and drink from the limited supplies Alinour had brought in his pockets. Nevertheless, Damien seemed on the cusp of being overwhelmed by the pain.

Nate looked over at his first officer as he sat on the floor against a wall, rubbing his outstretched leg. Sweat had begun to accumulate in beads all over his bald head and the warmth had drained from his dark brown skin.

*Hold on, Vance. We're nearly there.*

It was dark outside as well as inside. Their cell hadn't had an external window, but this dingy abandoned office had a large one to the west wall. A glance at his watch told him it was close to midnight.

Damien groaned and put his head back against the wall, his breathing heavy.

'Alinour, is there nothing we can give him for the pain?' said Petra in a hoarse whisper.

The undercover agent shook his head. 'I do not have enough privileges to access medical supplies. I would have brought some painkillers, but Larsen ensures they are tightly controlled.'

Bill crawled over to Damien. 'Sorry, buddy, let me check your dressing.'

He pulled the leg of his cargo pants over the injured knee. The bandage was soaked with blood from both sides. Bill then gingerly pulled it down from the top, looked under it, and contorted his face.

'This thing needs changing and it looks like he's reopened the wound. It's bleeding pretty badly.'

Nate grabbed Alinour's backpack and ripped out the inner cloth lining while Bill took the old bandage off Damien's leg and rubbed the wound as clean of blood as he could. Then Nate handed over the strip of cloth and watched as Bill tied it around the commander's thigh. The man was as close to a medic as they would get here; he knew more about field dressing than Nate or Petra anyway.

'It's not going to help much,' said Bill, rocking back onto his rear after it was done. 'It'll just keep bleeding if he doesn't rest it.'

'We don't have the time, Bill. Alinour, can we move yet?' said Nate, sliding over to the man.

The agent stretched up and peered out of the window in the door. 'They are gone,' he said as he came back down.

Nate looked over at Bill and Damien.

'I've got him,' Bill said before hoisting the commander up and supporting him by putting the injured man's arm over his shoulders.

'Then let's go.'

The troupe sneaked out of the room, once again following Alinour's lead. They found the corridor empty as he had said and made their way down a flight of stairs to the left.

It turned out to be the first staircase they had ascended when they had arrived, albeit blindfolded. The door at the bottom opened out into a spacious hangar. Nate's instinct had been correct. He recognised it from the smell of oil. The lights were off, but the moonlight shining through the open side gave them enough residual light to make their way through, though it was a fairly empty space. Tucked away in the corner, Nate could see the wing of the stolen cargo transport shuttle poking out of the gloom.

Outside, pulled across the runway, there were concrete crash barriers, as well as abandoned airport tugs, trucks, and loaders.

They made their way past the Tiger APC and two Jeeps towards the open runway. It seemed they would get away without incident. Nate thought it felt too easy, despite the last couple of hours of dodging and diving they'd already had to do.

He hurried up beside Alinour. 'How long before they notice we're gone?' he asked.

'I relieved the guard on duty, saying I would take his place. They should not realise for some time.'

And yet, as they crossed the threshold out into the clear night with its bright moon and crisp stars, Nate heard the sound of slow clapping behind them.

The group stopped and turned in unison. Fangevokter and a dozen guards stepped out from the shadowy places of the hangar.

The jailer continued to clap as he came fully into the light of the Moon. He had a huge grin on his face and laughed to himself quietly. Marissa, in her guise as Son of Adam, came out just behind and to the right of him.

'Well done, well done, Captain Rifkin! You have saved

your crew. Well done, indeed,' he said, swinging his arms to the side. 'And with the help of our faithful policeman Alinour, I see.'

Nate's grip tightened on his weapon. They were caught completely out in the open. If they ran, they'd be gunned down before they reached the runway's concrete barriers. Likewise, if they made any offensive moves. Being larger, the abandoned vehicles were their best hope, but the nearest of them was almost as far as the concrete slabs. Damien's condition was a concern as well.

'Oh, don't be shy, Alinour,' Fangevokter called as the agent shrank back. 'Be proud of all you've accomplished over this last year. And before you ask, yes, we've always known of your duplicity.'

'How did you know we would be here?' asked Petra.

Fangevokter put his hands in his pockets and kicked at the ground. 'Since we knew your mighty saviour was working for the police all along, we have kept tabs on him. As soon as he dismissed the guard outside your cell, we knew he would bring you here. It's the whole reason we allowed him to take duty as one of your guards in the first place. His usefulness as a source of disinformation for the police was wearing thin.'

Alinour stepped forwards, his fists balled. 'You played me, Larsen!'

'I do so enjoy games of strategy,' Fangevokter replied. 'You really must think several moves ahead of your oppo-nent if you are to win. Especially in games of life or death.'

'If you're so prescient, what are we thinking now?' said Nate.

Fangevokter laughed. 'You are the most easily read of your little team, Captain Rifkin. You are thinking that if you can just make it to the vehicles out yonder, you will find a defensive position. However, to your dismay, you will quickly discover them lined with explosives and I have the detonator. Though, we of course didn't do that with you in mind, but to deter incursion by road. Serendipitous, no? Now, if you would kindly lower your weapons.'

*Jesus, no wonder he always looks so pleased with himself. We need a new plan.*

'Guys, I think I'm about to do something really, really dumb,' Nate said in a low voice. 'Get ready to run for the loader.'

Petra looked at Nate as if he had gone mad. 'But he said it's rigged. He'll blow it as soon as we're near.'

'Trust me.'

'I don't think—'

'Probably best not to in this case.'

There wasn't any time left to weigh the consequences. It was this or nothing.

Nate made a show of lowering his submachine gun towards the floor. Then, in the blink of an eye, he flicked it forwards and fired. A full volley of bullets ripped through Fangevokter's body and he dropped to the ground.

'Run!'

*Weren't expecting that, were you, smug bastard.*

Nate scrambled up from his crouched position, his feet sliding on the grit on the runway, and he saw his team was already away. Taking advantage of the confusion, the group ran as fast as they could, Bill dragging Damien along with him and Nate bringing up the rear.

He continued firing into the hangar where Son of Adam and the guards had taken cover.

Bullets ricocheted around him off the tarmac and

there was a strange rumbling in the air.

A round whooshed past Nate's ear and planted itself in Alinour's back. The man went down with a thud and a yell in front of the loader, then crawled underneath it.

Bill, Damien, and Petra made it to the front end of the vehicle as rounds punctured the doors and windows.

'Stay behind the engine block,' Nate called out.

As Nate joined them behind the loader's cab, Petra knelt down and dragged Alinour out from under it.

He was bleeding from a wound in his back, below his right shoulder blade.

She sat him on the floor next to Damien and then, alongside Bill, popped up to return fire.

'How did you know Larsen was bluffing?' Petra yelled over the sound of gunfire. 'About the explosives.'

'I didn't,' said Nate, letting off a few rounds, which impacted the personnel carrier. 'Still don't.'

It was hard to aim in the darkness and Marissa and her guards had taken cover inside the hangar.

'I guess we just watch out in case any of them go near Fangevokter's body,' Nate said.

'We're out-gunned and running low on ammo, Captain,' said Bill as he regained cover. 'And neither the commander nor Alinour are in a fit state to help us. We can't hold this position. We need a new plan.'

The rumbling sound had gradually become louder and was close to drowning out the gunfire. It sounded like an aircraft, which didn't register as unusual for Nate, seeing as how they were in an airport. But the airport was disused. There shouldn't be any aircraft in the area.

He looked up to the sky in time to see a large, dark shape blot out the stars as it flew over from the direction of the hangar, casting a shadow over the runway. Nate knew that shape.

'It's the *Galileo*!' he cried.

'Finally,' said Petra, throwing down her gun. 'I'm out, we're pinned, and they're advancing.' Alinour made no protest as she took his gun from him.

She was right. Marissa's glowing mask bobbed up and down like a spectre in the gloom as she advanced with her guards. They had organised an effective covering fire as they walked and Nate had to keep himself down.

The *Galileo* touched down at the far end of the runway and the noise of its engines faded.

# CHAPTER FOURTEEN
## The Newton

T HE RINGED DWARF-PLANET Haumea hung before the crew of the *UNSV Newton* in its crimson-spattered magnificence. A bizarre, flattened world, far-flung from its closer planetary cousins, it was the Planet Hunters' latest target for detailed mapping. Many probes had been out this way on fly-bys over the decades and taken snapshots of the cosmic egg and its two moons, Namaka and Hi'iaka. But none had come so close as the Planet Hunters now had in their little spaceplane.

Major Iain Firth had brought the craft into a high equatorial orbit beyond the trans-Neptunian object's faint ring system, where Lieutenant Chris Vanson then engaged the ship's advanced topographical scanners.

Earlier probes had confirmed the presence of dark red tholins on Haumea's surface in a blotch on one elongated hemisphere, along with fresh, bright water ice—a product of a recent resurfacing event—and given astronomers a decent enough look at their distribution. The *Newton*'s task now was to test the various hypotheses for a mechanism by which this resurfacing could have occurred.

'I think we're going to see geological activity on Namaka,' said Specialist Leron Barnes, 'or maybe evidence that tidal stresses from Haumea caused an outgassing.'

Iain turned in his seat and stroked his greying lamp-shade moustache. 'My money's on whatever moonlet created those rings. What do you think, Lieutenant?'

'Comet impact,' Chris said in a flat tone.

Leron clicked his tongue. 'That's your answer for everything.'

'Well, I'll be right one of these days. It's simple statistics. What about you, Captain?'

Captain April Rose-Hartley stared out of the front window, her eyes on the celestial oddity but not really looking at it. One arm was wrapped around the back of her headrest and as usual she had one leg up on the dashboard with the other hand in the pocket of her flight suit trousers. She kept thinking about what James had said to her after Captain Queen's memorial. For once, the cockpit was devoid of music; her Gary Moore album had finished and she had neglected to put anything else on. No doubt something Chris would be thankful for.

'Are you alright, Captain?' said Iain as he leaned across and tapped her on the shoulder. 'You seem out of sorts.'

'I wonder if Nate's still sulking?' April said, half in reply to Iain and half to herself. 'Never seen him get like that before.'

Iain gave a pained expression that creased his brow. It was sometimes hard to tell he was April's elder despite his fading hairline, but his exasperation piled on the years.

'Oh, the investigation. You're still going on about that?'

April looked at him incredulously. 'What? Get off my case, dude. It's not like I wanted to get involved anyway.'

'Mhmm, whatever you say, Captain. It's not like you've been talking about it non-stop ever since we left Earth or anything.'

'I have not!'

April turned to look at the rest of her crew. They stared back at her with disbelieving expressions; Leron's head tilted with a smirk and Chris pursed his lips and scrunched his eyes.

'Et tu, dudes?' April groaned. 'This is mutiny!' She slumped back in her seat with her arms crossed.

The audacity. She hadn't talked about the investigation for the *whole* trip out to the Kuiper Belt. A snippet of conversation here, an explanation there; perhaps the odd ponderance or recollection and a few minutes of idle speculation, followed by a good laugh at Nate's idiotic behaviour. That was all.

Okay, maybe it was a bit much. April couldn't deny it had been at the forefront of her mind during this mission. The last April had heard on the topic had been Nate arguing the administrator should sanction an invasion to get Son of Adam. Ludicrous idea. Nate was being so hot-headed lately. It reeked of desperation. But she couldn't help wondering if Schreiber managed to get diplomatic permission in the end for James, Erin, and Nate to go over to wherever it was.

April shook her head to try to clear her mind. The thoughts wouldn't stop. She had told her fellow captains she wasn't interested in the investigation. The truth was, she'd only said that because she felt she had nothing to

offer, nothing that would help bring down the son of a
bitch who killed Austin, anyway.

No, she could best honour the old man's name by
continuing with the mission he had given her: to discover
new worlds out here on the outermost reaches of the
solar system and to broaden humanity's knowledge of
its own backyard.

Captain Queen had been like an uncle to her and
they'd been similar in many respects. They'd often ban-
tered and rankled each other and both of them had been
prickly at times but always there. Despite his age, he had
always been able to match her energy.

She loved and missed the old man dearly.

April was no detective. Neither were James, Erin,
or Nate, for that matter, but she felt like James's sheer
amount of life experience and Erin's drive would carry
them through. Besides, all three of them had personal
stakes in the matter: Austin had been James's best and
oldest friend, Erin had lost her wife in the attack, and
Nate had been right there in the midst of it when it had all
gone down. They were all much closer to it than she was.

There was simply no room for April in the mix and she
definitely didn't want to babysit Nate. Arcadia Landing
had really messed him up.

Erin was an enigma, though; she seemed far too
well-balanced for having just lost her wife. It could be
her way of grieving, but April could have sworn she'd
seen a slip of the mask when Erin had accidentally said
they were avenging Cheryl.

April was like a dog with a ball. Once something
caught her attention, nothing could tear her away until
she burned out on it. Now, the investigation was her

ball. It was ridiculous she would find something like that more interesting than Haumea, which sat right outside her window; it was probably the ADHD.

A pang of guilt hit her. If only the *Newton* hadn't been so far out the day of the attack, they might have been able to help with Nate's evacuation.

She sighed and turned around in her seat to face her crew once again.

'Look, guys. I realise I might have taken it a bit far with the investigation talk,' she said. 'I'll drop it.'

Chris barked a laugh. 'Wow, introspection? And not about ancient music! Who are you and what have you done with our captain?'

'Watch it, Lieutenant.'

Chris held his hands up apologetically and went back to his monitoring station. He was the youngest of the Planet Hunters by about ten years and just as impulsive as April. His lack of appreciation for (and knowledge of) rock music was a constant source of frustration, but he was handsome with his dirty-blonde hair, angular jawline, and pale blue eyes. And just like all her men, he rocked the stubble that marked their long-haul excursions into deep space, though she didn't think he could pull off a moustache like Iain or Leron. April often joked Chris was the himbo of their little troupe.

'Yep,' April continued, making finger guns at Haumea, 'we've got a job to do, boys. Keep mapping that egg.'

Leron and Iain exchanged a wary look and Chris glanced back around at her.

After a short moment, Leron said, stuttering, 'Great! So, what are your thoughts on the origins for Haumea's tholins?'

April regarded Leron for a long moment, her electric blue eyes boring into his deep brown ones. Leron was a scientist through and through: a specialist in planetary composition and formation. If April had to bet on who was right about the tholins—him or Iain—she'd pick Leron in a heartbeat. He was also what April referred to as the 'tank' of their party, owing to his tall, muscular physique. She liked to mix her metaphors. But her thoughts weren't really on the question at hand.

Her mind raced. The specialist began to squirm under her interrogatory stare, sweat glistening on the dark ochre skin of his forehead.

'Err, Captain?'

'You are absolutely right, Leron!' April cried, pointing at the man. Her outburst made him jump.

'About Namaka?'

'We absolutely should go back and help them get that bastard.'

Leron stammered. 'I didn't—'

'We owe it to Austin,' April continued, ignoring him. 'And what was I thinking? Of course I have something to offer. They'll be lost without me.'

'Oh, hell,' Leron muttered. He rubbed his hand across his short afro then closed down his station.

April whipped around to Iain. 'Turn this ship around, Major. We're going home.'

'But what about our mission?'

'Screw the mission,' said April, securing herself into her seat properly. 'Haumea will still be here when we get back. Its orbital period is two-hundred-eighty-four years, for Christ's sake. It'll barely even move. Lieutenant, close it up. We're leaving.'

'Are you sure?' asked Chris. 'It's at eighty-three percent. We could stick around until it's done and at least have some usable data—'

April glared at the Lieutenant.

With a sigh, Chris tapped on his screen and disengaged the topographical scanner. 'Ready to go, Captain.'

April clapped her hands. 'Excellent. Let's haul ass, Major!'

Iain oriented the ship away from the dwarf planet system and towards the dim light of the distant sun, then threw the throttle control forwards.

The stars shimmered and stretched; with a crack, the *Newton* leaped forward under the Austinium drive's impetus. Being the fastest-accelerating ship of the *Aurora*-class fleet, blue haze quickly accumulated over the front window as the ship exceeded the speed of light and hit its maximum of three-*c* in minutes. At a distance of forty-nine astronomical units, the journey back to Earth would still take them nearly two and a half hours.

There was little conversation on the journey home. The crew of the *Newton* was used to long periods of silence from one another, a silence usually filled by April's music.

Occasionally, as a concession, she allowed one of the others to put on a more modern album. And seeing as how she had now uprooted them at a moment's notice, this was one of those occasions.

This time, it was Iain's turn.

He bobbed along to the off-tempo rhythms and odd phrasing of the postbeat folktrance that filled the cockpit. Iain had explained to April that Imogen Tekas was a master of the genre and an artist he held an immense amount of nostalgia for.

April didn't get it. It was far too new for her tastes. But it was amusing to see Chris didn't get it either; it was still too old for him. Only Leron joined Iain in appreciating it, though he had broad tastes and enjoyed almost anything they put through the speakers.

Iain broke from his reverie and tapped the large screen in front of him, switching the music off. 'We're on our final approach, Captain. Standby for drop. Prepare for orbital insertion in three… two… one…'

With the distinctive crack of the Austinium drive's dissipation, Earth appeared before them, bright and blue, streaked with wispy white clouds. They had come in over Paraguay. It was just past midday, local time.

Iain pulsed the ship's thrusters to bring the *Newton* into low Earth orbit, heading east.

'Great job, Major,' said April, patting his shoulder. 'What would I do without you guys?'

'Hold on a second.' Iain tapped the screen then pulled a pair of headphones out of the storage compartment next to him. He placed one cup to his ear and held up his index finger to April.

'What is it?' asked Chris.

'Picking up some worrying comms chatter,' said Iain. 'Lieutenant, can you clean this up? Then I can put it on the speakers.'

Chris turned his chair from the forward position to port with a click and brought up his terminal. 'Lots of interference. It'll take a moment.'

A few minutes went by; April watched anxiously as Chris worked. He knew his way around an audio track. In a past life—pre-military—Chris had been an amateur audio engineer at his church in Bloomington, Indiana, which only served to highlight to April how strange his lack of appreciation for classic music was.

'Got it,' Chris said. 'Sending it back your way, sir.'

After a long moment, Iain nodded to April and tapped on the screen.

The sound played through the cockpit. They had intercepted a bunch of transmissions between the *Galileo* and ISA headquarters. Snippets of conversations interspersed with what sounded like shouting and gunfire.

A pit formed in April's stomach. As the messages continued, she was able to piece together and intuit something of what had happened. James, Nate, Erin, and their crews had gone after Son of Adam and it sounded as though it was because Nate had done something stupid. Either way, judging by the rattle of gunfire, they were in immediate danger, fighting for their lives. There had been one casualty and another injured; she couldn't tell who they were, but the prospect made her heart leap into her throat.

'Give me a precise location for the *Galileo*,' April said, panic now in her voice. Her heart raced. For the life of her, she couldn't recall exactly where Son of Adam's stolen transport had touched down.

Iain tapped on the console a few more times. 'The *Galileo* is transmitting from… Kazarman in Kyrgyzstan, a small village in the central region surrounded by mountains.'

That was it; the name had eluded her. She remembered then about the disused airport. If they could land, they might be able to help.

'We need to get down there,' said April. She didn't truly know what they could do, but the thought of leaving everyone down there to fend for themselves was unacceptable.

'Based on our altitude and position, we're looking at an hour to re-entry. But into a gunfight, Captain? We have no weapons.'

April hit her seat restraints. 'An hour? Jesus, dude, you heard what's going on down there. They could be dead by then. There has to be a faster way. We don't need to fight; we can get them out of there.'

'Isn't that what the *Galileo* is there for?' said Chris. 'If they wanted extraction, why not use that?'

'And what if they can't, Lieutenant?' April shot back. 'They could be cut off from the ship or it could be damaged. I don't know, but I don't like the idea of sitting this one out.'

'We could provide a distraction?' Leron said.

April glanced sidelong at the man. 'Elaborate.'

Leron cleared his throat. 'Iain could fly us in low. We'd kick up a hell of a dust cloud, make a lot of noise, knock the bad guys off their feet. You guys ever been to Maho Beach? Those jet blasts are mean, man. But we could take damage if they decide to shoot at us.'

'I could do that,' said Iain.

'Yes! That's what I like to hear, Leron. I'll take those odds.' April's spirits lifted. It was a good plan. Now they just needed to address the re-entry time. 'Major, any ideas on getting us down faster?'

Iain groaned and threw up his arms then pointed to the screen in exasperation. 'The laws of physics are the laws of physics, Captain. We're too high up and by the time we touch atmo, we'll have completed two orbits. We'll be going over Kyrgyzstan in another ten minutes.'

*The laws of physics…*

April fiddled absentmindedly with the frayed edge of

one of the band patches on her flight suit. As she did so, the view out of the window darkened as the *Newton* passed the terminator line and slipped into night.

There had to be a way. Iain was right, the laws of motion and orbital mechanics wouldn't allow the *Newton* to get down any faster. If only they had a way of breaking physics without actually breaking physics.

It was like a switch flicked in her mind. She thrust her hand in the air. 'That's it! Use the Austinium drive. It'll let us skip all the complicated manoeuvres and get us right where we want to be in seconds.'

Iain gawped at her. 'Have you gone mad? Do you know what that would even do during re-entry?'

'No-one does. It's never been tested,' said April with a shrug.

'And for good reason,' Iain cried. 'The Austinium drive warps spacetime. You know what else warps space-time this much? Mass. A lot of mass. It could be like slamming a black hole into the planet for all we know. And god knows all our flying around already caused problems for LIGO.'

'I know how the damn thing works, Major. I took Captain Fowler's class on the drive's physics. I'm confident it will not do that. And LIGO's a bad example; you know full well the Austinium drive's noise helped make the interferometers *better*.'

'Wait, what does she want us to do?' Chris muttered with a glance at Leron.

Leron leaned across to him. 'Captain wants us to make a jump down to the surface.'

Chris gulped and laughed anxiously. 'Well, it's not the dumbest thing we've ever done, right?'

'That depends.'

Iain huffed and looked up to the ceiling then wiped his face. 'The first thing they taught me about flying these ships was: "Do not activate the Austinium drive in the atmosphere." Those were the very first words out of my instructor's mouth. The first ones. Not "good morning" or "who's ready to learn how to fly a spaceship?" It was not to do the exact fucking thing you're suggesting… Captain.'

April snorted. 'Nice recovery, adding the "Captain" on the end there. Otherwise I might have thought you were being insubordinate.' She sighed and gave him a sympathetic smile while pointing to her chest. 'Look, man, if it causes a mass extinction, I will take the flak, alright?'

Iain raised an eyebrow. 'Oh, well, if you've got it all squared away with God, then I guess it's fine. What's a bit of world ending between friends?'

April reached across and smacked him in the arm. They both stared at one another then burst into laughter.

It died away quickly and after a brief silence, April said, 'So, you gonna get us down there or what? Our window's closing.'

Iain nodded and exhaled heavily. 'Fine, I'll do it.' He reached over to the dashboard and flicked one of the few switches. 'But can you at least give them some kind of a warning, Captain? Channel's open.'

April beamed from ear to ear and pumped her fist in the air. 'Yes! *Galileo*. Come in, *Galileo*. This is Captain Rose-Hartley of the *Newton*. Are you reading me?'

A panic stricken voice with a Welsh accent answered, 'Major Rhys Jones of the *Galileo* reading you loud and clear, Captain. I won't lie, you've caught us in a bit of a pinch about now.'

'We're aware of your situation, Major Jones,' said April. 'We're on our way. You've got thirty seconds to warn your team before we drop in on your asses.'

'Thirty seconds?' asked Rhys. April fancied she could almost hear him craning to look out of the window. 'But… I don't see you anywhere.'

'Oh, you will.'

April nodded to Iain and he closed the comms channel before bringing up a map on the main screen showing their real-time position above the land. He then pulsed the ship's reaction control thrusters and the veiled Earth came full front and centre in their view.

April gripped her seat restraints and closed her eyes. Her heart felt as though it would burst from her chest. The seconds ticked by in excruciating slow motion. This was a stupid idea, but it was the best one she could think of in such a short timescale. Iain was a great pilot and April trusted his instincts implicitly, but even so, she had to bite down the urge to remind him about reducing their relative velocity before they made the jump. In low Earth orbit, the *Newton* was travelling at twenty-eight thousand kilometres per hour and inside the Austinium drive's warp field, that velocity would be conserved. If Iain didn't halt them, they'd pancake into the ground and possibly obliterate the entire valley.

She opened her eyes. On the map, they passed above Kyrgyzstan and overshot, continuing on over China and finally Mongolia.

April breathed a sigh of relief.

'Commencing de-orbit burn,' said Iain. 'Are you sure about this, Captain?'

She shook her head. 'No way, man. Just get it over with.'

Iain pulsed the thrusters again and the ship turned opposite to their direction of motion. He pushed forward on the throttle control and the powerful rear engines rumbled to life.

April groaned against the crushing weight of her arrested momentum. It felt like her and the chair would become one. Out of the corner of her eye, the rushing Earth with its webwork of pinpoint city lights slowed to a standstill and then started to accelerate in the opposite direction.

'Coming back over Kyrgyzstan now,' Iain said, his voice weirdly monotone. It was clear he was masking his trepidation. 'Last chance, Captain.'

The *Newton* spun on its axis back around to face Earth. Here the city lights were less, especially around the central region. It would be impossible to pick out Kazarman if the map wasn't annotated.

This really was their last chance. What would happen on the other side of that jump? So many things could go wrong. The possibilities raced through her mind as she stared into miles of darkness below. On the map, mountain ranges capped with white snaked across the land; Earthen veins fed the Naryn River and its tributaries on their way to the Aral Sea.

An amusing thought arose: If the *Newton* were to have hit the ground without first aligning its vector, James and Erin would look up to see the ship appear from out of nowhere, only to zoom off sideways to the north-east into a mountain. An ignominious end but memorable and pretty funny. Not too bad a way to go, all things considered. All the same, April prayed she hadn't mistaken her own confidence in the matter for bravado.

'Hit it, Major.'

# CHAPTER FIFTEEN
## VELOCITY WEAPON

JAMES FILED OUT OF THE *Galileo* behind Erin and her crew. Rhys stayed behind in the cockpit to deal with communications and to keep the ship ready to go at a moment's notice. Prior to departure, Tom had popped in from the cargo bay and handed them all weapons. Elisabeth had pulled no punches with her acquisitions. James was used to handling sidearms for personal defence at the off-world bases; pistols mostly. He left the heavier weapons to the on-duty security personnel. Even then, it had only been necessary the handful of times he had visited Arcadia Landing in the past because of the potential clientele. He hadn't needed one at Catamitus Dock at all. The AAR-65 assault rifle he held now, though; this was a weapon of war.

He wore a black armoured vest over his flight suit with pouches of extra magazines all around and, just like the rest of the crew, he had a ballistic helmet on his head.

His weapon also had a powerful torch on the underside of the barrel in front of the foregrip.

Grit and sand crunched under his feet as he stepped down from the spaceplane and onto the runway. The night in Kazarman was cool and clear as the wind blew down from the shrouded snow-capped mountains. They had landed behind several abandoned vehicles and randomly-placed concrete barriers and were out of sight of the gunfight closer to the hangar.

Sharp cracks pierced the stillness almost rhythmically and shouts could be heard in the distance.

Erin took the lead. 'Right, you lot. Let's get our people out of here. No unnecessary risks.'

'What about Son of Adam, Captain?' asked Aisling.

A pained expressed came over Erin and she hesitated. 'No unnecessary risks,' she finally said. 'Move out.'

Following Erin's lead, James, Aisling, Tom, and Sai set off at a jog along the runway towards the nearest of the vehicles, a mid-sized fuel tanker. As they approached, the sound of gunfire intensified.

They crouched behind the tanker's cab and Erin peered out from around it.

'Can't see much,' she said. 'There's more cover up ahead, flashes coming from the hangar beyond.'

'That'll be the bad guys,' said Tom.

Aisling scoffed. 'How do you figure that?'

'Come on, Ash. The crew was escaping from the airport. They're bound to be on this side of the fight.'

'Let's go,' said Erin. 'Weapons ready.'

James tucked the rifle butt into his shoulder and flexed his fingers on the vertical foregrip. The rest of the group did likewise.

They moved out from behind the tanker in formation with Erin, Aisling, and Sai—all three former soldiers—up front. James and Tom were the least experienced in this kind of movement and so were towards the rear. In fact, Tom had no military background at all; he was a construction engineer with basic private firearms training. James had expected him to try to opt out of the operation and stay on the *Galileo*, but there had been no stopping him. At even the merest suggestion from Erin he do just that, his voice through the cockpit speakers from the cargo bay had carried a tone of absolute finality.

'You need everyone you can spare. I'm coming,' he'd said. Erin hadn't pressed the matter any further.

They snaked around the abandoned airport vehicles, checking behind each carefully before moving on to the next, making a beeline forward and keeping low.

Before long, Erin announced she had sighted the attackers firing out from the other side of the frontmost loader.

James joined her at the front of the group and peered around their vehicle. Nate, Bill, and Petra were trading rounds from their cover behind the second-to-front vehicle—a set of aircraft steps. Damien sat on the ground, breathing heavily and firing through a nearby low gap, and there was another man next to him James didn't recognise, but he was slumped and unmoving.

'What's the plan, then, Captain?' said James, glancing back to Erin. Even in the darkness he could see the hardness of her expression. This was not the jovial and easy-going Erin he knew. This was someone else, perhaps a hearkening back to the warrior she used to be before joining the ISA. James knew that, unlike him, she had seen action during her military service: two tours of duty in the British Army.

'Nate's team is pinned and we've got two injured. We still have the element of surprise, so we're going to outflank them,' she replied, then turned to Sai. 'Commander, you and Simmonds go out to the right, behind those concrete barriers; I'll go left.'

'Yes, Captain,' Sai and Aisling said in unison.

'What about me and Tom?' said James.

'Forward. Let Nate know we're here. Render whatever assistance you can.'

Erin gestured to Sai and Aisling. The three of them glided silently off to their positions and were lost in the darkness.

'Just the two of us now,' James said to Tom, who stood with his back to the vehicle and held his gun raised across his chest.

'Yes, sir. Ready when you are.'

James nodded and turned on the torch on his gun. 'Weapons free.'

They went out either side of their vehicle, James to the left around the cab and Tom to the right.

James immediately spotted the Sidera Silere attackers. He took the first shot, which was followed by a volley of several cracks from Tom's weapon.

None of the rounds found their targets, but the attackers took cover.

'James!' Nate cried. He was crouched behind the vehicle's engine block. 'You got here right on time. Bill and I are out of ammo; Petra's down to her last few rounds.'

James knelt down beside him. 'We've got you. Erin and her crew are going to give those guys a little surprise.'

Suddenly, Nate grabbed James by the shoulders, his face ashen, panic in his eyes. 'Son of Adam's out there,

James. It's Marissa, Marissa de Beek.'

'The corporal? That—that doesn't make any sense.'

'What does that matter? She's right there. We have to get her and end all of this. Now you and Erin are here, we've got the numbers.'

James shook his head. 'Our mission is extraction only. They have the advantage right now. We'll regroup back at HQ and have another crack at it.'

'Please, James!' He sounded desperate and gripped James's shoulders harder.

James pushed Nate off of him and the man fell to the floor. 'You have two people injured, for crying out loud.'

'Dead,' said Nate. 'Alinour is dead.'

'Alinour?'

Nate pointed to the slumped figure next to Commander Vance. 'Undercover police. He helped us escape. Bled out moments before you arrived.'

'Damn. I'm sorry we didn't get here sooner. What about Commander Vance?'

'Shot in the leg; all this moving around made him lose a lot of blood and it's in danger of becoming infected.'

'With all due respect, Captains,' said Petra as she stood next to Tom, firing at the enemy position, 'we've got more immediate concerns.'

She was right. They couldn't spend a moment longer holed up behind this staircase.

'Sergeant Milakova, you and Tom keep up the suppressive fire for as long as you can. Bill, help me get Commander Vance up. We need to vacate this position.'

James handed his weapon and fresh magazines over to Petra, then hoisted Damien up. The man was drowsy and his left trouser leg was soaked crimson. He grunted with every movement. Even in the pale moonlight his face was sickly. Bill joined James on the other side.

A shout went up into the night from Erin, followed by a mighty burst of gunfire, then all went silent.

James paused.

'Drop your weapons!' Erin called out.

The reply was a clatter of metal and plastic. Erin, Aisling, and Sai's manoeuvre sounded like it had worked.

*Finally, some good news.*

James breathed a sigh of relief and nodded to Bill. They started shuffling back along the runway towards the *Galileo*.

'Where's Son of Adam?' said Erin, her voice harsh and guttural like a crack of thunder.

As James continued along, he heard Nate's confused voice. 'What? She's not there?'

Before long, Bill and James came within sight of the *Galileo*. Bill was panting and wheezing from dragging Damien along, which James thought was a bit rich, considering he was taking most of the weight. He had to remind himself it was his augmentation that allowed him to take the strain without tiring and his perception of Commander Vance's weight was skewed by his slightly enhanced strength. The man was huge and all muscle and barely supporting himself.

With a tap to his earpiece, James said, 'Major, this is Captain Fowler. Open up. We have wounded. Get the med-kit.'

'Right-o, sir,' Rhys replied through the earpiece.

Bill and James lifted Damien up the steps into the *Galileo*'s cockpit together and rested the man in one of the seats.

Rhys looked him over. 'He's lost a lot of blood,' he said. 'Single entry wound. Nothing on the other side. The bullet's still in his leg. It'll be doing all sorts of damage.'

'Hospital?' asked James.

Rhys pulled out a syringe and measured out some local anaesthetic. 'There's one in the village. I'll make the call for an ambulance. I'll change the dressing and see if I can stop the bleeding.'

'I wouldn't trust them,' said Bill as he brushed Damien's forehead. 'We don't know how many of them are in league with Sidera Silere. Can't you operate here?'

'Does it look like I can operate here, *mun*?' Rhys snapped as he cleaned Damien's skin with a wipe, then put the needle into his thigh.

'Where'd you learn to do that?' James asked.

Rhys snorted. 'I was an army medic back in the day, would you have it? Now I pilot a spaceship. It's strange the way life goes sometimes.'

'Can't argue with you there. Can you contact Elisabeth? I'd like to update her on the situation.'

Rhys gestured to the console. 'Help yourself, Captain. He'll need antibiotics, too, by the looks of things, though they won't do much with his wound this filthy. Whoever treated this had no idea what they were doing. I've got to clean it properly once I've got the bleeding under control.'

Bill put his hand on Damien's shoulder. 'You'll be fine, buddy. Big, strong lad like you.'

Damien shivered and groaned. It sounded like he'd tried to laugh but he clearly couldn't muster the energy.

James manoeuvred himself into Rhys's pilot seat and opened up a satellite communications line to Budapest.

Elisabeth answered the call promptly. '*Galileo*, what's

the situation?' she said.

'It's Captain Fowler,' said James. 'Situation has improved. Erin and her team have secured the hostiles and I should imagine they'll be making their way back to the ship soon.'

'That is good news. Well done, Captain.'

'There's more. Commander Vance is injured and in need of medical attention. Rhys is doing what he can. Sadly, it seems your local police contact didn't make it. It's too dark to tell how many of the Sidera Silere people Nate's crew put down before we got here, but I imagine there'll be quite the body count.'

'Damn it. Alright, Captain. Keep me informed as to your progress. I have some calls to make.'

Just as the line went dead, a bright flash erupted in James's peripheral vision and a bang shook the *Galileo*'s windows.

Further towards the hangar, one of the abandoned vehicles exploded and was now aflame. A fresh crackle of gunfire pierced the night.

'Oh shit! They *were* rigged,' cried Bill.

'What?' said James, rising from the seat.

'Fangevokter—the guy that ran this place—said he'd rigged the vehicles with explosives and that he had the detonator. But Nate killed him.'

James moved towards the back of the cockpit and grabbed some spare assault rifles from the storage box Tom had brought through from the cargo bay.

'Someone else must have gotten hold of the detonator,' said James as he thrust a gun and magazines into Bill's arms. 'Looks like our celebration was premature. Major, keep us apprised. Bill, let's go.'

Grit skidded and cracked as James jumped down from the *Galileo* into a full sprint, Bill following close behind. His feet hammered the tarmac in sync with his pounding heart.

A plume of black smoke poured from the smouldering wreckage of the airport loader, covering the road ahead like a shroud.

James and Bill snaked around the first few vehicles, giving them a wide berth in case they too should explode, and vaulted the lines of concrete barriers.

As they came closer, shadows moved in the cloud, silhouetted by the glow of lingering flames and the occasional muzzle flash.

James was first to drop to his knees behind a slab of concrete and take aim at the shifting shadows.

Then out of the smoke burst Erin, backing up and firing intermittently while ducking gunfire. She was followed by Nate and Petra, who were unarmed, stumbling, and coughing. Aisling then emerged backwards like Erin had, firing into the gloom and dragging an injured Sai along the ground. They took cover behind their own concrete slabs just ahead of James and Bill's position.

More figures moved in the smoke and were immediately put down by Erin.

'Bill, go cover your team,' said James.

Without another word, the man got up and ran to where Nate and Petra had ducked down. Petra took the gun out of Bill's hands straight away and pointed silently to Nate, who lay panting on the ground.

James then moved up through the barriers to Erin. The smoke thinned with the changing of the wind and James could see the bodies of three Sidera Silere acolytes on the ground.

Rounds zipped past them as the attackers broke cover from behind the vehicles ahead and fired.

James took aim without thinking and squeezed the trigger. His volley felled one, who stumbled back behind the cab of the aircraft stairs.

'What the fuck happened?' he said, glancing sidelong to Erin. 'You had them bang to rights.'

Captain Pritchard ducked down behind the barrier and James joined her.

She was panting hard and wiped the sweat from her face with the back of her hand. 'We'd only caught a dozen of them. Then the rest of the bastards came out of the hangar like a fucking swarm. Son of Adam himself hung back and picked something up, the coward. They—' Her voice caught in her throat. 'They killed Tom.'

'Shit.'

'Then the absolute maniac blew up the loader. Nate was knocked down by the blast and I think he's burned. Then Sai got shot, but Ash managed to drag him out of there. I don't know how serious it is. The smoke helped us escape.'

James propped his gun on the topside of the barrier and took aim again. In three bursts he dropped two more Sidera Silere attackers.

'We need to leave. Now,' he said.

'But what about Tom?'

'You just told me he's dead.'

Erin grabbed James by his body armour and dragged him back down to the floor. 'Are you fucking mental? I can't just leave his body here,' she screamed.

James scrambled up and pointed towards the hangar. 'Oh, so you want to fight through all that lot to get to him? Have some sense, Captain. We've got Nate and his team. Mission complete.'

'And sacrificed one of mine in the process!'

'So let's go before we lose any more.'

'No.' Erin's dirt-stained face was hard as stone, her voice a growl. 'I will fight through them. I will kill every last one. I will make Son of Adam suffer for what he did to Tom, to Austin… to my Cheryl.'

James stared at her agog. 'Get in, rescue Nate and his team, get out; quick'n tidy, you said.' He jabbed her with his finger for emphasis. 'This mission isn't about vengeance, Erin.'

'Not for you, maybe.'

She moved to get up, but James pulled her back down. 'Don't make me drag you back to the ship.'

Erin glared and tilted the barrel of her gun towards him. 'Try it.'

James kept eye contact with her and his heart ached. He understood her rage and her drive; he walked a fine line himself and would like nothing more than to be able to go along with her, to avenge Austin and all those other innocents Son of Adam had killed. But what would be left in the wake of their righteous fury? Martyrdom for Son of Adam? An invitation for Sidera Silere to strike vengeance on the ISA? More death. And what would become of Erin and James? They'd be struck off, possibly imprisoned; he feared that more for Erin than for himself. Instead, for himself he feared giving in to that deep-seated god complex, becoming a monster.

The world hardly needed yet another of those.

Gunfire continued to clatter all about them; Aisling and Petra, and now Sai once more, held their positions while James and Erin sat behind their barrier.

'Erin,' he said, easing the gun-barrel away after a long moment had passed. 'I'm going to pretend you didn't just point that gun at me.'

His fellow captain's eyes were red and watery and she looked as though she could burst.

'Captains, come in. It's urgent,' said Rhys through their earpieces, breaking their rumination.

Erin blinked away the tears and activated her earpiece. 'What is it, Rhys?'

'I got a proper weird message from the *Newton* just now, so I did.'

James scratched his bearded cheek and then tapped his earpiece. 'April? Are you sure, Major? She's supposed to be on mission way out.'

'It was definitely her, sir. She says you've got about thirty seconds to clear out before she arrives.'

With a frown etched on his brow, James glanced upwards. The sky was clear and the smoke had thinned. Stars twinkled in the shroud of the night. If the *Newton* was barely thirty seconds out, surely he'd be able to see it by now?

'I'm not seeing them anywhere.'

'That's what I said, Captain. Oh, I've got the commander's bleeding under control now and he's passed out. I can't do nothin' about the shrapnel though, so we'd better bog out of here soon, like.'

Bullets ricocheted off the edge of the concrete behind which they hid, sending chips and dust flying.

Erin rose up over the edge and fired off a volley. 'Is April bringing backup?'

'She didn't say,' said Rhys. 'Bloody well hung up on me, she did.'

*What on Earth is April up to?*

James tapped Erin on the arm. 'I don't know what's going on, but we can't stay here much longer.'

Erin chewed her lip and absentmindedly tapped the barrier with the side of her fist a few times. 'Oh, alright,' she finally said. 'But next time… Next time, he's mine.'

'Agreed,' said James. 'Now, can we get out of here?'

Erin and James jumped up to their feet and laid a barrage into the enemy's position.

'Fall back!' Erin cried, backing up.

James glanced to his right and behind to see the others abandon their places and start to retreat. Aisling, Sai, and Petra joined Erin and James in maintaining the suppression on the enemy. Sai seemed relatively unharmed, but James noted the bullet impact mark on his armoured vest. Bill dragged Nate, who hobbled as fast as he could. James only hoped Rhys would have the *Galileo* ready for take-off as soon as they got there.

A blinding white flash from above lit the entire airport for a split second, turning night to day. The image was seared onto James's retinas: Sidera Silere running after them with Son of Adam bringing up the rear, pointing their way.

A sharp, deafening crack followed, reverberating through the entire valley.

Everything seemed to move in slow motion as James picked out the briefest glimpse of a silhouetted space-plane against the flash as it rocketed overhead.

Then the sky fell.

The crash shook the ground like an earthquake.

The next thing James knew his face was scraping along the tarmac. He tasted dirt and smelled blood.

A prickling heat blasted over him as he rolled. His

vision alternated black and orange before he finally
came to a halt in some smouldering grass to the side
of the runway.

His ears screamed and his skin burned. Even after he
stopped rolling, the world still spun around him.

After what felt like an eternity, he planted his hands in
the dirt and blackened grass and lifted himself up to his
knees. The grounding helped his world to stop spinning,
but his ears still rang. Where was his gun? Hadn't he
just held it? It must have been torn from his grasp in
whatever had just happened.

As he staggered to his feet, the sight of the hangar
made his heart skip.

*I've died and gone to hell!*

Everything was aflame. The hangar, the airport
buildings, the runway, grass, and vehicles. Fat, inky
plumes rolled skyward from the hangar as the fire danced,
lighting up the inside. The transport and vehicles within
flickered in the haze caused by the intense heat.

A secondary explosion ripped the lunar transport apart
and took what remained of the roof with it, spewing sparks
and embers up through the smoke like glitter on the wind.

His mind raced and he patted himself down. He
wasn't dead. Were there other bombs? Did Son of Adam
set them off?

There was a grating roar as the skybridge between two
of the airport buildings crumbled and fell like a great
beast. Then the walls of the right-hand building behind
the hangar caved in and the whole thing gave itself up to
the flames, throwing up yet more dust and sparks.

This had not been a mere vehicle bomb. A nuclear
blast maybe? No, that was a stupid thought. He would

have been vaporised, along with the whole valley.

In the fiery glow, he could see bodies littering the ground all the way towards the hangar. This couldn't have been Sidera Silere's doing. Not that they wouldn't kill themselves to prevent them all from escaping—they'd already proven they were capable of that kind of madness—but because the destruction had rained down from above. Apart from the remains of the lunar transport now burning within the hangar's hellfire, there was no sign Sidera Silere had any way to drop bombs from the sky.

James touched his face and winced. It stung badly. His beard was slick with blood and his head pounded. It was rare these days for anything to overwhelm his enhanced durability.

As he blinked, flashes of the silhouetted spaceplane lit the darkness behind his eyes.

'Jesus, April,' he muttered through a groan. As his mind reconstructed the event, he understood.

He looked at the runway. Aside from the scorched tufts of grass, the area around him was free of fire. The blanket of flames from above had come down moving northeast and missed half the runway. The concussion that had thrown James off his feet must have set off the explosives in the other vehicles. Thankfully, it meant the *Galileo* was safe.

The flash he recognised, though. He'd seen enough FTL jumps over the last few decades for it to be unmistakable. He hadn't realised how loud and bright they truly were.

*Probably amplified by the atmosphere.*

April must've used the *Newton*'s Austinium drive to get down from orbit. It was the only logical explanation and the reason for the thirty-second warning. A shiver of fear went through James as he comprehended the risk. April was smart; she had grasped the physics exception- ally well when James had trained her. Still, he wondered: had she taken the risk out of confidence or desperation? Had she known the destruction it would cause or was this about giving them all a fighting chance?

The use of the Austinium drive within an atmosphere was a topic everyone in the ISA—including Austin him- self—treated with a wide berth. There was no good way to test it and a lot to lose if any of the numerous worst-case scenarios played out. At least now they knew what would happen, which included a blast wave of re-entry plasma.

It was lucky any of them had survived.

James scanned the sky, but the thick smoke obscured his view and the *Newton* was nowhere to be seen. He was sure the ship was intact, which meant it would prob- ably land soon.

*Better check on the others.*

Instinctively, he tapped his earpiece, only to find it missing.

'Damn it,' he muttered.

He held up his hand to shield his vision from the bright orange hellscape and scanned the moonlit end of the runway. The *Galileo* sat unscathed at the far end just as he had predicted. There were bodies on the floor nearby and his heart sank.

He ran to the nearest of them and dropped to his knees. It was Erin. She had been further along in their retreat when the *Newton* had come crashing through the atmosphere.

James checked her over. She was still breathing. As he touched her neck to feel for a pulse, she groaned and rolled onto her side.

'What the fuck happened?' she said, holding her dust-blackened forehead and blinking in the orange glow. 'I've not had a headache like this since Cheryl and I went on that pub crawl in Barry after Pride.'

James laughed, more out of relief than amusement. At least she hadn't lost her sense of humour. 'April happened.'

Erin rubbed her eyes. 'April? *Y lembo*! Oh, where is she? I swear she and I are gonna have some words when she gets down here.'

Over her shoulder, James noticed bodies were beginning to stir. Nate was already sitting on his knees, staring into the flames, his form lit by the wavering orange luminescence.

James helped Erin to her feet and the two of them checked on their team. Aside from cuts, bruises, headaches, and horrible tinnitus, everyone seemed unharmed. A good result, considering how the night had progressed thus far.

Erin spoke to Rhys through her comms and relayed that everyone was okay, if a little shaken. The wail of distant sirens—firefighters and police, most likely—could be heard cutting through the crackle of the flames.

Nate rose to his feet a few minutes later, having refused help up. Without taking his eyes from the fire, he marched towards the wrecked vehicles and ruined airport buildings as though in a trance.

'Nate? What are you doing?' James asked, watching him as he passed them.

The mesmerised captain ignored the question and continued on his way.

Giving her best attempt at a commanding tone, which faltered into a croak, Erin said, 'Captain Rifkin, stand down. Stand dow—Nate, you prick! Get back here!'

Nate stopped and glanced back towards them, his frame silhouetted by the carnage ahead.

'I have to find her,' he said. 'She's out there.'

Erin pulled a face with a mix of exasperation and disgust. 'Who?'

'Marissa—Son of Adam. I can't leave without her. This can't all have been for nothing.'

He turned away and continued on without a further word.

Petra bolted after him, knocking into James with surprising force as she passed. She reached Nate in no time. It was as though she hadn't felt the impact of the *Newton*'s velocity weapon at all.

Then Nate was on the ground and Petra stood over him, panting hard, her fist out to the side.

'Did she just deck him?' said Erin, her mouth flapping open like a goldfish.

'For fuck's sake,' said James before jogging over to the two *Magellan* crew members.

It was hard to hear what Petra was screaming over the sound of the roaring fire, wailing sirens, and James's own tinnitus, but she was giving Nate an earful.

'Sergeant Milakova,' James said as he approached. 'You need to step away.'

She rounded on him with the look of an unjustly scolded child and opened her mouth to retort. Her face was a mix of emotions, from rage to incredulity and despair.

James simply held up his hand and said in a much gentler tone, 'Step away, take a breather. I'll take it from here.'

Reluctantly, after a long moment of staring into James's eyes, she huffed and nodded and flexed her fingers.

As she walked back past him, James said in a low voice, 'I saw nothing and neither did Captain Pritchard.'

She stopped and looked at him, her eyes darting, searching. 'Thank you,' she mouthed and then made her way back towards the *Galileo*.

'She's dead, Nate,' said James, turning to the man on the ground. 'No way she survived that.'

'We did.'

James put his hands on his hips. 'Well, it didn't come down right on top of us, did it? Look at those buildings.'

'I need to see the body,' Nate replied, looking up at James, his eyes glistening in the dark. 'Then I can put this all behind me.'

'Put it behind you? You think anyone will let you put this shitshow behind you?'

'I mean Arcadia Landing. I don't care what happens to me now.'

There was a rumbling on the air and the *Newton* came into view, its running lights twinkling in the smoke as it flew over them. It banked wide and came around before finally landing near the *Galileo* on the rougher ground beside the runway.

*At least the Newton survived re-entry. April, you absolute crackpot.*

Nate stood.

'Come on,' said James, grabbing hold of Nate's arm. 'Let's get back to the ships, get ourselves sorted, eh?'

They had barely taken a step when Nate wrenched his arm out of James's grip and ran in the opposite direction, back towards the burning hangar.

James gave chase. By the time he caught up, Nate was kneeling beside a body. He stopped short and his heart leaped into his throat. Could it really be?

Nate rolled the body over. The person was wearing a mask, covered in luminous green paint, a face defiant to the last. Son of Adam.

Approaching slowly, James watched in confusion as Nate pulled the mask off, revealing the soft, youthful face of Corporal Marissa de Beek.

James turned away, holding his hand to his mouth. Nate had been right. Marissa was Son of Adam? How? This didn't match with anything he thought he knew about the terrorist leader. It didn't match with any of their research, any of the—admittedly circumstantial—evidence. Moreover, it didn't match with James's experience on Le Guin.

'James?'

He chewed on his lip. James could have sworn he'd recognised Son of Adam's voice. Colonel Zhu had seemed to recognise Son of Adam, too. Had she known Marissa? It hardly seemed likely, but Zhu had known a lot of people. He'd have to check that connection when he got home.

'James!'

Nate had called him. He turned to see him in a state of panic, holding his fingers to Marissa's neck.

'She's alive.'

# CHAPTER SIXTEEN
## VAINGLORY

'HOLY SHIT, GUYS. LOOK AT THAT!' April cried, admiring her handiwork. There was an orangey glint in her eye as James and Nate returned, having carried the unconscious Marissa through the swirling embers of the airport and back to the *Galileo*.

James gave her a withering look as he passed and shook his head.

'Aw, you're welcome, dude,' she said.

In the cockpit, James turned Marissa over to Rhys, who roused and examined her.

She remained silent throughout, her expression vacant. Her hair was a tangle of vines and her face was cut and splotched with colourful bruising. She had a dislocated shoulder, which Rhys was not gentle about resetting. Marissa shrieked as it cracked. Under the body armour, her clothing was singed, torn, and dirty and her arms and hands carried blistering burns.

Erin and James helped to clean her up, then bound her arms and legs and sat her in the rear of the cargo bay. The whole thing was a silent affair, the two captains barely able to look at her, much less say anything.

Once they had dealt with Marissa, they turned their attention to seating Nate and his crew between the *Galileo* and *Newton*. It wasn't difficult, but it wouldn't be a comfortable ride. The *Magellan* had been the true passenger craft of Austin's little fleet. The cargo hold of the *Galileo* was primarily to assist with engineering and maintenance, though there were fold-out seats along the back wall. The *Newton* had even less room since its bay was fitted for deep-space exploration, holding a large folded robotic arm and various small satellites, probes, planetary rovers as well as supplies and miscellaneous equipment.

Damien remained resting peacefully where Bill and James had placed him, in the seat immediately behind the *Galileo*'s outer airlock door—Tom's former station—which meant James had to go elsewhere.

Nate had already perched himself in Sai's seat at the back of the cockpit and sat forward, crumpling the tattered Son of Adam mask between his hands.

'Don't you dare think you have the right to sit up front with us,' said Erin, standing over him with her fists balled and shaking, tears still in her eyes. 'You can fuck right off to the cargo hold with Marissa.'

Nate started to protest, but Erin cut him off and pointed to the cargo bay hatch. 'You're lucky I'm not throwing your arse out on the runway and leaving you here. Now get back there.'

Without a further word, Nate got up and skulked through into the bay.

Erin blew out her cheeks and looked up to the ceiling. Shaking the anger away with her hands, she said, 'Sai, I hate to ask this of you, but…'

Lieutenant Commander Suresh nodded and started to move through after Nate. 'I'll keep an eye on them,' he said, picking up his assault rifle as he went.

'Right, James, that means you can take Sai's seat,' said Erin, turning to James.

James crossed his arms and grunted in agreement. 'What about Bill and Petra?'

'They're coming with me,' said April, popping her head through the open outer door. 'They wanna be as far from Nate as possible and I don't blame them. One of them'll have to go in the cargo bay though. I think there's at least one seat in there behind all the equipment.'

The *Newton* had a single spare station in its cockpit; April had never chosen a fifth crew member for the Planet Hunters. Four was all they needed, she'd said, much to Austin's chagrin. The old captain could've overruled her and assigned someone, but in the end he'd decided to respect April's wishes.

'Thanks, April,' said Erin. She tapped Aisling on the shoulder. 'Ash, let's go get Tom's body. Looks like the fire's died down now. I can't leave him out there on the runway all burnt up, like.'

'I'll get a container ready,' said Rhys.

Erin and Aisling dropped down from the *Galileo* and retrieved Tom's charred body from the runway. They brought him back to the ship that had been his home and placed him in an environmentally-sealed container with as much dignity as they could. Rhys and James stood as a guard of honour while he was lowered into the box.

As the last of the burnt-out husks of the airport vehicles were hauled away in the pinkish dawn light, James approached April, who stood watching on the runway.

'You really know how to make an entrance,' he said, putting his hands in his pockets and sidling up next to her. 'What were you thinking? Did you even consider what might happen if you used the drive down here?'

April gave an exaggerated shrug. 'Plenty. Iain thought it would be a lot worse. In hindsight, I probably should've thought about the particles collecting on the front of the field. But we didn't go FTL, kept it strictly sublight.'

'You could have killed us, April.'

She rounded on him then and jabbed him in the chest with her finger. 'No. You are lucky I did what I did. Saved your asses. Tell me you'd have won the engagement if I'd have been here an hour later. Go on. You can't, can you? Nate and Watkins disarmed, Vance critically injured, Lando dead. And that Alinour guy. Do you know how many Sidera Silere bodies they recovered? Eighty. Thirty out on the road, the rest still inside the buildings. Another fifteen survivors who have now been arrested. Watkins said they had this village in a fucking stranglehold. And it gave you and Nate a chance to get that bitch. You. Are. Welcome.'

'You killed eighty people with that stunt?' said James, agape. 'Christ, we're not trying to level the score.'

April scoffed and folded her arms, taking another sidelong glance at the gently smoking ruins. 'Hardly. Eighty to seven hundred don't sound level to me.'

She then looked down at the ground and kicked a pebble. Lowering her voice, she said, 'But no. That... That wasn't the plan.'

James noted the contrition; there was pain there. The true impact of what the *Newton* had done hadn't hit her yet, but he could tell she was starting to feel it.

'Then what was the plan?' he asked.

April cradled herself, took a deep breath, and looked back towards the two ships sitting side by side at the end of the runway. 'I'm… I'm a murderer. Oh, god. I've never killed anyone before.' Her face turned pale and she put her hand to her mouth.

'Leron's idea was to fly in low, knock them off their feet with our exhaust. Give you guys a chance to book it. Using the drive to get down faster was my idea.'

April didn't have a military background; like Specialist Barnes, she had come straight into the ISA from her work in astrophysics and planetary science. Before being scouted by Austin to lead the *Newton* team, she'd been working on a paper for a scientific journal about trans-Neptunian objects. Austin had simply asked her— after seeing the raw data she had been working with—if she wouldn't rather see the objects for herself. When she'd taken command of the *Newton*, the customary rank of captain had come along with it.

James put a hand on her shoulder and shook his head. 'You're not a murderer, April. And those fatalities aren't entirely yours. We all put down our fair share.

'You wouldn't believe it, but I'm in the same boat as you. But we did what had to be done to get our people out of there. You *did* save our lives. I'm sorry. I shouldn't have given you a hard time for that. So, thank you.'

The tension visibly slipped from her and she wrapped her arm around James in a side hug, leaning her head against his shoulder.

'Damn straight,' she said through a weak smile.

The two of them pulled away from one another and James said, 'Y'know, I still can't believe Marissa is Son of Adam. It doesn't fit.'

April cocked an eyebrow. 'Did you take my advice and look at the police records?'

James nodded. 'It all points to something far older. Marissa is too young. I need to get to the bottom of this.'

'Maybe Son of Adam isn't a person. Maybe it's like a mantle or something, passed down through generations of whack jobs,' said April.

As she sauntered away towards the ships, she called back, 'Take the win, dude.'

James surveyed the wreckage of the airport, still cloaked in the shadow of the mountains as the dawn's salmon-coloured clouds faded to white against the crisp blue sky.

He puffed out his cheeks and blew out air, then muttered, 'Yeah... Maybe.'

The sound of trilling sirens met James's ears as the *Galileo* touched down on the runway in Budapest, just ahead of the *Newton*. As the spaceplane coasted along, out of the window he spotted a fleet of police cars and an ambulance approaching at speed.

The moment the two ships came to a halt, they were surrounded.

Erin had already updated Elisabeth on the situation while they'd been in the air, so the reception was expected.

Rhys helped Erin haul Marissa out of the cargo bay and handed her over to the waiting officers on the ground.

At the same time, Damien was lowered down and the paramedics rushed to see to him; Elisabeth had already apprised them on his condition.

James and Nate stepped down from the cockpit in time to catch Marissa glancing back at them with a smirk before she was lowered into the back of a police car. Her attitude filled James with a sense of unease and Nate too looked unsettled.

They didn't have time to consider what this could mean, however, as Elisabeth marched along the runway towards them, her expression inscrutable.

'This is the part where I would be saying "well done" for a successfully completed mission if it had not turned into such a catastrophe,' she said to James, folding her arms.

April hopped down from the *Newton* with Iain, Leron, Chris, Petra, and Bill.

Erin walked over to stand beside James and Nate.

Nate made to speak, but Elisabeth cut him off with a finger and a piercing look, then raised her voice. 'Full debrief in the MCC in half an hour. All of you. I want to know what the hell happened and how yet another one of our people ended up in a box!'

The four captains got themselves ready and made their way to the little room off the Mission Control Centre where James and Nate had been debriefed following Arcadia Landing.

Elisabeth once again sat at the head of the table and James took up the first seat beside her, with Erin opposite, Nate next to her, and April next to James. April alone reclined, picking at a hangnail.

The crews of the *Magellan*, *Newton*, and *Galileo* stood around the table.

In Damien's absence, Petra and Bill reported first on their ill-fated adventure, their capture, escape, and the death of the undercover police officer, Alinour.

Nate remained silent throughout, his face grim but dignified and his hands together on the desk.

Erin and James went next, detailing the events after they had landed, including Tom's death.

April's report was brief. 'Saved all their asses,' she said, feigning dropping a microphone.

Elisabeth listened intently and stared at April until long after she had finished, then rolled her eyes as though in realisation of the foolishness of expecting more.

'Thank you,' she finally said, addressing the assembled crews. 'You are dismissed. Sergeant Milakova and Specialist Watkins, rest assured there will be no repercussions for you or Commander Vance. You have been through enough.

'Lieutenant Commanders Simmonds, Suresh, and Major Jones: Please accept my condolences on the death of Specialist Lando; we will sort out a memorial for him when this is all over. Take some time.

'Major Firth, Specialist Barnes, and Lieutenant Vanson: You should prepare to return to the Haumea system as soon as is practicable. I will not keep Captain Rose-Hartley long.'

The crews nodded and murmured their thanks then filed out of the room. When the last of them had left and the door clicked shut, Elisabeth glared at Nate.

'Explain yourself,' she growled.

Nate fiddled with his fingers, then spread out his hands on the tabletop and rapped them on the surface. 'I am sorry,' he said, finally.

'It's a little bit late for that, Nate,' said Erin. 'People died. Good people. Our people.'

'What did you expect me to do?' Nate said in a low tone. 'I was desperate. None of you were doing anything useful and Son of Adam—Marissa, oh my god I still can't believe it—was about to get away. We needed decisive action. I did what I thought was best.'

James scoffed. 'You don't sound very contrite.'

'You just can't handle the fact I got results,' Nate spat, giving James a sidelong glare. 'I did more to move this investigation forward in these last couple of days than you have since Arcadia Landing. I found out Son of Adam's identity. I made sure she didn't get away again.'

Flabbergasted, James cried, 'None of that was you, you great pillock! Get your head out of your arse. We've just heard it first-hand from Petra and Bill. You got yourselves captured by being the most conspicuous people in the entire village, then the rest of us muggins here had to fly in to rescue you.'

Nate closed his eyes and breathed deeply. 'However we got there, the results are the same. Son of Adam is in custody, she will face justice for what she did, and I will finally be able to sleep.'

'Over eighty people dead and an airport destroyed,' Elisabeth began. 'You disobeyed direct instructions from me and the Kyrgyz government is now accusing the ISA of espionage. In short, you have caused an international incident with untold political ramifications.'

'I didn't destroy the airport—'

'Oh, fuck you, too, Nate,' April said nonchalantly, kicking her boot up onto the table top. She looked to Elisabeth. 'But espionage? Nah, that's bullshit. We saved that town from Sidera Silere occupation.'

'I am getting to you,' said Elisabeth with a glance to

April. 'You are not entirely innocent either.'

She pointed at Nate and continued, 'Do you know what the most painful aspect of all this is? On the morning you went missing, I was about to authorise a mission for you to retrieve the *Magellan* from Skyport. Yes, it is now in a fit state for re-entry—not fully repaired, it will need substantial refitting down here—but I thought you would appreciate being able to get it yourself, considering everything that has happened.

'But now I have no choice but to take it from you. Mr Rifkin, you are no longer the mission commander for the *Magellan* and I am placing you on a six-month suspension, effective immediately. When you return, you will be reassigned to security.'

Nate's gaze didn't waver; his expression remained flat and grim. If anything, James thought he saw the remotest flicker of relief in his eyes.

'I understand, Administrator,' Nate said after a long moment, his voice level and measured. 'I know I deserve to be reprimanded for my actions, regardless of the results. They were unacceptable, unprofessional, and my desperation cost lives. I appreciate you sparing the others.'

'Mr Rifkin, you are fortunate to have a job at all after what you have done. In fact, you are lucky I did not have you arrested the moment you set foot on the runway. Now, get out.'

'Yes, Administrator.' Nate rose from his seat at the table and strode to the door. There was a notable lightness to his steps as he left the room.

The air in the room remained thick and stifling. James had expected the suspension and for Nate to be chastised heavily, but Elisabeth's calm demeanour was more terrifying to him than if she had shouted. Stripping Nate of his captaincy was the right move. With his rash decision-making and reckless desperation that had nearly resulted in their deaths, the man had proven himself unfit to lead his crew.

With Nate gone, Elisabeth then rounded on April. 'Captain Rose-Hartley,' she began. Her energy faltered and she leaned her head forwards to rest in the palm of her hand and groaned. 'Your sheer dumb luck is astounding. The risk you took with the extremely volatile technology we employ may have worked out for you this time, but it will not always be so.

'Nevertheless, you have provided us with useful new data on the Austinium drive's operation and the potential dangers of weaponisation… Unlike the records from your Haumea expedition. Lieutenant Vanson told me you ordered him to shut off the topographic scanner in order to get back here faster. As such we have nothing usable, so you need to re-do it.'

April chuckled. 'Fine by me. Haumea ain't going nowhere.'

Elisabeth drew her fingers together and closed her eyes. 'A little contrition would be appreciated, Captain. At least some self-awareness.'

'For what?' said April, giving one of her exaggerated shrugs. 'I'm a fuckin' hero.'

'Consider this your only warning,' Elisabeth snapped. 'Take a risk like that again and you will be joining Mr Rifkin.' She huffed and calmed herself before continuing, 'I will update the mission roster. It is likely you will be flying again before the end of the week.'

'Not tomorrow?'

Elisabeth squeezed the bridge of her nose. 'April, if I could send you to the edge of the solar system this afternoon, god only knows I would. You are dismissed.'

April stood, somehow managing to scrape her chair back despite it being on casters and carpet, then gave James and Erin a mock salute and a grin before retreating from the room with a skip in her step.

'Are you okay, Administrator?' asked James, interlinking his fingers on the desk.

'It has been a day.' Her tone softened. 'Well done, both of you. Erin, I understand the loss of Specialist Lando must still be raw. Take some time off. And I suggest you both get in touch with our therapist since you have both engaged in combat resulting in fatalities.'

James nodded. The fact he had taken his first life hadn't truly impacted him yet. He was still focused on the moment and doing his job. But Elisabeth was right. It would be prudent to talk it through with someone.

Elisabeth continued, 'At least Mr Rifkin was right about one thing: We have Son of Adam now and she will be prosecuted to the fullest extent of the law. Perhaps something good may come of this. I must say I was not expecting it to be Corporal de Beek.'

'I have my reservations about that,' said James. 'I've already shared with April and Erin that it doesn't sit right. It doesn't fit the evidence we've gathered.'

Erin nodded. 'Marissa isn't augmented either. But equally, she could have been wearing an air supply under her mask at Le Guin. Plus, our "evidence" is really circumstantial. Even if we could definitively tie Son of Adam to the *Magnum Opus* murders, it still doesn't rule out Marissa.'

'April suggested "Son of Adam" could be symbolic and not just one person. It sounds a plausible way to explain the half century timeline, but I'm not convinced. There's just something about the Son of Adam I met in that spaceport...'

'We will see how it all shakes out,' said Elisabeth. 'Get some rest for now.'

James made his way along the Budapest streets towards home. He alighted from the bus at an earlier stop to usual and wandered, hands in pockets, kicking stones along the road. The evening was cold and the breeze ruffled his open jacket, but he ignored it. There was a certain simplicity to it, a serenity he desperately needed after the chaos of Kazarman, which still weighed heavily on his mind. In just one day, everything he knew had gained a new twist.

It felt as though the very ground on which his life stood was soft and uneven, like the dirt path through a country park after a storm. He'd agonised over taking lives and what it would mean for him so many times, but in the end, the moment had passed by and was gone. Where had that chilling flash of divine supremacy been? Nowhere. The descent he'd feared hadn't happened. No metamorphosis into some mad, twisted, and wrathful god. Three lives—mere shadows in the fog—extinguished in a fraction of a second and the world had carried on like always. Perhaps the great barrier he had erected in his mind was not tied to the act but the intention.

And then there was the investigation. The facts had unravelled themselves and now lay strewn in a tangled heap at his feet. He had been so sure. So goddamn sure.

Every smoking gun now had an alternative that was more plausible than his conclusion. Moreover, they would be easier to prove. The simplest solutions were usually the best. Perhaps, therefore, he'd been wrong after all, for his solution was both nigh-on impossible to prove and vastly more complex.

In turn, it would mean Nate had been right. Not that this justified the way he had—quite literally—burned the place down to achieve his result. But he *had* done what James had failed to do, there was no denying it. In fact, it seemed James had not just been behind but flat-out looking in the wrong direction.

Before he knew it, he arrived at his apartment building, trudged up the steps, and pushed open the door.

Angela came to meet him then and he dropped to his knees before her and sobbed. Chaos begat chaos. What was he even crying for? Mourning the people he had killed? Perhaps for the loss of Tom—a man he had barely said a word to—for Nate's demotion, or, more selfishly, for his own failure?

She held him tightly without a word, stroking his hair and kissing his head.

Eventually he rose and kissed Angela on the lips, then pulled away and took her hands to lead her into the lounge.

'Are you okay?' she asked, gripping his hands as they sat together on the sofa. 'For the first time in a long time, you actually look tired.'

'I am. Exhausted, even to my soul. It's all so overwhelming.'

'What happened out there?'

She listened intently as he recounted the rescue mission and all that had come out of it.

Angela continued to stare at him long after he had finished speaking.

She lowered her head and shook it, her long white hair waving in front of her face. The way it caught and filtered the warm light of the room seemed to grant back some of its former glory.

She gave a light chuckle. 'Well, shit. I guess that means you don't need to know what I found out.'

James looked at her askance.

'Sorry! I don't know why that was the first thing that came to my mind after everything you said,' she said with a furrowed brow and raised bottom eyelids. 'We can talk about something else to take your mind off of things or—'

'No, I'll be okay. Besides, I'm booked in to see the therapist in the next few days to talk through all this,' said James, drying his eyes with his jacket sleeves. 'There's no way you can drop a bomb like "I've found something" and leave it at that. I'm intrigued now. Show me what you've got.'

Angela beamed and even bounced a little on the sofa. She hadn't changed much from before they were married, not really, not at heart. It was good to see her excited about something again, given something to think about other than her health problems. James recalled how she used to get like this when talking about her new D&D stories, then her livestreams, and later, her crime novels.

'Well, I was doing some searching around online like I said—'

'Like I told you to be careful about,' James interjected with a smirk.

'Oh, exactly,' said Angela. 'So I was looking into Sidera Silere activity and—'

James sputtered and held his hands up in disbelief. 'You

what? That's the exact opposite of careful! These people are murderers, Ange. They're a full-blown terrorist organisation now, the likes of which hasn't been seen since Daesh.'

Angela rolled her eyes. 'For fuck's sake, I'm not stupid, James. My eyes might be failing me, but I've still got them and for the time being, they still work. Don't be such a prick.'

James tipped his head back and closed his eyes. 'Fine, but what's this got to do with the *Magnum Opus* murders?'

'Turns out, not a lot. But I did find something else: a set of photographs featuring Marissa de Beek meeting with known Sidera Silere, err, operatives? Acolytes? Agents? What do we call them?' She then waved her hand dismissively and continued, 'Never mind, that doesn't matter. Check out the picture. It's on the network.'

James pulled his phone from his pocket. It had already connected itself as usual to their home network server upon entering the building. He tapped through to the downloads folder and brought up the picture Angela was talking about.

James's eyes bulged and he gasped.

It was a view across the street of a coffee shop in the Budapest city centre. Marissa half-stood, leaning over a table out front and shaking the hand of an older woman with brown skin, white-tinged black hair in braids, and wearing sunglasses. Marissa wore a bright blue, flowy sundress, while the other woman had on a red leather jacket and black jeans.

'There was a whole set, but I only downloaded this one,' said Angela. 'When I saw them, I thought she looked familiar. That led me to looking back through ISA staff records and it turned out to be her. I then realised no-one at the ISA had had any contact with Marissa since she resigned.'

'Well, she seemed pretty shaken up at the time,' said James, thinking back to the argument he'd seen on Skyport in the immediate aftermath of the attack. 'But now we know from Nate, Petra, and Bill's testimony that it was all an act. She just wanted to distance herself from Arcadia Landing, to disappear, and did so under the guise of being traumatised by it.'

Angela slapped him on the knee. 'I know that *now*. But that's why I said you wouldn't be interested in what I found anymore.'

'But the other woman… That's Ilona Illes,' James said, tipping the phone towards Angela and pointing at the screen. 'I thought she was gone for good. Why was Marissa meeting with her?'

'Yeah, well, she's back in town,' said Angela, folding her arms and crinkling her nose in disgust. 'And evidently still in deep with Sidera Silere.'

'They weren't called that back then, though,' James reminded her. 'It was just a motto. How long was her sentence?'

'They charged her with attempted murder after what she did to the *Aurora*. It was supposed to be twenty years, but she got out after about five and served the next fifteen on parole. After that, she moved away.'

'Wait, where did you say you found this picture?'

Angela shrugged. 'I didn't. It was on some deep web message board. I got chatting with some people on there and one of them provided the set.'

James crossed his arms. 'And you're sure it's safe?'

'Clean as a whistle, near as I can tell. Oh, don't look at

me like that. All downloads run through the ISA security software automatically. Like I said, I'm not an idiot.'

James rubbed his chin. 'So, essentially, what you found out… is the same as what we found out in Kazarman: that Marissa is with Sidera Silere?'

'Yep, pretty much. I'd have bet money Marissa was a mole in the ISA and Ilona was her handler, just like before. Though I guess my evidence isn't as compelling as literally finding her wearing a Son of Adam mask. I mean, wow. I'd have totally lost that bet. Make that shit make sense.'

'I know, right? It doesn't, does it?' said James.

He then shared with her April's suggestion.

'No,' said Angela, shaking her head. 'It might sound plausible, but I still don't think it fits with the pattern of the murders. Even the police were only looking for one person. Nothing there suggests the killings were being carried out by multiple people.'

Her face broke into a gentle smile and she patted James's hands. 'Never mind all that for now. Take the time off you've been given to rest. Perhaps, if we keep an eye on how the case against Marissa progresses, there'll be some clue as to whether she's legitimately Son of Adam or just a scapegoat.'

James shifted uncomfortably in his seat. 'I wouldn't say it's that simple. I believe what Nate said about her role in the bombing. Whether she's their leader or not, she definitely bears some responsibility for the attack. She's no mere scapegoat. I don't like the idea of waiting; it's dangerous.'

'I know, I know. But Elisabeth wants to wait, too, by the sounds of it. You'll sound like a crazy person if you started badgering her about it now. We have no hard evidence.'

*No hard evidence...*

She was right, of course. It was the same conclusion Erin had drawn. All they had was a potential line stretching back to Dr Hales's murder, linked by Project Augment. They needed the ballistic analysis from the Le Guin massacre. It was their last chance to provide something concrete, but even then, how would it prove Marissa hadn't been the one in the mask at the time?

As much as he hated the idea of waiting around, potentially giving the real Son of Adam the opportunity to strike again, he didn't have much of a choice.

He'd have to watch the criminal proceedings for Marissa carefully, though he suspected it would be hard to miss.

# CHAPTER SEVENTEEN
## EPOCH

MARISSA'S TRIAL WAS FINALLY OVER. Following her arrest on the runway in Budapest, she had been extradited by international agreement to the Netherlands, her home country, where she was formally charged and tried.

James sat alone on a bench in a secluded green space outside the courthouse in Schiphol. He had managed to avoid the flock of journalists hanging around like vultures by slipping out of a side door while they were preoccupied with barraging Elisabeth with questions. He and his ISA colleagues had done their part in the proceedings over the last several months, providing evidence and testifying to Son of Adam's crimes, including the lunar massacre. Nate in particular had recently given an enthusiastic account of Marissa revealing her identity. And now she awaited sentencing.

It was supposed to be an auspicious day; the whole world

was watching. In fact, the whole world had been watching since the start, making it the most heavily televised public trial in recent decades. But James remained troubled.

As he stared sightlessly into the clear blue sky, numb to the sights and smells of summer around him, he couldn't shake the feeling something was amiss. The evidence presented by the so-called expert analysts made it pretty clear Marissa was who she claimed to be. The recovered mask was shown to contain space for a small breathing apparatus in addition to the voice changer; forensic reports from Le Guin and Angela's research were used to tie the pistol there to the *Magnum Opus* murders, which added yet more charges to Marissa's already-impressive list. James, Erin, and Angela's hypothesis regarding Project Augment and the connection to Dr Hales was dismissed as conjecture, outweighed by the overwhelming evidence that Marissa was indeed Son of Adam.

*It all adds up perfectly. Too perfectly.*

The bench shook and creaked, breaking James's train of thought.

Erin sat forwards, elbows on knees, holding her head in her hands. 'Those bloody journalists,' she muttered and then sat up and looked at James. 'How did you get around them? Is that another augmentation of yours? Invisibility?'

James chuckled and reclined against the slatted wooden backrest.

'Looking forward to the results?' she asked, matching his posture. 'God, this bench is uncomfortable.'

James shrugged and put his hands behind his head. 'It helps me think.'

'Thinking? Looked to me like you were zoning out. I wouldn't blame you; this has been a lot. I just want to get back on the *Galileo*, y'know? Go back to what I'm used to. Give me a chance to put all this behind me.'

'It doesn't feel right to me.'

Erin sat up straight and gawped at him. 'Oh no. Come on, James, not this shit again, *butt*. We were wrong. You need to get over it.'

'I can't, Erin,' said James, shaking his head and sighing heavily. He closed his eyes with a deep frown and put his head back. 'Why hasn't Marissa—at any single point in this trial—made any effort to defend herself, despite pleading not-guilty? She just spouts nonsense Sidera Silere rhetoric to every question.'

'I'll agree with you there; she has been pretty incoherent.'

'It's more than that,' said James, glancing sidelong at Erin with one eye open. 'Where are the reprisals, eh? Sidera Silere has gone totally silent.'

'Because we cut off the head of the snake, obviously.'

'Did we, though?'

Erin stared at him open-mouthed for a long moment. James understood her desire for this all to be over. She wanted closure; she deserved it. They all did. But James's refusal to believe they'd simply been wrong about Son of Adam wasn't mere egotism. If only he had solid proof, but he alone had the longevity and experience to make the necessary connections. And that was all it was: his personal experience, which amounted to little more than a gut feeling. Where could he go from here?

'Erin, you know I can't let this go,' he said.

'I know,' she replied, standing and looking towards the courthouse. Her phone buzzed. 'Jury's finished deliberating. We'd better head back in.'

Marissa was found guilty on all charges and sentenced

to life imprisonment without the possibility of parole.

'James, walk with me,' Elisabeth said, touching his shoulder.

It had been two weeks since the trial had ended and James stood with his arms crossed in a darkened Mission Control Centre, staring out at the empty chairs and computer terminals, particularly to where Austin had sat during the early days.

Sidera Silere activity had diminished to almost nothing. It was as though they had all but vanished from the face of the Earth. James still couldn't let go of the feeling something was wrong, despite the trial. He remembered what he had said to Erin on the day of the sentencing. If it were true, why hadn't Marissa defended herself? That was the strangest thing about it all. If she wasn't going to defend herself, why not plead guilty in the first place? And if she was their leader, why didn't Sidera Silere make any attempts to get her out? There was no sign of jury tampering, blackmail, threats, or any protests at all. If Sidera Silere were everywhere as they'd always claimed, surely they would never have let her go to jail. The same went for the handful of other survivors from the airport. Unless that had been the plan.

*It was all a distraction, I'm sure of it. It's so obvious. But I can't prove it.*

'James.'

He jerked up then and turned to Elisabeth. 'Sorry. Lost in thought.'

'You miss him,' she said. 'I miss him, too, despite him having been a constant thorn in my side.'

James snorted and turned to leave with her. 'He was the best of us,' he said.

'No, you are the best of us and he knew it,' Elisabeth replied as James opened the door for her. 'But Queen did more for this project than anyone else. Which makes what I have to say to you all the more difficult.'

They walked along the corridor a little way; Elisabeth remained silent and James waited for her to elaborate. He knew her position came with a lot of stress; he'd never envied her nor Dr Azzopardi before her. But they were both masters of the art of saying what needed to be said. Elisabeth knew how to say difficult things to even more difficult people. The way she carried herself now gave James pause. Something was weighing her down in a way he had never seen before.

She stopped in the corridor and stepped in front of him. 'I am being replaced,' she said.

James came to a dead halt. 'What? Why?'

'The Kyrgyz government put on a good show, but they're not happy, and that is not all.'

'Oh god, what else?'

'With Marissa in jail and Sidera Silere scattered, the UN believes it is now time to revisit the signing of the UEC treaty. They have scheduled it for the thirteenth of April, marking the first anniversary of Arcadia Landing. It represents the perfect time to do away with all the old things in favour of the new. So, at the treaty signing, I will be honoured and a new administrator will take my place.'

'Another UN—or UEC—ambassador?'

Elisabeth shook her head. 'No, not this time. Remember, the UEC is establishing a new military arm for the ISA with a new rank system. There will be a lot of restructuring going on. From what I have heard, however, they are still looking for a scientist to be the administrator. But it is likely our security teams and space crews will be overseen by a military commander under the civilian administrator.'

'Austin would hate that.'

'Oh, he did. Argued with me until he was out of breath about it, in fact—on more than one occasion. But I have no say in it and, broadly, I support it.'

James cleared his throat and held out his hand. 'Well, I'm sorry to see you go, Administrator. It has been an honour to work with you. And I'm sorry we've given you such a hard time recently.'

Elisabeth ignored his hand and stared at him. Nothing she had said seemed to take away the weight.

'There's more?' James asked, lowering his hand.

Elisabeth looked away from him and paced back and forth. 'This is the part I hate,' she said. '*Gott*, I have spent my entire career negotiating and debating all kinds of political bullshit, but this… This breaks my heart.'

'What is it?'

Closing her eyes, she took a deep breath and drew herself up to full height. She exhaled slowly and looked up into James's eyes. Elisabeth had never made a secret of her perpetual exhaustion, as though she ran on pure stress, but the weariness he could now see behind her bright hazel eyes was different.

She spoke slowly, clearly; she had rehearsed this. 'The *Aurora* has always been a test vehicle, administered in whatever way Captain Queen saw fit. But technology has moved on; we have the *Newton*, the *Galileo*, and the *Magellan* now. Catamitus Dock has already begun their first shipbuilding project and the facility isn't even complete yet.

'In short: the *Aurora* is no longer needed, especially

now that Austin is gone. The UN has moved to officially decommission it.'

James's blood ran cold. Whatever he had expected her to say, it wasn't this.

'Surely they can't do that?' James stammered. 'It would be an insult to everything we've worked for. Just because Austin's gone, it doesn't mean the *Aurora* is suddenly useless.

'May I remind you it was the *Aurora* that towed the *Magellan* to Skyport following the attack? I was the only one who could get there! And they want to knock us down to three?'

Elisabeth reached out and squeezed James's arm. 'I am sorry, James, truly. It will happen at the treaty signing and there will be a fitting tribute to Captain Queen. I will make absolutely sure of that. I can only hope my successor will give the ship pride of place in the aviation museum.'

'Aviation museum? Mothballed like the *Magnum Opus*? Left as a desiccated husk?' James scoffed, running his hand through his hair. 'And what about me? Am I to be entombed with the ship? Will the United Earth Confederacy pay for my mummification? Out with the old, in with the new, after all.'

'Teaching,' said Elisabeth. 'They want you to use your vast experience to continue teaching and training new crews, like you did with our current brood.'

James crossed his arms and looked at her with scepticism. 'Are you sure? Because if I were any good at teaching, maybe April wouldn't have nearly cratered a village.'

'You know the physics behind the Austinium drive better than anyone besides Captain Queen. You have literal decades of first-hand spaceflight experience and your background is in particle physics. Perhaps it is the right time to retire Captain James Fowler and become Instructor James Fowler instead? Perhaps this is the way to honour Austin's legacy: by ensuring our next generation of astronauts—or generations, in your case—can benefit from it, too.'

James regarded her for a long moment and she held his gaze. She had a point and he had helped to train the current crews. Austin was all about his little fleet; even if James couldn't fly anymore, at least he could keep Austin's dream alive.

'Oh, and speaking of the *Magellan*,' Elisabeth said. 'I thought you should know Commander Vance will be taking over from Mr Rifkin as the ship's mission commander. I am not waiting for the treaty signing; it is effective immediately. I want that ship back down here so we can finish refitting it. It must be made mission-ready for the signing. It has been sitting at Skyport for far too long already.'

A flash of envy passed through James then, making him shiver. It occurred to him the *Magellan* could have been his ticket back into space after the treaty signing. But it wouldn't have been fair on Damien. He felt ashamed of himself. 'I'm sure *Captain* Vance will be overjoyed. I know he's had his eye on the position since before Nate came along.'

'Yes, he has. I will never understand why Queen chose Mr Rifkin over him.'

James nodded. 'Considering everything that's happened, I'm inclined to agree.'

Elisabeth then slapped her hips lightly and said, 'Well, that is all I had for you. I am sure these next few weeks will be both interesting and difficult in equal measure.'

'Where are they holding the treaty signing this time?' asked James.

'Catamitus Dock.'

# III.

III.

# CHAPTER EIGHTEEN
## CATAMITUS DOCK
### *12ᵗʰ April 2067*

T HE BILLOWING BLUE HAZE in the front window faded as James dropped the *Aurora* safely from FTL. The cockpit then was bathed in the welcoming glow of the gas giant beyond. It was a view that never got old, no matter how many times he saw it.

Jupiter, known since antiquity as the most majestic of the planets—huge beyond the grasp of human understanding—hung reigning in well-deserved glory as the inner solar system's staunch protector. It was impossible not to stop and admire the bands of warm colour, from the brightest scarlet to the deepest brown— the swirling, chaotic beauty of fluid dynamics in action on a mind-bending scale.

The *Aurora*'s scanner bleeped as it registered three contacts, quickly identifying them on the screen as the *Galileo*, *Newton*, and the newly refitted *Magellan*. The ships drifted into James's view, the three white hulls gleaming in the reflected sunlight, tinted with the gas giant's colour.

James opened a communications channel to the other ships. 'Here we are, people. Drink it in while you can. We're heading on to Ganymede.'

The *Aurora*'s speakers burst into life with loud rock music as April responded from the *Newton*. 'Dude! You're killing our vibe out here. I've just put on the perfect tune; we're all rockin' out.'

'No, we're not,' Lieutenant Vanson cried. He sounded in pain. Just how loud did April have it over there?

James chuckled. 'Alright, Captain, five more minutes—Wait a sec, is that Manfred Man?'

'Yes!' April cried in jubilation. 'See, I knew you being immortal was gonna be great. I bet you remember all the best bands.'

'Hey, watch it. I'm not that old.'

'Oi, you two, just shut up and enjoy the view, would you?' Erin radioed from the *Galileo* amid laughter from her crew. 'We can all hear you, you know.'

James fell silent with a smile on his face. He looked around the cockpit of the *Aurora*, taking in its familiar features, noting scuff marks and chipped controls. He stared into every crevice, determined not to overlook any detail no matter how small. It was hard to believe this would be his last flight in the ship, taking it to its official retirement. Sure, it may look a little worse for wear on the inside after two decades, but it had been well-used and, as far as he was concerned, it was still up to snuff.

Still, if there was a final sight to see in this ship he had made his own, he couldn't have picked a better one. He watched as Io, the innermost of the Galilean moons, drifted lazily across its gargantuan parent; a tiny yellowish dot, almost silhouetted against the bright clouds.

*Man, Austin… If only you could've seen this.*

He sighed and tapped the comms unit. 'Time's up, people. Everyone ready to go?'

'Born ready,' said Captain Damien Vance from the *Magellan*.

James nodded to himself, fired up the ship's main drive, and turned away from the magnificent view. He saw the others follow suit on the scanner. Together, they headed further out in the Jovian system, continuing towards Ganymede.

It was almost a year to the day since the attack on Arcadia Landing—a year since they had lost Austin; a year since Erin had lost Cheryl. In fact, the disaster had left a deep and bitter wound in the collective consciousness of society. James knew everywhere would be marking the occasion with a memorial of some kind. The treaty signing at Catamitus Dock was to act in dual purpose as that memorial and as the new facility's official opening.

The sizeable dark grey moon, Ganymede, soon came into view, its surface pockmarked with white and light brown patches all around. The moon's most prominent feature was the expansive and ancient dark region known as the Galileo Regio, which stretched across most of its surface.

It was within this region—in the moon's northern hemisphere—that Catamitus Dock resided.

As James and his wing of ships drew closer, small flecks of light could be seen glinting in the orbit of the moon, like stars disturbed by an atmosphere. The sparkles—easily mistaken for floating debris—gradually resolved themselves into a single mass: a huge metal structure so large it would have dwarfed the old International Space Station.

The huge claw-like frame was clearly still unfinished in places but featured an internal space large enough to hold a spacecraft many times the size of the *Aurora*. Along one side of the frame were the beginnings of a command centre. On top was a spin gravity ring and a cable stretched from its centre still further out, away from the moon and beyond James's sight.

'What the hell is that?' asked Damien through the comms.

'That,' said James, 'is what I was out here helping to build last year: humanity's first orbital shipyard.'

Now, as James brought the *Aurora* round, leading the others in a loop around the shipyard, the clawed frame was clearly visible. So, too, was the long line from its base leading all the way down to the moon's surface: the space elevator connecting it to the rest of the facility below.

Two pods could be seen going up and down the inside of the tether, each going separate ways, probably still delivering construction materials up to the floating promontory.

'Catamitus Dock, this is Captain James Fowler of the *Aurora* requesting permission to land.'

'One moment, Captain,' said one of the base's air-traffic controllers. After a minute or so of silence, she continued, '*IXS-17 Aurora*, permission granted. Prepare for de-orbit burn and proceed to landing pad zero-two. Welcome back, sir.'

James brought his ship in lower, heading towards his designated pad, while the others moved off to their own. The approach to the ground base was smooth and uneventful, owing to Ganymede's negligible atmosphere and gravitation.

As the *Aurora* soared over the base, the ship passed a

new addition to the dock that had not been present the last time James had been here. In fact, it hadn't been in the plans at all.

On the outer perimeter, just beyond the prefab tubular walkways and outbuildings, sat a large turreted cannon emplacement. Its thick cabling snaked across the rocky terrain directly to the building that James knew housed the base's fusion reactor.

As he studied the rest of the base out of the side window, he could see two more such emplacements. They bore a remarkable similarity to the Achelon derelict's particle cannons, but on a smaller scale. The sight gave him a chill that stirred the hairs on the back of his neck.

He reasoned the ISA must have taken Zhu's recommendations seriously following both massacres, but he wasn't aware they had successfully replicated the alien ship's weapons systems already. If that was the case, then those incredible cannons would be more than capable of vaporising any external threat. Were these to become the new standard air defences at humanity's off-world outposts?

It was clear the ISA was reacting to the public calling into question its preparedness to protect its on- and off-world staff. The UN had put heavy pressure on Elisabeth in getting things ready for the treaty signing and for her successor. They were determined another Arcadia Landing would not happen.

It was a move that puzzled James since the threats to both Arcadia and Le Guin had come from within. Perhaps they had also taken into account the damage the *Newton* had done in Kazarman? He wasn't used to not being privy to this kind of information. For all Elisabeth had said about James being 'the best' of them months ago, he felt increasingly shut out. After the treaty signing, he would no longer be a mission commander, or even a pilot, so the ISA were pulling back. It was all 'need to know' and James no longer needed to know.

James finally hovered the *Aurora* above the pad with the ship's vertical thrusters and gently lowered it until the magnetic locks clamped down with a dull thud.

As the ship's engine powered down, James unfastened his restraints and rested his head back against the seat.

Silence, broken only by the residual tinnitus from April's arrival at the Kazarman airport. At first, he'd wondered why his augmentation hadn't healed the ringing, but it was such a small thing that he'd eventually managed to train himself to ignore it.

Outside, the landscape was bleak and grey but given a slight warm tint by the eternal presence of the gas giant above. Catamitus Dock had been built on the Jupiter-facing hemisphere of this tidally locked moon so its spectacular views could serve as a morale boost for those who would spend months of their lives working out here.

The ground facility itself was reminiscent of a smaller Arcadia Landing but with the utilitarian aesthetic of Le Guin. Its modules and prefabs blended in with the landscape well.

He found himself looking around the cockpit again as though he would forget what it looked like: the now-faded 'plaid' sticker over the cover to the Austinium drive spool switch; the piece of burnt circuitry he'd glued to the left window frame to remind him of his first harrowing adventure; the photograph of him, Austin, and Angela from the project's earlier days tucked into a gap in the main screen's bezel.

The *Aurora* had taken him to nearly every major celestial body in the solar system and back over the last two decades.

He smiled. All except Uranus. That one had been left to April for the *Newton*'s first mission. Every pre-mission meeting, she brought some kind of terrible pun.

*God, she must have been insufferable on that trip.*

To his right, secured into a mesh pocket on the wall, was a clear soft pouch filled with water. Inside, a singular tiny fishlike creature swam happily around, darting to and fro.

James had named it Frank.

A kindred spirit, Frank needed little in the way of food and was seemingly immortal. A peculiar specimen from an early mission. James had been tasked to bring back a sample of subsurface water from Enceladus using a hole already drilled by a previous autonomous mission. Inside had been Frank and several others of its kind. James had handed over the specimens but had kept one for himself as a sort of cockpit companion. It was something Austin had scolded him for since no-one had known anything about the creature's biological needs at the time. James had tried a number of different fish foods to no avail but eventually had found success with instant dry yeast.

As cold as Enceladus was, Frank's species thrived in the warmer currents pushed up by deep hydrothermal vents. Enceladus was the first place in the solar system known to host extra-terrestrial microbial life and then, following James's mission, multicellular life. So far, only Frank's species had been discovered in terms of complex lifeforms, but there were theories larger creatures—perhaps Frank's predators—inhabited the deeper depths.

*You are coming with me, buddy.*

James lifted himself out of his seat awkwardly, adjusting himself to the Moonlike gravity, and shuffled around to the back of the cockpit. There, he grabbed his things from storage and placed Frank's pouch in his bag.

He gave one last forlorn look to the inside of the *Aurora*, patted the doorframe, and said, 'Thanks for all the memories,' before activating his mag-boots and disembarking into the docking bridge of Catamitus Dock.

He met the others where the docking bridges joined in front of the entrance to the arrivals lounge.

Much like Le Guin, the arrivals lounge was laid out as a large atrium with check-in desks and crewed security barriers at one end. A few rows of chairs with unfilled gaps for planters took up space in the middle of the room and the left wall held a panoramic window looking out on the starlit landscape beyond.

He hadn't spotted it from the *Aurora*, but from here James could see the chunky base of the space elevator with its mast stretching up beyond the limits of the window's field of view and into the heavens.

The solar system's small moons with their much lower gravity were the only places where such a system was viable. Ganymede was especially good, being tidally locked to Jupiter. Its rotational period was slow enough to not place a huge centrifugal strain on the elevator.

After checking in, they were escorted by security through utilitarian grey corridors to their quarters, diminutive lodgings grouped together into their own block. The crews went off to their own rooms further along the block, but the officers' quarters were next to each other.

'This place is impressive but a bit... spartan,' said Damien.

James leaned against the cool metal of his door. 'Yeah,

well, early days yet. This place isn't meant for tourists, after all, and as far as I remember, these blocks are temporary. This is eventually going to be turned into a storage area; that's what's on the blueprints. The actual residents' area is further around the central ring.'

'So the place isn't finished yet?' asked Erin.

'The important bits are,' said James. 'But this has all had to be put in extra for the ceremony. Hence these glorified storage containers for bedrooms. Let me put my stuff down and I'll give you a tour.'

'Nah, I think I'm gonna hit the hay,' said Damien. 'Thanks, though.'

'Alright. Do you know where to go for the ceremony tomorrow?'

'Yeah, I got a map on my phone. It doesn't look too complicated,' said Damien as he moved off to his room. 'Good night, all.'

Erin put her hands on her hips. 'Well, I for one am well up for a tour! You coming, April?'

'You know it,' April replied. 'Ain't missing this for the world. Lead the way, Jimmy.'

A stab of pain went through James. Austin had been the only one who had ever called him Jimmy and he hadn't realised how much he associated it with the man.

Nevertheless, he opened the door to the room and put his bag down. He took a moment to pull Frank's pouch out and placed it on the tiny desk before locking up. Inwardly he groaned at the prospect of having to come back to this little pod-room to sleep; it looked cramped and uncomfortable. It was a shame the residents' area had no rooms to spare; he knew from experience those were much nicer.

James, Erin, and April set off further into the facility, down the narrow cylindrical corridors, with James narrating the history behind the making of the place, their magnetised footsteps sucking to the floor. Many of the staff and construction crews they passed along the way walked similarly and the familiar noise faded into the general hum just as it had at Le Guin. Some staff, however, had already abandoned the use of their mag-boots and loped haphazardly along the corridors instead, often leading to the trio having to stop and move aside.

'I wonder if we'll be able to use the technology in the Austinium drive to give these places Earthlike gravity in the future?' Erin pondered aloud as she watched the latest bounding engineer fail to stop himself as he hit the door at the end of the passageway.

April shrugged. 'Maybe. Hell of a field to generate though and what would it do to the landscape?'

'It's not like there's anything out there to preserve,' said James, gesturing to the heavily cratered vista out of a small window. 'Anyway, like I was saying: the ISA wanted to build this shipyard in Arizona originally, obviously without the space elevator. Then the Moon was suggested to bring down launch costs, but ultimately they picked Ganymede, because it's the only moon in the solar system with its own magnetic field.'

April and Erin nodded approvingly and they continued.

James followed the wall signs pointing arrows towards the central plaza where tomorrow's ceremony would take place. The corridors weren't much to look at and being all very similar, it was easy to lose sense of where you were.

He looked back at the others. Erin, who had initially seemed fascinated and excited by the new facility, now looked subdued and peaky, so he dropped back to walk alongside her.

'You alright?' he asked.

Her lips tightened to a thin line and she made a lilting 'Mmm' sound and said nothing more.

The grey corridor opened out into a huge domed area with Jupiter visible high above. The two women stopped at the threshold and each let out a small gasp. It was an unfinished garden zone with small patches of synthetic grass that had already been installed and empty premises around the perimeter, excepting one small coffee shop and eatery, but the potential was undeniable. In the centre was a large stage with seating in rows out front. People milled about, clearing away construction materials and setting up lighting, sound, cameras, and more. This was to serve as both the administrative nexus of Catamitus Dock and its recreation grounds. The evolution of the Arcadia Landing project had shown the ISA the benefit of having such wide-open spaces for the morale and mental wellbeing of the facility's resident workers. After all, who wanted to spend years at a time scurrying rodent-like through narrow halls of stark grey? Le Guin didn't have a garden, but that was because it was so close to Earth that it wasn't deemed necessary. The domed zones were instead reserved for the larger-scale off-world habitats.

'Woah! This is so cool,' said April. She pointed to the sky. 'And you can see the elevator from here, too. Fuckin' rad, man.'

James laughed and followed where her finger was pointing. The space elevator was much clearer to see from here, stretching up to an infinitesimally small point.

The claw of the shipyard was too far away to resolve clearly with the naked eye, but to have Jupiter, its closer moons, and the shaft of the elevator all in the same field of view was breathtaking.

'I can get us on if you'd like?' said James, flashing his security pass. 'They gave me this when I worked on it.'

'Fuck yes,' cried April. 'Let's go!'

'It's a long trip though; a couple of hours each way.'

'Dude, I don't care! Erin, how about you? James can get us on the freakin' *space elevator.*'

'It's just like Arcadia Landing,' Erin said softly. The awestruck glint in her eyes had given way to something darker, a melancholy, and she now looked glum.

James bit his cheek and exchanged a look with April. Something was wrong. The tour was supposed to cheer them all up, but it seemed to be having the opposite effect on Erin. And if James was honest with himself, it put him out a bit. Was this not impressive enough? Immediately, he felt ashamed of himself for thinking that way. It was clear something deeper was going on.

Before he could think any further on the matter, Nate approached the three of them. He was dressed in the immaculate white uniform of the security team and carried a sidearm in a holster on his belt. The lightly armoured uniform was form-fitting, with grey and black accents down the arms and legs. The new UEC logo was visible on his chest next to one for the ISA.

He stopped before them with a smile and crossed his arms. James had wondered how well he'd take the transfer but judging by his neatly trimmed beard and fresh top fade, it had revitalised him. At least, he looked happier, more relaxed, and less unkempt than the last time James had seen him.

'It's good to see you guys here,' he said.

Nate's presence seemed to jolt Erin out of her funk and she launched forwards to give him a hug. 'Nate! Oh, it's so good to see you. How're you getting on, *cariad*?'

'Damn, bro,' said April, eyeing the man up and down. 'That suit is cold. How's security treating you?'

Nate peeled himself from Erin and said, 'Honestly, best thing that could've happened to me.'

'How so?' asked James.

'Less pressure, would you believe it? Y'know, what with Marissa being in jail now and all this new stuff on the horizon'—he gestured around the dome—'it's taken a lot off my mind. I wasn't coping. I needed the change. I wasn't happy about it at first, but it's turned out for the best.'

'Really happy for you, mate,' James said, gripping Nate's shoulder. 'At least it's looking like a brighter future for some of us.'

Nate nodded solemnly. 'I heard about the *Aurora*. I'm really sorry, James. I didn't see that coming. Not something I'd have done.'

'Yeah, well. It is what it is.'

'Listen, guys,' said Nate. 'I wanted to apologise for the way everything went down. I caused a lot of trouble and a lot of hurt.'

'You needed help,' said James. 'More than we could give at the time. With so much going on, we dropped the ball.'

Erin and April both nodded.

'Yeah, man,' April said finally. 'You might've acted like a fuckin' idiot, went off books, raved like a lunatic, and got people killed—'

'April!' James and Erin cried simultaneously.

Unperturbed, she continued, '—but you're still our bro. We're a family; Austin's crew. And we'll always be.'

'Thanks, April,' said Nate, rubbing the back of his neck.

'That's Captain Rose-Hartley to you, Private,' April said with a smirk, punching him lightly in the shoulder.

The four carried on talking and laughing for a while longer, then Nate went off to continue his security patrol. He'd explained he would be working behind the scenes, keeping things running smoothly for tomorrow's ceremony. Not that anyone expected anything to go wrong, given Sidera Silere's almost total silence over the last few months. It seemed they really had cut the head off the snake.

James then led April and Erin out of the dome's northern exit towards the terminus for the space elevator. April was positively vibrating by then and managed to get Erin to agree to give it a try. There, thanks to James's pass, they boarded an industrial-looking pod and strapped themselves in for the initial jolt of movement. There were seats enough for ten people with fold-out chairs or space for a couple of tonnes of supplies.

Erin, James, and April sat alone as the elevator accelerated upward. It maintained a constant acceleration akin to Ganymede's gravity—about a seventh of Earth's—creating an almost seamless experience as they rose higher into the sky.

Soon they unclipped their restraints and were free to move about the pod. Out of the windows, Catamitus Dock receded quickly below them. The layout of the base was clear to see in a way James hadn't been able to fully appreciate while flying over in the *Aurora*, and he could see his old ship parked on its pad, along with the *Magellan*, *Galileo*, and *Newton* further around the perimeter.

April seemed to be thoroughly enjoying herself, pointing out things on the ground and otherwise squishing her face up against the glass. Erin, however, turned away from the window and rested her head back against the seat rest and closed her eyes.

'Long way up,' said James, prodding Erin in the arm. 'Journey takes a good two and a half hours and the pod will flip over at the halfway point. Got plenty of time to talk.'

April slumped back into her seat and whistled. 'Man, I never thought in my wildest dreams I'd be riding a freakin' space elevator. How crazy is that? I mean, how does it work? Doesn't Europa fuck with the counterweight?'

James stared at Erin for a long moment. She hadn't responded and now looked completely spaced out with a wan expression. He'd have to try again later.

He sighed and turned his attention to April. 'The shipyard isn't that far out. There's no way to have a true surface-stationary orbit over Ganymede; the distance is outside of its maximum for satellites. The ISA put the shipyard at the Ganymede/Jupiter L1 Lagrange point instead, which is a bit closer and less affected by tidal forces from Europa.'

'But the counterweight is further out, right?'

James nodded. 'The counterweight is actually a captured asteroid; it was the only thing heavy enough. That was part of my job here. We strapped an Austinium drive to the thing, towed it to L1, and built downwards with carbon nanotubes, then pushed it out a bit beyond the Lagrange point.

'The plan was to disconnect the drive after the cable was connected to the base, but some clever dick worked out they could use it to counteract tidal perturbations, so it stayed. Cheaper than burning propellant on station-keeping for that amount of mass. Then, the rest of the elevator and shipyard have standard ion-stabilising thrusters to deal with the subtler forces and radiators along the length.'

'Incredible!' April went back to looking out the window in wide-eyed wonder.

They continued to rise in silence for another half an hour. A soft alarm then sounded in the pod, screens flickered on with a red seatbelt graphic, and a computerised voice warned them to strap in again.

April and James joined Erin in securing themselves down and a few minutes later, the gentle downward pull faded away as the pod stopped accelerating.

After a short moment of weightlessness, the whole pod turned about its axis with April laughing and cheering. Soon after the pod had flipped, the downward pull returned as it began to decelerate towards the shipyard. The screens turned green and then flickered off.

'That was the halfway point,' said James, taking off his seatbelt once again. 'They only flip it when there's people inside, otherwise the cargo is just secured from floor to ceiling to prevent it becoming unbalanced.'

'You sure you're feeling alright, Erin?' April asked, kneeling next to the other woman.

Erin sniffled and shook her head. 'Sorry, guys. I don't mean to be a proper downer and I know I said I was well up for the tour, but I'm not feeling right at all.'

'Do you want to talk about it?' said James. 'We're here for you.'

She looked up and stared at the opposite wall of the pod, her eyes red and damp. 'It's Cheryl. Being down there in the facility reminded me of her. It looked so much like Arcadia Landing, I couldn't stop thinking about how we'd walk around that garden whenever I went to visit her. We'd sneak kisses behind the shrubs, have date nights in the entertainment district, go to the club, and all that.'

'They sound like nice memories,' said James.

Erin nodded. 'They were, but I realised I'll never get to do that with her again and it got me all in a state.' She sighed, wiped her eyes, and leaned back. 'Y'know, we finally held a memorial for her? After Marissa's trial, I could finally say goodbye properly; get some closure. Being here, though, it reminds me of where she died and it's brought back all the pain. I can't believe it's been a whole year already.'

'Anniversaries are always gonna be hard,' said April. 'We're all feeling it. But we're all here together; we can support each other and share the fun memories of the people we've lost. Don't keep it all locked up in here'— she prodded Erin in the chest—'or you'll burst.'

Erin put her hand on April's and leaned her head on hers. April then wrapped her in a big hug and let her bury her head in the crook of her neck. Erin began to sob.

'Let it all out, babe. That's what a clutch is for.'

The sobs quickly turned to a burst of laughter barely muffled in April's neck.

'It's a *cwtsh*!' Erin cried, pulling back, and the two women then dissolved into a fit of giggles.

Erin sat up and dried her eyes once again, but this time from the tears of happiness. 'Aw, you guys are the best,' she said with a smile.

The three continued talking and laughing for the

rest of the journey up to the shipyard, sharing fond memories of Austin and Cheryl and all their adventures. Ganymede was no longer visible through the window, as its curve had shrunk beyond the confines of the upper frame. Even Jupiter itself was obscured below. All they could see were stars; it felt like they were in the middle of nowhere and the only indication they were moving at all was the gentle force of pseudo-gravity keeping them to the floor of the pod.

When the pod eventually came to a stop, the weightlessness returned and the three companions used their mag-boots to walk themselves out into the shipyard's atrium. It was much smaller and darker than the one at Catamitus Dock above their heads.

April regained all of her excitement and now Erin seemed much more eager to explore as well.

James led them out of the atrium and to the nearby viewing deck, which looked out on the giant empty claw-like cage. There were large unlit lamps just visible on all the hinged limbs. It was like an inverted celestial hand, ready to hold a spacecraft of colossal size. The long window was tilted forwards so they could lean out and look upwards at the moon above.

'One day soon, there'll be a spacecraft in that,' James said. 'Bigger than any of our ships. Elisabeth said work has already begun and they're going to announce it at the ceremony tomorrow.'

The rest of the facility was unfinished and out of bounds for visitors. Construction up here had paused and everything was locked up. So with little else to see, they boarded the elevator again and made their way back down to the surface.

The journey back dragged on and they were all tired from their long day. James had been so excited to show his friends everything, he hadn't factored in the lateness when he'd taken them up.

When they finally returned to the surface, they made their way back to their separate rooms. By this point, James was so tired he didn't bother to unpack; he just flopped straight on the bed and went to sleep.

# CHAPTER NINETEEN
## THE UNITED EARTH CONFEDERACY

EARLY THE NEXT MORNING, James stepped out of his quarters, stretching and yawning. Around the same time, the others joined him in their narrow, empty corridor.

Damien and Erin were, like James, fully dressed in their normal flight suits, but April had come out barefoot in a white crop-top with a unicorn on the front and pink shorts. James had to stifle a laugh; it was a very un-April-like design.

'How'd you guys sleep last night?' Damien asked, rubbing his neck and wincing.

Erin grinned and stuffed her hands in her pockets. 'Oh, I slept like a log. I won't lie to you; most restful sleep I've had in weeks.'

'Do you sleep on a literal stone slab at home or something?' said James, flexing his shoulders. 'I think someone nicked all the padding out of my mattress.'

A bleary-eyed April lifted her top to scratch her side, exposing a boob with a nipple piercing; Damien blushed and turned away. 'I slept on top of the covers,' she said, nonplussed. 'Gave me a bit more padding.'

'Sounds like a great idea,' said Damien, looking up to the ceiling.

April shuddered. 'Not when you sleep in the nude! Fuckin' freezing, bro. Hey, what's wrong with you, anyway?'

Damien stammered and refused to turn back around. 'Err, shouldn't you be getting dressed, Captain?'

April scoffed then and glanced at James and Erin with a smirk. They were used to this kind of thing from her.

'*Tits is tits, and I don't give no shits*,' she sang with a wagging finger. A line from a modern song was unusual for April. 'Grow up, man.'

When Damien still refused to look at her, she continued with a groan, 'But, if it's making you feel uncomfortable, I'll get my flight suit.'

April then turned around, whipped off the crop-top, and strolled half-naked back to her room, grumbling about having to get dressed before breakfast.

'She is extraordinarily comfortable in her own skin, isn't she?' said Damien, finally relaxing.

Erin giggled.

'If only we could all be so carefree,' said James. He slapped Damien's arm and looked at Erin. 'Come on, let's get some grub. She'll know where we've gone.'

A couple of hours passed and a call went out for a final rehearsal for the ceremony, of which James was a part. The group accompanied James into the domed garden and behind the stage, where things were still being made ready.

April juggled a length of navy-blue fabric in her hands, pulling, tugging, wrapping, turning, and tying. She'd had to bat James's hand away several times already, but the ordeal was finally over.

James's neck-tie looked neat and tidy at last.

She stepped back to admire her work and smiled as she received a light smattering of applause from Erin and Damien.

'Honestly, dude,' she said with a wry smile, 'nearly eighty-three years old and you can't tie a tie properly? Angie always do this for you?'

'Thanks, April,' said James, trying not to injure himself from the irony while craning to look into a window behind her.

April herself wore her normal patch-covered flight suit and had made no effort whatsoever to dress formally for the upcoming occasion. At first, James had thought she would go back to her room to change again, but when he'd asked, she'd merely looked at him askance.

Of course she wouldn't.

Though, he did notice she had refreshed the dye in her hair and put in some new studs, which were more ornate than her usual.

What she'd said wasn't quite true, either; James did know how to tie a tie, but they always came out looking wonky—it was a fact of life he'd learned to accept. In all their years, Angela had never said a word about his inability to tie a tie well either.

This time, however, James had to admit he'd done a worse job than usual. He blamed it on the gravity on Ganymede being a seventh of Earth's.

April had spotted the mess immediately though and

taken it upon herself to make adjustments. He had no idea what she'd done, but it now sat perfectly straight and symmetrical, secured down onto his blue RAF dress uniform.

Damien and Erin had already changed into their smart clothes. The former wore an impeccably tailored US Navy full dress blue uniform with gold accoutrements and a bright white hat. Erin's was similarly exemplary but in the form of a khaki British Army number two service uniform.

'Good luck with the rehearsal, *bach*,' said Erin, stepping up and giving James a hug. 'We're gonna have a wander before the ceremony and show Damien about a bit. Won't be going back up the elevator though!'

James heard his name being called from the other side of the thick, claret curtain, the shrill voice of the emcee echoing across the stage. He waved off his fellow captains and watched them go as April threaded her arm into Damien's and started excitedly pointing at things.

He chuckled and shook his head then turned his attention to the voice behind the big curtain. Despite squawking at people all morning, telling them where to stand, what to say, and how to say it, the emcee's voice still hadn't given out. A blessing in disguise, really, since the urgency of it had kept the rehearsal moving along smoothly thus far.

The moment James pushed the curtain aside and stepped out onto the stage, he was grabbed by the arm and hurried into position opposite another, taller man. This was the man who would take over from Elisabeth as administrator of the ISA. Slim, balding, with a thin pencil moustache and round glasses in front of keen eyes, Dr Robert Stimpson carried himself with an air of dignity, standing ramrod straight with his hands behind his back. His suit was non-military but formal and the impression he gave was of an old Victorian schoolmaster.

However, the man gave James a sympathetic look and rolled his eyes at the emcee who had manhandled him.

The emcee, a shorter man, needed no introduction: renowned showman, presenter, and television personality, Erik Ivory. James had never been one for following celebrities, but it was well known Mr Ivory was an eccentric and a fusspot in the world of show-business. He was a stout man with a slightly orange complexion and wild hair, immaculately dressed in his classic red tuxedo with gold trim. He wore thick-rimmed glasses at the tip of his nose, which James thought was so he could look up through them at everyone while screeching his directions.

As Mr Ivory moved off, James took a moment to look around the large, semi-circular stage on which he stood just off-centre. The flooring had a wood effect to it but was clearly metal to accommodate standard mag-boots. The now fully constructed auditorium was lit by several high spotlights, which were beating down with an oppressive heat. Front and centre on the stage was a lectern with multiple microphones attached and beyond were the rows of seating he had seen before. This time, there were television cameras between some of the rows.

To the other side, above the curtain, was a wide banner that read, 'A United Earth for a Better Future'.

'It's nice to finally meet you, Captain,' said Robert; he had the posh RP English accent to match his looks. 'I've been following your career with great interest.'

'And I yours, Doctor,' James replied, shaking the man's hand. 'Astounding work negotiating this treaty.'

Robert gave a slight courteous bow of the head and said, 'Finally, someone in the ISA who appreciates this incorporation. I spoke to Captain Pritchard earlier this morning in the mess hall. She seemed… suspicious of it.'

'I think we're all a little apprehensive,' said James. 'And Erin's got a lot on her plate right now. Besides, she's not the most politically-minded.'

'Well, I hope I can assuage your collective apprehension. The ISA will always primarily be about science and exploration. But as we push further out, we do need to ensure we can defend ourselves, both from without and within. Surely, you of all people could appreciate that.'

A sharp clap came from Mr Ivory, which made James jump. 'Captain Fowler, come over here, please.'

'We can debate it later if you prefer,' said Robert.

'I do have some concerns I'd love to pick your brain about,' James replied. 'I mean, I understand the need for extra security since Arcadia Land—'

'Enough. That is enough idle chitchat,' said Mr Ivory, his voice piercing. 'You are disrupting the flow of the rehearsal. Remember, you may be rubbing a lot of elbows, but this is not a meet-and-greet; it is a momentous occasion of solemn reverence. Now get over here before I drag you over here.'

James rolled his eyes and marched over to the side of the stage where Mr Ivory stood pointing to the floor.

The emcee twirled his finger. 'Turn around, good. Stand up straight,' he said, trilling his r's excessively. 'Now, walk over to the administrator.'

'What?'

'You heard me, Captain. Walk. Left, right, left, right.'

Bristling, James made his way back across the stage

towards Robert. About halfway, he was grabbed and pulled back roughly.

'No, no, no. Precisely four steps, please. And make sure to start on your left foot. I know you military-types aren't known for your brains, but try to think of this as a sort of dance and me as your choreographer!'

James growled quietly to himself and tried to brush off the remark. He repeated his steps, this time making it across in the requisite four. He stood still, frozen in place before the soon-to-be administrator, daring not to make even the slightest of movements. Mr Ivory seemed as though he could smell fear.

'Shake hands, please. And loosen up, Captain. You're receiving a commendation for your years of service and bidding a sweet adieu to the *Aurora*, not facing court-martial.'

James and Robert shook hands once again, this time with a much stiffer movement, but it was evidently acceptable enough.

'Robert,' Mr Ivory said, orbiting them both. 'Now is the part where you pick up the medal. No, with your left hand. Left. Yes, that one. Pin it to the captain's left breast. Oh god, *his left*, you imbecile! Haven't you ever given a medal before?'

'No, I cannot say I have had the pleasure,' Robert said, his voice dripping with condescension.

He tried again, this time with James struggling to contain laughter. They both got through the ordeal; James then stood to attention and saluted Dr Stimpson, who made his best attempt to do likewise and immediately drew the ire of the presenter.

'Robert, at least try to look like you've been in the

military before,' Mr Ivory implored him. 'Captain Fowler's salute is tight, swift, accurate. Your arms have all the grace of an orangutan trying to fling a turd.'

Half an hour later, they were done. James stared up through the dome at the starry sky from a park bench far from the stage, on the outskirts of what would eventually become a green space.

Mr Ivory had made him and Dr Stimpson practice their routine four times. In truth, they had done it perfectly the second time, for fear of being berated some more, but the presenter had remained unconvinced. He insisted on the extra attempts to make absolutely certain they wouldn't forget the steps to his self-styled dance by the time of the ceremony in the evening. The brief respite of the park bench was very welcome. His gaze fell from the ever-present gas giant above to the edge of the dome, where he could still see the *Aurora* sitting on its landing pad.

He then lowered his head, fiddled with his hands, and bounced his leg. Nothing lasts forever.

*Except for me.*

A light tap on the arm brought him from his reverie as Robert sat down next to him, holding two takeaway cups.

He handed one to James, who responded with a confused expression. An earthy aroma drifted up through the opening in the lid, rich and enticing.

'Coffee,' said Robert. 'Looked like you could use one.'

'Oh, thanks,' said James before taking a sip. It was a hot latte and he could taste the cocoa powder sprinkled on the top. He thought he detected a hint of caramel, too. It wasn't usually James's drink of choice, but it hit the right spot. 'Where'd you get this?'

'There's a shop on the far side of the dome called Joybringer Café or some such, in which they have some rather ludicrous names for the drinks and their sizes.'

James examined the side of the cup. Sizes were printed in a list with checkboxes next to them. 'Gany-Medium?' he said through a chuckle, then gave a deadpan 'Wow'.

Robert snorted. 'Yes, and mine is "Catami-Tall". I've never heard the like.'

The two remained in silence for a long moment, drinking their beverages and staring up through the dome.

'So,' Robert said, placing his now-empty cup down on the floor next to the bench. 'You had some concerns?'

James took another sip of his warming latte. 'Yep. Militarisation concerns me, Doctor. It is a concern to all of us in Captain Queen's troupe. Austin himself hated the idea and April proved out his worries with her stunt in Kyrgyzstan. The Austinium drive is a potentially deadly weapon. In the wrong hands—'

'And you feel military hands are the wrong hands.'

'Bingo,' said James.

'I don't see how military hands could be any worse than what we have right now. The ISA has a great many spacecraft equipped with the Austinium drive already. Any one of them has the potential to cause a world-ending catastrophe if one of our pilots were to go rogue. Captain Rose-Hartley also "proved out" that concern, to use your own words.'

James remained silent. The man had a point and his knowing smile said he had James over a barrel.

Robert continued, 'Militarisation means greater discipline and tighter control over this dangerous technology. And the necessity for such control will only grow as the scale of our ventures expands. If our forthcoming project is successful, we will be branching out into interstellar space. What, then, would you propose a ship full of scientists, untrained and unprepared for combat, should do in the event it comes across an Achelon warship?'

'Space is big, Doctor—'

'Yes, remarkably so,' said Robert, shifting to better face James on the bench. 'So remarkably huge, in fact, we will probably never encounter another spacecraft in a million years. And yet, there is one half-buried in the surface of Mars right now, just one planet from our home. And of all the myriad extraterrestrial intelligences that may be out there in this improbably vast universe, the first ones we happened to encounter were hostile zealots with enough firepower to blink us out of existence. Yes, space is big, Captain. But it is a very small world.'

James stared at him for a long moment. It was a good argument and there was no denying this guy was eloquent and knew his stuff. 'That may be true, but I wouldn't want to risk being driven into open conflict with whoever we find out there. We're clearly a young species in terms of our space-faring capabilities. I don't think it would go very well for us if we were the aggressors.'

Robert nodded sagely and linked his hands together. 'Defence is a far cry from aggression, Captain, especially when one involves personnel trained to make credible threat assessments.' He stopped and considered his words. 'If I may be so bold… Could it be that your close relationship to the late Captain Queen is influencing your judgement on these matters?'

'Austin's distrust of the military was no secret,' said James.

The two continued discussing and debating the whys

and wherefores on the park bench until lunch time, at which point Dr Stimpson left to attend to other matters.

Left with much to consider, James meandered through the unfinished parkland in the direction of the mess hall. He met with April, Erin, and Damien once more and they sat together to eat. He told them all about his part of the rehearsal and the subsequent discussion with the new administrator.

'I dunno, seems like an old fossil to me,' April said between bites of her sandwich. 'Definitely towing the same line as Schreiber. Austin wouldn't have stood for it.'

Erin shrugged. 'I won't lie to you; I couldn't care less. As long as I get to keep pootling around in the *Gal*, that's fine by me.'

'Well, I, for one, see the wisdom in his words,' said Damien, pushing his tray aside and leaning forwards onto the mess table. 'But I understand the concerns. We're not Sidera Silere and we have to guard against adopting their dark forest mentality.'

James grunted in agreement as he finished his lunch. The administrator's words had affected him more than he cared to admit. Perhaps his ability to see the bigger picture had been clouded by his loyalty to Austin.

He then heard his name being called and turned to see a member of the communications team marching towards him.

'Captain Fowler, you've received an urgent transmission from Earth, sir,' said the man, giving an awkward salute.

James waved him down. 'There's no need for all that nonsense, mate. But are you sure it's for me? I'm not expecting any long-range messages, especially not with all the ISA staff here already.'

'Definitely for you, sir. It's your wife.'

The man's remark took him off-guard. How would Angela contact him out here? It's not something she could do from home; it would require a powerful transmitter of the kind only available at the ISA headquarters.

Erin glanced back and forth between James and the communications officer, utterly perplexed.

'Alright,' said James, lifting his hands. 'I have no idea how Ange got access to a long-range transmitter, but I'll take a look. Lead the way, mate.'

As he got up to go with the communications officer, Erin touched his hand. 'Keep us in the loop, won't you?'

'I will.' He glanced down at his lunch tray.

'I'll clear it, don't worry about it,' said Damien. 'Go see what she wants.'

James bade farewell to the others and followed the man across the dome to the southern exit where the comms tower was located. It was a familiar location to him, as he'd received regular work updates here. It was here, too, sitting in one of the cubicles, he'd last heard Austin's voice, telling him all about his arrival at Arcadia Landing. The delay-time had been significant and there had been a lot of work to do, so James hadn't felt the need to make a response.

He wished he had.

The communications officer left him alone in one of the booths. He could have had his pick of any of them since most were unoccupied, but he chose the one closest to the door anyway. After shutting the curtain behind him, he started up the machine and retrieved the enigmatic message.

Angela's face shone brightly on the screen. The

background answered his first question: she was definitely at the ISA headquarters. As for what she wanted to convey, her voice had a worrying urgency to it and she spoke as though she'd run all the way there.

'James, oh god, I hope you get this message. I think I'm onto something big. Remember I told you how I got hold of that picture of Marissa with Ilona? Well, the person who provided the whole set of images reached out to me again late yesterday. They wanted to know if I'd found them helpful or if anything had come of it at all since they'd seen the trial and the image wasn't part of the presented evidence.'

James paused the recording; his heart raced. A random person whom she had met on the deep web was now reaching out to her? Not only that, but someone with some kind of connection to Sidera Silere. Someone whose motivations and intentions were impossible to know. His mind raced through all the possibilities: was she in danger? Had something happened to her and she'd just managed to get away? He almost didn't want to hear it.

Tentatively, he let the recording continue.

'I replied to them to say the images hadn't been used because the same information came to us through other means,' Angela said, gesticulating wildly. 'They then asked if I'd checked the date stamp in the image's preserved metadata, which, of course like a complete chump, I hadn't!

'But, James, I should have done. It would have blown this case wide open. How stupid was I? The date the picture was taken—the date Ilona met with Marissa in that little café in the Budapest town centre—is smack-dab in the middle of when you were chasing down Son of Adam on the fucking Moon!'

'What!' James cried. He stood up so quickly he bashed his head on the ceiling of the booth. 'Ow, Jesus.'

He paused the recording again while he rubbed the top of his head and sucked in his breath.

*How the fuck could we have missed something like that?*

Maybe he was getting old. It was understandable Angela might miss such a crucial detail. After all, technology had moved on so quickly, and though she had always been good with computers, some of the subtler changes had proved difficult for her to adapt to. But him? He should have known better. He was basically trapped in his early forties, mind and all. He should have adapted better.

The implications of that little date in the metadata were huge. If Marissa had met with Ilona during the Le Guin massacre, then that meant she couldn't possibly be Son of Adam. It had all been a subterfuge. All to throw them off the scent of a perhaps deeper plan the real Son of Adam had for Sidera Silere.

He sat down and resumed the recording.

'She can't possibly be Son of Adam!' Angela cried. 'You were right. You said you recognised the real Son of Adam's voice, that the real one was augmented like you, and that Colonel Zhu knew who it was. And now, with the ballistics report on the pistol used on the Moon in the mix, it absolutely has to be someone connected to Project Augment. Marissa is a red herring.'

'Excuse me, Mrs Fowler,' said another voice from behind Angela. 'What are you doing here?'

She turned around. 'I—I'm sending a message. It's important.'

'Civilians aren't allowed in here. Please come out.'

Angela then turned around and hissed into the microphone, 'The real Son of Adam is still out there, James. Whatever he's got planned, I'll bet it's to do with the treaty signing again. Watch yourself. I love you.'

Then the recording ended.

*Shit, I need to get to Elisabeth.*

James leaped to his feet again and bolted from the booth. The next thing he knew, his vision swam and his body jerked unbidden. The feeling was familiar. He slumped forwards as his whole body cramped and he was caught in the arms of the communications officer whom he had followed. What was he doing outside the booth? Then he was thrown off the man and flopped to the floor, his limbs twitching. As his vision gradually cleared, he saw the man putting a TASER back in its belt holster.

'I'd hoped it wouldn't come to this, but I heard every word of your wife's message, Captain, and I couldn't just let you go ahead and ruin our plans.'

James's faculties returned to him quickly, more quickly than his attacker expected, and he lunged, bowling the man over.

They wrestled with one another on the floor of the cramped communications centre corridor. But James's superior strength won out.

He lifted the man up by the scruff of his neck and punched him in the face. The man stumbled back into the booth and slumped to the floor, unconscious.

James shook away the residual dizziness and leaned back against the wall to centre himself.

*Fuck me, they really* are *everywhere. Now, Elisabeth. Better warn the others, too.*

James stumbled out of the communications centre and,

finding his feet again, bolted back into the domed garden.

He raised Erin on his earpiece and said, 'Erin, we have a situation. I want you and the others to meet me at the UN administration buildings. I need to speak to Elisabeth.'

'That doesn't sound good. What's happened?'

'I'll tell you in a bit. Just meet me there.'

Before long, he was outside the UN building at the eastern edge of the dome. He burst through the door and called out for Elisabeth.

The administrator popped her head out of her temporary office just as Erin, April, and Damien appeared in the doorway behind James.

'We need to stop the treaty signing,' said James, gesturing vaguely to the door. 'Son of Adam is still out there.'

From behind Elisabeth stepped Secretary-General Masahiro. 'What is the meaning of this?' he said.

'Secretary-General,' James said, running his hand through his sweat-soaked hair and advancing cautiously. 'I have reason to believe Son of Adam is still on the loose and presents a threat to today's ceremony.'

'How'd you figure this out?' April asked.

James proceeded to tell them all about the message from Angela and the attack by the communications officer.

'No.'

James did a double-take. Masahiro stood ramrod straight, his arms crossed, jaw set into a hard expression with a piercing gaze.

'We cannot stop the treaty signing,' he continued. 'Come what may, it must happen today. If I move to postpone it again, it will spell the end of the dream of the United Earth Confederacy. The other member states will simply not have it.'

Elisabeth's face had drained of all colour and she stammered, 'But, Mr Masahiro, if what Captain Fowler says is true and we have prosecuted the wrong person as Son of Adam, then continuing with the ceremony as-is would be foolish.'

'I agree,' said the secretary-general. 'We must tighten security and instruct them to be extra vigilant. I will not let these terrorists dictate our actions. I will not shrink back in fear again. There can be no repeat of Arcadia Landing. Catamitus Dock is where we draw the line.'

And so, later that afternoon, the ceremony began right on time with Erik Ivory's squawking-but-dignified tone. The portion of the ceremony involving the treaty signing seemed to go by in no time at all and with no incident. There was an air of caution covering the proceedings and an anxiety to the very atmosphere that had everybody in the audience on edge. Extra security had been brought in. At the secretary-general's order, armed guards had been placed along the sides of the seating area and flanked the table on the stage on which the treaty document sat.

In the audience sat first the dignitaries and their support staff and then, further back, specially invited journalists and high-ranking ISA staff members, including James, Erin, April, and Damien.

Secretary-General Masahiro gave a short and furtive opening speech. Despite his bravado in the UN building earlier, it was clear he was nervous. The other UN ambassadors and world leaders filed up from the front row onto the stage. They signed the document and stood for a few minutes to pose for photographs.

The document was hurried away backstage and the dignitaries returned to their seats.

The mood shifted in the room at that moment, the oppressive atmosphere dissipating like mist in the morning sun. What had been a nervous silence morphed into an excitable chatter. The worst was over. But James couldn't relax yet.

Mr Masahiro returned to the lectern with a look of relief and wiped sweat from his brow. He then straightened his tie and grunted, casting an irritated glance directly at James.

'I apologise for having the treaty signing truncated like this,' he said with a slight bow to the audience. 'Some concerns arose before the ceremony and we felt it prudent to increase our security presence and keep the signing short. I am glad it seems our fears were unfounded.

'And so, I welcome you all into this bright new future that we have ratified before you today, here, in the shadow of one of humanity's greatest engineering achievements. A shining monument to what we can achieve when we work together as one people. With our new international ties, we will forge ahead into a better tomorrow. Thank you.'

The secretary-general smiled and waved to the audience. There was thunderous applause and a standing ovation. As he stepped back from the lectern and marched off backstage, the orchestra that sat to one side began to play. It was, appropriately, a rendition of the first three movements of Holst's *The Planets* suite.

James gave a nervous glance to Erin and April, who shared his confusion. They had believed him unquestioningly and trusted Angela's word. Erin in particular was convinced by the new evidence placing Marissa in Budapest when Son of Adam had been on the Moon. But no threat from Sidera Silere had materialised. For whatever reason, they had allowed the UEC treaty to be signed. And aside from James's attacker in the communications centre, who had been arrested and taken into custody by the security team, there was no sign of any further mischief.

Near to the end of the musical interlude, James stood and made his way backstage. There, he met with Dr Robert Stimpson. As they had practiced, he would be inducted as the new head of the ISA and his first act would be to commend James and officially decommission the *Aurora* with a tribute to Austin.

The music ended with a light smattering of applause. James heard Mr Ivory return to the stage, his footsteps clanking on the magnetised stage floor. The eccentric presenter announced the next portion of the proceedings.

James and Robert walked together onto the stage and performed their movements flawlessly. Elisabeth came up on stage for Dr Stimpson's induction and made a short speech reflecting on her tenure, ending with a ringing endorsement of her successor.

A short moment later, as James shook the new administrator's hand, his ISA Exceptional Service Medal pinned to his uniform, Robert muttered, 'I can't see anything out there, can you?'

James grinned and looked out across the audience through the intense glare of the spotlights. 'No,' he said through his teeth. 'Nothing.'

'I appreciate you raising the alarm, Captain, but it seems you were wrong on this occasion.'

'I hope so, Administrator.'

James then moved away to one side while the administrator officially announced the *Aurora*'s decommission.

The giant screens to each side of the stage lit up with a series of photographs of Captain Queen. Another short speech exalted him as the genius inventor of the Austinium drive as well as the driving force behind the creation of the *Aurora* and its sisters.

James imagined the old man turning beet-red under his beard at the implication and sputtering to give equal credit to the various teams he'd worked with over the years. The drive may forever bear his name, but he'd never considered himself its true creator.

'Congratulations, James,' Erin said, squeezing his arm as he returned to his seat in the audience.

'Yeah, well deserved, dude,' said April, turning to the side and propping her foot up on the seat. 'Beautiful tribute to the old man, too, isn't it?'

James nodded and relaxed back in his seat. Still no sign of Sidera Silere. Perhaps his defeat of the communications imposter had scared them off?

'So what happens now?' asked April, reaching across Erin and jabbing him in the shoulder. '*Aurora*'s off the board, so what they got you doing after this?'

'Teaching,' he said, a little less enthusiastically than he'd intended. In truth, he hadn't given much thought to what Elisabeth had said. There was so much going on it was better to take everything one step at a time. Besides, he didn't know how he felt about the prospect of instructing full-time; he hadn't done it since Nate had taken over the *Magellan*.

'Teaching again?' said April, giving him an impressed

look. 'Nice one, Jimmy. You're well good at it.'

The irony.

James chuckled. 'Call me "instructor".'

# CHAPTER TWENTY
## THE SELIDOR

NATE'S HEART ACHED AT THE TRIBUTE to Austin and he agreed with every word. He sniffled and lifted the visor of his helmet to wipe the tears from his eyes. It was no time to get emotional. He needed to keep an eye on the proceedings. Through the grapevine he'd learned James had raised concerns about some kind of potential threat from Sidera Silere, which would be why Nate now stood in full combat gear at the far corner of the seating area for the ceremony.

Nothing yet, but he was struggling to remain vigilant.

He flexed his fingers on the grip of his submachine gun; it was a familiar weapon, the same model he'd used in Kazarman: the VAS-67 bullpup. Visions flashed in his mind of that experience: watching Specialist Lando gunned down; Alinour bleeding out, taking his last breath in agony and amidst failure; tankers exploding; everything on fire.

It was all too much. He'd thought he was over this, thought he'd managed to make a better pace of life out of his punishment. But Austin's tribute had made him vulnerable and combined with the feeling of the gun in his hand brought it all flooding back.

*Why did it have to be this particular gun?*

He shook himself to clear away some of the visions; cobwebs he called them. It was apparent to him he was no longer in a fit state to monitor what was going on and there was no telling how he would react if Captain Fowler's portent of doom came true.

He tapped his earpiece. 'Sergeant, it's Private Rifkin. I'm gonna need to take a breather, sir.'

'The visions?'

'Yeah. We wondered if this might happen.'

'Okay. Take care of yourself, son. Have five in the break room.'

'Thank you, sir.'

His new security squad had been good to him. Almost everyone was his superior since he'd been busted down, but they all understood the need for good mental well-being and had supported him the whole way.

The ISA had provided counselling, which had helped somewhat, but there was still a long way to go. Being part of an understanding group was the biggest help of all. Almost all of them had had their fair share of traumatic experiences during their service.

Nate removed himself from his position and was quickly replaced by another private, who tapped him on the shoulder and gave him a thumbs-up as he passed.

The break room was bare; white walls, white ceilings, strip lights, a table, and some fold-out chairs. Some of the other security team members were already here, waiting to be called upon. Some weren't members of Nate's squad, but they all got along well enough, even if they weren't quite so understanding.

There was a single small screen on the wall broadcasting the ceremony live as the newscasters portrayed it.

'Hey, Rifkin,' said one of the other guards as Nate removed his helmet and scratched his head. The man sat with his boots up on the break room table facing away from Nate, watching the show and chewing gum. His skin was a deep tan and his brown hair slightly longer and spiked with pomade. He idly held up his right hand balled into a fist.

Nate stowed his weapon and bumped the man's fist with his own. 'Hey, Rodriguez. Enjoying the show?'

'Yeah, man, great stuff so far. Pull up a chair. You want a brownie?'

The chair next to Rodriguez scraped loudly as Nate pulled it out. 'No, thank you,' he replied. 'Gotta watch my figure, y'know?'

Rodriguez barked a laugh and turned his head to look sidelong at him with a shit-eating grin. 'You sure? More for me, then. Well, we've all had one. Actually, I don't think there's any left, come to think of it.'

'Oh, all y'all? Shit, I really missed out, then. Where'd they come from?'

Rodriguez shrugged and coughed. 'Kitchen, I guess. We're working extra hard and they're furnishing us with snacks.'

Nate sat down, closed his eyes, and laid his head back. He inhaled slowly, holding his breath a second, then exhaled, repeating this until he felt a bit less tense. It had been a long day and he'd come overtired as well, which probably wasn't helping.

* * *

Austin's image faded from the screens and the orchestra swelled once again, playing the opening bars of *The Planets'* fourth movement, *Jupiter*.

James closed his eyes and listened, allowing the music to wash over him. It was the most familiar movement of the suite to him—a firm favourite of his father's. That and Jeff Wayne's *The War of the Worlds*. He'd always put something on while they watched the stars together.

*The chances of anything man-like on Mars… Funny.*

The orchestra brought the section to a close and the audience expressed their polite appreciation.

Mr Ivory pranced back onto the stage and said, 'And now, my friends, we come to the official opening of this grand facility in which you are seated. I am told that for some time now, the inner factory workings have been complete and work has begun in earnest on the shipyard's first project.' He gave an exaggerated shrug and added, 'Clearly that was more important than tending to the amenities.'

This received a few chuckles from the dignitaries in the front row.

Mr Ivory grinned and pointed to a few of the people there. 'Yeah, you know what I mean. Anyway, may I please welcome Dr Robert Stimpson back to the stage, who will take us through this exciting announcement.'

The new administrator stepped up to the lectern and leaned over the microphones. 'Catamitus Dock

362

represents the frontier of human achievement. It is the most distant facility we have and, as I'm sure you'll agree, the view above is positively alien. This moon, one of the largest in the solar system, has allowed us to realise a concept that the esteemed rocket scientist Konstantin Tsiolkovsky thought up while considering the Eiffel Tower almost two hundred years ago. That is, the space elevator you see outside this dome.'

Two assistants marched onto the stage carrying two brass posts, between which was suspended a short, bright red ribbon. They put the posts down in full view of the audience, a few feet from where Robert stood, the ribbon held taut.

Robert picked up a large pair of orange-handled scissors from the lectern and held them up.

He continued, 'It is truly astounding how far we've come in just a few short decades and it is my pleasure to officially announce Catamitus Dock is now open.'

With a single, swift cut, the ribbon separated down the middle and the audience erupted in applause.

Robert motioned for calm and then resumed his speech. 'As our distinguished presenter has teased, we have a further announcement to make. Ever since the ISA became aware of the incredible potential of the Austinium drive, we have striven towards making it usable for interstellar travel. And for the last ten years, we have been hard at work designing a new generation of spacecraft to realise that potential. I am, therefore, excited to announce that engineering work on our newest spacecraft began on the second of March this year. Behold, your first look at the *ISF Selidor*.'

The screens either side of the stage lit up once again,

this time with rendered concept images of the proposed new spacecraft.

An energetic chatter arose from the crowd, turning the atmosphere electric.

By the scale, it was at least as long as the *Magnum Opus* but a lot sturdier. It had two retractable spin gravity pods at the mid-section, with spherical supply tanks fore and aft. Radiators extended between the large rear engines and the cockpit—or, rather, 'bridge', for it was so large—was buried deep within the ship's front end. Everything was kept close to the centre to reduce its cross-section. The main body of the craft was covered in a sort of angular composite armour.

James recognised the material from the ISA's research on the *Bitter Authoritarian*. The derelict's armour had the benefit of being inordinately light, strong, and good at absorbing radiation. It seemed the Arcadia Landing R&D teams had managed to reverse-engineer it before the attack.

Definitely the kind of ship that would fit inside the orbital claw at the top of the elevator.

The administrator waited for the chatter in the audience to quieten down. 'I now invite Captain Olivia Burton, mission commander for the *Selidor*, to give you some more information about the new ship and its proposed mission.'

A young woman got up onto the stage amid polite applause and took Robert's place at the lectern. She was much shorter than the administrator and almost disappeared behind the bevy of microphones. Her hair was a light brown bob and she had pale skin and round features.

'Thank you, Dr Stimpson,' she said, her voice deep and mid-western. 'The *ISF Selidor* will be the first in a new line of Jupiter-class starships. Utilising all the advantages Catamitus Dock affords, we expect her to be mission-ready by 2072. That means, in just five short years, humanity will be an interstellar civilisation.

'The *Selidor*'s mission—hopefully the first of many—will be to visit and survey the Alpha Centauri trinary system, the journey towards which, with the ship's updated Austinium drive, is projected to take six months.

'This may be a purely scientific mission, but we will not be going unprepared. The *Selidor* will be equipped with four CIWS point defence turrets, two smart missile tubes, and a particle beam cannon, all powered by the ship's fusion core and all fully retractable within the frame.'

*Science? It sounds more like they're going for war.*

Captain Burton continued, 'We already know Proxima Centauri plays host to at least one rocky exoplanet. The ship itself is not rated for atmospheric flight, but that is why we're planning to house a small landing craft in the rear payload bay. And of course the starship has all expected safety features, redundancies, and escape systems. With our crew so far from home, we cannot skimp on safety.

'After the ceremony, the ISA is opening applications for key personnel positions for the mission and, sometime next year, for support staff. So, if you want in on the adventure of a lifetime, get to writing those applications, people!'

Captain Burton then thanked the crowd and walked off-stage to a standing ovation, the biggest yet. The dignitaries in the front row remained seated, clapping politely, but the ISA staff behind cheered and whooped and hollered.

James couldn't deny it was an exciting prospect, though one he had no chance of taking part in. His fate was already decided. It was a bittersweet feeling; on the one hand he was infused with a nervous energy and a renewed optimism, but on the other, there was a deep and pervading envy. It was a shame that in order for the *Selidor* to get its wings, he had to surrender the *Aurora*'s.

It was then, amid the clamour, he noticed the security officers coughing. All of them.

* * *

Rodriguez cleared his throat twice, then got up to grab a drink of water from the other room. There was a sink in there. All the tap water on the base was drinkable. It didn't make sense not to be. It all came from big storage tanks and the base's wastewater reclamation plant wasn't operational just yet.

Two others in the room started to cough, too, then a third. By the time Rodriguez came back with an empty cup, he was having a coughing fit.

'You guys alright?' asked Nate, opening one bleary eye.

'Yeah, yeah, fine. Just a tickle in the throat,' Rodriguez said, coughing even harder. 'Does seem to be getting worse though. Must be the dry air.'

Nate made a face. The air wasn't that dry.

Then Rodriguez began to wheeze and turn red. Nate shot out of his chair to help the man. He was struggling to breathe and gesticulated and pointed at his throat.

Nate tapped his comms. 'Medic! We need a medic to the break room. Rodriguez is choking. Looks like his airway's closed up.'

No response.

*What the fuck is going on?*

The other three guards in the room then started wheezing, too, holding their throats and doubling over.

A short moment later, Rodriguez stopped making noise and fell to the floor.

Nate bent down to check him. No breathing.

He put his fingers to the side of the man's throat. No pulse. At that moment, the others keeled over as well and became still.

'Shit!' Nate cried as he rolled Rodriguez over onto his back and started chest compressions. Into the comms he shouted, 'Help! Medic! Medic to the break room! Rodriguez has stopped breathing; I can't feel a pulse!'

Still no answer.

After a long moment, Nate stopped the compressions. No one was coming. If he left to get help, Rodriguez would certainly die, if he wasn't dead already.

He checked again for a pulse but found none. Then he moved over to the others in the room.

All dead.

Nate stood, hyperventilating, his mouth parched and his heart hammering in his chest.

Could this be Sidera Silere?

*I have to find James.*

* * *

After a few minutes, Erik Ivory returned to the stage. People sat down in dribs and drabs as they finished clapping until only one man remained.

He stood in the middle of the crowd, some ways ahead

of James and the others, clapping slowly and deliberately with a condescending rhythm.

Even from the back James could see the man's head was covered in a black fabric and he was dressed in a smart suit with a deep grey blazer.

The presenter glared from the front with his hands on his hips before raising a finger and opening his mouth.

He faltered, however, as the man began to chuckle and shake. His voice grew louder—almost maniacal—and his movements erratic, but still he continued to clap.

Then, he stopped.

As he did so, the security officers around the perimeter collapsed to the floor one by one, choking and wheezing until they all lay still.

A frisson of fear ran visibly through the audience like a wave and worried, high-pitched murmurs arose.

With the voice that James had recognised all the way back at Le Guin Base, the man boomed across the auditorium.

'Well done. Well done indeed. What a marvellous achievement. You are all, here and now, complicit in the downfall of humanity and yet you cheer it.'

The man turned around, revealing a glowing green grotesque on his black mask, and continued, 'The irony would be amusing if it wasn't so tragic.'

*Son of Adam!*

'You can play here all you want,' the terrorist leader continued, 'making alliances and grand plans, impotent declarations of a brighter future. But here I am to remind you that you are not in control. Not in the slightest. You ignored the messages of Arcadia Landing and Le Guin, instead opting for this trite gesture of commemoration, and went ahead constructing great beacons to the gods, inviting a wrath that will consume us all.'

Alarms began to sound across the dome and Son of Adam raised his hands.

'If this is the path humanity chooses for itself, then so be it. I wash my hands of it. In fact, I will give you a helping hand. Arise, my brothers and sisters!'

At his word, a multitude of people from the audience donned masks of their own and stood in unison, creating a panic.

Son of Adam turned to the stage where Erik Ivory held a phone to his ear. Without hesitation, the masked man pulled a pistol from his suit blazer and fired a single shot, which rang out and reverberated around the dome.

Mr Ivory dropped to the ground.

Those remaining seated in the audience flew into a full panic, screaming and pleading and crying.

Son of Adam's acolytes filed out from the seating area and retrieved the dropped submachine guns of the security team.

'Any of you guys armed?' James whispered to the others.

'No,' said Erin, scowling at the terrorist leader.

Son of Adam threw his gun arm high and waved the pistol. 'Now, now, I urge you all to remain calm or more of you shall die. I reiterate: you are not in control. Look around you at the empty seats where your loved ones, acquaintances, and colleagues have stood for our righteous cause. We are legion. There is nothing beyond our touch.'

He paused and brought his arm down, moving it across the crowd; each person ducked and whimpered as the pistol passed over them.

'Remember this as you burn in the fires of divine

retribution. Sidera Silere will not try to save you. Instead, we will let you be consumed and out of the ashes we will rise as the penitent to start anew. This is the better future for humanity. Oh, and we'll be taking the *Aurora*.'

Son of Adam then moved through the audience towards his acolytes. All of a sudden, there was a roar as an older man on the edge of the seating area grabbed him and tackled him to the floor.

The nearest acolytes rushed forwards and wrestled the man to his feet. They held his arms and kicked the back of his legs as Son of Adam lifted himself from the floor and looked down at the kneeling man.

'You'll never get away with this, you filth!' the old man spat.

'A hero? No, just a pretender.' Son of Adam chuckled as he lowered the gun to the man's head and pressed the barrel into his temple.

Throwing caution to the wind, James leaped up from his seat and bellowed, 'Stop! No-one else needs to die.'

Son of Adam looked over at James, the smiling grotesque cocked to one side in curiosity.

'Ah, the true hero at last,' he said. 'Always too late to save the ones you love. Perfect in impotence.'

Without taking his glowing green painted eyes from James, Son of Adam pulled the trigger. Blood spattered the suits of his acolytes. They let go of the old man, allowing his body to drop the floor. More screams erupted from the audience and James looked on with a white-hot rage, his heart pounding.

Son of Adam and his followers then retreated through the dome's exit towards the spaceport.

*No… Just executed him in cold blood like that.*

'James,' said April, rising from her seat and moving next to him. 'There's nothing you could've done, man.'

'We have to go after them,' said James as all four of them moved out of the seating area. 'Stop them from taking the *Aurora*. Take him down once and for all.'

'We can use the *Galileo*,' said Erin. She scooped up one of the submachine guns the acolytes had left behind. 'She's got weapons now, too. If necessary, we shoot it down.'

'Weapons?'

Erin checked the gun's cartridge and sighed. 'When they refit the *Magellan*, they added weapons to our ships based on those little particle pistols from Mars.'

James nodded. Part of Zhu's posthumous recommendations, no doubt. He didn't like the idea of destroying the *Aurora*, but if it was the only way to stop Son of Adam from getting away, then so be it.

*At least that's one good thing to come out of the decommission: The* Aurora *didn't get any weapons.*

'Shouldn't the base's defensive cannons take care of them?' said Damien.

James shook his head. 'The ships were approved for landing, registered and everything. They'll need a manual override.'

'We'll do it,' said April with a little too much enthusiasm.

Damien smirked. 'Just because you want to fire one of the big guns.'

'Natch! Who wouldn't?'

'It's a sound plan,' said James. 'While you're at it, see if you can find out what happened to the security teams and...' He hesitated. Another thing he didn't want to think about. 'See if Nate is among the dead.'

The three of them glanced at one another, enervated

and wide-eyed. They all knew it was a strong possibility, but where was he? The last James had seen of him, he'd been at the corner of the seating area just before the ceremony had begun. The dead guy in his place was someone else entirely.

Just as he thought of this, he heard someone call his name. A collective weight lifted as all four of them looked up in unison to see Nate running towards them.

He stopped to catch his breath.

'Nate, you're alive!' Erin cried, throwing her arms around him.

Damien clapped a hand to his former captain's shoulder. 'Glad you made it, sir—I mean, Nate. Sorry, force of habit.'

'They all just dropped dead,' Nate said, his voice shaking as he looked around at the bodies of the security guards. 'I think it was something to do with the food.'

April raised an eyebrow. 'Poison? How?'

'Rodriguez—a guy from my squad—offered me some snacks, brownies or something. He said they'd come from the kitchen. But then he realised there were none left. That was just before he… I tried to save him, but… What happened here?'

'Son of Adam,' said James. 'He's on his way to steal the *Aurora*. I'm glad you're alive, mate, but we've gotta go after him.'

'Wait, Son of Adam? But… Marissa?'

'She's not the one. I'll explain later, or maybe these guys can.'

Nate nodded and thrust his gun into James's hands. 'Godspeed.'

Newly armed, Erin and James sped off in pursuit of

the terrorists, out of the dome and through the various connecting hallways towards the spaceport.

On the way, Erin radioed her crew to go and help out with the investigation in the dome, calm people down, and gather information. There wasn't time for them to meet her at the ship. She and James would have to go alone or they'd lose Son of Adam; they'd wasted enough time already.

They soon caught up with the group in the spaceport's atrium. Bullets flew the moment they burst through the door, ricocheting off the walls behind them and ripping into the benches.

James grabbed Erin and dragged her behind the check-in desk as submachine gun rounds obliterated computer screens and tablets. Plastic and metal shards rained down on them.

Erin popped out low from the side of the desk and returned fire. James followed suit by reaching up, resting the gun on top, and blindly firing.

'They're already at the tunnel,' said Erin. 'They're going to get away.'

Sure enough, the gunfire ceased. James tested the waters by peeping over the desk. The room was empty and still; only the sound of the alarm blaring remained. This, too, cut off a short moment after, leaving nothing but James's ever-present tinnitus ringing and Erin's heavy breathing.

'Come on, let's get to the ship,' said Erin, pointing to the exit at the far wall.

'Right.'

James vaulted the desk and the two then bolted for the door. Their footsteps thundered down the gangway until they reached the airlock to the *Galileo*.

James bobbed up and down impatiently as they waited for the second door to open. It was an excruciating moment. As soon as he glanced at the control panel and considered hammering some buttons, the door opened and they passed through into the *Galileo*'s empty cockpit.

Erin took the pilot's seat on the left and James the captain's chair on the right. As they strapped themselves in, a low rumble shook the ship. They watched out of the window as the *Aurora* and two other private passenger craft lifted off from their pads and blasted off into the sky in close formation.

'Shit,' James hissed.

'Hold onto your butt, *butt*. We're not done yet!'

Erin powered up the ship, disengaged the magnetic locks, and lifted it off the pad. She then oriented the spacecraft towards the stolen vehicles, now just three specks of light in the starlit dayside sky.

She slammed the throttle forwards and the *Galileo* shot away with a blast.

# CHAPTER TWENTY-ONE
## One Trick Pony

THE *GALILEO* ROSE RAPIDLY into the sky, tearing through Ganymede's vanishingly thin oxygen atmosphere. It was a much smoother experience than lifting off from Budapest. The lower escape velocity of the moon meant spacecraft could lift themselves to orbit using only their advanced ion engines. There was no need to burn propellant with the rocket motors.

'Erin, we need to get to them before they jump to FTL,' said James.

Erin hit the throttle control with the palm of her hand. 'Enough with the backseat driving. I'm going flat out here.'

Another couple of seconds went by in the deafening silence of the cockpit, wrought by the ship's ion engines. James had never gotten used to the lack of noise. At least in the *Aurora*, when he pushed hard enough, there was a whining resonance they'd never fixed. He'd always said to Austin it gave the ship character, but the truth was he preferred it to the dead silence.

Erin tutted as she glanced at her screen, which displayed the ship's scanner and showed a rising distance measurement for the stolen vessels. 'We're not making any headway on them. I'm gonna burn it. Clench those cheeks.'

She placed her finger underneath one of the few physical dashboard switches and counted down.

'Three. Two. One.'

She flicked the switch and the solid rocket boosters in the rear of the craft ignited with a thundering roar.

James was immediately crushed into the back of his seat as he sat on the precipice of the explosion. The small lights that were the stolen ships grew brighter as they closed the gap.

'Another few seconds and we'll be in weapons range,' Erin said, pointing at the terminal in front of James. 'On your console. Controls left to right: button to deploy, screen and stick for manual targeting, trigger on stick to fire.'

Erin had barely finished barking the instructions when James slammed his palm on the button to deploy the weapons. Hatches opened to either side of the ship's nose and the machinery locked in place with a great 'ka-thunk'.

Taking control of the nubbin of a stick, he aimed the *Galileo*'s two small beam cannons at what the targeting computer had identified as the *Aurora* and squeezed the trigger, but it was too late.

The back of the leading spacecraft erupted in a dazzling display that briefly overwhelmed the targeting computer's view. The *Aurora* blasted away from them at great speed, followed soon after by the two passenger ships. The

*Galileo*'s particle beam fire found only empty space.

'Goddammit, they used their rockets right then. Can they tell we're targeting them?'

Erin shook her head. 'No, it's not that sophisticated. Just shit timing, innit. Try again while we're still in range.'

'We need to go faster.'

'For fuck's sake, James, what did I tell you about backseat driving? We're nearly out of propellant as it is. Shoot 'em down or we'll have to chase them halfways across the system.'

James barked back, 'The last time I played this game, it was all wireframe graphics and chiptunes.'

'Well, this is real life, not a Diso to Lave trade run.'

Her words made him do a double take and he gawped at her.

She returned his dumbfounded stare with a wink.

'Alright, then,' he said and tried again with the weapons, but the ships were too far away to accurately target. He swore and punched the console.

A few seconds later, the boosters disengaged and all fell to silence once again. The *Galileo* had caught up somewhat, but the *Aurora* and its companions were moving away rapidly, up to jump altitude.

James brought the weapons to bear a third time and fired.

'Did you get them?' Erin asked.

'I don't think so. All I've got are these poxy bright spots to aim at and I can't see the actual beams,' James said, adjusting his aim up a fraction.

Then the stolen ships began making evasive manoeuvres, dodging and weaving around the targeting screen. He could barely keep the ships in the reticule.

'Looks like they figured out we're shooting at them,' said Erin. 'Must be reading the energy surges. Someone over there's at least got half a brain.'

'Jesus, Erin. Why didn't you get the engineers to install a lock-on system? They don't even have manual targeting on fighter jets anymore.'

Incredulous and sputtering, Erin's voice went up in pitch as she cried, 'Don't blame me! I didn't want the bloody things in the first place.'

James groaned and swore again under his breath, but he continued fighting with the darting lights and discharging the particle beams whenever they crossed the reticule.

*I suppose I should be thankful these things are even gimballed. Where the fuck's April with those base cannons?*

After a few short moments, they reached jump altitude. The stolen vessels could evade no longer. Now, with them flying straight forwards, James took his chance to aim carefully. He knew he only had a matter of seconds before they engaged their FTL drives and disappeared. They were still at such a distance it was difficult to get a clean shot.

Then, one of the beams connected with the leftmost passenger ship, causing the light of its engines to flicker and fade as it spun out and was left adrift in low orbit around Ganymede.

'Great shot, but that's the wrong ship,' said Erin.

James flexed his shoulders and said, 'Just a warm-up.'

But the moment he brought the *Aurora* front and centre in the crosshairs, it and its remaining escort disappeared in a flash of light.

James stared into the night, confounded. He'd had them right there in his sights, a millisecond away from pressing the trigger.

Erin reached across and slapped him on the back of the head. 'A warm-up! Fannying about, more like. Looks like we're doing this the hard way, then. At least you got one of them.'

James groaned and slumped back in his seat, rubbing his face. Now they could only guess at where Son of Adam was going. The very nature of the Austinium drive's operation meant they couldn't be tracked nor could they communicate with anyone else when they jumped. The warp field created by the drive scattered all incoming and outgoing signals. The stolen ships were effectively invisible. Why hadn't he focused harder on stopping the *Aurora*? Was it because he didn't want to damage his one remaining link to his friend? Or was it truly not for lack of trying?

Erin activated the Austinium drive with a flick of a switch and pressed the button on the dashboard screen to spool the engine. The familiar whirr of the charging drive system grew in its usual intensity until the 'Ready to Engage' light came on.

*Funny, it's not labelled 'Plaid' in here...*

Erin pressed the button to make the jump to FTL and waited, gripping the flight stick and staring intensely out of the front window.

Nothing happened.

The two of them shared a glance and then a great mechanical coughing and sputtering sound emanated from the rear of the craft.

Instead of jumping after the stolen vessels, the cockpit of the *Galileo* was plunged into darkness and silence.

The emergency power kicked in a second later and the lights returned at a flicker. The main screen lit up, but the console LEDs remained blank.

James and Erin stared at one another in confusion, the latter with wide eyes and breathing heavily.

'That's not supposed to happen,' said James, darting his gaze around the cockpit.

Erin tentatively tried the throttle control to no avail. Her expression shifted then; her lips flattened, nostrils flared, and cheeks turned red.

She roared and slammed her clenched fists onto the dashboard, cracking the screen. 'What have those bastards done to my ship?' she cried.

In an effort to bring the *Galileo* back to full operation, Erin pressed and flicked any and every button, toggle, and switch within reach. But still nothing happened.

James instead focused on the unblinking night sky. The stars remained as staunch as ever, the universe unsympathetic to their plight. No matter how much they pleaded, the fabric of the cosmos would not yield.

Looking down, he examined his hands. 'They're gone...' he said softly. 'Gone. We'll never find them now. It's over.'

'They played us,' said Erin, her teeth now bared. 'They knew we'd try to follow them and they made sure we couldn't. And we fell for it.' Her temper rose again and this time tears came to her eyes. 'But how did they even get aboard my fucking ship?'

James reached out a hand and touched her shoulder. Instantly her hand gripped his. Erin threw her head back and screamed. Tears floated away in globules, some splashing on the front window.

Her next words came in heaving sobs. 'I'd just gotten closure. Just begun to feel normal again. We got justice for Cheryl. We put an end to it. But no, we did nothing; her killer is still out there and always has been. Why? Why is this happening?'

James's heart broke for her and tears came to his eyes. The look of pain on her face was unbearable; all the hurt and shock and grief was dredged to the surface in the realisation their efforts and sacrifices had been for naught. 'I don't know,' he said, his voice cracking.

He cleared his throat. 'I'm sorry, Erin. It's my fault. I let them get away all over again.'

Erin laughed, a bitter half-sob, then sniffled and wiped snot on her sleeve. 'Don't be stupid. Not like me...'

'You're not being stupid. I can't imagine how much this hurts... Hey, we should probably warn April and Damien. If Sidera Silere got to the *Gal*, they probably did the same with their ships, too. Are the comms working, at least?'

Erin nodded. 'You're right, erm...' She tapped a few times on the cracked screen. It was still working despite the damage. The communications panel started up with no problems and showed nominal.

'Small mercies,' she said before opening a channel to April on the ground, putting it on the loudspeaker. She motioned for James to take over.

'Captain Rose-Hartley, this is the *Galileo*. Are you receiving us?' he said.

April's voice crackled at first then cleared up. 'Loud and clear, dude. You get em?'

James glanced at Erin, who had brought her knees up to her chin and now stared out of the side window. 'One of the two escort vessels, but the *Aurora* got away. You and Damien should check your ships, though. The

*Galileo*'s been sabotaged.'

'Sabotaged? Shit, that's cold. What's the situation?'

'Not sure yet, but when we tried to jump after them, the ship shut down instead. I'll need to examine the drive cavity and make repairs. We'll keep you posted. Any luck on your end? What happened to the cannons?'

'Yes and no,' said April, her voice losing all brightness. 'Those assholes disabled the base's defences. One of the technicians must've been in league with them, because we were totally locked out of the controls. As for the security officers... It's bad. Real, real fucking bad.'

James glanced again at Erin, who had now turned to face him, her eyebrows furrowed and head tilted. 'Go on.'

'Almost every security officer on duty at the ceremony is dead. The sergeant and the higher-ups escaped unscathed as well as others posted elsewhere on the base. They couldn't get to the dome, though, because someone had locked the doors.'

'Christ alive,' said Erin.

April continued, 'We had a little chat with your attacker—the one from the communications centre. He was most enlightening after a little, ahem, persuasion. Led us to some of the kitchen staff. James, they honestly could've killed everyone on the base. Nate was right. It was the snacks, laced with a fucking neurotoxin.'

James held his temples and said, 'Jesus. How's Nate holding up?'

'He's not.'

'Alright. Thanks, April,' James said after a long moment. 'We'll reconvene when we've got ourselves moving again.'

He motioned for Erin to kill the transmission, then

the two of them sat in silence for a good while.

'What a way to start the "new era",' Erin said, breaking the silence. 'New treaty, new ship… New massacre.'

James threw up his hands. 'What the fuck does Son of Adam even want with the *Aurora* anyway? He could have stolen literally any other FTL-capable transport or shuttle from any other base between here and Earth. But no, he chose to come all the way out here to Jupiter, kill a bunch of people, then disappear again with *my* ship. I don't even know what he wants with me. Back on Le Guin, he said he had plans for me specifically, bigger plans that meant he didn't want to kill me there and then. I was so caught up at the time I didn't think about it.'

'I reckon they stole it to hurt us. The *Aurora* is more than just a ship. It's a symbol of progress, a legend in its own right. You said you thought you recognised his voice? What's the deal with that? Do you think you could've known him way back? Know anyone who's holding a grudge against you?'

'It's possible,' James said with a shrug, 'but at my age, most of the people I've known are either extremely old or dead. I don't feel like I've made enemies with anyone. Angela did, but me? Can't think of any. Besides, none of you young'uns have a voice like his.'

Erin cackled at that. 'Young'un? I keep forgetting you're, like, ninety.'

'Eighty-two and a half, thank you very much.'

With a smile, Erin unbuckled herself from the seat and clapped her hands together. 'Well, the *Gal*'s not gonna fix herself, is she? Let's un-strand ourselves.'

Half an hour passed and the two friends carried out a thorough inspection of the ship's control systems.

Erin donned a spacesuit and went outside to check for damage while James examined the drive cavity in the payload bay.

There was already something familiar about the situation they found themselves in and the sensation of déjà vu only grew stronger for James as he continued the inspection.

There was nothing wrong with the wiring or the mechanical control systems. Mercifully, the service hatch was larger in the *Galileo* than it was in the *Aurora*. But when he took the panel off, there was a whiff of smoke that instantly cast his mind back two decades.

His very first trip out in the *Aurora* had been marred by sabotage from a Sidera Silere mole. At that time, they had placed a small explosive device next to the Austinium drive in an attempt to get the ship stranded around Neptune. It had taken James hours to figure out what the problem was and how to get around it and he'd almost lost his life in the process. Now, he suspected a similar mischief.

Reaching into the cavity was much easier owing to the larger opening and the fact he wasn't wearing a full spacesuit. The tips of his index and middle fingers gripped either side of a flat board and he pulled. Slowly, with a bit of wobbling, it came loose. What he pulled out was a burnt and broken shard of silicon, exactly alike to how the *Aurora* had been interfered with all those years before. He went in for more and found the remaining pieces, plus shrapnel from the explosive.

Then, he looked inside, shining a torch to the back. The Austinium drive unit itself was undamaged and he could see the ribbon cable ports he needed to get the ship back to full working order.

*Sidera Silere really are a one trick pony. No imagination whatsoever.*

'Erin, come back inside. I've found the problem and I know how to fix it,' he said into his comms. At least this time it should be easier to fix without micrometeorites punching holes in the fuselage.

'Oh? Tidy. I was just about to come back anyway. Everything looks fine out here. No signs of tampering; they must've got inside somehow.'

James considered this as he flicked the largest piece of charred circuit board, allowing it to spin in the microgravity. 'I'm more concerned with the fact this has happened twice to two different ships over twenty years apart and that's not even counting the *Newton* and *Magellan*. I swear to god, if Austin were alive right now, I'd give him a clip round the earhole for this design.'

'Twice? What do you mean?'

He chewed the side of his lip and clicked his tongue. 'I'll show you when you're back inside.'

Fifteen minutes later, Erin was back in the cockpit. She remained in her spacesuit as she floated through into the payload bay to join James.

He explained to her the details of the historic sabotage on the *Aurora* and showed her how it was almost the exact same situation. The exception this time was that the explosive was set to go off on activation of the FTL drive.

At his direction she drifted over to a tool cupboard on the side of the bay and retrieved a spare ribbon cable. She plugged either end into the ports that James had pointed out and immediately the ship's lights brightened.

'Yes!' Erin cried, thrusting her fist into the air. 'She's back in business.'

James replaced the panel to the service hatch and then the two of them floated out of the bay, back to the cockpit, and closed the door.

Erin strapped herself into the helm seat and tried the manoeuvring thrusters.

The *Galileo* rocked this way and that, causing James to have to grab onto the back of one of the seats. Then the ship yawed and rolled until the view out of the front window was centred on the damaged passenger craft.

It was close enough to see it was side-on to Ganymede with its topside adjacent to the *Galileo*, but it also had a slow, oblique rotation. There was a gradually expanding cloud of debris emanating from the back end of the ship. Some of the larger chunks were clearly pieces of engine nozzles.

Erin glanced sidelong at James with a smirk and pointed at the stricken vessel. 'Oh, I know you're thinking what I'm thinking.'

James nodded and dragged himself back to his seat. He couldn't help but smile as a frisson of excitement passed through him. 'We need information about where Son of Adam's going with the *Aurora*; what his plans are for it and for me. I bet someone on that ship knows.'

'Exactly—if you didn't space them, that is.'

James shrugged. 'There's only one way to find out.'

# CHAPTER TWENTY-TWO
## INFILTRATION

THE SHIP'S RETROGRADE THRUSTERS FIRED, pushing hard against its forward momentum as the *Galileo* drifted over to the stricken passenger craft. Slowing the craft, Erin brought it in as close as she dared.

Once it had matched the damaged ship's orbital velocity, the manoeuvring thrusters hissed, attempting to align with the other craft's axis of rotation. The *Galileo* kept low, deliberately back from the cockpit so as to avoid being spotted by any survivors upon approach. The approach was a strange and dangerous cosmic dance, bringing the ship close enough to the stolen vessel for boarding while avoiding the small shards of debris that hung nearby to the damaged hull.

The strange rotation of the other craft made it impossible to line the *Galileo* up perfectly. There was a hole in the dorsal hull of the ship through the cargo hatch, which James had created when he'd used the

*Galileo*'s particle beam to cripple it.

Erin remarked it looked large enough to be a good entry point and so lined up her ship as well as she could with the hole.

James suggested connecting the two vessels with a tether and using the *Galileo*'s thrusters to halt the other craft's rotation, but Erin objected. Bringing the other ship to a halt would alert any survivors inside to their boarding attempt, and besides, they had no tether aboard nor a means of attaching one. Their only option was to go EVA.

'The tricky bit,' said Erin, concentrating hard on the screen's external docking view, 'is aligning it just right with our airlock.'

'I guess Austin never banked on the need for ship-to-ship docking,' James muttered.

'Yeah, we're pretty much space pirates now. Avast!'

'And now you're gonna make us walk the plank.'

Erin poked her tongue out at him. 'Wouldn't be a very good pirate captain if I didn't, now, would I? Almost there… Ahah!'

The docking screen showed the opening pass by, right through the centre of the crosshairs.

'I think I've got it. Now we just need to get our timing right,' she said, crossing her arms and wearing a smug expression.

'Nicely done, Captain,' said James as he reached down beside his seat and grabbed the stowed submachine gun.

Erin shook her head as she unstrapped from her seat and floated towards the back of the cockpit. 'I don't want us using those. If the main body isn't depressurised already, those slug-throwers will be a great way to do it.'

She opened a small locker between two of the computer consoles. Inside was a small collection of guns that set James on edge. They were pistols made of a single piece of smooth, chromed metal. The short barrel blended into the handle and grip and the guard joined back up with the muzzle, making a slightly rounded triangle.

He knew this weapon well.

As Erin handed one to him, visions flashed in his mind, brought on by the coolness of the metal and the alienness of the design. A huge mechanical mass with a bioluminescent head marched towards him at great speed amid utter darkness and the stench of death. He raised the weapon towards the monster, but it was knocked aside before he could fire.

'James! What the hell are you doing?' said Erin, holding his outstretched arm down. She wrenched the gun from his grip and drifted back, horrified.

James came back to his senses and looked at his now empty hand. He then looked to Erin. 'I—I'm sorry.'

'You could've shot me!'

He held his hands up in an apologetic gesture. 'I am so, so sorry. It was a vision, a flashback from the Achelon ship. I still get them, even half a century later.'

Erin's horrified look softened and she examined the weapon she'd wrested from his grip. With sympathy in her voice, she said, 'You've used one of these before, haven't you?'

James nodded. 'Maybe Nate was right; maybe I am a liability. When I touched it, I felt like I was back there with that… that *thing* bearing down on me.'

But it wasn't only that. He recalled how Nate had told him and Elisabeth that Austin had been shot by one of those particle weapons. All those years ago, in the med bay on that derelict spacecraft full of horrors, he hadn't realised how nasty those things were. If they didn't kill you outright, you'd die of radiation sickness soon after; it almost didn't matter where you got shot with one. Now he knew these things, it was a big surprise Erin had this little cache on the ship at all.

'No! No, you are far from a liability,' said Erin as she floated back towards him. She rested the gun down on one of the seats. 'C'mon; your turn for a *cwtsh*. Everyone needs one now and again, right?'

The two embraced briefly and Erin said, 'We don't have to use these if it'll be a problem.'

'No, you're right. We can't risk blowing holes in the sides of the ship,' said James, puffing out his cheeks. He gestured to the alien weapon. 'Besides, these might give us an advantage.'

He picked up the pistol; no further visions came.

Erin closed the locker with a clatter then turned to the main screen. Pointing, she said, 'Right then, see this hole in the cargo hatch right by here? That's our target. It should offer us the element of surprise. The more I look at this, the more I suspect we *did* depressurise the cabin. So we can use the normal guns if you want?'

James returned her quizzical expression with a shake of his head.

'Okay, as long as you're sure. If that's the case, I don't expect much resistance unless we're unfortunate enough to be boarding a ship full of safety-conscious criminals.'

'In which case, we're in for a right shitshow,' said James. They then moved to the back of the cockpit and pulled themselves into a couple of spacesuits.

'Hold on a minute. You don't need one of these things, do you?' said Erin as she locked her gloves into place. 'You went without air in that spaceport on the Moon. Or is space different somehow?'

James laughed as he placed the helmet onto his head and locked it down with a click. His next words came through his suit radio. 'No, you're absolutely right. I don't need it, but there's just something about going out there into the great fathomless void without it that feels wrong, y'know?'

'So it's a security blanket? Mind over matter, *butt*.'

'Easy for you to say. Do you know how much radiation Jupiter puts out?'

'Yes,' Erin said, now also through her suit radio as she clipped the pistol to the outside of her suit. 'That's why I'm wearing one. The radiation won't kill *you* either, though.'

'Neither will the common cold; I still don't want it. Let's get this over and done with. You ready?'

'Ready as I'll ever be,' Erin muttered.

The two of them floated around and oriented themselves either side of the heavy cockpit door.

Erin punched a red button on the wall and the cabin depressurised with a long, drawn-out hiss that faded into silence. Once the light above the door turned green, she turned the handle until they heard a dull thud.

Then she pressed another button—with yellow and black stripes this time—and the door slid open.

The sight chilled James to the bone; the passenger ship's burnt hull made its slow pirouette in front of them against a backdrop of thousands of stars while the Jovian moon loomed below.

'You alright, James?'

'Nah. Nah, I'm pretty far from alright. This is a first for me.'

He wondered then what would happen if he missed. It was probably the most terrifying prospect he could think of. He'd remain tumbling in orbit around Ganymede for what could be—depending on the stability of the orbit—thousands of years, getting slowly baked by the gas giant's radiation. And the worst part was he wouldn't die; he'd be conscious the entire time.

Alternatively, he could bounce off the wrong way. His orbit path would then intersect the moon and he'd hit the ground at hundreds of kilometres an hour.

Then again, being so close to an inhabited settlement, someone might be able to come and get him in relatively short order if either of those scenarios were to happen.

'Never done EVA before? Not even on the *Magnum*?'

'Well, not jumping across to a spinning ship, I haven't! I know it's not really going that fast but...'

Erin laughed. 'It's not that far. Just focus on the timing of the hole's rotation. Oh, and don't push off too hard. You don't want to bounce.'

*No kidding.*

'Have *you* done this before?' James asked, perplexed.

Erin leaned forward out of the opening. 'Nope. Saw it in a movie.'

And with that, she pushed herself lightly away from the *Galileo*'s cockpit towards the passenger ship as the hole rotated around to her position.

A few seconds later, she bumped into the hull, jolting a little, but she grabbed hold of what was left of the cargo hatch to steady her movement and lifted herself inside.

*Well, here goes nothing.*

James leaned forwards and watched the hole pass him by, but the sudden increase in field of view afforded by poking his head outside meant taking in the vertigo-inducing background through his peripheral vision.

It was enough to halt him.

His heart pounded and he felt his hands become clammy inside his gloves. The hatch passed behind the ship and he would have to wait until it came round to his side again.

'You coming or what?' came Erin's voice over the radio a minute later as the hatch passed James by for a second time. 'Can't do this without you.'

*Damn it.*

James waited until the hole appeared on the left once more, closed his eyes, and took a deep breath. He exhaled slowly, fogging up the inside of his helmet. He opened his eyes just as the condensation dissipated, focused hard on the entry point, and pushed off.

The opening grew larger in his view, coming at him from the left—faster than he would have liked. He put out his hands and grabbed the sides of the hole but couldn't stop himself. With a grunt, he hit the wall and jolted hard. If he hadn't just about kept his grip, he'd have gone flying off into the black.

He took a moment to steady himself and, not wishing to stay outside any longer, hoisted himself inside. He floated upwards through the hole. All of a sudden, as he was staring upwards, a pair of hands burst out from the shadows and gripped his shoulders, stopping him in his tracks. Erin pulled him down and into the darkened alcove, setting him on his feet.

'Sorry for the fright,' she said. 'Any further and you'd

have floated right up into the cabin. It's totally spaced.'

'That's great news,' said James, panting.

'If only. Turns out sod's law even applies out here. We've got four hostiles in spacesuits arguing above us and two dead.'

James shot her a look.

'Don't worry. I wasn't seen. They're too busy freaking out, but they're still heavily armed.'

With a heavy sigh that fogged his visor again, James unholstered his alien pistol. 'Alright. Shitshow it is. Let's move.'

'Up and to the right, behind the seats,' said Erin.

The two floated through into the passenger cabin. At the far end of the lengthy area were the four masked and suited members of Son of Adam's retinue. Their conversation was inaudible due to the vacuum, but it was clear from their animated body language they were having a contretemps. They waved around the same weapons they had taken from the bodies of the security guards in the dome.

Between them and the two companions were rows upon rows of airline seats in three columns across the width of the fuselage.

James and Erin came up through the burn-hole that had barely missed the internal floor hatch for the ship's cargo space and drifted into the back row of the centre seating column.

Ducking down behind the backrest, they looked at one another and nodded. Then they pulled themselves around the column in different directions; James to the left and Erin to the right, keeping low as they floated along the gangway floor, edging closer to the enemy.

James moved into the leftmost column and rose up from the row, eight back from the group. Erin did the same on the right-hand side.

Unnoticed, they both raised their pistols in unison.

'How do we get their attention?' said James, looking over at Erin.

She shrugged with one of her hands, taking it off the pistol. 'I don't know. You're going to have to think of something. I don't feel comfortable just shooting them when their backs are turned.'

James looked around his immediate vicinity and spotted a closed-top cup, magnetised to the tray on the backrest nearest the window. He prised it from the surface and examined it for a moment. It was of a brushed metal and emblazoned with a black corporate logo on it that read 'Spaceline Interplanetary'.

He then wound back his arm and lobbed it at the nearest hostile. It flew in a perfectly straight trajectory and bounced off the back of his helmet, causing him and all the others to turn around.

The armed acolytes each shouted something inaudible and pointed their weapons at James and Erin. Realising they couldn't be heard, one of them made a hand gesture for the two captains to lower their weapons.

James raised his finger and wagged it, pointed at them, and returned the instruction.

'No, *you* put your guns down,' he hissed.

The other side's gestured commands became more emphatic.

'I don't think they're gonna,' said Erin.

'And neither are we. Open fire.'

James pulled the trigger of his own raised weapon,

which fired its invisible beam, burning into the first man's suit.

He staggered and his body floated back into the other acolytes.

Erin fired her own pistol and neutralised the second.

Then both she and James ducked down behind the rows as a volley of assault rifle rounds ripped through the seats and punched holes through the walls of the cabin.

James went low, shoving his hand out from the bottom corner of the row and into the gangway.

He fired and scorched the wall, missing one of the gunmen, who dragged himself behind the front row.

James gasped as bullets ripped through the seat to his right, catching another cup and evacuating its reddish contents. The dark red liquid flew in small globules above the row, their trajectory causing them to spatter on the ceiling.

'James, you alright? Hope that's not blood,' Erin radioed, panic in her voice. 'You're not leaving me alone in here.'

'No, it's just wine. But that was a close one. Hold on, I've had an idea that might just fool these guys.'

'What—'

He grabbed one of the remaining globules of the liquid and smeared it on his suit then picked up the cup and tossed a little more of the contents above the seat.

Orienting himself sideways on the floor, he pushed himself up, trying to remain as limp as possible.

He closed his eyes tight as he floated into the line of fire, not truly expecting his insane idea to work. But no gunfire came his way; he felt no bullets penetrate his suit.

*These people are a few sandwiches short of a picnic. What*

*are they even doing out here?*

'James, what the fuck are you doing?' Erin cried.

He opened his eyes then thrust the gun forwards as he fired. The beam burned a hole through the chest of the terrorist behind the seat.

By the time the other hostile had noticed his deception and turned away from Erin, James had the weapon trained on him and dispatched him without hesitation.

*That's another three I've killed now. I don't really want to make a habit of this.*

'Fucking hell, James,' said Erin, popping up from her hiding spot. 'If you'd have told me what it was you were doing, I'd have told you what a stupid idea it was. What would Angela say if I went home and told her she'd outlived her bloody immortal husband?'

'If it looks stupid but works…'

'Oh, shut it,' Erin said, jabbing her finger towards him. 'Just because you're augmented doesn't mean you get to take dumb risks. I don't want to lose any more of my friends either.'

'I'm fine, Erin. But I take your point. I'll be more careful in future. Come on, there should be at least one more in the cockpit,' said James.

The two pulled themselves along the rows of seating and arrived at the doorway leading to the ship's cockpit. It was the same colour as the rest of the cabin, which was a warm white, and its rounded rectangular shape was framed by a thin strip of aluminium.

James turned the latch gently and eased the door open. He peered through the helmet-sized gap and saw two seats, both of which were occupied.

Staying low and gripping the edge of the door, he

opened it fully and he and Erin sneaked in.

They came up in unison and pressed their weapons to the back of the cockpit crew's heads with a tap. The two acolytes turned and stared at the barrels of the guns with terror in their eyes.

Erin motioned for them both to get up.

As they lifted themselves from their seats, the man to the right, who had been sitting at the helm position, darted his hand down to his holstered sidearm, but Erin was quick on the draw and blasted a hole in the helmsman's chest, which burned through and punctured the cockpit glass.

James stared the remaining man in the eyes and shook his head.

Erin disarmed their prisoner then grabbed him by the arm. James did likewise on the other side and the two of them escorted him back through the cabin.

They moved slowly, taking just long enough for the prisoner to comprehend the fate of his shipmates.

Erin then shoved him head-first through into the cargo bay, bumping and scraping him on the lip of the hole.

'Careful,' said James. 'You don't want a rip in his suit before we've had a chance to question him.'

More confident of his abilities this time around, James went first across the void and back to the *Galileo*'s airlock. As he went, he glanced at Ganymede below. Without the anxiety of becoming lost in space, he realised how magnificent it was, all dark grey and pockmarked in white, an unobstructed view he had experienced neither in the *Aurora* nor the shipyard.

Then, the *Galileo*'s hull obscured the view. He'd timed the jump much better this time and didn't jar himself as he came to a halt outside the airlock door.

Once he was settled in the opening, he turned and motioned for Erin to send the prisoner at the next rotation, holding out his arms.

A minute or so later, they came around again. With clear protest from their captive, Erin shoved him across the gap between the two spacecraft and he came flailing towards James.

The man continued to flail after James grabbed him. His fearful movements then turned malicious as he groped for James's helmet fastener.

James heard the distinctive hiss of air escaping from his suit. He allowed his helmet to come completely off and float away into space.

The man went sheet-white. Clearly not all of Sidera Silere's members were knowledgeable of the extent of James's abilities.

Far from stunning him into compliance, the sight of James's uncovered head smiling back at him from the vacuum of space made him fight all the harder.

He kicked and shoved and pushed, but James held fast onto him with his augmented strength and bundled him into the cockpit. After a short scuffle, the prisoner was strapped to a seat with his hands and feet bound with cable ties.

Erin returned to the cockpit, closed the door, and re-pressurised the room.

Together, they pulled off the man's spacesuit helmet so they could talk. He had pale white skin and thin, gaunt features. A scraggly goatee covered his pointed chin and his hair was short and styled back into a duck tail.

'Now,' said James after slipping out of his own spacesuit

and sitting back down with the pistol in his hand. 'We're all going on a little trip back down to Catamitus Dock and you, my friend, are going to sing for us.'

'Like a damn canary,' Erin added.

The man scoffed and looked her up and down. 'I'm not telling you a damn thing, you fucking bitch.'

Erin gave James a lurid smile then pulled back her arm and slammed her fist into the man's face. Spit and blood flew from his mouth.

'Oh boy, you deserved that,' said James with a chuckle.

The man spat blood on the floor. 'Fuck you, freak. What are you, anyway?'

'That sounds like something you should have asked your boss before you got involved in all this.'

Rubbing her hand, Erin swivelled the helm chair around and sat down, leaning back and putting her boots up on the prisoner's knee with her legs crossed.

Her expression hardened, all trace of sympathy removed, and she examined the particle gun with seeming disinterest.

'You know your colleagues died in agony, right?' she said to the man, placing the weapon in mid-air and spinning it around idly. 'Horrible things, these. An atrocity waiting to happen. If they weren't lucky enough to have been killed outright, they'll be vomiting themselves inside-out while they suffocate.'

'Erin?' James hissed. 'Where are you going with this?'

The prisoner narrowed his eyes then raised his eyebrows. He stuck his tongue into his cheek and snorted. 'You think you can intimidate me?'

Erin tapped the gun again and slowed its spin. 'James? Did you know there's a second mode on these things?'

'What?'

'Yeah, it's proper lush. You see, there's a dial at the back here. You can't normally see it because it blends in, but if you turn it like so...' She grabbed the gun from the air and turned the dial just behind the grip. Red lights came on along the barrel and Erin continued, 'You've got yourself a plasma-cutter of sorts.'

James couldn't mask his surprise. He'd had no idea the weapon was a multi-tool, not that the knowledge would have helped him when he'd needed it. By the time he had been thrown across the room into the chamber that had given him his augmentation, he'd no longer had possession of the weapon. Perhaps if he had, then Yula... No, there was no need to replay all that yet again.

'Here,' said Erin, taking her boots from the prisoner's knees and leaning forwards. 'I'll show you how it works.'

She rested the barrel against the prisoner's knee.

'What? Are you fucking insane?' the man cried, trying to shake his leg away to no avail.

Erin gripped it with her other hand and pulled the trigger. There was a loud searing sound and soon the cockpit was filled with the smell of burnt clothing and flesh.

The prisoner screamed so loud it made James wince and continued until Erin removed the weapon from his leg.

He panted and gulped. 'You can't do that!' he gasped. 'The Geneva Conven—'

Erin darted forwards and pressed the still-hot barrel of the alien plasma cutter to the man's cheek, singeing the skin a little and causing him to whimper.

'Geneva's half a billion fucking miles away, sunshine,' she growled. 'I'm queen of this particular castle. You're going to tell me what I want to know or you and I will be having a lot more fun.'

James reached out and gripped Erin's shoulder, giving her a stern look.

'Stay out of it, James,' she said, shaking his hand away. 'You have no idea how long I've waited to get one of these arseholes alone.'

The man then spat in Erin's face. 'I told you, I ain't saying a goddamn word.'

She wiped the spit from her cheek and smirked. 'That's just what I'd hoped you'd say.'

With a lightning-fast swing, she brought the gun back and smacked the man across the face with it. She did it again and again until his cheek was bruised, split, and bloody.

She went to do it a fourth time, but James grabbed her by the arm and held her off. 'Erin! What the fuck's gotten into you?'

'Leave me alone, James. He doesn't deserve your mercy.'

'No, you need to stop before you do something you'll regret.'

'Something I'll regret?' Erin scoffed, trying to wrench herself away from him. 'This whole year has been full of regrets. Let go of me.'

James gripped the gun and wrestled it free of her grasp, then dragged her kicking and screaming to the back of the cockpit.

He opened the door to the payload bay and pushed her through, then followed her and shut the door behind him.

Erin flew at him in a rage and punched him square in the jaw. But he was undeterred and before she could bring her arms back, he had hold of her again.

'Stop, Erin. I can't let you torture him.'

'Why the fuck not?' she cried, scrambling for the door

again as James held on to her. 'He deserves all the pain I can inflict on him.'

'Yes! Yes, he does,' James cried, shoving his friend to the other end of the payload bay. 'That's not the reason I'm holding you back. You'll never get anything out of him that way. You'll end up killing him first and all you'll have is blood on your hands.'

'I don't care!'

'What about Cheryl? What would she want?'

'She knew I'd killed before—'

'In the military, yes. To help us rescue our people, yes. But as a cold-blooded murderer? As a torturer? This isn't the Erin I know and not the Erin that Cheryl and Austin loved.'

She huffed but stayed back this time, glaring at James and clenching her fists as she floated above the floor of the bay.

'That Erin died with them,' she said with a bitter sting in her voice.

James floated towards her. 'No. No, she's still very much alive. She's gone through hell—more than anyone should be expected to endure—but she came out all the stronger in spite of it.'

'I don't feel very strong.'

James reached her and put his hands on both her shoulders. With a smile he said, 'You don't have to be, because you still have people who love you and can understand a little of what you're going through. People who can be strong for you when you need it. Like me and April and even Nate. If you'll have us.'

Erin looked away from him and whispered, 'Of course I will. I love you guys.' She then looked James in the eye, all her anger and darkness displayed through the intensity of her stare.

After a short pause, she said, nodding towards the door, 'He's not worth my wrath, him in there. But when the time comes, when Son of Adam is as close to me as you are now, there is nothing in all the universe that'll stop me from tearing him apart. And as much love as I have for you, I will kill you if you stand in my way again.'

James's heart broke for his friend. There really was no stopping her now, but he didn't want to. He may have got her to back down for the time being, but he recognised she was only delaying her vengeance. When it came to Son of Adam, the gloves were off.

'Fair enough,' he said, putting on a smile and tapping her arm. 'Come on. Let's get some *useful* information out of that guy.'

They floated to the end of the bay, where James opened the door and they passed through back into the cockpit.

'Finished your little lover's quarrel already?' said the man, craning over his shoulder as they came in behind him. 'Or were you in there having a quick fuck?'

'I'd be careful what you say, mate,' said James as he sat down opposite the man in the captain's chair. 'You realise you people killed her wife, right? I wouldn't advise pissing her off any more than you already have.'

He faltered but then tried for some extra bravado and stammered, 'Hey, that wasn't me. I—'

'Or maybe we can wait until we get down to Catamitus Dock and you can explain to the captain of the *Newton* all about how you sabotaged her ship as well as the rest of them. If you think Captain Pritchard, here, is scary…'

'Oh, April definitely won't be happy,' said Erin, turning

her chair around to face away from the prisoner. She started up the *Galileo* and turned it to face the Jovian moon. As soon as the ship stopped turning, she pushed forwards on the throttle and it began to move.

'But if you help us, we can help you,' said James. 'Why'd you get into all this, anyway? What's in it for you?'

The man sighed. 'It's those damned aliens. They're coming and I just want to be in the group that survives.'

James nodded and leaned forwards, his elbows on his knees. 'Okay, I can get behind that. Hey, what's your name, anyway?'

'Adrian,' he replied.

'Well, Adrian… They're not coming, trust me,' said James.

The prisoner threw his head back and laughed, then winced at the bruising and swelling around his cheeks. 'Trust you? Aren't you an alien, too? They say you're immortal.'

'Oh, so you do know who I am. Then what the fuck was all that out in the airlock?'

'I didn't know you could breathe in space.'

James rubbed his temples and groaned. 'Right, well, anyway. I was there when we discovered the Mars wreckage. I went aboard, explored the inside, and, unlike you, I actually met the aliens. Their long-range communications system has no power. They're not coming.'

'But how do you know?'

'Because I'm the one who destroyed it,' James lied. 'You have nothing to fear from the aliens.'

Adrian seemed to consider James's words for a long moment, shooting glances at him as though trying to verify from his expression whether he was being sincere or not. The internal struggle was plain on his swelling and darkening face.

Eventually, he closed his eyes and lifted his head, then looked James in the eye and said, 'Alright, how can you help me?'

'Ten minutes out,' said Erin. She flicked on the comms and requested docking permission, then hailed April and told her they were on their way with a prisoner.

'How, indeed,' said James. 'Well, there's no doubt you'll be facing murder charges for all those security guards, but maybe that wasn't you either.'

'It wasn't—'

'Telling me the information I want to know will go a long way to convincing me and therefore a long way to convincing the authorities.'

'F-fine, I'll… I'll talk.'

'Good lad.'

# CHAPTER TWENTY-THREE
## Imminence

'WHAT THE FUCK DID YOU DO to my ship, dude?' April screamed as she punched Adrian to the spaceport atrium floor. She had her flight suit open with the arms tied around her waist, revealing the black short-sleeved *Nirvana* t-shirt underneath.

He spat a tooth out of his bloodied mouth, his face already swollen and black and blue from Erin's assault. 'Screw you, bit—'

April cut his insult short with a swift punt to the stomach, knocking the wind out of him with a groan.

Chris and Leron rushed around her and dragged the heaped prisoner to his feet, then led him away to the security station where a holding cell awaited.

'He told us everything, April,' said James, putting his hands on his hips. 'You didn't need to mess him up even more.'

'Uh-huh,' she said, gingerly prodding her bruised

knuckles. 'What happened to his face?'

'Besides the magnificent decking you just gave him, you mean?'

April gave a wry smile and pointed to her cheek.

'Oh, that... Just a little persuasion,' said Erin, bringing her finger and thumb together.

April's eyes shot wide open and she pointed at Erin, mouthing, 'That was you?' then, out loud, 'Damn, girl. Remind me never to piss you off.'

A flush crept across Erin's cheeks and she shuffled her feet sheepishly. 'Son of Adam got away again and I may have gone a little overboard.'

Overboard was an understatement, but Erin had calmed somewhat during the approach to the facility. It seemed not looking at the man and allowing James to work with a little more diplomacy had helped her order her thoughts. He still couldn't blame her for her outburst, though. She may have punched him, but due to his augmentation it didn't hurt and there was no lasting damage. No hard feelings. But despite her resipiscence, James had no doubt she would make good on her threat in the payload bay.

Nate may have been the loose cannon of their group, but he had been so focused on his own redemption it had broken him and compromised his judgement.

April was fierce in her loyalty to what she considered her found family, but mostly she just liked to be where the action was; she was carefree and impulsive but not cruel.

Damien was new to their inner circle: a capable combatant but a stickler for the rules.

Erin, though... Erin was out for vengeance. That much was clear. Behind her soft, playful exterior, she was everything April and Damien were, without the limiting factors. It would be wrong to call her a loose cannon like Nate; no, hers was a targeted, implacable fury. How had James missed it before? She'd even spoken of revenge two times previously, but he'd never really taken her seriously, instead putting her words down to a slip of the tongue or an immediate reaction to grief. He'd made the mistake of thinking they were on the same page with the investigation. But the reality was, where James was out to stop Son of Adam and get justice for Austin, Erin would repay blood with blood.

James walked with April and Erin through the uniform grey corridors and out into the dome, where once again they met Nate. He was still dressed in his full security gear, though a little more dishevelled.

As they approached, James shoved the submachine gun back into Nate's hands and said, 'I believe this is yours.'

Weary, the five of them walked through the unfinished garden still bustling with dignitaries and UEC ambassadors, who had been instructed to remain while the situation was being resolved.

They agreed to accompany James as he turned towards the communications centre. He needed to check in with Angela, or at least send her a message to let her know he was okay and to thank her for the intel. The news about the attack on the ceremony would be reaching Earth soon—or perhaps it already had; it was difficult to keep the delay times in mind. Whichever way, he'd rather Angela not have to worry about him for too long. It was unlikely she would be able to sneak back into the ISA headquarters to send another message to him. Hopefully, the security guards who had found her had simply sent her home; she was known and well-loved around the base, so they would have ensured she got back safely, even if it had come with a stern talking-to.

He recorded his message and sent it off. The others couldn't help but insert themselves into the message, too—Erin telling Angela she would look after James, Nate assuring her they'd get the guy, and April telling her to make James tie his own ties from now on. Damien alone remained outside the booth for the whole time.

After the message had been sent, they left the communications centre and made their way back through the garden, this time towards the outer edge of the dome, which looked out on the great space elevator.

Towards the curved edge of the dome was a small seating area with a coffee table and a freestanding flag with the logo for the Joybringer Café on it. The café itself was on the complete opposite side of the plaza, but since it was the only coffee shop on the entire moon, it could afford to stretch itself out a bit.

The armchairs were of a soft and comfortable patterned fabric and had been arranged in a circle around the glass-topped table. Every one of them groaned in relief as they sank into the chairs. It had been an extraordinarily long day for all of them.

'So, sit-rep,' said Nate, reclining and rubbing his top lip. 'The remainder of our security forces have the situation handled here for now. Total casualties, including Erik Ivory and the aide to the Argentinian ambassador—the old guy Son of Adam executed—came to thirty-seven. The bodies are piled high in the medical centre, all waiting for autopsy. Ships are on standby, ready to repatriate, with more on the way. A fleet of damn funeral barges.'

'The whole facility is shaken up, man,' April added, leaning into the centre and tapping her nails rhythmically on the coffee table. 'People have been scared to go to the mess for their food in case it's been tampered with. But we're pretty sure we got all the kitchen staff responsible.'

'I wouldn't want to be the one informing the families,' said Damien.

James sat forwards with his head in his hands and then swept back his hair. He looked up and his gaze rested on the stark landscape outside the window. It was now night on Ganymede and Jupiter was in its waning phase. The small impact craters close by were lit dimly by the artificial lights emanating from the facility. The lit area faded after a short way and the Ganymedian surface blended into the night sky, where the stars shone with mesmerising clarity.

*Thirty-seven. What a waste of life.*

James could picture clearly in his mind's eye the horrible painted grin on Son of Adam's mask. He almost felt as though he could see right through it to the monster underneath, into his dead, soulless eyes; a picture of the loss of one's humanity if there ever was one.

'And what about you guys?' said April, nudging James in the arm. 'You said your prisoner gave up some information?'

He snapped out of his introspection and looked at April. In truth, Adrian had been generally co-operative, if a little guarded, following James's convincing lie about destroying the *Bitter Authoritarian*'s long-range communications system. In reality, it had been damaged in the crash.

Adrian had come across as a genuine guy, terrified for his safety but driven to action by a stream of cultic propaganda. His testimony wasn't as helpful as James had hoped; he had no idea why James was so important to his boss. Perhaps it was too much to expect Son of Adam to share details like that with his underlings. But it wasn't completely useless.

'According to our little songbird, the *Aurora* is a key piece in Son of Adam's plan to give us a "helping hand" in our own destruction,' said James. 'Apparently the three ships were to rendezvous at a Sidera Silere stronghold in Belize, where they'd gather as a larger group and Son of Adam himself would explain the next stage of the plan.'

'We can assume that's out, then,' April said, flinging up her hands. 'Wouldn't take a fuckin' rocket surgeon to figure out we've captured one of his guys. I ain't gonna pretend Son of Adam's dumb; he's always one step ahead of us. He'll have planned for an alternative meeting point.'

Erin nodded, ignoring April's mixed metaphor. 'Right. But aside from the symbolic value of the *Aurora*, it's functionally no different to the other passenger transport he stole or even any of our ships, right?'

James rocked his head back and forth. 'Well, that's not quite accurate. The *Aurora* is a test vehicle. Austin was always adding new prototype tech to it, like more efficient power generation to potentially allow for higher FTL speeds, for instance.'

'How much more efficient?' asked Damien.

James glanced at everyone in turn. 'About double that of any ship currently flying. The ISA has been using the findings to design the Austinium drive for the *Selidor*. The goal was always to go interstellar with it.'

'Double the speed!' cried April.

'No, double the *output* in the fusion reactions. The

*Aurora* can't go much faster than any of your ships. Its drive can't harness that power. It was only ever run at full power for short times during experimentation and the extra power dumped into batteries. The rest of the time, it was limited to a lower output the ship could handle.'

'Do you think he could use it to attack Earth?' asked Nate.

James shrugged. 'I don't see how. It wouldn't help him get anywhere faster and if he tried to land at an installation, he'd get shot down instantly. Plus, the *Aurora* doesn't have any weapons.'

'Unless the *Aurora* is the weapon,' said Damien with a chill in his voice.

Thinking for a moment, James conceded the point and said, 'Our top lad did say Sidera Silere's massacres so far haven't hit the message home, so… maybe? Where, though?'

'Budapest seems likely,' said Erin. 'ISA headquarters. All of Sidera Silere has probably heard about the *Newton*'s stunt in Kazarman by now, so my guess is he'd use the *Aurora* to level the city.'

April's face went pale and she stared at James. He recalled their brief conversation on the runway during the aftermath of the—for want of a better word—firestorm. 'Water off a duck's back' was usually an apt descriptor for the effect anything had on April, but this had stuck like oil.

'Where else?' she said with a gulp.

'There's a new astronaut training centre just outside of London,' James said. 'I think that's where they want to put me. Maybe he'll hit that city and kill off the next generation of candidates so we can't launch the *Selidor*.'

Erin crossed her legs and interlinked her hands over her knee. 'Our biggest problem is that we have no way of knowing where Son of Adam's gone. We can't track ships when they're inside the warp field.'

'So you're saying we're stuck waiting around until someone spots them dropping out somewhere? I can't accept that. We have to do something,' said April. 'We have to move now!'

'Move where, April?' asked Damien.

Nate stood and paced back and forth. 'They don't think we got their message yet? I think we got it loud and fucking clear.'

James squeezed the bridge of his nose. 'Personally, I don't think Sidera Silere knows what their cause is anymore. Isn't it supposed to be about keeping humanity safe by not doing anything to attract attention from aliens? I'm not sure how hitting Earth or butchering security guards serves that goal.'

'I agree,' said Nate, nodding. 'It's starting to feel more like a vendetta against the ISA. Anyone else get that feeling?'

There was a general murmur of agreement as everyone fell silent in thought. Erin was right, not knowing where Son of Adam and the stolen ships were going was the biggest problem. Even if they waited until the ships dropped out somewhere and were picked up by a satellite, data transmission was still limited to light-speed and so would come with a huge delay time.

April then snapped her fingers and stood. 'I've got an idea,' she said. 'I could get my Planet Hunters to access satellite data across the system in real time. Even if they took one each, it'll help not having to hear it through the grapevine.'

James clapped his hands together and pointed at her.

'That's a great idea,' he said. 'But I think we're going to have to spread out across the system to minimise the delay times. Then at least one of us has a decent chance of getting to Son of Adam before he sets anything in motion. Erin, you happy for me to join you on the *Galileo*? Again?'

'Always.'

'I think one of us should speak to Marissa,' said Nate. 'When we were in Kazarman, she talked about you, James. She might know something about what Son of Adam wants with you.'

'I remember,' said Damien. 'We can take the *Magellan* back to Earth. You can go and see Marissa while Petra, Bill, and I will contact the General Assembly of Budapest to order an evacuation.'

James watched the interaction with interest, then got up from the armchair and said, 'Nate? Can I talk to you for a minute? Privately.'

'Sure thing… sir?' He rubbed the back of his neck and chuckled. 'I can't tell if we're pulling rank or not.'

'Nah, no need for all that.' James put out a hand and led Nate a little way away from the group until they were out of earshot, then continued, 'Listen, if you're going to see Marissa and then help with the evacuation on Earth, you know you're probably taking yourself out of the fight, right?'

With pursed lips, Nate stared off into the distance and put his hands on his hips. Bobbing his head, he said, 'Where are you going with this, James?'

Examining the taller man's expression closely, he answered, barely above a whisper, 'A year ago, I asked you what was bothering you after Arcadia Landing and

you said you weren't ready to talk. After all that's happened, we never did have that talk.'

'I remember,' Nate said after a long exhale. 'Obviously
I was shouldering a lot of guilt and responsibility. I felt
like I needed redemption for what happened.'

'And that's why you were so desperate to get Son
of Adam.'

Nate nodded.

'And what about now?' asked James. 'Like I said,
you're pretty much taking yourself out of the fight to
work support instead.'

Lifting his head to make eye contact, Nate said, 'I
told you working security has been good for me. I've
grown. I realised a long time ago now that I don't need
absolution for Arcadia Landing. It would've gone down
the same way with or without me. Would Marissa still
have done what she did? Yeah, she was a piece of shit to
start with and none of us are to blame for being fooled;
she was just that good at it. Would Austin still have died?
Probably, because his actions reflected the kind of man
he was. He wanted to help save the city and he died a
hero. I didn't push him into it and no-one would have
had the power to stop him.'

'Not even me,' agreed James with a wistful smile.

Nate shook his head and nibbled his thumbnail
while cradling himself with the other arm. 'I made an
ass of myself getting that desperate and I made some
big mistakes—those were my fault and I've been
rightly chastised for them.' He looked down at his feet
and shuffled. 'All this to say that I no longer feel the
overwhelming need to be the one to take down Son of
Adam. I think that's what you're asking, right?'

'Yeah. I just needed to be sure you're alright.'

'I appreciate the concern. The only thing left is Marissa and I should be the one to talk to her before Sidera Silere decides she's a loose end.'

Nate walked back to the group, clapped his hand on Damien's shoulder, and nodded. 'Thanks for offering me a ride, Captain. When that's done, we can monitor the inner planets. The way they're arranged right now, we'll be in good striking distance of all of them.'

Satisfied, James sat back down on the armchair.

April then looked like she had an epiphany and pulled out her phone. She placed it down in the middle of the coffee table and tapped the screen. A holographic projection rose up from the phone about two feet above the surface. It flickered into a real time to-scale representation of the solar system.

Controlling the orrery from her watch, she shifted and rotated it around, then zoomed in until they could see the inner planets.

'Wow, dude, you're right. Impressive,' she said, her lips drawn down. 'They're all pretty close together. How did you know that?'

Nate leaned in and examined the map, cupping his hand to his chin. 'I keep tabs on where the planets are in relation to each other. Wait, don't you?'

'Nah, bro. Why would I?'

Sitting back, he raised an eyebrow and folded his arms. 'You mean to tell me the legendary Planet Hunters don't keep track of the planets?'

April reclined and put her feet up on the coffee table. She winked at Nate and said, 'We just bag 'em and tag 'em; let nerds like you do the telemetry.' She stuck out her tongue.

'April,' said Erin, getting closer to the table and resting her chin on her linked hands. 'Pull out the view to include the outers.'

She put her tongue away. 'Sure, babe,' she said, pinching on her watch's screen. The orrery zoomed out until the gas giants were visible and the terrestrial planets were barely distinguishable.

'That'll do,' said Erin, holding up her hand. She surveyed the system map for a short time, mouthing her thoughts silently.

'What are you...' James started, staring at Erin's finger moving around the hologram.

'I won't lie to you. It's gonna be tricky with this configuration' she replied, shuffling back in her chair and gesturing at the map with an open palm. 'See how the planets are grouped into three rough sectors?'

'I see it,' said James, catching her drift. 'So the *Magellan* can cover the inner solar system as Nate said, then we can take Jupiter, Ceres, and Uranus in the *Galileo*, and April, you can take Saturn and Neptune in the *Newton*. How does that sound?'

'What about Hecate?' asked Nate, prompting April to pull the view out even further to show the Kuiper Belt and the ninth planet.

Erin shook her head. 'All the Kuiper Belt objects are too far out and there's no settlements out there. Why bother? I reckon he'll lay low around the inner solar system until he knows he's not being followed, then move on to the new rendezvous point. I don't think he'd ever venture out further than Saturn, to be fair, and that's a stretch, considering there's nothing out there but satellites and probes.'

'And this pattern to the outers will make it easier for all of us to fly straight for wherever he ends up,' James added.

'Good enough for me,' said April, switching off the hologram and grabbing her phone.

'And me,' Damien said, rising from the armchair and turning away from the group. He put his finger to his ear and spoke something inaudible. After he was done, he turned back and motioned for Nate to follow him.

'Let's go pay our ersatz Son of Adam a visit.'

'Should we not check in with our new administrator?' said Nate, rising from his seat with a stretch. 'Surely we need to get this mission approved?'

It was a surprising turn for the former captain, considering everything he'd put them through last year, but James kept his poker face.

April and Erin shared an inscrutable look and Damien slipped his hands into his pockets and cleared his throat.

After a long moment of Nate looking at the group expectantly, James said, 'No. Not this time. I know we dragged you about going off half-cocked with Kazarman, but right now we have a solid plan we all agree on. Time is of the essence. We can fill in our superiors on the way.'

A look of understanding passed quickly between the two men, then Nate and Damien bade the group farewell and marched off together in the direction of the spaceport.

After they had gone out of sight, April stood up as well. 'Leron and the others must've finished repairs on the *Newton* by now—thanks for the tip-off, by the way. I'm gonna check up on them, then we'll head on out and get in position. Catch you later, dudes,' she said before setting off at a jog.

Only James and Erin remained in the seating area.

They both stared at the empty coffee table and chairs opposite. Two times now they had failed to catch Son of Adam when he was within their grasp. James felt this failure keenly. Now, for a third time they were going after him. The difference was this time they had a plan, or at least the semblance of one. Still, he couldn't help but wonder what fresh surprises their enigmatic foe had in store for them.

Erin leaned towards James and said in a half-whisper, 'Have you had any more thoughts about who Son of Adam could be?'

James shook his head. It was something he'd tried not to think about. Nothing fit anyway. Dr Hales back from the dead was something he'd briefly considered. But that was ridiculous and he didn't fit the profile either.

Erin continued thinking aloud, half to herself. 'We're looking for a man who knew Colonel Zhu somehow; who evidently knows—and hates—you well enough for you to feature in his long-term plans; was around at the time of Project Augment, was a military sniper, and doesn't show up on any facial recognition software.'

'Colonel Zhu was very surprised to see him, too,' said James, tugging on his beard. 'You didn't see the look on her face in that video. It was like she'd seen a gh—'

Something clicked in James's mind. He recalled Son of Adam's words at the ceremony: 'Ah, the true hero at last. Always too late to save the ones you love.'

*Always too late... Always? But I've only loved Angela. Hyperbole. Who else could he be talking about? Austin and Zhu perhaps? Or could it be...*

'Yula,' he said aloud.

Erin looked up in surprise. 'What?'

'No, it doesn't make sense,' said James, his mind racing. He stood, scooting the armchair back with a squeak, and began to pace back and forth. 'No, no, no… It can't be him. He's dead. Same as Dr Hales. Long, long dead. But then, if he was dead, he wouldn't show up on facial recognition, because he doesn't exist!'

'What on earth are you going on about? I won't lie to you, you're rambling like a proper madman now, James. It's freaking me out, it is.'

'Oh boy, if that's the case, then he's even more pathetic than I thought he was. Holding on to that candle all this time.'

'James!'

'I think I know who it is,' said James, fixing Erin with a manic glare. 'Gather your crew. Let's go catch ourselves a ghost.'

# CHAPTER TWENTY-FOUR
## The Greek Camp

The *Galileo* floated amid the darkness, suspended near a small cluster of some of the larger Trojan asteroids at the Jupiter/Sun L4 Lagrange point leading the gas giant. The reddish-brown rocks were hundreds of kilometres wide and featureless but for one or two pockmarks from small impacts dating back to sometime in the distant past, before the system stabilised. The sheer size and asymmetry tricked the mind into perceiving the huge distances between them as much smaller and wayward explorers would be forgiven for thinking they were in danger of a catastrophic impact.

The reality was the cloud made for a good vantage point, allowing the ship to stay gravitationally bound to the gas giant while masking its profile among the rocks.

For Major Rhys Jones, however, simply blending into the amorphous clumps of silicate wasn't enough. Immediately upon arrival, the *Galileo*'s pilot tipped the ship on its end relative to the ecliptic plane so the dark, heat-shielded ventral hull of the craft faced towards the inner planets.

'What are you doing, Major?' asked James as the smearing view beyond the front window settled down.

'Reducing our albedo,' Rhys replied, turning in his seat to face James. 'And I'll tell you for why. You see all these big rocks out by here? Dark as anything and very hard to spot. Us, on the other hand? Blinding. At least, our top-side is, anyway. So, by showing our darker underside, we lower the chances of being spotted.'

James nodded, impressed.

'It's also quite unnecessary for this stakeout,' said Erin with a chuckle.

Rhys spluttered. 'No offence, Captain, but you'd be singing a different tune if Mr Adam came knocking because he spotted us blinking at him through a telescope. Leave the piloting to the experts, why don't you?'

Erin rolled her eyes and slapped James's knee.

The helmsman continued to grumble to himself about Erin having one taste of piloting experience and thinking she knew it all.

It sounded to James as though the man felt a bit threatened to be reminded of Erin's prowess. It shouldn't have been a surprise she knew how to fly her own ship.

For hours, the *Galileo* remained in place, steadfast in its monitoring of satellite data from across the solar system. Almost every celestial body in the system had a satellite of some kind in orbit; Jupiter and all its moons had so many by this point it was impossible to check them all. There were even active probes flying within the upper cloud layers of the gas giant itself.

There were similar probes inside Uranus and Neptune and landers on the latter's largest moon, Triton.

James recalled one satellite in particular, far above the darker ice giant, orbiting just beyond its faint rings. It was amazing it was still collecting data so many years after James had put it there using the *Aurora*. And within this satellite remained the memento he had hidden for his father.

Throughout the stakeout, the crew of the *Galileo* said barely a word to one another, the time instead going by in a kind of sombre expectation.

From here, on the inner trailing edge of the Greek Camp Trojans, Jupiter was a bright point of light in the sky, only a little more luminous and closer than when viewed from Earth, such was the enormous diameter of the gas giant's orbit.

James stared out of the window, eyes unfocused, with his head in his hand. He was at war with himself. The more he thought about his suspicions for Son of Adam's identity, the more sense they made. And then, in an instant, they became just as ridiculous as thinking Dr Hales had risen from the grave and he tried to come up with more alternatives. It was a circular thought process and it was driving him mad. For this reason, he hadn't given Erin a name, for fear of looking foolish if he turned out to be wrong. Instead, he would wait and see. If he was right, it would make no difference to anyone else who was under the mask, anyway. It only concerned him as the last remaining link to the original *Magnum Opus* expedition. The frustration was, it required conjuring a situation in which the individual behind Son of Adam had faked his death and believing it without any supporting evidence. The mental gymnastics were astonishing, but he couldn't shake it. And then, how would Son of Adam have found out about Project Augment after that? How would he have recruited Dr Hales? And how would he have gone on to become the leader of Sidera Silere? The man James had known hadn't had even a fraction of the required charisma.

Pulling himself away from the window, he turned his attention to other things. There was no point in dwelling on it; right or wrong, he would soon find the answers he sought.

* * *

It felt strange, being back aboard the *Magellan* again after so long. It was almost exactly as Nate had left it, but now he saw it from a new vantage point at the rear of the cockpit. Petra's old seat. Damien sat up front in the helm position as he always had, but now Petra took up the seat beside him, which had formerly been Nate's. Bill was in his usual spot on the port side of the craft and Marissa's seat remained empty. For the last year under Captain Vance, it had stayed just the three of them, though Damien had made it known he wasn't averse to filling the vacancies; he simply preferred to wait until after the treaty signing when the new state of affairs would settle down.

Seeing the ship from the outside on approach down the docking tunnel on Ganymede had been a treat. It looked good as new and the engineers had taken the opportunity to make some minor design changes for the refit. The rear fins were now curved and leaned in at a slight angle, connecting over the top of the fuselage like a spoiler where before they had stood up straight and proper. The wingtips had an upwards turn to them that hadn't been there before and the dome marking the position of the Austinium drive was flattened down, flush with the roof the ship. The things that excited Nate the most, however, were the hatches either side of the nose cone, concealing the spacecraft's new particle beam cannons.

*Unnecessary? Probably. Reactionary? Almost certainly. Cool as hell though? Definitely.*

For the first time, Nate felt the sting of regret at no longer being the *Magellan*'s mission commander and he found himself pining for the captain's chair, thinking perhaps a time would come again when he would command a space vessel. And he allowed himself the flight of fancy, envisaging standing on the bridge of a Jupiter-class, charting courses unknown.

Soon, they dropped out of FTL in low Earth orbit, speeding along over Namibia. Marissa had been imprisoned in the Netherlands, so Damien began the process of adjusting their orbit vector while Petra radioed Mission Control.

'This is Commander Milakova of the *UNSV Magellan* checking in,' she said and gave them details of the ship's status.

'We have your telemetry, Commander, but we don't have you scheduled for return yet,' said one of the flight controllers. 'We're currently dealing with a lot of emergency space traffic going out to Catamitus Dock following the attack. Have you been advised to bring survivors or the deceased?'

'Neither. We need you to get us a landing slot at

Rotterdam The Hague airport, then get us a patch through to the General Assembly.'

'You're… going to the Netherlands, but you want to talk to the local government here?'

'Yes, it's urgent.'

The flight controller stammered. 'I'm not sure about this. It's a very unusual request. Is Captain Vance there?'

'Goddammit, man, for once would you do as she asks?' cried Damien. 'We have reason to believe an attack on the city is imminent; we need the Assembly to order an evacuation.'

'Yes, sir… and the airport?'

Damien's temper flared. 'We're going to see Marissa de Beek. We think she may have pertinent information about the attack. What is the point in making Petra the on-board communicator if you're just going to badger me anyway? Every damn time.'

After a few minutes more, the flight controller backed down, promising to get in contact with the local government. The *Magellan* was given permission to land at the airport in Rotterdam and, after an hour and a half, was tearing through the atmosphere, the view out of the front window glowing and shimmering with re-entry plasma.

The ship landed with a bump on the runway at the airport and Nate, Petra, and Bill disembarked. Damien stayed behind to wait for communication from the General Assembly in Budapest.

Taking a taxi, the three of them made their way to the UEC Detention Unit in Scheveningen. Petra got them entrance and the guards directed them to a waiting room while they prepared Marissa to receive visitors.

'So it's Commander Milakova now?' asked Nate, sitting

on the edge of the hard plastic chair. He had his elbows resting on his knees and his hands clasped. 'Congratulations.'

Petra eyed him warily. The last time they'd spoken had been on the runway in Kazarman, where she had screamed at him and punched him.

Nate knew she wasn't over it. He could feel the effusion of resentment and the look told him she just wanted to get this over and done with, hoping for as little interaction between them as possible. He'd broken her trust. She'd known Kazarman had been a bad idea and had told him so long before they'd gone.

'What do you hope to get out of her?' she said coolly. *No small talk; got it.*

'She got close enough to Son of Adam to become him in her little performance. She has to know something about his plans and why Captain Fowler is so important to the guy.'

Bill sat with his arms crossed, one arm up and thumb caressing his bottom lip. 'You think she was part of his inner circle? If he even has an inner circle. Do Sidera Silere themselves even know who he is under the mask?'

Bill was more cheerful; he was always quick to chide but equally forgiving. Nate felt no lingering negativity from him.

Nate glanced sidelong at Petra. The arrangement probably worked in her favour. With Bill being more talkative, she'd be able to find out anything she wanted to know about what they were doing here without actually having to talk to Nate herself.

'Son of Adam must have an inner circle,' Nate said finally. 'An organisation like Sidera Silere doesn't get this big without a hierarchy of trust and confidantes. I'm hoping Marissa is one of them.'

'And if she's not?'

Nate began picking at his fingers. 'Then we've wasted our time and we'll have to hope that by the time we find out where he is, he hasn't already launched an attack.'

The door to the waiting room clicked open and a couple of prison guards entered. 'She's ready for you,' said one. 'Follow us.'

The three of them got up and followed the guards through the plain corridors of the prison to the visitation room with a floor-to-ceiling divider across the middle.

There, behind a plexiglass screen, sat Marissa in a plain grey t-shirt, her hands cuffed. Nate almost didn't recognise her; the formerly shoulder-length blonde curls were now substantially longer and were matted and tied back. Her face was gaunt and she now sported a tattoo on her neck, but Nate couldn't make out exactly what it was. Her arms were covered in scars from the burns she'd suffered at Kazarman.

At the sight of her former shipmates, she scowled.

They sat down before her on the opposite side of the screen, Nate taking the central seat a little forward of the others.

'To what do I owe this displeasure?' Marissa said, leaning her cuffed, scarred hands on the desk in front of her. 'I'm a very busy woman. I was just about to go to the gym.'

'Then I'll keep this brief,' said Nate, matching her posture. 'We know you're not the real Son of Adam, so you can drop the act.'

Marissa scoffed and looked away from him with an impish smile. 'Took you long enough. I suppose I was just that good.'

'Your little charade cost hundreds of lives.' Nate could

feel his temper rising. He'd always wondered how he would react to seeing her again and he discovered he had no patience for her. 'What was the point of it? Was this the plan, to get yourself captured and give us the run-around?'

Marissa scoffed. 'This? You think I wanted to get thrown in jail? Not the plan, no, but you gotta roll with the changes if you want to get ahead in life. That's his philosophy. I'm happy to be a sacrifice for the cause.'

'So why play decoy?' asked Petra, leaning forwards next to Nate.

Marissa sighed and hung her head. 'He came to us in Kazarman fresh from Le Guin. Knew he was being tracked. Needed an escape. It was Larsen's idea—he ran the place. As his right-hand woman, I would take up the role of decoy so that idiot Alinour would think Son of Adam stayed in the airport. His reports would keep all the attention firmly on Kazarman so the real Son of Adam could leave undetected. We knew someone would come after us eventually. Win or lose; victory, death, or capture—it didn't matter. All outcomes would keep you off his trail. I'd rather not have gotten blown up for it, but as it happens, my capture allowed me to keep up the act and take the heat off him even more.'

'And now the real Son of Adam has struck again,' said Nate, trembling with rage.

Marissa made no reaction to the news. Nate had no way to know whether she had already heard about the attack on Catamitus Dock in here; there had been a significant delay in the reporting of it due to the long distance. In either case, she was clearly unsurprised.

She pointed with both her bound hands at the three

of them and laughed. 'You people, though? Oh, you people had us going. We didn't think you'd be so stupid! Larsen swore that you using your ISA credentials to get through the checkpoint must have been a ploy, some kind of bluff or strategy—he loved those. If we'd have known you were just being exceptionally dumb, you'd have been gunned down in the market.' She sighed and shook her head ruefully. 'Assuming you had a strategy was Larsen's downfall.'

Nate slammed his hand down on the desk, causing the security guards to take a step forwards. 'This isn't a game, Marissa! We didn't come here just to listen to you gloat. You clearly spent time with the real Son of Adam. You were a key player in the Arcadia Landing attack. What is he planning?'

Ignoring the question, Marissa examined her fingernails and picked at bits of dirt under them. She looked at Nate with her head tilted to one side and a wry smile. 'Well now, Nate. What should I call you? That's an ISA security uniform.' She threw her head back and cackled. 'They demoted you! What are you now? A private? Oh, that is precious. All for coming after little old me? Maybe this visit of yours was worth it, after all.'

Petra stood with such force the chair clattered away from her. 'What is he planning, Marissa?' she screamed.

Marissa licked her lips with a sadistic glee. 'I know the answer to this one: I have no idea what you're talking about!' She laughed again and stamped her feet. 'Go on, ask me another.'

'Why did he attack Catamitus Dock?' said Nate as Bill moved to calm Petra.

The other woman looked thoughtful for a moment,

flicking her bottom lip with her finger, then, with a malicious grin, repeated in a sing-song voice, 'I have no idea what you're talking about. Another!'

He knew she was just toying with him by this point, but he couldn't have this be a wasted trip, so he asked anyway. 'What does Son of Adam want with the *Aurora*? Why is James Fowler so important to him?'

At this, Marissa stopped and reclined in the chair. 'Now *that* is the right question. I thought you'd never ask. Son of Adam suspected you would come to me, though he expected it to be the hybrid himself. He has relayed to me a message for your alien friend: "Find me at the changing of the world, where gold rings stained crimson cry eternal condemnation for the god that failed". He'll understand.'

Nate raised an eyebrow. 'What does that mean?'

'I'm done.'

'Done? No, you're not. What does it mean?'

Marissa glanced around at the guard behind and nodded at him. He stepped forwards and, grabbing her by the arm, pulled her up, scooting the chair back.

The guard then led her towards the door to go back to her cell.

Nate jumped forwards and pressed his face against the plexiglass as she passed through the doorway. 'Wait! We are not done. We are not—Marissa! Fuck!'

'I don't think you'd get any more out of her anyway,' said Bill.

'I agree,' said Petra. 'She's lost it. Let's get back to the airport, see if the captain's had any more luck getting that evacuation started.'

Nate stared after Marissa, distraught. This wasn't how he'd imagined the conversation would go. In truth, he'd had no idea what to expect. He knew it wouldn't be easy, that Marissa would play hardball, but he'd thought they'd get more time. With more time they could have come away with something more useful than a nonsense riddle. A message for James? It sounded like Son of Adam wanted a meeting, so it must have been a clue to his whereabouts. Nate wasn't in the right head space to give it much thought.

*It's nice to finally have closure on Kazarman, though.*

He felt a slap on his shoulder; it was Bill. 'Still, it wasn't a total waste. We've got something to pass on, at least.'

Nate made a non-committal grunt, then tore his gaze away from the closed doorway on the other side of the screen.

He followed Bill and Petra out of the visitation room and out of the prison building to their waiting taxi.

On the way back to the airport, Petra pulled out her phone and called Damien, putting him on speaker so Nate and Bill could hear.

'We're on our way back. Marissa was a waste of time, sir,' said Petra, holding the phone between the three of them. 'Looks like her time on the inside hasn't softened her any yet. Got a few tidbits but mostly rambling. How's it going on your end?'

'Not well,' said Damien; he sounded exasperated. 'I've spent nearly this whole time arguing with clerks and being put on hold. I went back to Mission Control and got them to call all the emergency services, just to see if we can get this thing off the ground. But it's going to need a local government order. So, I'm trying again.'

'Damn bureaucrats,' said Bill as the taxi juddered on a pothole. 'I once dated a filing clerk. Strange guy, really anal and a tad obsessive. Didn't last a month.'

'That could be the tagline for your entire love life,' said Petra. 'Didn't last a month.'

'Harsh. May I remind you what one of your previous girlfriends said about you?' Bill snapped back. 'I believe it was, "Petra possesses a unique mixture of qualities off-putting to every man or woman she's ever dated and is ever likely to date".'

'Oh yeah, the one who left the online review? Toxic bitch. You're a terrible wingman.'

Nate bit his knuckle to stifle laughter. He didn't want to upset Petra any more than his very presence on this mission already had. The journey gave him some time to think on Marissa's message. What could 'the changing of the world' mean? Everything of world-changing signif-icance these last few decades had happened on Mars, so it was the most likely candidate, and even more likely to be amongst the ruins of Arcadia Landing. But he had no idea what the second part of the clue could refer to. He struggled to think whether there was a place in the city with 'gold rings stained crimson' but he didn't know the city that well.

*James has been there more than I have; he'll know.*

'Guys?' said Damien from the speaker.

Petra looked down at the phone. 'Err, sorry, sir. We'll be with you in about twenty minutes. Then we need to send a transmission to Captain Fowler.'

'You have something?'

'Just a puzzle piece that maybe he can fit into place.'

The taxi slowed to a crawl in the late-afternoon rush hour traffic.

'That doesn't sound very promising,' said Damien.

'Hopefully I'll have made some progress by the time you get here.'

* * *

'Anything on the receivers yet?' asked James, his hands clasped behind his head and his eyes closed. He'd never been on a stakeout before; they always seemed so much more fun in the movies.

'Nothing,' said Aisling and Sai simultaneously.

'Damn. We should've brought stakeout snacks,' James said, opening his eyes and looking at the two officers. 'They always have pizza or doughnuts or something at these sorts of things.'

Erin snorted. 'Where on Ganymede would we get either of those from?'

Aisling hit her console. 'This is a waste of time. We're not gonna get anything from Jupiter or Uranus. Son of Adam just left the Jovian system; why would he come back? And why would he go to Uranus?'

'He wouldn't,' Sai replied. 'But we haven't heard anything from the others either. I wonder how Captain Rose-Hartley is doing...' His voice trailed off a little too gradually.

Aisling's eyes widened and she reached across and jabbed him in the arm. 'You like her! Sai, that's wildly inappropriate. She's a superior officer.'

Sai stammered, 'I, err, what?'

'And what would she even see in you anyway? You're not old school enough for someone like her. Have you heard the music she's obsessed with?'

'Ash, what are you—'

Erin called to the back. 'The Lieutenant Commander

doth protest too much, methinks.'

Aisling's freckled cheeks flushed a deep crimson and she turned away from Sai back to her console.

Sai looked around bewildered. 'What just happened?'

James couldn't help but laugh at his obliviousness. It had been a long day for them all.

A long moment passed. The pregnant anticipation that had been present at the start of their stakeout had given way to boredom over an hour ago and most of it had been spent in silence.

'Hold on,' said Aisling, shattering the quiet, all trace of her former bashfulness gone. 'I'm receiving something. A transmission from Earth. It's the *Magellan*.'

James sat up straight and saw everyone else do the same.

'Patch it through, Ash,' said Erin as she tapped on the screen in front of her to put the audio on the speaker system.

Damien's voice came through clear. '*Galileo*, *Newton*, this is the *Magellan*. I'm sad to say we've been unsuccessful at getting the local councillors to take us seriously long enough to get an evacuation going.'

'Idiots,' Erin muttered. 'They'll red-tape themselves into a crater.'

Then Nate took over the comms and said, 'Bill, Petra, and I went to see Marissa in prison. She was remarkably unhelpful.'

'Is there *any* good news in this message?' said James. It seemed a shame to wait a nearly full hour's delay just to send a message of failure.

'But,' Nate continued, 'she had a message for Captain Fowler, so I will pass it on as it was given. She said, "Find me at the changing of the world, where gold rings stained crimson cry eternal condemnation for the god that failed". Pompous nonsense. I hope to god it means something to you, James. Otherwise we're all fucked. *Magellan* out.'

James's heart sank and his expression turned grim. He knew where Son of Adam was.

Erin and Rhys looked at one another and then turned their chair around to stare at James in anticipation. Aisling and Sai both stopped what they were doing and looked at him too.

A cold chill went through him and threw his mind into crystal clarity. His gut reaction to the riddle connected the dots to his crackpot identity hypothesis perfectly. The changing of the world; the gold rings; failure.

James stared Erin dead in the eyes and said, 'He's going to Mars.'

'What? Why would he be going to Mars? There's nothing there anymore apart from the shipwreck,' she replied.

James nodded and grimaced. 'The shipwreck, exactly. Remember how Nate said Xander Levine fired the big particle cannon at the *Magellan*? Well, there were always two of those things on the ship. What if Son of Adam plans to use one?'

'But how would he power it, like?' said Rhys. 'The city's gone. It's just a pile of ruins and rubble.'

A look of horror came over Erin and she put her hands to her eyes. 'Oh my Christ, he's gonna use the *Aurora* to power the gun. It's the only thing with enough juice.'

'What's the range on those things?' said Aisling. 'What's he gonna shoot?'

James turned in his seat and shrugged. 'They're planet-killing weapons. I think we need to assume he's going to try to hit Earth with it. The two planets are approaching opposition.'

'But still, fifty million kilometres…'

'I know it's a stretch, but I can't think of anything else,' said James, shaking his head. He realised it all sounded totally bonkers, but what else was there? Why else would Son of Adam go to Mars, if not for the ship's weapons? 'It's the only thing that fits. We need to get a message to April, tell her to meet us there.'

'It'll be faster if we fly,' said Erin, locking her chair back in the forward position. 'Rhys, lock in on the *Newton*'s position and get us out of this bloody asteroid field.'

'Right you are, Captain,' Rhys said, giving a quick salute. 'Plotting course now.'

'What about the *Magellan*?' Erin asked, glancing back to James.

'It didn't sound like things went well in Budapest. Knowing Damien and Petra, they'll keep on trying. Besides, I think Nate would rather sit this one out.'

Erin gave a perfunctory nod and faced forwards once more.

The *Galileo*'s nose pitched down towards the bright sunlight and the few asteroids in their field of view disappeared behind them as the ship's rear engines ignited and pushed them full-throttle out of the cloud.

'All set and ready, Captain,' said Rhys as he spooled the Austinium drive.

'Punch it, Major!'

And the ship jumped with a crack.

# CHAPTER TWENTY-FIVE
## A Race Against Time

AFTER OVER AN HOUR'S FLIGHT from the Jupiter Trojans, the *Galileo* returned to normal spacetime over Saturn, far above the gas giant's magnificent ring system. They had already passed by Mars and many of the other inner planets on their straight-line path from their stakeout point. It seemed redundant, but at twice the speed of light, the Austinium drive meant it was faster to speak to April in person than send a radio transmission across the vast interplanetary distance.

Rhys made the necessary orbital adjustments with the ship's thrusters to prevent them from falling down the gravity well, pushing them into a roughly circular orbit around the amber jewel world below.

The sudden appearance of the planet in the forward view drew gasps from the crew. From here they could see the hexagonal polar region and the delicate bands of clouds ranging from yellow to a light brown. The rings themselves cast caliginous shadows on the upper cloud layers, appearing to cut into the planet.

It was a sight James had seen a precious few times before. He thought of Enceladus and the immortal Frank still hanging out in his quarters at Catamitus Dock. Back when he'd landed on the ice-covered moon, he'd only seen Saturn's rings in passing. Enceladus, like most of the other moons, orbited in the same plane as the ring system, so from the frigid, icy surface, they were invisible. Creatures like Frank, if they could have looked up through the thick ice sheet of their homeworld and out into the night sky, would have seen a large yellow orb sixty times as large as Earth's Moon. They would never know it had rings at all.

Staring out of the side window, he tried to identify the moons he could see. Enceladus was nowhere to be seen—likely on the other side of the planet—but there was what looked to be Tethys and closer in towards the edge of the rings tiny Mimas.

'Raise the *Newton*,' said Erin, craning to take in the view. 'They should be around here somewhere.'

'Nothing on the scanner?' asked James with a momentary glance away from the moons.

Rhys shook his head. 'The navigation lock isn't that accurate. It got us in the general vicinity; we don't need to be within visual range. Just close enough that we can talk without a significant delay. Ah, got 'em.'

'On speaker,' said Erin.

Crackling with static, the cockpit speakers then burst to life, the piercing scream of a face-melting guitar solo causing the *Galileo* crew to wince and hold their ears.

*Van Halen, definitely April.*

The music stopped abruptly and Erin rubbed her ears, groaning and muttering something in Welsh.

'You said it,' said Rhys, nodding at her.

'Hey dudes,' April cried through the speakers. 'I guess this is about Nate's message, huh? Mars, right?'

Erin replied, 'That's right. We think Son of Adam is going back to the derelict. We need all hands on deck. You coming with?'

'You know it. Let's ride.'

Half an hour later, the *Galileo* dropped out around the red planet, followed by the *Newton* after a few more seconds. Again, the assiduous helmsman circularised their orbit and the rest of the crew set to work opening the more advanced active scanners.

'I'm picking up the *Aurora* on the surface, Captain,' said Aisling after a short moment, tapping her screen. 'Looks like it's parked right next to the derelict.'

'It's weird the alien ship survived the explosion, isn't it?' asked Sai, twisting in his seat to look at his fellow lieutenant commander. 'Everything else for ten kilometres was destroyed.'

'The armour on that thing is strong,' said James, turning his chair around. 'Apart from losing a few exposed sections in the blast, it's mostly still intact. It's one of the reasons they're using a reverse-engineered version of that armour on the *Selidor*.'

'Makes sense,' said Sai. 'Do you think Son of Adam is down there waiting for us?'

James cast his gaze down at the gleaming rufescent planet below. They'd dropped out over the right spot; the Milanković Crater could be clearly seen, the largest feature of the Arcadia Dorsa plain.

'The message means he anticipated us going to Marissa, which means he knows we're coming for him,' he said. 'We need to be ready for anything. No doubt it's a trap for me and he knows I have no choice but to spring it.'

'Uhh, sirs?' said Aisling. 'I'm detecting an energy surge from the location of the ship. The ISA database says it's a match for the *Bitter Authoritarian*'s main gun.'

Sai spun back to his console. 'Confirmed. I sent a request to Lieutenant Vanson on the *Newton*. He's got their more advanced surface scanners trained on the site. Imagery shows the dorsal hardpoint bays opening and one of the cannons deploying.'

'He's activating the cannons with the *Aurora*'s power core,' said Erin. She motioned for Rhys to open a line to the *Newton*. 'April?'

'Yeah, we're seeing it,' she replied over the radio. 'Can't believe he's got that thing up and running. What's the plan?'

'Split into two teams. We'll land, infiltrate the wreck, and take Son of Adam down. You take the *Newton* down there and'—Erin gave James a sorrowful look and clasped her hand to her chest—'destroy the *Aurora*. He can't fire the cannon if we cut the power. I don't think we have time for anything else.'

James knew the words were coming. He thought he had prepared himself for the *Aurora*'s demise when they had chased it out of Ganymede, but he suspected some part of him had held back on the weapons. Now it was out of his hands and, coming from Erin, the words cut like a knife.

He must have looked pained because Erin reached

out and grabbed his hand. 'I'm sorry, *cariad*. I know it's your ship and your last remaining link to Austin. It is for all of us.'

'It's his legacy.'

Erin shook her head and smiled ruefully. 'No, *we* are his legacy. I agree I'd much rather see the *Aurora* given pride of place in the aviation museum, but if Son of Adam gets even one shot off—'

'Captain, the cannon's moving,' Sai interjected. 'It's hard to tell from the satellite footage, but it's definitely not pointing towards Earth.'

Without taking her eyes from James, Erin's brows crumpled. 'Then where *is* he aiming, Sai?'

'Captain, I don't mean to be an idiot or nothing, but can he see us up here?' Rhys asked with a nervous chuckle.

Remembering the *Magellan*, James's eyes widened and he threw off Erin's hand. 'He's targeting us!'

'Oh shit.' Erin launched herself back into her forward seated position. 'Rhys, evade, evade!' she cried, reaching across her pilot and slamming her hand into the comms controls. 'April, he knows we're here. Shift your arse.'

The radio crackled with April's voice. 'Copy that. Iain, haul ass.'

The powerful rear engines of the *Galileo* erupted and began an erratic descent, pushing the crew into the backs of their seats. The cabin rumbled and bucked as the ship plunged into the thin Martian atmosphere.

Out of the side window, the *Newton* shot past in close proximity, rocking them more, its rear engines a blinding cyan.

A flash of light came from the surface and in an instant, a bright stream of particles appeared between the two evading craft like a bolt of lightning.

'That was a little bit too close, Rhys,' said Erin. 'Good call, James. April, you've got to get down there and take out the *Aurora* before he can fire again.'

The aggressive guitar riff of Led Zeppelin's *Immigrant Song* came through the ship's speakers and April howled, then said, 'Chill, babe. I know what I'm about!'

Erin switched off the ship-to-ship comms and they were left with the ominous roars and moans of atmospheric entry.

The *Galileo* twisted and turned, its front end gleaming from the friction and windows hazed with streaking plasma jutting this way and that as it cut a turbulent path through the thickening air.

James kept his hands locked onto his restraints, knuckles white as he juddered and swayed. 'This was a lot easier the first time.'

'Well your MEM wasn't trying to outmanoeuvre a big fucking gun. How did he know we were there? And how did you know he knew we were there?'

'I didn't,' said James, wincing, buffeted around in his seat. 'But Xander Levine managed to track and hit the *Magellan* with one of those things and it wasn't even attached to the ship.'

'Good point.' After a few seconds of nothing but rattling machinery, she continued, 'Well, either we're really good at dodging or that cannon hasn't fired again.'

Aisling piped up. 'Nothing more on the sensors, but it's probably still tracking us. Based on the damage to the ship, the turret should have a limited range of motion.'

'Won't be long now. Couple of minutes at the most and we'll be down,' said Rhys, flicking switches above his head.

Erin nodded. 'Bring us in low, Major. If he's having

trouble getting a bead on us, I'd like to keep it that way.'

The glow from the atmospheric drag dissipated and the *Galileo* swooped in close to the ground and wide of the derelict warship, following tight behind the *Newton*.

Little remained of the great city that had only a year ago stood on this site. Scattered debris of modules and the mangled remains of buildings littered the landscape, much of it now covered with ruddy Martian dust. Blast lines were still visible emanating from the area near the horizon that had housed the city's power plant.

All that remained of the public transportation system upon which the city had relied were half-buried tracks and the rib-like arches of tunnel supports.

At the edge of the blast zone, close to the *Bitter Authoritarian*, were more complete sections of buildings, low walls, ruined foundations, and buckled steel pillars.

*Mars, truly the Bringer of War.*

As the two ships banked around and the *Galileo* came up over some of the taller ruins, there was a crack like thunder. Instantly, another brilliant line of particles rent the sky just above the starboard wing.

'Rhys! Christ alive, that nearly cooked us,' Erin cried, her arms spread wide in indignation.

'Sorry, guys,' said Rhys, bringing the ship in for a rough vertical landing near to the city ruins, facing the derelict. 'Guess he was still tracking us after all.'

The huge cannon atop the profiled remains of the gargantuan alien warship glowed and fizzed violet and moved ponderously skyward, having lost the *Galileo*.

'Where's the *Newton*?' asked James, taking off his restraints. 'I could have sworn it was right in front of us a second ago.'

Erin unbuckled herself from her seat and came back through the cockpit towards him. 'April said she knew what she was doing. We proceed as planned. Son of Adam was preoccupied with us and if we've lost track of the *Newton*, he probably has, too.'

The crew donned spacesuits and locked down their helmets. Rhys had set the ship down a good walking distance from the alien spacecraft.

Erin went to the locker by the door and distributed submachine guns among the crew, but James declined, opting instead for one of the silvery alien pistols.

He didn't fully know why; perhaps he had developed an affinity for the weapon. There was something about being back here that made him feel like it was more appropriate.

When everyone was ready, they depressurised the cockpit and all except Rhys jumped out of the hatch, down to the rust-coloured Martian surface.

The familiar grit met James's boots as he took his first steps and a plume of dust puffed up around him. The sky was bright and clear, just like it had been on that day forty-two years ago when he had become the first human ever to stand on this desert world.

More plumes of dust; the others joined him. Another loud crack made them all jump and the muzzle flash bathed everything around them in a sickly blue.

The *Newton* zoomed overhead, kicking up dust as it came low. It went past the ruins and veered off in an arc to the left across the orange Martian sky while the crew of the *Galileo* set off towards the wreck.

James stopped in his tracks and stared at the sand-coloured alien ship. Its winged front section, tiled with ceramic heat shielding, was half-buried in the dirt. Its huge kilometre-long portside wall, towering over everything in the region, cast long shadows over the ruins of the city. The was a weathered and broken observation tower atop the rear, what remained of the composite glass glinting in the sunlight.

The *Aurora* sat within its deepest shadow, completely dwarfed by its bulk.

Erin walked over to him and placed a hand on his shoulder, speaking through her suit radio. 'You feeling alright, *butt*?'

'Just weird,' he said. 'Coming back here after all these years. The place where it all began, where Yula died, where my life changed forever. It hasn't changed at all.'

Erin glanced at the wreck and back at James. 'It must be hard, but this is no time to reminisce. Are you sure you're up for this?'

Blowing out a long sigh, he said, 'Yeah. Let's take him down.'

He allowed his gaze to linger on the alien ship a moment more, then he slapped Erin on the arm. The two walked together, catching up with Aisling and Sai.

As the group traversed the barren, debris-scattered landscape, the cannon thudded into place again and sparked.

'April, it's gonna fire again,' Erin said, looking for any sign of the ship in the sky. 'It's now or never, lady.'

'Get down,' cried April through all of their suit radios. 'Coming in hot.'

The group dove face-first onto the rocky ground as the *Newton* came around again with a blast of dust and dirt. This time, the ship's beam weapons discharged invisibly, cutting through the parked *Aurora*.

The sparks on the barrel of the cannon flickered and

crackled but, apart from that small power flow interruption, continued on, waiting for its chance to fire on the *Newton* again.

'Hit it again!' cried Erin as the ship banked.

It came around in a tight turn and fired its beams straight into the back end of the *Aurora*. The ship exploded in a dazzling burst of light and a deafening boom. The ground trembled and huge clouds of red dust blasted away.

Still on the ground, the crew of the *Galileo* covered their helmets with their hands.

James shut his eyes as the impact of thousands of tiny grains rattled his helmet and shoulders.

The ground stopped shaking and the shockwave passed.

Picking themselves and each other up off the ground, the crew then peered through the slowly settling dust.

The cannon was dead and dark and the *Aurora* was gone. All that remained of James's precious craft were a few sections of blackened hull.

He fell to his knees.

*I'm sorry, Austin. We tried.*

'Woo, yeah! Got the sucker,' cried April over the suit radios. 'And not a moment too soon. Great shooting, Leron.'

'April,' said Erin, 'give it a minute. James is pretty torn up right now.'

'No, it's okay,' said James as Aisling, Sai, and Erin walked over to him. He picked himself up from the ground once more. 'There was nothing else we could do. At least Earth is safe.'

Was the planet safe? Staring at the cannon, which had stopped where it had last pointed, James realised that at no point had it looked like it had ever been targeting

Earth. It had been a longshot hitting the planet had been part of Son of Adam's plan, anyway. If not to attack Earth, then why was he here? What else could he possibly want inside the alien ship? All the data relating to the elysian enzyme had already been extracted years ago.

'I'm really sorry, dude,' said April over comms as the *Newton* circled overhead. 'That was pretty insensitive of me, huh?'

James sniffed and blinked his tears away. 'Don't worry about it; I'm fine,' he lied. His heart ached; it felt like he had lost Austin all over again. But the job wasn't finished and he needed to be strong. There was no sense in falling apart. 'Like Erin said, there's no time to get sentimental right now. Let's go and get—'

His speech was interrupted by the sound of gunshots, the bullets burying themselves in the dust all around them. Out of a small opening in the *Bitter Authoritarian*'s hull poured a dozen heavily armed and suited Sidera Silere acolytes.

'Oh, for fuck's sake,' Erin shouted. 'Ruins. Go!'

As they ran, April implored them in their ear for their status, but her voice was drowned out by the sound of panting, continued gunfire, and boots skidding on the ruddy dirt.

James reached cover amongst the ruins of Arcadia Landing, diving behind one of the larger pieces of charred debris.

There were less than a hundred yards between the combatants, and the *Galileo* crew was outnumbered and outgunned. But the cover gave them the advantage, as the Sidera Silere troops were out in the open.

'Weapons free, return fire,' Erin said, drawing up her

submachine gun. She leaned around her small section of aluminium girder and fired, clipping one of the attackers' suits. The person dropped their gun and made a desperate attempt to stem the escape of air from their suit, but they were unable to get a seal around the hole and soon fell to the floor and lay still.

The others of the group had managed to find themselves a modicum of cover—overturned, burnt-out Martian buggies or slabs of lacerated metal.

But the *Galileo* crew's cover remained superior.

Aisling and Sai crouched together behind a low reinforced wall and took turns firing off rounds. The terrorists had them under heavy suppression, so they couldn't get off more than a few shots before ducking again.

James sat on the floor with his back to another length of wall and pulled out his pistol. The group of them had taken cover in what had formerly been the northern spaceport arrivals lounge. Shattered glass from what had been a large panoramic window lay scattered around and further into the room sections of buckled magnetised floor remained.

Closing his eyes while his heart hammered in his ears, he brought up the pistol and repeated to himself, 'I am not a monster. I am just doing what needs to be done. Kill or be killed.'

Taking a deep breath to steel his nerves, he rolled himself away from the wall. He crawled on his front to a gap between his cover and another mangled piece of debris. There was a clear line of sight to three of the enemy combatants.

Pointing the alien gun out in front of him, he took careful aim, then fired. The chest piece of his target burst open as the particle beam burned through it. In this way, he took out the other two before he was forced to roll back behind cover by the gunfire of a fourth.

'Erin,' said James as bullets ricocheted off the metal and debris around him. 'There's a small crater, twenty metres to the front-right. Give me an opening and I'll be able to flank them.'

'Another one of your stupid plans, it sounds like,' she said, shoving her suited arms around the pillar and firing blindly.

'At least I'm telling you this time. I gladly invite you to think of a better one.'

Erin groaned and glanced about. 'Sai, Ash, get over to Captain Fowler's position. Suppressive fire on my mark.'

'Yes, Captain,' the two said in unison.

Aisling and Sai ducked low and moved between chunks of broken wall. The hammering of rounds followed them and broken shards fell at their feet. Moving carefully, waiting for gaps in enemy fire, they made their way to James.

With their backs to the wall, James looked Aisling in the eye and, after a small gap in the assault, nodded.

'Now!' she cried.

The crew of the *Galileo* sprung from their positions and laid into the enemy force with their submachine guns.

At the same time, James moved out from cover as fast as he could and, crouching low, dodged and weaved among the city's remains. In less than a minute, he reached the crater and jumped down into the depression before slamming himself shoulder-first into its facing wall.

Huffing and grunting inside his suit, James rolled onto his front, scrambled up, and poked his head and pistol just above the rim of the crater. Taking careful aim once again, he fired into the remaining acolytes.

In the confusion they split their attention, enough to wipe them out entirely. Between James and his companions' counter assault, the Sidera Silere faithful soon lay dead or dying on the rough and rocky ground.

After the guns fell silent, James turned over onto his back and slid down the wall of the crater, sending little stones tumbling with him.

James's helmet speaker crackled. It was Rhys. 'Everyone alright over there? Nobody got any bullet holes they need patching, like?'

'We're good, Major… I think,' said Erin. 'Least me, Ash, and Sai are. James, you about?'

Rhys grunted. 'I've got his vitals here on the screen. So I know he's not dead.'

By the time James opened his eyes again, the *Galileo* crew had made it to his position and now stared down at him from the rim.

'Having a kip, are we?' said Erin.

James couldn't see through her helmet visor because of the glare, but he could tell from her tone of voice she was giggling. He got up and brushed himself off, then, taking Erin's hand, he came out of the crater.

'Taking a breather, actually,' he said. 'I can't believe that worked.'

'It was *your* plan, sir,' said Aisling with a wry smile.

'That it was,' he said, looking pointedly at Erin.

She rolled her eyes, then tapped on her suit radio. 'Oi, April, what gives? Where the hell have you been? We could've used some air support down by here.'

'Hey, our armour's paper-thin and we were starting to take fire,' April replied. 'We needed to bug out. Iain set her down just on the other side of the shipwreck.'

'Alright, listen, we're heading inside to grab Son of Adam. It's probably best if you and your crew are back this side, waiting for us to bring him out.'

'Roger that.'

Erin then turned to James and said, 'Right then, how do you want to play this? You say you think you know who this guy is; what should we do?'

She was keeping it as dispassionate as possible, he could tell. But he could see from the twitch in her eye and the furrow of her brow she was troubled. It had all come to this. There was no escape for Son of Adam here and they'd finished off his best and brightest. Dragged away in irons or in a body bag, he was coming with them one way or another. Erin's promise hung over James like a sword. There was no telling how she would react when confronting the man directly. Knowing Son of Adam's modus operandi by now, there would probably be another surprise in store for them before this was all through.

'If his welcoming party is anything to go by,' said James, gesturing to the bodies scattered around them, 'I think we need to go in with overwhelming force. Always assume he's got an ace in the hole.'

'I like the sound of that,' said Erin as she swapped the magazine in her submachine gun with a fresh one. 'You'd better take point, though. You're the only one of us who's been here before.'

'Here' was a relative term. James looked into the shadowy hole in the hull where the Sidera Silere troops had come out of. He didn't recognise this part of the ship at all and there was no telling where it would lead.

'I'm fairly certain I've never been in *there*,' he said.

# CHAPTER TWENTY-SIX
## REQUIEM

THE FOUR GAZED INTO THE oppressive darkness of the derelict vessel's chthonic portal. The opening in the hull was just large enough for a person of average height to pass through. The additional bulk of spacesuits and the inflexible, sealed helmets made it more of a challenge. It was a wonder the acolytes managed to get through so quickly. The hole, wrenched in the normally insuperable composite armour of the hull, was a recent addition. While most of the armour had held up during the destruction of Arcadia Landing, this section of plating was already buckled and weakened from the initial crash. This vulnerability had allowed the explosion to shear off one of the panels, ripping apart the internal reinforcements and exposing part of a corridor.

James lit the torches on either side of the top of his spacesuit helmet. Not for the first time today his heart was in his throat and it thundered in his ears. Holding his pistol outwards with both hands, he crept down the small slope to the opening.

Across the threshold by a few steps, he stopped and took in his surroundings. It was pitch black, save for the light coming from his suit and the minor illumination from the outside world. The interior was just as he remembered from his last visit over forty years ago—just as he remembered from the nightmares that had plagued him in the weeks and months that had followed; the nightmares and waking visions that had returned sporadically over the intervening years. He was now ensconced in the heart of his deepest fears, the pure white walls and baroque etchings that covered them, the atavistic and barbaric religious texts of the Achelon.

The corridor sloped upwards towards an open door arch he could not yet see into.

He took a step and his mind flashed with images and emotions so intense he dropped the pistol to the carpeted floor and had to steady himself against the wall.

Just like on the *Galileo* when he had grasped the alien pistol for the first time in decades, he saw visions of the alien warrior with its mechanised armour and lurid cranial displays. The metallic scraping of the huge blade as it erupted from its forearm housing. The pervading stench of rotten flesh, of death, in whatever passed for a medical facility for these implacable zealots. Screams as Yula fought for her life and the imagined crack of bone as the blade punctured her chest. His airways saturating as he drowned in the chamber covered in spiderlike drones.

Grunting, he closed his eyes and tried to regulate his breathing.

*Focus, James. Focus. It was decades ago. All the aliens*

*are gone. Just breathe.*

After a few moments, the visions faded and the fog in his mind cleared. He was grateful his team hadn't heard him just then; the comms were miraculously off. He must have knocked the control by accident.

Sweat dripped down his forehead and off the end of his nose, but with his helmet on he couldn't do anything about it. He thought to take the helmet off, but the memory of the fusty atmosphere within the ship made him retch.

Instead he pushed himself off the wall and scrambled in the darkness on the floor for the gun.

*You're here to lay this whole affair to rest. To get justice for Austin, for Zhu... For Yula.*

'Corridor's clear,' he said after clearing his throat and switching his comms back on. His voice trembled and his mouth was dry. 'Form up behind me.'

The others entered the passageway behind and he listened to the sound of their boots clunking along towards him.

Erin gripped his shoulder with her gloved hand and rested her helmet visor on his. 'How're you holding up?'

His dim reflection in her visor showed him pallid and clammy. 'I'll be fine,' he stammered. 'It's this place. I wasn't prepared for how intense it would be seeing it all again. Even the things I thought I'd put behind me came flooding back. But I think as long as I keep my mind on what we're here to do, I'll be fine.'

Turning back towards the open doorway at the end of the corridor, he motioned for the others to follow him. One after another they stepped through. It was more of the same: a long, dark passage with uneven carpeted flooring, loose ceiling panels, and exposed electronics in the walls. On the left-hand wall were closed doors leading to other rooms.

Aisling and Sai tried a couple but found them sealed shut. This was the lower deck of the ship and had borne the brunt of the impact. Many of the walls were compressed and fractured. It was the most likely reason why they couldn't access those rooms—the doors were jammed in place.

Some of the white material covering the walls—on which the alien script had been carved—was cracked and flaking away. Large chunks and fine powder littered the floor in some places, exposing the bare metal underneath.

There was a bend in the passage leading around to the left and after a while, more inaccessible doors appeared along the right wall.

There was no light at all here. Around the bend even the subtle illumination from the hole they'd entered through had vanished. Turning off their helmet lights would mean being plunged into absolute darkness, but the white walls reflected their beams, making it less claustrophobic.

'I don't understand,' said Sai, swinging his light beams from wall to wall. 'Humans could have made all this. I mean, the graffiti on the walls is a bit extra. It's giving me cultic vibes. But there's nothing inherently alien about this. They've even got carpet on the floors.'

'I wonder if the inside of the *Selidor* will be anything like this?' Aisling said. 'Minus the weird scrawl.'

James turned to face them and continued walking backwards. 'Probably a bit more utilitarian for the *Selly*. Grey, boring, military. But have either of you ever seen a picture of one of the aliens?'

Aisling and Sai shook their heads.

James continued, 'They're humanoid... after a fashion. With their suits, they're quite a bit taller than us, but their actual physiology is a little shorter. They have four arms—two big ones similar to ours and two smaller vestigial ones nearer their chests. They're bipedal, have pale skin, little in the way of fur... Like a much scarier version of the classic Roswell greys.'

'What's a Roswell grey?' Erin asked.

James chuckled. 'Oh yeah, I forgot you kids never learned about all those twentieth century alien conspiracy theories. It was back before we knew about all this, when many people still thought humans were alone in the universe.'

'We're the alien generation,' said Erin. 'This ship has been on Mars for my entire life. I remember learning about Arcadia Landing as a kid in preschool.'

'My nephews haven't even been taught about the first Mars landing,' said Sai, 'or the Moon landing. And they're eight and ten respectively.'

James spun back around to face the direction he was going. 'The world has moved on so quickly and that's all ancient history. I never learned all that much about the Victorians at school. Everything was either before or after that era. We seem to have a blind spot for learning about stuff from eighty to a hundred years before.'

'But the Mars landing was only forty-odd years ago,' said Erin.

'Yes, but in the grand scheme of things, it wasn't that important. And to be candid, it was a bit of an embarrassment for the space agencies at the time, what with all the deaths and cover ups. The second Mars landing, however... Now that was the notable one for establishing Arcadia Landing as a small research outpost. And we learned a great deal more about this ship and its former tenants from that time onwards. The space agencies grew out of their embarrassment and knowledge of the existence of sapient species far in advance of our own became commonplace. Our first landing became little more than a historical footnote in the chapter of Arcadia Landing.'

'That's quite sad,' said Aisling. 'You have no-one left to remember what you all went through.'

'I remember,' said James. 'And I'll remember for a whole lot longer than any of you will be alive for. That will have to be enough. Anyway, that's getting a bit melancholy. In answer to your question, Sai, there's no reason why we couldn't eventually build something like this.'

'Other than good taste, of course,' said Erin.

The group then came to a split in the corridor with an offshoot heading off to the right, as the passage they were in continued around to the left.

There was a faint light emanating from the new section and James gestured for the others to follow it around.

As they rounded the corner, the passage ended in a wide double doorway. It was open and there were cables on the floor snaking out from the room and around in a different direction from where James and his team had come.

Through the door, the space opened out into a huge room almost the width of the entire ship, with a high vaulted ceiling. Spaced evenly throughout in rows and columns were tall, cylindrical metal containers standing on their ends, with giant pipes connecting them at the top and bottom. They were subdivided into sections across the whole area of the room.

At the base of each container were mechanical devices, analogous to valves, as well as monitoring stations on etched, white plinths.

With his torches, James followed the line of cabling through the room. They connected to the light-sources that had spilled their illumination faintly into the corridor, free-standing spotlights that definitely were not in-keeping with the alien aesthetic.

'Someone's been here,' said James, pointing to the lights. 'Humans, I mean. Doesn't look like Sidera Silere's doing either.'

'Could have been from the reclamation teams,' Erin suggested. 'Cheryl said they were always in and out of the ship, stripping the place for study. Maybe they were examining whatever this is.'

Aisling froze. 'Wait, you don't think there could still be city personnel here, do you?'

As she said this and they moved as a group down one of the columns of containers, Sai's suit lights passed over something white on the ground, tucked behind one of the monitoring stations.

'What's that?' he said, pointing. 'Captains, there was something down there.'

Erin and James walked over to where his lights were shining. As they moved around the terminal, their own torches illuminated a human spacesuit, emblazoned with ISA and Arcadia Landing insignia, lying slumped against the base of the container.

James knelt next to the body, tilted the helmet back, and looked into the visor. Within was the sunken brown face of a man, trimmed black beard, bushy eyebrows, his eyes closed.

'He's dead,' said James, looking down at the oxygen tank readout. 'Power to the suit has long gone. Poor guy probably asphyxiated. I reckon he was trapped here after the city was destroyed.'

'I know him,' said Erin, her voice clipped.

'What?'

'I. Know. Him!'

James watched as her chest heaved up and down and her breaths came ragged and panicked.

Aisling rushed to her aid and put her arms around her shoulders. Erin sank to the floor.

'What do you mean you know him?' said James, standing, hands raised in caution. He could see her head darting back and forth and could hear her desperately gulping down air.

He looked back at the dead salvager and then at Erin.

'That's Imran Hassan. He was part of Cheryl's squad. Oh god. Oh god, no.' She gripped Aisling's arms and tried to slow her breathing, but it was only making her worse.

'Sai, check around to see if there are any more bodies here,' said James, catching Erin's horrific implication.

Lieutenant Commander Suresh moved off out of sight, the beams of light from his helmet flashing between the containers as he searched.

Erin looked up at James, her eyes wide and fearful. 'Is she here, James? Is she here?'

'It's going to be okay, Captain,' Aisling said, trying to make her voice sound soothing, but there was an edge of terror to it. The possibility was too much to bear. 'We're here.'

A long moment passed in silence as Erin stared at James and Aisling cradled her.

Then, Sai's voice came over their suit radios. 'I've located three more bodies back here,' he said. 'All Arcadia staff, same salvage unit.'

Erin's voice went up in pitch as she murmured softly, 'No, no, no. Please.'

'Captain,' said Sai. 'I'm—I'm sorry. You'd better come over here.'

Her ragged hyperventilation stopped instantly and she froze. It was as though time itself had come to a screeching halt. Then, without a word, Erin lifted herself up from the ground and trudged around the containers. She moved on autopilot, almost mechanically.

James and Aisling followed her closely until they came upon a huddle of spacesuits propped up like Hassan.

Erin fell to her knees and crawled towards the three as Sai stood to one side. Touching the visor of the body in the middle with her own, she peered inside.

And screamed.

Sai shuffled up next to James and opened a private comms link to him. 'It's horrible,' he said over his captain's shrieks. 'Looks like they huddled together as they died. I don't know what's worse. Being vaporised out there or surviving that only to be trapped in here.'

'This,' said James, glancing sidelong at him and pointing to the ground. 'This is definitely worse.'

Erin tugged and pulled at Cheryl's suit, pushing over the bodies of the other two salvagers. Away and clear, she removed the helmet, letting it clatter to the ground, and stroked the pale face with her gloved hand, muttering to herself. Then she wrapped her wife's body in a tight embrace and sobbed.

James knelt down beside her and said, 'I'm so sorry.

I can't imagine how it must have felt for her to be stuck in here like this.'

'It was easier,' said Erin, not slackening her grip on Cheryl, her voice cracking as she spoke. 'It was getting easier to accept. We had the memorial. I said goodbye. We knew there would be no body and that she would have died instantly in the blast. I took solace from that. No pain, no suffering. But here she is, intact, whole. I was so, so wrong. And now I know the truth—that she died slowly, painfully, gasping for air, probably calling my name. Huddled in fear, far from anything resembling home, lost in the dark.'

'Erin, I—'

She looked at him then and barked a harsh laugh. 'And you know what the worst part is? Nobody came for her. She's been here for a whole year. If anybody had come looking in the immediate aftermath, they might have found her, rescued her. But we all assumed everyone had died together, never imagined anyone would still be in here on the day of the treaty signing. We abandoned her to death!'

It was true; the ISA had abandoned the site after the city's destruction. Other projects had taken precedence. It had taken forty years to build Arcadia Landing as it had been and there simply weren't the human or material resources available to deal with the wreckage and rebuild. Especially not with Catamitus Dock, the investigation into Sidera Silere, the treaty signing, and the *Selidor*. There were plans for the new ISA administration to come back to Mars and clear up; the alien wreckage was still a valuable resource, after all. But it was a process that would take time.

'It's unfair,' said James. 'It is the worst of all worlds. The best we can do right now is to get justice for her. We can take her back to the *Galileo* and bring her home after we've dealt with Son of Adam.'

Erin's voice lowered to a growl. 'Son of Adam. Mark my words, I am going to take my time with him. How much punishment can an immortal take? You seem pretty durable.'

'He will be hard to kill.'

She laid Cheryl down on the cold floor and brushed her face with her glove one last time. James could see her trembling in fury. 'He will beg for death by the time I'm done with him.'

James sighed and hung his head. There was a raw energy coming off of Erin he knew couldn't be contained any longer. Mollifying her wouldn't be useful, anyway. She was at a breaking point. If he tried to bring her down, he was sure she'd have no energy left for the coming fight and then neither of them would get what they wanted.

But they needed to find Son of Adam first. All they could do was follow the path through. He vaguely remembered seeing a map of the ship on one of the screens when he and Yula were investigating one of the upper decks years before. This area seemed to be part of the cooling system. Beyond, power distribution. If Son of Adam was anywhere, it was most likely there.

'Come on,' he said, getting up and tapping her on the shoulder. She didn't move, so he tapped her again.

'I can't.'

'We will come back for her. I promise.'

Reluctantly, Erin stood and stepped away from Cheryl's body. 'James, remember what I said about getting in my way.'

'Noted. Lead on, Captain.'

Then they were marching through the rows and columns of containers again. Aisling and Sai brought up the rear, with James following Erin.

At the far end of the room, they ascended the stairs and passed through another open doorway. They were met with yet another long corridor with two rooms going off to each side from the middle. The doors were open and the team popped their heads around the frames in turn. They were control offices linked to the previous room. At the end of the passage was another huge doorway.

James and Erin went through first. The space had opened out once again, similar to the room with the containers; just as tall but not as deep. The gargantuan machine towards the back glowed faintly—the only light in the room.

The door then shot closed behind them with a bang, trapping Aisling and Sai on the other side.

James and Erin sped back and hammered on the door.

'Commanders? You guys alright?' James called.

'Yes, sir, but we can't get through,' Aisling said. 'Is there anything you can do to open it on your side?'

James searched around the edges of the doorframe, running his hand along the walls for a control unit. 'No, nothing this side,' he said, shaking his head. 'No panels, buttons, or anything.'

'Damn, nothing on our side either,' said Sai. 'Hold on, it looks like there's a panel above the door. Ash, if I give you a leg up, can you reach it?'

'Yes, I think so.'

While he listened to the commotion on the other side of the door, Erin tapped him several times on the back.

'James,' she said with urgency.

He turned around and followed where Erin pointed. At the end of the room, at the base of the huge machine that James assumed to be a reactor, was a collection of lit computer terminals. Wires trailed from them and they had been jury-rigged to work with the horseshoe-shaped alien desk behind. Beyond the desk was the see-through tank of the reactor. The liquid inside produced the eerie glow.

'What am I looking at?' he asked.

Erin tutted and pointed again.

This time he noticed a figure in a spacesuit standing in the centre of the mix of human and alien computer systems. The suited figure was facing the both of them and from within its helmet glowed the grotesque smiling mask of Son of Adam.

Without dropping his gaze from the terrorist leader, James banged on the door behind him. 'Hey, we have eyes on Son of Adam. Keep working on getting that door open. Erin and I are going after him.'

# CHAPTER TWENTY-SEVEN
## SON OF ADAM

ERIN TREMBLED. SHE HAD HER WEAPON raised and pointed directly at Son of Adam. The terrorist leader remained statuesque, seemingly unaffected by the threat, staring at them with his glowing green eyes.

Wary of his friend, James followed her lead and levelled his pistol at the man, steadying it with both hands.

'Can he even see us?' James asked with a glance at Erin. Her face was lit in profile by only the feeble glow from the reactor, but he could make out her stony expression.

She didn't answer his question but stalked towards their prey. If Son of Adam couldn't see them for the shadows, he soon would.

Resigned to whatever would happen next, James kept in step with Erin, watching their target like a hawk for any signs of movement. A difficult prospect, since his masked face was buried within the spacesuit's helmet.

Flicking the comms control on her chest to encompass

any frequency Son of Adam might be using, Erin said with a snarl, 'Down on the ground with your hands behind your head.'

'It's over,' James said, doing likewise. 'The *Aurora*'s destroyed, your cannon's dead, as are your followers. You're done and you're coming with us.'

James's words hung in the air while Son of Adam regarded them both with his inscrutable painted expression. The seconds dragged on with such viscosity, it was like watching pitch drip.

He finally moved, raising both of his gloved hands into the air. Surrender? Was it really that easy? The two companions had powerful weapons trained on him, after all, and he appeared unarmed. But instead of lifting them above his head, Son of Adam brought his hands inwards and unsealed his suit helmet with a click and a hiss. Assiduously, he removed it and placed it on the computer terminal before him, then proceeded to remove the suit's gloves in the same manner.

*Of course he wasn't surrendering. He's like me, doesn't need the helmet at all.*

The masked man tilted his head, looked at James, and chuckled, the sound coming through his earpiece. The laugh grew louder and more deranged then stopped dead.

'I said get on the fucking ground,' Erin roared, jabbing her trembling gun forwards.

James looked between the two of them and added, 'I'd do as she says, Grant, or you'll die for real this time.'

'No.'

With a flick of his wrist, Son of Adam sent a knife flying towards Erin. It knocked her gun aside with a clang and she dropped it to avoid a suit puncture. The weapon clattered to the floor and was lost amid the darkness.

Moving with incredible celerity, Son of Adam vaulted over the computer terminal and launched himself at James.

He pulled the trigger of his pistol. The beam missed. It burned a streak in the wall next to the reactor. Before he could recover, Son of Adam was on him. He held James's arm in a vice grip and they wrestled for control of the alien weapon.

Erin screamed and barrelled into Son of Adam with her shoulder. The impact wrenched the pistol from James's grip and it too was lost on the floor.

Son of Adam wheeled away, still on his feet. Giving no quarter, Erin swung her gloved fist and connected with his jaw, which sent him reeling.

James sprang forwards as Erin advanced. She grabbed the man by his helmet's connecting ring.

'Oh, I'm going to enjoy this,' she said, pulling back her other arm.

Linking his hands, Son of Adam then brought them down into the crook of her elbow and followed it up with a knee to the abdomen.

Erin had the wind knocked from her and Son of Adam threw her aside.

James swung out at him. In the same moment, Erin kicked with her boot, connecting with the side of his leg and knocking him down onto one knee.

Despite the distraction, Son of Adam dodged James's swing then jumped on top of Erin. He pulled another short-bladed knife from his suit and raised it, ready for the kill.

James leaped across, tackling Son of Adam to the ground. The masked man rolled James onto his back and came at him with the knife. With both hands, James knocked his attacker's arms aside at the last second, causing him to plunge the weapon down to the floor. A tell-tale hiss erupted from James's shoulder; his deft manoeuvre had come at a cost. For a brief moment, he panicked about his air escaping, but he came to his senses and pushed Son of Adam off of him.

Both combatants rose from the ground. With a raw ferocity, Erin came at Son of Adam again, throwing punches and kicks as fast as she could.

The man gave a good account of himself, defending each and every blow. Then he grabbed Erin by the shoulder and pulled her towards him.

There was a sharp intake of breath. Erin stopped. Everything came to a halt. All James could hear through his speakers were stammers of surprise.

Son of Adam let go of her and she stumbled back, clutching her stomach. The knife in his hand was slick with blood.

'Erin!' James cried, rushing towards her. He caught her before she fell and he could hear the air rushing out of the stab wound.

Son of Adam backed away with a skip in his step and repeated Marissa's prophecy, 'Find me at the changing of the world, James.'

Then he strode off to one side of the room and opened a service hatch.

As he passed through the opening, James thought to go after him, but he couldn't leave Erin. He pressed tightly against the wound in her stomach with one hand and pulled out a roll of duct tape from his suit with the other.

'Erin! Erin, hold on.' Grabbing her hand, he directed her to put pressure on the wound while he ripped off a length of the sticky black tape.

With it, he sealed the puncture in the suit and stopped the air from escaping, but there was nothing he could do about the injury.

'Keep your hand there. I'll get you out of here.'

Erin grumbled and shook her head. Her eyes were wide and her face was pallid. 'No,' she grunted. 'No, you go after him. Promise me. He dies today.' Her gaze rolled up to the sky. 'I'm sorry, Cheryl, my love. I failed you.'

'No, no, no, you stay with me now,' James said, his voice cracking. If he didn't get her back to the *Galileo* soon, she'd die.

She locked her eyes on James. 'Go after him. Make him pay. I failed her; you won't. Leave me.'

'Fuck that! I'm not leaving you to die.'

She mustered whatever strength she had left and shoved James away, screaming at him, 'Kill him! I swear to god, James, if you don't and I survive, I'll kill you myself.'

'Oh yeah? And what if you die?'

'Then I'll fucking *haunt* you. Go!'

It was no use. She would never let him take her back to the ship like this.

James scrambled to his feet. 'Sai, Ash, you have to get in here right now and take Erin back to the *Galileo*. She's gravely injured. I'm going after Son of Adam.'

Sai's voice came over the radio. 'Two seconds and we'll have the door open, sir. This damn panel is—Ah, got it!'

The door at the far end of the room whooshed open and Aisling and Sai burst through.

Backing away, James looked from them to Erin.

She smiled and nodded at him. 'Thank you,' she mouthed.

He returned the nod then spun on his heel, scooped

the pistol up from the floor, and set off at a run towards the hatch Son of Adam had retreated through.

The passage was narrow and dark. His helmet torches illuminated pipe and conduit-lined walls. There were no engravings here, no appointments or aesthetics. This area of the ship was naked and industrial. Bare metal, gratings and rails, gauges, and rivets.

Some sections were narrower than others. As he ran, his boots clanged on the walkway floor. Then he slowed and squeezed past pieces of machinery. There was no way the Achelon in their power armour would have fit through here. Their engineers would have to have been without suits, crawling through ventilation shafts and scurrying around pipes.

James followed the eerie passage for what seemed like forever, ducking under pipes, squeezing, jogging, climbing, and then crawling. Eventually, it opened out into a wider segment with a corroded industrial staircase and he was met with a choice. He could either continue along this deck, further towards the front of the ship to sections unknown, or he could go up a deck.

*Where did he go?*

There had been no sign from Son of Adam he'd recognised the name James had tested: Grant. It seemed ridiculous and impossible. But there had been no denial either.

*Where* would *he go?*

What had Son of Adam meant when he'd repeated those pseudo-prophetic words? Where had the world changed if not here on Mars? Inside the *Bitter Authoritarian?*

A chill made its way up James's body. He recounted in

his mind the second part of the phrase and he knew: where gold rings stained crimson cry eternal condemnation for the god that failed.

First contact wasn't the world-changing event Son of Adam was interested in. The world hadn't changed when humanity had found out it wasn't alone in the universe. For Son of Adam, the world had changed when James had become immortal. When he'd become a god.

If the masked man truly was Grant Oliveras back from the dead, there was only one place on the whole ship he would go.

*The med bay.*

James darted up the stairs, his footsteps ringing with each step, and he bolted along the new corridor. As far as he could remember, the med bay was close to the crack in the hull through which he, Austin, Yula, and Grant had entered all those years ago, but two decks higher. Here, though, he was nearer to the back of the ship. He had a lot of ground to cover and no clear way of knowing exactly where he was. What he did know, however, was that he needed to go up several more decks.

During their expedition, James had never seen this part of the ship. He recalled how when he and Yula had made their way up to the med bay through the armoury, they had ascended in a lift, which subsequently had fallen back down its shaft. If there was any way to get to that deck again, it would have to be through these maintenance tunnels.

What would he find at the end of this chase? It was likely he was being lured into a trap half a century in the making, but he didn't care. There was no way he could just leave. Erin would never forgive him and Son of Adam would be free to launch more attacks.

As he ran, his suit radio crackled and Son of Adam's menacing voice came through. 'Come and find me, James. You know where I am.'

Maintenance tunnels branched off this way and that, but he kept to his path. Eventually, he came to another set of stairs and went up. There were unlit signs in the script he couldn't read above each section he passed through. Soon, his passage turned back on itself and he went up a third set of steps.

At the far end of this new corridor stood Son of Adam, his glowing eyes piercing the gloom, and James came to a halt.

'Good, good,' he said through James's earpiece. 'Look at you, congratulating yourself on shutting down the ship's cannon as if you know the extent of my plans. But you have not escaped death yet.'

James raised the pistol and fired. He saw burn marks and sparking appear at the end of the passage, but Son of Adam was gone.

*Shit.*

He sprinted, vaulting pipes as he went. 'This was all just about revenge for you? All this death and destruction just to get to me? I always knew you were an arsehole.'

'I'm simply restoring the poetic order of things,' Son of Adam replied. 'Your life should have ended here, just like hers did when your failure took everything from me.'

Another set of stairs.

'So all this Sidera Silere stuff is just bollocks. Got you,' said James, launching himself around a corner and past machinery.

'Sidera Silere gave me new purpose and now they

thrive under my leadership.'

James scoffed, clanging up yet more stairs. 'Right, except you're clearly augmented like me. I doubt your followers will be too impressed to learn they're being led by a "filthy hybrid".'

'Needs must, Captain. Needs must. I am the voice of the stars, and you and I are the alien threat they fear. We are gods, James. And I will show them the way.'

*He's fucking lost it. Forty years of brain rot.*

He then caught another glimpse of his prey. Son of Adam ducked down and out through a maintenance hatch.

James redoubled his pursuit, skidding to a halt where the man had exited. He crawled through the gap and was stunned by the shock of familiarity.

He had emerged out into the armoury. It was almost entirely unchanged from when he had last been here. The only difference being that the Arcadia reclamation teams had gutted the place of weaponry, suits, or anything else technological. The rooms were bare.

Picking his way along, he couldn't help but glance into the laboratories. In one he saw the overturned unit where he and Yula had eaten what was to be their final meal. He stopped and smiled, recalling their conversation— the most light-hearted part of the expedition. She had wanted to come to his wedding. In fact, she had vowed to beat him if he failed to propose to Angela the moment they landed. Blissfully unaware of what was about to happen, both he and Yula had fully expected to find their way out of the almost-lifeless vessel.

What did Grant want, anyway? If the chance to kill James was a bonus, then what were his true plans? What had he missed? He'd said James had taken everything from him with his failure—the same failure which had haunted James for the past forty years: Yula's death. He'd known Grant had been attracted to Yula, and in fact secretly obsessed with her, which had been creepy enough, but making her death all about him was a whole extra layer of awful. Then to hold on to it for all these years?

James shuddered.

Eventually, he came to the corridor leading to the wide-open triangular double doors of the med bay. As before, it was dark within, the flickering lights throwing sharp shadows across the floor.

He stood at the threshold.

Last time, the ship had been pressurised with an oxygen atmosphere, but James realised he hadn't passed through any airlocks and no doors had closed behind him. It stood to reason the entirety of the dilapidated vessel was exposed to the near vacuum of Mars. Over the course of decades, the ship had slowly been falling apart. Martian weathering was minimal and ponderous, but dust storms—coupled with the constant in-and-out of salvaging teams and, most recently, the nuclear blast that had annihilated the city—had begun to take a toll.

Looking up and around at the doorframe, noticing the imperfections and scratches and dings made by humans carting machinery back and forth, James considered he might just live long enough to see this ludicrously-sized spacecraft become a crumbled ruin.

*On the plus side, with the ship depressurised, I won't have to smell the med bay.*

He removed his helmet and gloves, leaving them in the doorway, and stepped through. It was almost as he remembered it: still a gruesome tableau of torture.

Rows of hospital beds covered in blue blood, the strange medical instruments gone, taken for study. There was the clear central area with its domed ceiling and concentric gold rings above and below.

Despite the fractional atmospheric pressure, his ears rang at an unbearable pitch. To the left, the chamber that had given James his augmentation stood open with panels torn off the side, exposing the device's complex internals.

At the sight of it, his vision blurred and shimmered and he looked away, fighting to keep his composure.

A figure stepped out from the shadows into the middle of the golden ring on the floor. Son of Adam. In the hostile darkness his painted mask glowed bright.

As James held the side of his head with one hand to stem the oncoming headache, Son of Adam raised both of his hands. The man grabbed the top of the fabric and pulled the mask forwards and off.

Grant Oliveras looked almost exactly as he had forty-three years ago. Round, clean-shaven face, olive skin, and prominent ears. The only differences that indicated the passage of time were his hair, now a mop of black curls, and his green eyes that carried the same weariness James recognised from his own reflection.

At the sight of his old crewmate's malicious grin, his headache intensified and his vision swam. Instantly, he knew this had been a bad idea.

'Here we are at last, back to the start. This room, where the world changed forever,' Grant said, his voice still coming through James's earpiece, a necessity owing to the lack of air pressure. It was the same tone as he had heard at Le Guin but much clearer.

The man spread his arms and turned on the spot as

though in ecstasy.

James did his best to glare at him while he fought with his own mind.

'Do you remember it?' he continued, lowering his arms and facing James, who now dropped to one knee. 'Let me give you a refresher.'

Grant grabbed the rigid collar of James's suit and dragged him a short way across the floor, then shoved him down onto his hands and knees above a reddish-brown stain.

James groaned and grunted as flashes of memory assaulted him.

'Look here,' said Grant, his voice turned guttural and commanding. He gripped James's hair and pushed his cheek to the cold metal of the med bay floor, right into the stain. 'Yula's blood. This is the exact spot where she breathed her last, where Queen and I found her.'

James's mind and senses flared: the reverberating clang of metal on metal, the memory of the room's putrid odour, the tang of iron, and the pain of being thrown back by the alien's mechanised arm. They all flashed into his mind and he screamed.

'Does it haunt you still? The knowledge that you couldn't save the woman you stole from me?'

'She was my friend.'

'Bullshit. I saw how close you were. She should have been mine.'

'You're obsessed.'

'I loved her!' Grant pulled James up to a kneeling position. 'You had a duty to protect her and you failed. But it was not just you, no. The ESA, NASA, Roscosmos... All of them failed her. They treated us like shit. They ordered us down here even when it became clear we were laughably untrained and ill-equipped for the task.'

'And that's why you've been killing them all,' said James, his voice strained and mouth dry. 'Everyone who worked on the *Magnum Opus* project.'

'Yes, but not before I engaged the services of a certain doctor,' Grant said, sauntering back and forth. 'After my first dramatic performance—'

'Your suicide.'

'—I took my father's savings and paid Dr Hales to kill you. It didn't take much; he was a man of few scruples. But as the particulars of your condition became clear, I saw a greater opportunity.'

'And when Hales completed the serum to make you immortal, you killed him.'

Grant shrugged. 'The old man was dead weight and I needed a change of scenery. I couldn't have him running around London while I went to America, now, could I? Even worse, he might have followed me like a lost puppy. He really was pathetic. Ruthless, useful for a time, but ultimately pathetic.'

There it was, the confirmation of what James had already suspected; it had been him. Grant had been Dr Hales's mysterious employer and the one who had put a sniper round through his brain.

'You were quite right,' Grant continued, 'when you said this was about revenge. But the scope of my vengeance is much larger than just you.'

James shook his head, trying to clear the flashes of memory, but it only made his headache worse. 'Why join up with Guy Furious? You said he was a moron.'

'I had the pleasure of meeting him at a rally in Montana.

Many of his ideas always were pure and utter nonsense, but even a stopped clock is right twice a day. Like I said, his movement gave me a greater purpose than simply taking revenge on those who had wronged me. And it happened that our interests aligned.

'So I joined and rose up the ranks, brought my own ideas, carefully whispered over years to radicalise those who would otherwise give in to their languor. I knew I could mould them into a weapon and in bringing down the ISA, I would achieve both our goals: revenge for myself and protection for humanity from the alien scourge.'

'You're the reason for the ISA sabotages,' said James.

Grant tutted. 'Come now, I can't possibly take all the credit.'

'And the cults?'

'You know as well as I do how easy it is to make the deeply religious hate something, especially when they feel their eternal salvation is on the line.'

'You're insane.'

Grant came close to James then, so close the microphone in his ear would have made no difference.

'No, James. I have a clarity of mind and vision you and your friends seem to lack. That bleeding heart Queen raised a sorry bunch.'

Heat flared within James and the brain fog cleared. 'You keep his name out of your fucking mouth,' he said at a growl.

Grant pulled back and a malevolent grin spread across his face. 'Oh, I see I've touched a nerve. If it's any consolation, I didn't mean for the good captain to die at Arcadia Landing. That was simply... a happy accident. It meant I could move Zhu up my list.'

Taking the chance afforded by the respite and his fury, James launched himself forwards, knocking Grant onto his back. Grasping the front of the man's suit, James punched him with his other fist. Again and again he struck, unleashing a primal rage. Then, straddling him, he drew his weapon from the belt of his suit and levelled it at his former crewmate. The gun shook in his hands and sweat poured from his brow.

Grant laughed, his face none the worse for James's assault. 'I see we're back to this again. I told you on the Moon you wouldn't pull that trigger.'

'How can you be so sure?'

'Because you're weak!' Grant spat, malicious glee in his eyes. 'You lack the fortitude to dispense life and death at a whim. You've squandered the gift the Achelon bestowed upon you. You've fought your very nature and you fight it even now. A pitiful excuse for a god, as pathetic as those mortals you call friends. What does the wildfire care for the grass? They couldn't kill me and neither can you.'

'You've lost, Grant. Get some perspective. You have no way to attack Earth without that cannon. Your grand plan is dead in the water.'

With disarming speed, Grant seized James's wrists before he could get off a shot.

The two rolled, wrestling once again for control until Grant pulled up his knee and shoved James away.

Back on his feet, he made to bring the alien gun up, but Grant was faster. He rushed forwards and tackled James, carrying him backwards towards the chamber.

A punch came James's way. He dodged. His own fist came up and connected with Grant's jaw and the man stumbled, catching himself by gripping the chamber's computer terminal.

The device whirred to life behind James and a frisson of fear shot through him.

Grant came up with a gut punch and, with his hand grasping James's face, shoved him through the opening to the chamber.

The glasslike door slammed shut between them.

James launched forwards and beat uselessly against the glass.

*No, not again. Not again!*

Grant stepped away, victorious. He tapped a few controls on the terminal and then prowled back and forth in front of the chamber.

'It's incredible you've come all this way and really have no idea what my plans are,' he said, rubbing his jaw. 'You think you've stopped me from attacking Earth with the ship's cannon? That wasn't what I was doing at all!'

'Then what was this all for?' James cried, his eyes darting around the chamber, which had now begun filling with liquid from the bottom.

'The communications system.'

James stared, dumbstruck. Surely not? Grant might have been crazy and looking for revenge, but there was no way he'd be insane enough to reactivate the ship's long-range transmitter.

'You're lying. It was destroyed in the crash.'

'Wrong again, James! Damaged, certainly, but not beyond repair. Did I not tell you on Ganymede I would wash my hands of you? You people didn't listen. Arcadia Landing and Le Guin were warnings meant to make you shut down operations. You continued without regard for the harm you would do. Did I not say I would give you a helping hand in bringing about your own destruction?'

James stared agog at Grant as he gesticulated in frustration. The liquid in the chamber was nearly at his knees now, but he could do nothing about it. He couldn't believe what he was hearing.

'I realised,' Grant continued, 'the only way to make you listen, the only way to make you see the threat before your very eyes, was to bring it to you.'

'No! No, you can't. You cannot send that distress call, Grant. They will destroy us all.'

'Yes, they will. And Sidera Silere, under my eternal leadership, will rise from the ashes of a dead Earth and reclaim the land. It is already done.'

'What?'

'I sent the distress signal before you and your friends arrived. You lost before you had even begun. It might take decades, or perhaps centuries, before the Achelon will come. It's a shame you will not live to see it, unlike me.

'I've spent a great deal of time over the years reading through the ISA's research into this miraculous machine. Gaining access wasn't hard. Can you blame me? After all, it bestowed immortality to the both of us in a roundabout way. It seems the Achelon really hated imperfection and their medical ethics are completely at odds with ours. This machine is capable of both giving life and taking it. Their medical records indicate that anyone they found to be inferior was placed in here and summarily destroyed like a problematic animal. And so, *adios*, James.'

Pulling on his mask once again, Grant turned away and marched towards the airlock.

James banged on the door to the chamber and swore

under his breath. The liquid was halfway up his thighs now. He knew the spider drones would drop in soon and then it would be too late. This was just like the last time; how did he allow himself to end up in here again? He'd sprung Grant's trap to perfection and now there was nothing to stop him.

*Wait! The pistol!*

He still had it in his hand and he recalled Erin's words in the cockpit of the *Galileo*. The alien gun doubled as a plasma cutter!

Checking the back of the gun revealed the dial Erin had used. He turned it and the barrel lit up. He pushed it against the door and pulled the trigger. A hiss and sparks erupted from the end, cutting into the window. Slowly, he sliced the bottom curve of a large circle so the rising liquid would leak out first. Perhaps the spider drones wouldn't drop into the chamber if it wasn't full enough. Then, he proceeded to cut upwards and round. The liquid reached his waist and started to pour from the cut he'd already made.

After a short while, he completed the circle and switched off the pistol. With a push, the cut section of window fell to the floor.

James clambered out of the chamber and, still holding the gun, ran to the airlock. It opened easily and he passed through into the bright sunlight of Mars.

Now on the outside of the *Bitter Authoritarian*, he ran down the beige hull towards the fleeing Son of Adam.

Before he got within two hundred yards of his prey, the second stolen passenger vessel rocketed in, its long white fuselage gleaming in the warm noonday sun. Its hatch was open as it slowed to a hover just off the portside of the derelict.

Using the reduced Martian gravity to his advantage, Grant jumped the gap. The moment he was aboard, the passenger ship closed its hatch and shot off into the air.

As James reached the edge where Grant had been, he was blown onto his back by the *Newton* in fast pursuit.

*Get him, April. Shoot him down.*

He watched as the two ships rose higher into the Martian sky. Then, before they had reached the edge of space, there was a blinding flash of light. A few seconds later, a sharp crack reached him, dulled by the thin atmosphere.

The light cleared and the passenger craft was gone.

# CHAPTER TWENTY-EIGHT
## CONVERGENCE

THE *NEWTON* RETURNED FOR A landing next to the *Galileo* near the remains of the city. It kicked up clouds of dust and dirt as it came in. Sitting atop the derelict's hull, James had a clear view of the ruins stretching out to the south for miles. It was the kind of devastation he'd expect to see from an ancient site on Earth, not a modern settlement on Mars.

It was a strange feeling to be here without the protection and security of a spacesuit, but there was something natural to it despite the frigidity. The Martian wind whistled faintly, picking up the lightest dust and depositing it all around him like ersh from a tree. The ship's hull slanted downwards towards the ground where its front end was buried, but he was still very high up. It really was unfathomably huge.

In the distance, the odd short mountain stood proud at the horizon and rocks of differing sizes, shapes, and colours scattered the landscape. Otherwise, the area lived up to its description as a desolate, barren plain. To the north stood the ridge of the enormous Milankovič Crater, stretching for miles to either side.

Below was the wreckage of the *Aurora*. He didn't know how long he'd been staring at the twisted shards of burnt and broken metal, but it didn't feel like enough. Not enough time to do justice to the remarkable little ship that had been his for the last twenty-three years.

He picked at the tiny pebbles by his feet, turning them over in his fingers before flicking them away off the side of the ship. It was over. Sidera Silere had won and Grant had escaped his grasp for a third time. All the clues had led them here. This was the point of convergence for all the disparate threads. Without them—with no onward path to follow— there was no hope of knowing where Grant had gone. They'd ditch the stolen passenger ship at the first chance and, because Grant couldn't be seen by facial recognition systems, he would slip into a crowd and disappear.

Sidera Silere had always been a step or more ahead of James and his companions and they wouldn't make the same mistakes again. Worse still, Grant had locked humanity onto a single track of fate by sending a message to the Achelon. Sidera Silere had become a self-fulfilling prophecy, so afraid the aliens would return due to the actions of humanity they'd made it a reality.

What would Sidera Silere do now? Would they go to ground or continue to be the thorn in the ISA's side? James's money was on the latter. It was doubtful Son of Adam would inform his followers of what he had done. First of all, that would require admitting there wasn't already a risk of the aliens returning. And secondly, for all his talk of protecting humanity and of having his cabal rise up to reclaim the world, Grant didn't give a shit about people; they were a means to an end. At least, perhaps the world would get a reprieve from Sidera Silere's large-scale atrocities for a while.

James understood the anger, the sorrow, the frustration, and the blame. He'd held his own share of bitterness and resentment towards the former space agencies for the way they'd handled the first expedition. He even understood Grant's attraction to Yula, though the man had never stood a chance with her. What he couldn't fathom was the level of jealousy, selfishness, and hatred that had driven him to become a serial killer. He'd spoken of love, but it was clear he hadn't understood or respected Yula at all and nor did he care to. Grant didn't see her as a person, just a means to an end.

James's earpiece crackled. 'James! Where the fuck are you, dude? Oh, wait. Iain, is that him all the way up there? Shit. You want us to come get you or are you all good?'

It was April. James cracked a smile; he couldn't help it, he always appreciated her alacrity.

With a kiss of his teeth he said, 'Not doing so hot, April. I think I'm gonna sit here a while.'

He then explained what had happened inside the ship after Son of Adam had stabbed Erin. She already knew as much from Sai and Aisling.

'Damn, that's cold. So the guy faked his own death over forty years ago and has been running some shadow play ever since? Jesus. Don't beat yourself up over it, man,' she said. 'There's nothing more you could've done. We'll get him. As long as we're still breathing, there's always another chance. But… How are you gonna get down from there?'

How indeed. Remembering his fall from the roof of his and Angela's former house in Chigwell, jumping was an option that he'd probably survive, especially at one third the velocity. But he didn't much feel like testing it.

'I'll make my way back through the ship the way I came,' he said, turning on his backside to look at the airlock. 'How's Erin doing?'

'She's weak but stable. Gave everyone a fright there. Thankfully, the wound isn't as deep as it could have been, but she's pretty despondent. Should I tell her?'

'No, I'll tell her. She should hear it from me. I'd like you and your crew to meet me in the coolant room. We need to retrieve the salvage team's bodies. Just give me five, first.'

'No problemo.'

After some more time observing the bleak Martian scenery, James picked himself up off the surface of the ship and shuffled back inside. He barely registered the now-empty med bay as he walked its length. At the doorway he recovered his helmet and gloves and, carrying them in his arms, he passed the laboratories of the armoury. The recent events had disarmed them of their menace. It was like walking through the corridors of his own apartment building. A secure familiarity.

World-weary, he grunted and groaned as he crawled on his hands and knees through the maintenance hatch. And now he had to remember the route back to the reactor room. It wasn't difficult, but it was a lengthy walk. In his haste to pursue Grant, he hadn't appreciated what he'd passed. He didn't stop this time either, but he turned his helmet lights back on while he carried it and marvelled at the alien industrial technology as he strolled by.

Down and down he went, back through the turns

and twists and along the starboard maintenance tunnel until he reached the reactor room at last.

Ignoring the glowing contraption and all the computer terminals, he stalked the corridors.

In the room with all the containers, he met with April, Lieutenant Vanson, and Specialist Barnes. They had been joined by Sai and Aisling; Rhys was looking after the captain, they explained.

Together they picked up the bodies of the Arcadia reclamation team, starting with Erin's wife, Cheryl. They carried her and the others back to the ships. James had put his helmet and gloves on again, more to get them out of the way than anything else. But perhaps there was a little self-consciousness in there, too. He didn't want to make the others uncomfortable by seeing him without them on.

Aboard the *Galileo*, in the cargo bay, James knelt next to Erin. She lay on a pallet with a cover over her body. As soon as he came down to her level, she turned her wan face to him.

'Is it done?' she asked, her voice weak.

James bit his bottom lip and lowered his head. 'Cheryl's aboard, as promised, and the others are divided between us and the *Newton*.'

She rolled her eyes and took a deep breath, then reiterated her question with emphasis. 'Is it done?'

He took a moment, fighting with himself about what to say. Deciding on a gentle approach, he told her about all that had happened. Son of Adam's identity, the med bay, his true plans for the doom of humanity.

Throughout, Erin's expression never changed by even a millimetre. And when he finally finished, she closed one eye, then lifted her right hand and pointed two fingers at him with her thumb raised.

'Pow.' She lowered her thumb as she spoke, then dropped her arm. 'There, you're dead now. Told you.'

'Grant must have killed me over there, because I didn't feel that. Am I a ghost?'

Erin shook her head. 'Turns out he was more than either of us bargained for, eh?'

Tears drew down James's cheeks and his face crumpled. 'I'm so sorry, Erin.'

She closed her eyes and shook her head again. Managing a small smile, she said, 'You brought my Cheryl back to me. Thank you.'

'We can't give up,' James said, sniffing. 'He's too dangerous to be left out there. But I just don't see a way forward, especially since I'm being reassigned.'

'And we won't—I won't. But, this time, not out of revenge. I've said some truly awful things to you, *bach*— things I regret. I let my anger take hold of me and now I've seen where it leads. Nothing like a knife to the gut to make you consider a few things. I can't live with this darkness inside me any longer. Can you forgive me?'

'Of course,' said James. 'And for the record, I've never thought any less of you for it.'

Wincing and groaning, she shuffled herself up to a half-seated position. 'As for your reassignment, we'll all keep you in the loop and you're welcome aboard the *Gal* anytime.'

'Thanks, Erin. How about we get out of here? I've gotta see Ange, let her know we're all fine.'

Erin nodded and James helped her to secure herself down. Then he made his way back to the cockpit and, sitting in the captain's chair, gave the order to Rhys.

James took one last look at the burnt out husk of the *Aurora* while the helmsman initiated the ship's launch sequence.

*I promised I'd take good care of her and now she's ended her life like this. I'm sorry, Austin.*

After a few minutes and a liaison with April, the *Galileo* lifted from the ground and rose into the air with the *Newton* following close behind. The two spaceplanes climbed through the thin Martian atmosphere. Upon reaching Mars orbit, Rhys spooled the Austinium drive and the ship lurched away from the planet.

Minutes later, Earth was in full view. It was good to be home. Back on the ground at the Budapest airport, James and Rhys helped Erin into an ambulance and then unloaded the bodies of the salvage team.

Dr Robert Stimpson met them just as Elisabeth had done upon their return from Kazarman, demanding a full and immediate debrief.

James's mind was still reeling. All he wanted to do was go home to Angela and ignore the world. But the threat humanity now faced, and Grant's escape, couldn't wait.

He marched along the runway beside the administrator with April trailing behind.

'Captain Vance and Private Rifkin are already here,' said Robert. 'They briefed me on their meeting with our decoy Son of Adam just before you arrived.'

The doors opened for them automatically and they stepped out of the afternoon sunlight and into the flickering fluorescence of the airport. It seemed like they flew through the facility; in no time at all, they were seated around the familiar table in the Mission Control

Centre. Damien and Nate watched with grim expressions as James and April recounted what had happened.

Robert showed no reaction when James told them about Grant sending a distress call to the Achelon.

He simply steepled his fingers, raised them to his lips, and said, 'A troubling development. Can you confirm the veracity of this?'

'No, sir,' said James. 'But some of our satellites or ground stations may have intercepted it. It's unlikely it was anything more than a burst, but it should be omnidirectional. We don't know where the Achelon fleet is, after all.'

'At the very least, we have some years before we could reasonably expect them to arrive?'

'Decades, centuries, perhaps never. The signal will propagate through space at the speed of light. But we can't sleep on this; we need to start our preparations now.'

'I agree, Captain, and we shall do our utmost,' said Robert, maintaining his dignified air. 'Now, about Grant Oliveras...'

The debrief continued for another hour with suggestions—both helpful and unhelpful—from every corner until eventually they were dismissed. The details had yet to be worked out, but the administrator was in favour of April's suggestion to put together a specialist taskforce to track down the Sidera Silere leader.

Each of them was given time off to recover and James made his way home.

Angela met him at the door and shuffled into his embrace. Being in her arms again spread warmth through his body and he melted.

They held onto each other as they walked through to the lounge and sat together on the sofa.

'I got your message,' she said, stroking his beard. 'Almost as soon as the news broke.'

'I hope I didn't make you worry.'

'Going after Son of Adam? You're damn right I was worried.' She gazed deeply into his eyes and then looked sullen at his expression. 'Is something wrong? What happened out there?'

With a sigh he looked way, allowing his gaze to fall on the mantelpiece displaying the group photo from the *Magnum Opus* expedition, the five of them smiling together. There was Grant, standing between James and Yula, with Austin and Zhu seated in front. It was just supposed to be a meteorite, nothing more. An astronomical oddity worthy of study; an expedition that would hail them all as heroes and pioneers like so many before them. Instead, it had not only changed James's and Angela's lives and the fate of the entire world but birthed an honest-to-god supervillain. Sometimes it made James question the worth of it all.

Angela nudged him.

'Sorry,' he said, then shared with her all the details of the race to capture Son of Adam, who he turned out to be, and what had happened in the med bay.

A look of horror came over her when he told her how Grant had been behind everything Dr Hales had put them through.

'I always got creeper vibes from him,' she said, finally. 'So, in a way I was right about him being the first victim of the *Magnum Opus* killer.'

James tilted his head.

'Grant Oliveras had to die so Son of Adam could live,' she explained.

'How poetic. But let's not frame him as a victim,' he said with a groan. 'He's still out there and dangerous. Worse, he succeeded in his plan; a plan so out-of-pocket none of us even had a clue. There's no telling what he'll do next.'

Angela pawed at his arm and laid her head on his shoulder. Some of their questions had been answered: the identity of Dr Hales's enigmatic employer, the reason for his murder, and where James featured into those schemes had all become clear. But the answers brought little solace. With it came the knowledge that another immortal existed in the world—one with the power and influence to pose a threat to humanity.

Their optimistic hopes for the future had been dealt a severe blow. Just like it had done all those years ago as they'd watched the launch of the second Mars expedition from the beach in Florida, the world faced uncertainty anew. There was no way of knowing how far away the rest of the Achelon fleet was. But however long it took, James was certain they would come in force and the United Earth Confederacy would need to be prepared.

James wondered then about the other ship—the second light in the sky that had shot down the *Bitter Authoritarian* all those years ago and vanished without a trace. An enigmatic people; that the Achelon had clearly been in conflict with them was all anyone knew of them. Who could they be? What had brought them to blows in the first place? He couldn't fathom it: another species, one more powerful than the Achelon.

*The enemy of my enemy…*

Such beings could be potent allies, if only there was more information on them. Perhaps the *Bitter Authoritarian* had not yet given up all its secrets.

In the meantime, the hunt for Son of Adam would continue and Sidera Silere had now unknowingly become the number one obstacle to countering the Achelon threat. The answer lay not in pulling back but forging ever forward. In April's words, 'As long as we're still breathing, there's always another chance.'

But where would James feature in this new future? His impending reassignment would take him away from it all and he doubted it would afford him any chance to accompany Erin again, despite her promise to keep him apprised.

For now, at least, he resolved to enjoy the time he had left with Angela.

*The Augment Saga continues in*
*Legacy of the Gods*

# ABOUT THE AUTHOR

Alan K. Dell is a British sci-fi author and creative person with far too many hobbies. He writes science fiction described as 'by, and for, sci-fi geeks' and loves to explore interesting high-tech concepts in his work. Outside of writing, he is a book blogger and reviewer, avid videogamer, archer, photographer, and musician. For his day job he works as Parish Administrator for his local church. He lives at home in Essex with his wife and two children.

**Get in touch (he doesn't bite!):**
Website: www.alankdell.co.uk
Social Media: bio.site/alankdell
Goodreads: www.goodreads.com/alankdell

Please take the time to leave a review on Amazon or Goodreads. It would be greatly appreciated and it's a brilliant way to support authors.

# MORE IN THE AUGMENT SAGA

## THE RE-EMERGENCE
*An Augment Saga Novella*

## FROM THE GRAVE OF THE GODS
*The Augment Saga: Book One*

## THE FLIGHT OF THE AURORA
*An Augment Saga Novella*

## NEWTON'S REACH
*An Augment Saga Short Story*

❧

## LEGACY OF THE GODS
*The Augment Saga: Book Three*

# OTHER BOOKS BY THE AUTHOR

## THE GOD SUN
*A Cosmic Horror Sci-Fi Novelette*